CITY OF GHOSTS

tacia Kane was born in Illinois, raised in St. Louis MO, ad lived in South Florida for a dozen years before ioving to the UK with her British husband and two aughters. *The Downside Ghosts* is her first urban fantasy ries.

isit her authorized website at www.staciakane.net

Also by Stacia Kane

THE DOWNSIDE GHOSTS

Unholy Ghosts

Unholy Magic

City of Ghosts

STACIA KANE

CITY OF GHOSTS

Book Three Of the Downside Ghosts

WOLVERHAMPTON PUBLIC LIBRARIES	
XB000000068047	
Bertrams	11/08/2010
	£7.99
~~PF~~ ALL	01111295

HARPER
Voyager

HarperVoyager
An imprint of HarperCollins*Publishers*
77–85 Fulham Palace Road,
Hammersmith, London W6 8JB

www.harpercollins.co.uk

This paperback edition 2010
1

First published in Great Britain by
HarperCollins*Publishers* 2010

Copyright © Stacia Kane 2010

The Author asserts the moral right to
be identified as the author of this work

A catalogue record for this book is
available from the British Library

ISBN: 978 0 00 735284 5

This novel is entirely a work of fiction.
The names, characters and incidents portrayed in it are
the work of the author's imagination. Any resemblance to
actual persons, living or dead, events or localities is
entirely coincidental.

Printed and bound in Great Britain by
Clays Ltd, St Ives plc

All rights reserved. No part of this publication may be
reproduced, stored in a retrieval system, or transmitted,
in any form or by any means, electronic, mechanical,
photocopying, recording or otherwise, without the prior
permission of the publishers.

FSC is a non-profit international organisation established
to promote the responsible management of the world's forests.
Products carrying the FSC label are independently certified
to assure consumers that they come from forests that are managed
to meet the social, economic and ecological needs
of present and future generations.

Find out more about HarperCollins and the environment at
www.harpercollins.co.uk/green

Chapter One

> Not all of your duties will be pleasant. But that is the sacrifice you make, for as a Church employee you must always remember that you are privileged above all others.
>
> —*The Example Is You,* the guidebook for Church employees

The guillotine waited for them, its blackened wood dark and threatening against the naked cement walls of the Execution Room.

Chess limped past it, trying not to look. Trying not to remember that she deserved to kneel before it, to place her neck on the age-smoothed rest and wait for the blade to fall. She'd killed a psychopomp. Hell, she'd killed *people.*

Only the death of the hawk meant automatic execution.

But nobody knew about that. At least, nobody with the authority to order her death knew about that. She was safe for the moment.

Too bad she didn't feel safe. Didn't feel the way she should have felt. The dull ache in her thigh with every step she took in her low-heeled Church pumps reminded her of the almost healed gunshot wound; her limp reminded everyone else, drew attention to her at a time when she wanted it even less than usual.

Elder Griffin's hand was warm at her elbow. "You may sit while the sentence is read and carried out, Cesaria."

"Oh, no, really, I'm—"

He shook his head, his eyes serious. What was that about? Granted, an execution wasn't exactly a party-it-up event; very few Church events were. But Elder Griffin looked even more solemn than usual, more troubled.

He didn't know, did he? Had Oliver Fletcher told him about the psychopomp, about what she'd done? If that bast—No. No, she was being stupid and paranoid. Oliver wouldn't have told him. When would he have? As far as she knew, the two men had only shared one conversation since that night, the night she'd killed the psychopomp, the night Terrible had been—

Her breath rasped in her chest. Right. This wasn't the time, or the place. This was an execution, and she had testimony to give, and she needed to calm the fuck down and give it.

So she sat on the hard, straight-backed wooden chair, breathing the disinfectant stink heavy in the room, and watched the others file in after her. Elder Murray, the rings painted around his eyes as black as his hair, almost disappearing against the rich darkness of his skin. Dana Wright, the other Debunker who'd been at the bust at Madame Lupita's, her light hair curling around her face.

For Lupita herself, no one came. Any who might have cared about her, who might have wanted to be there for her in the last moments of her physical life, had either already been executed themselves or were locked in their cells in the prison building.

Last—last before the condemned woman herself—came the executioner, his face obscured by a heavy black hood. On his open right palm rested a dog's skull—his psychopomp, ready to take Madame Lupita down to the spirit prisons. Clenched in his left fist was a chain, and at the end of that chain was Madame Lupita, her legs and wrists shackled together with iron bands.

The door thunked shut behind them, the lock popped; it would not open for half an hour. Time enough for the execution to take place and the spirit to be taken to the City of Eternity. The timelocks had been instituted in the early days of the Church, when a series of mishaps had led to a ghost opening the door and escaping. Like everything the Church did, the timelocks made sense, but Chess couldn't help the tiny thrill of panic that ran up her spine. Trapped. Something she never wanted to be.

The executioner fastened the chain-end he held to the guillotine and began setting up the skull at the base of the permanent altar in the corner. Smoke poured from his censer and overpowered the scent of bleach and ammonia; the thick, acrid odor of melidia to send Lupita's soul to the spirit prisons, ajenjible and asafetida, burning yew chips to sting Chess's nose. The energy in the room changed, power slithering up her legs and lifting the hair on the back of her neck, that little rush that always made her want to smile.

She didn't, though. Not today. Instead she pressed her teeth together and looked at the condemned woman.

Lupita had changed since Chess saw her last, in that miserable, hot little basement that stank of terror and burned herbs and poison. Her big body seemed to have shrunk. Instead of the ridiculous silver turban Chess remembered, Lupita wore only her own close-shorn hair; instead of the silly sideshow caftan, her bulk was hidden beneath the plain black robe of those sentenced to die.

But her eyes had not changed. They searched the little crowd, found Chess, and glared, hatred burning from their depths so hot that Chess almost felt it sear her skin.

She forced herself not to look away. That woman had almost killed her, slipping poison into her drink; had almost killed a roomful of innocent people, summoning a rampaging, violent ghost. Fuck her. She was going to die, and Chess was going to watch.

Something slithered behind Lupita's eyes.

Chess's breath froze in her chest. Had she seen that?

That flash of silver? That flash, which meant Lupita was Hosting a spirit in her body?

Her eyes widened; she stared at Lupita now, focusing. Waiting. It shouldn't be possible. Lupita hadn't been Hosting when she was arrested—they would have caught that immediately when she was brought in—and there was no way in hell she would have been able to pick up and bond with a spirit in the Church prisons. It simply wasn't possible.

The flash didn't reappear. No. She was imagining things. All the stress, the tension of her personal life—what there was of it—and the overbearing sympathy of the Elders and the other Debunkers, crushing her beneath their concern for her leg and their good intentions. Add to that a few extra Cepts and a Panda, and half a Nip to keep her awake . . . No wonder she was seeing things. What was next, pink elephants?

Elder Griffin stood before the guillotine, cleared his throat.

"Irene Lowe, also known as Madame Lupita, thou hast been found guilty by the Church of the crime of summoning spirits to earth. Further, thou hast been found guilty of the attempted murder of Church Debunker Cesaria Putnam. Cesaria, is this woman responsible for those crimes?"

Chess stood up, despite the protests of her right thigh and Elder Griffin's slight frown. "Yes, Elder."

"Thou testifiest this based on what?"

"I saw this woman commit those crimes, Elder."

"And thou swearest thy word to be Fact, and Truth?"

"Yes, Elder. I do."

Elder Griffin gave her a curt nod, turned next to Dana Wright while Chess sank back onto her chair. A woman was about to die based on her word. When her word—the word of a junkie and a liar, the word of someone who'd betrayed her only real friend in the world—wasn't worth shit.

He was never going to speak to her again. She'd given up calling the week before. She'd given up hoping she might see him out at Trickster's or Chuck's, given up hanging around the Market in the cold, waiting to see if he turned up. He was still out there, of course. People had seen him.

People who weren't her. She'd never known anyone could avoid another person so thoroughly. It was like he could sense her coming.

Shifting movement in the standing crowd drew her attention back to the proceedings. The execution itself was about to take place.

The room thrummed with power now, beating like a heart around them, steady and slow and thick. No need for a circle; the room itself was a circle, a fortress with iron sandwiched into the cement walls.

Elder Griffin started pounding the drum, letting his hand stay in the air for so long between beats that Chess felt herself waiting, breathless, unable to move or allow her lungs to fill until the next heavy thump. The room's magic slid into her, finding those empty spaces and filling them, making her something more than she was. It felt good. So good she wanted to close her eyes and give herself to it completely, to forget everything and everyone and do nothing but exist in the energy.

She couldn't, of course. She knew she couldn't. So instead she watched as the executioner's psychopomp formed, the dog growing out of the skull, flowing like a river from a mountain peak to become legs, a tail, hair sprouting glossy and black over the bare skin and bones.

The drum beat faster. Drums . . . there had been drums at Lupita's séance that night, played by a duo of speedfreaks with eyes like ball bearings. Now the drums again, keeping monotonous, dragging time under Elder Murray's voice.

"Irene Lowe, thou art found guilty and sentenced to die by a tribunal of Church Elders, and this sentence shall now be carried out. If thou hast any last words to speak, speak them now."

Lupita shook her head, staring at the floor. Chess reached out with her own power, trying to get some sense of something from the woman. Some fear, some anger. Anything. Lupita was too quiet. Too calm. This didn't feel right.

The executioner helped Lupita to her knees, placed her neck on the divot. The drum beat harder, louder even than Chess's blood in her veins or the thick sweet magic air rasping in her lungs. Louder than her own thoughts.

She reached out farther, letting her power caress Lupita's skin, trying to find something—

Oh, fuck!

Her leg gave when she leapt to her feet, almost falling over. "No! No, don't—"

Too late. The blade fell, its metallic *shnik* slicing the air as cleanly as it did Irene's neck, thudding into place like the slamming of a prison door.

Irene's head tumbled into the basket. Blood erupted from the stump of her neck, poured over her head, over the dull cement floor.

Her spirit rose; her spirit, the spirit that had been Madame Lupita. The dog lunged for it, ready to drag it below the earth, into the prisons outside the City of Eternity.

The other spirit rose as well. The spirit Lupita'd been Hosting. The one there was no psychopomp to take care of, no graveyard dust to subdue. The one an entire roomful of Church employees were helpless against in that room with its iron walls and locked door.

Chess's scream finally escaped, bursting into the air. It

was drowned out by the others, the shouts of surprise and fear.

Elder Griffin dropped the drum. The dog grabbed Lupita's spirit—she had a passport on her arm, she was the one he'd been summoned to retrieve—and dove into the patch of wavering air behind the wall. The last thing Chess saw of Lupita was her mouth stretched into a horrible grin as she left them all to die.

The ghost hovered in the air before the guillotine. A man, his hair slicked back from his forehead, his eyes blank, his face twisted with savage joy. Elder Murray shouted something, she couldn't be sure what; her skin tingled and itched and threatened to crawl away from her body entirely. A powerful ghost, too powerful. What the fuck was he, how the fuck had she—

"I command you to be still!" Elder Griffin's voice rang out, echoed off the walls, speared through Chess's body. "By my power I command it!"

It wouldn't work. She knew without even looking that it wouldn't. But the executioner . . . did he have another skull? Some graveyard dirt?

Dana screamed. Chess glanced over and saw the ghost fighting with Elder Murray, its mouth open in a ghastly smile, its eyes narrow with effort. The ghost held the ritual blade in its hand, the one the executioner had used to summon his psychopomp.

No time to watch. No time to look at them, and it wouldn't do any good anyway. The room was filled with noise and energy and heat, a confusing mishmash of images her brain couldn't process. She focused on the smoking censer, the stang in the corner, the black bag beside it. The executioner dug through it frantically, pulling things out—

Someone fell into her, she tumbled to the hard floor with a thud.

More screams, more shouts. Something clattered to

the floor. The energy was unbearable. It wasn't a rush anymore, wasn't a high. It was an invasion, shoving her around, distorting her thoughts and her vision and infecting her with everyone else's panic.

She had to calm down. Her hands refused to obey her. Her tattoos prickled and burned, as they were designed to do. The ghost's presence set them off, an early warning system she was usually grateful for but would gladly have done without at that moment. Chaos reigned in the execution room, carrying her along on a wild riptide of blood.

Okay. Deep breath. Pause. She closed her eyes, dug down deep to the emptiness in her soul. The place where things like love and happiness and warmth should be, the place that was an almost empty room for her, the place where only two people lived, and one of them hated her.

But it was enough. It was enough to have that moment of silence, to tune out the terror and noise around her and find her own strength.

She opened her eyes. Her limbs obeyed her. She sprang to her feet, ignoring the pain—and almost lost her hard-fought calm.

Elder Murray was dead. His body lay stretched across the floor like a corpse ready for cremation. A gaping bloody wound leered at her from his throat.

Behind him the executioner slumped against the wall, his robe soaked with blood. She barely saw him through the ghost, blazing white, bloated with the energy he'd stolen. Chess groaned. A ghost with that much power was like an ex-con on Cloud-laced speed—unstoppable, without feelings, without logic. A killing machine who wouldn't stop until he was forced to.

And they were locked in with it.

Oh, shit—they were locked in with *them*. The iron walls kept the spirits of Elder Murray and the executioner locked in just as surely as the rest of them; Chess saw them out of the corner of her eye, faint shapes struggling to come into being.

There was a chance they wouldn't be hungry, that they wouldn't become murderous, but the odds were about as good as the odds that she'd be able to fall asleep that night without a handful of her pills. In other words, not fucking good at all. In a minute or so the ghosts would find their shapes, find their powers, and things would go from worse to totally fucking awful.

Blood spattered the walls, dripped off the shiny blade of the guillotine, and ran in thick streams along the cement. It dripped from the ceiling where it had sprayed from Elder Murray's neck; it formed a glistening pool around the body, outlined footprints in a dizzying pattern, and smeared around the broken remains of the dog's skull. Fuck. No psychopomp. Did he have another?

Elder Griffin was covered with blood. Dana too, her eyes wide. But Chess wasn't the only one who'd rallied. Dana's eyes were dark and fierce with determination; Elder Griffin fairly glowed with power and strength.

Chess caught Dana's eye, jerked her head toward the bag. Dana nodded and took a step forward.

"By my power I command you to be still," she said, each word loud and clear. "I command you to go back to your place of silence."

The ghost turned to look at her, and Dana edged back, drawing it away. Chess inched to the left, trying not to catch the ghost's attention. She had to get to that bag. Had to get to the bag or they would all die. Maybe they'd die anyway, but she was damned if she wasn't at least going to try to save them. Life might be a pool of shit but the City was worse—for her anyway—and she had no intention of going there. Not that day.

Her feet in their stiff shoes slipped in thick blood; the scent of it filled the air, a coppery tang beneath the herbs. How long would those burn, and was there more?

The ghost moved toward Dana, who kept talking, words of power flowing from her mouth. He clutched the knife in one semi-solid hand, blood dripping down the blade and covering his spectral skin. Viewed through him it looked black, like ink.

She glanced at the ghosts of Murray and the executioner again. They were almost fully formed now, slowly squirming into being like maggots erupting from a slab of rotting steak. She—they—didn't have much time.

Dana screamed. The ghost jumped at her. Elder Griffin leapt to the side, joining the struggle, as the ghost attempted to slice Dana's throat.

Chess dove for the bag. More herbs first—she grabbed the little baggies, dumped them on the dying fire in the censer. The smoke thickened. Another psychopomp, please let him have a spare. She threw things from his bag, not watching where they landed, the hair on the back of her neck practically pulling itself out of her skin. She couldn't hear much, what was happening? Were Dana and Elder Griffin dead? Oh, shit—

Her hand found something solid and her body flooded with relief. Another skull. Thank the gods who didn't exist, he had a spare. She yanked it out, tore at the inert silk wrapping it, barely glanced at it as she set it down.

A roar behind her. The ghost had spotted her. Dana and Elder Griffin tried to hold it, but it made itself transparent and sprang at her through the guillotine. She ducked out of the way. "I call on the escorts of the City of the Dead," she managed, stumbling, trying to keep within reach of the skull but away from the ghost's grabbing hand. "By my power I call you!"

The skull rattled. Chess pushed more power out, as much as she could—not an easy task when trying to keep from being turned into an energy snack for a rampaging dead man.

Another problem faced her as well. No passport. The

spirit hadn't been accounted for, didn't have a marking on his body; there was a chance the dog wouldn't know which spirit to grab when it came. It had happened to Chess once before, a few months previously, and the dog had gone after her. She would never forget that feeling, the horrible sensation of her soul being pulled from her body like a banana from its peel . . .

Not to mention the additional spirits forming not five feet away, the executioner and Elder Murray.

"No passport!" she said with a gasp, and Dana's eyes widened. She glanced at the knife in her hand, raised her eyebrows, and Chess nodded because she had no choice.

Dana tossed the knife. The ghost spun around when it clattered to the floor, leapt for it. Chess grabbed the executioner's Ectoplasmarker and popped the cap, held it ready in her fist, and shouted.

Just as she'd thought, the ghost wheeled back around and came after her with the knife. Dana and Elder Griffin moved, Chess didn't see where. She was too busy watching the ghost, seeing his solid hand raise over her head, grabbing his wrist with her left hand and bringing the marker up with her right.

He didn't have a passport—they hadn't expected him, hadn't designed one. Oh fucking well. The blade hovered above her eye, its point tacky with coagulating blood, while she scrawled a series of *X*s on the spectral skin. The ghost's face twisted with rage.

Now for the worst part. With every bit of strength she had left she pushed herself to the side, to the skull, and, dropping the marker, brought her right hand to the blade's point.

She hadn't expected it to hurt instantly but it did. Ow, it really fucking did, and her blood poured from the wound onto the skull, and she shoved all of that pain and all of her power into her next words.

"I offer the escorts an appeasement for their aid!

Escorts come now! Take this man to the place of silence, by my power and by my blood I command it!"

The dog roared into being, huge and shaggy, its fangs bared. This wasn't just a dog, it was a wolf, what the fuck was the executioner doing with an unauthorized psychopomp—

The ghost's eyes widened. His mouth opened in a silent scream as he tried to jump away, all thoughts of killing forgotten. The dog—the wolf—went after him, its body moving low and fast like the predator it was.

The ghosts of the executioner and Elder Murray were fully formed now, huddled in the corner. Chess could see the last vestiges of sanity, of who they were in life, draining away, could see them trying to hold on.

It didn't matter. The wolf howled. A hole ripped open in the thin veil between her world and the spirit one, the wolf snatched the original ghost in its massive jaw. Ectoplasm burst from the ghost's body under the wolf's teeth. The ghost screamed, an act somehow more horrible because of its silence.

The wolf turned toward Elder Murray and the executioner. They huddled together, trying so hard. Tears sprang to Chess's eyes. She'd never known Elder Murray well, never dealt much with him, but his last act was to struggle to retain some humanity, and she couldn't help the surge of affectionate sadness, of pride, that threatened to overwhelm her.

Dana and Elder Griffin were beside her, Dana squeezing her hand. The wolf leapt, still clutching their unwelcome visitor in its teeth, and caught Elder Murray and the executioner in a bizarre bear hug; he carried them through the wavering hole and it snapped shut behind them, leaving the three still alive to stare open-mouthed at where it had been.

Chapter Two

[The most sacred vows are those given to the Church, and overseen by the Church, for those involve not just the heart and mind but the soul.
—*The Book of Truth,* Laws, Article 331]

"I don't understand how it could have happened," Elder Griffin said again. They'd returned to his office, the welcoming, soothing room full of skulls and books. For once the television mounted by the ceiling was off; usually the Elder kept it on all the time to keep him company.

Apparently he didn't feel much like companionship at the moment. Neither did Chess, but then, she never did. What was the point? You let people into your life and you ended up getting hurt. Or hurting them. Either way, the road to pain was paved with other people, and she wanted no part of it anymore.

At least that's what she kept telling herself. Just then it worked. Usually of late it didn't. Once the decision was made to open up to someone, to welcome them . . . it wasn't so easy to accept that the place she'd opened for them was empty. And always would be.

Especially when it was her fault.

"I don't see how she could have made it past the detectors," Dana said, echoing something Chess herself had wondered earlier but without providing the answer Chess had come up with.

She gave it now. "She didn't. She wasn't Hosting when we busted her."

"But that isn't—"

"I was there, Dana." Chess paused, gave the other woman a small smile in an attempt to make her words less harsh. She'd never had a problem with Dana and wasn't interested in starting one. "I mean, I know you were there too, but I felt her energy. She stole mine, remember? So I know she wasn't Hosting. There was nothing inside that woman but Dumpster cag-mag and that awful tea."

"Cag-mag?" Elder Griffin looked puzzled. Shit. She shouldn't have said that. He knew she lived in Downside, of course, but didn't really know what that meant. Nobody did. And that was the way she liked it.

"It's a— It just means, scraps of whatever meat's about to go off. Like you get in the butcher's Dumpster."

The Elder's eyebrows rose; his shoulders relaxed. Like she'd said something that pleased him.

Which made no sense at all. Why would that make him happy?

"So you have managed to learn something about the area," he said. "You're not so isolated from your neighbors there as I had assumed."

For the first time in a while, Chess felt almost like laughing. Yeah, she'd found a way to fit in with the rest of Downside. That was one way to look at it.

"Yes," she said finally, dragging her tired mind back to Elder Griffin. Shit. Only ten at night and she was exhausted. She had more speed in her bag; hopefully they'd be done with this soon and she could go bump up.

Or, fuck that. She could go sleep. Drop an Oozer, drift away . . . Maybe she'd even get lucky and not dream. Her dreams didn't tend to be cheerful these days. But then they never really had been.

Elder Griffin smiled, the kind of smile that made Chess wonder even more what exactly he was up to, but he didn't speak. Muffled voices came through the door, the scuffle of feet on the shiny wide floor of the hall outside the office.

Dana shivered. "I still can't believe it," she said. "Elder Murray . . . It doesn't seem real."

Elder Griffin's face rearranged itself into more sympathetic lines, but when he spoke, Chess heard the steel beneath his bland tone. It made her own eyes widen. She didn't think she'd ever heard him speak to anyone like that—at least, not anyone still living. "Remember, Dana, Elder Murray will still be with us in spirit. There is no reason to mourn."

"Of course not." Dana straightened in her seat, pushed her light hair back from her face. "I wasn't—I wasn't implying anything. I'm just shocked. I liked Elder Murray."

"I liked him as well. And for that reason, Dana, and because I know the Truth, I rejoice for Elder Murray. The peace he's found in the City, the quiet . . ." Elder Griffin shook his head. "I envy him."

With difficulty Chess suppressed a shudder. The City—ugh. What Elder Griffin thought was peace, she thought was emptiness. What he thought was quiet, she thought was horrifying loneliness, with no pills or anything to make it bearable.

"We'll set the ceremony for"—he flipped the pages in the daily calendar sitting on the shiny wide desktop before him—"Saturday. Yes. Five days from now is Saturday—'tis so late I forgot for a moment what day it was. Saturday, Dana, you shall have your chance to see Elder Murray's happiness for yourself."

Dana nodded, her expression cleared. Meanwhile Chess felt as if someone had shoved a blender into her gut. With everything else, the deaths and the wondering where that damned wolf had come from and—okay, and her stupid babyish whining about her personal life, what a fucking joke—she'd forgotten about the Dedication ceremony. About what the death of an Elder would entail.

"Cesaria? Are you well?"

Chess nodded, opened her eyes wide and met Elder Griffin's blue ones with as much innocence as she could muster. "Fine, sir. Fine. Just a little tired."

"You do look tired."

She didn't respond. What was she supposed to say? Thanks?

"How is your leg, my dear? Do you feel well enough to come back to work officially?"

"Yes!" The word came out a little too loudly, a little too eagerly. She couldn't help it. Yes, she wanted to get back to work. Wanted to have something to do besides sitting around her apartment being mocked by the empty walls, by the empty spot next to her on the sagging couch. Wanted something to do aside from avoiding having Lex inside, because she knew if she invited him into her apartment he would expect to be allowed into her body as well, and she didn't think she could face that conversation.

Wasn't even sure she wanted to have it. Why? Why give up a friend and perfectly serviceable bed partner for one who couldn't be avoiding her more obviously if he'd hung up signs around her neighborhood telling her to stay the hell away from him?

Elder Griffin didn't seem to think she was overeager, though. "Excellent. Excellent. Wait here, please."

Chess and Dana exchanged mystified looks as he unfolded himself from behind his desk and crossed the floor. In the pale yellowish glow from the gentle lamps, his stockinged calves flashed, dried blood spatters from earlier forming lacy patterns the color of dead leaves against the white. He left the room and closed the high dark wooden door behind him with a quiet click.

What was he doing? She would have thought he was going to get a new case file for her, but he wouldn't assign her a case right in front of Dana, not on a whim like that. She had no idea where she even stood in the case queue; two weeks of hospitalization and another two weeks of enforced rest had taken her pretty far out of the game.

"So, back to work," Dana said, in the weary, flat tone of someone talking simply because she thought it would be rude not to talk.

Luckily for Chess, she didn't have the same concerns, or the same discomfort. She just nodded, pressed her palms together, and glanced around the room. Glanced at Dana, taking in the other woman's blond curls and expensive rings. Well, why not? Most Debunkers spent their money on actual things, rather than just buying anything they could swallow, smoke, or snort.

Unlike Chess.

Speaking of which . . . Three hours now since she'd taken the Panda and Cepts. She had plenty of time, a few more hours, but it never hurt to be aware.

The door opened, and Elder Griffin came back in, followed by Elder Thompson and a red-haired woman Chess had never seen before.

Not that it mattered, because the woman was clearly a Church employee. Her bare arms were decorated like Chess's, like Dana's, with one striking exception: the black snake, coiled up the length of her arm from wrist to shoulder, each scale perfectly delineated in a silvery magical ink that gave off a faint shimmer in the dim light.

A member of the Black Squad. Church law enforcement—Church government, as opposed to Debunkers like Chess and Dana, who were regular Church employees.

Her blood turned to ice. Had the woman come for her—had they found out? She'd been so careful all this time, all these years, never letting anyone get too close, never letting anyone see her take so much as a fucking aspirin, and now—and in front of Dana, of all people?

They were busting her in front of— No. No. She was being stupid, acting like some panicky moron, and she needed to stop it.

Preferably right that second, because the red-haired woman was looking at her rather oddly. Examining her, as if she could see the guilt. Not good. Chess tightened her grip on her own fingers to calm herself, and held the redhead's gaze. The woman wanted to play power games, wanted to have some dumbass little staredown? Fine. Her loss.

The woman smiled; then, very deliberately, she broke the contact and looked down at the floor. Ohhhkay. What did that mean?

"Dana," Elder Griffin said, breaking into whatever the hell was happening, "perhaps you should go back to your cabin. Get some rest."

Dana opened her mouth, then stopped. Elder Griffin's dismissal hadn't been rude, but it had been a dismissal just the same, and Dana wasn't stupid. She left in a flurry of muttered goodbyes.

Chess was alone with two Elders and a woman who probably had the power to throw her into prison just for looking at her funny, and the silence in the room pounded into her skull like a speedfreak with a hammer.

Elder Griffin sat down. "Cesaria, may I present Lauren Abrams? She just arrived from New York this morning."

The woman—Lauren—held out one thin pale hand. Her tattoos went all the way down the back of it, like a fingerless glove; at the end of those bare fingers her nails were short like a man's, and shiny. "Nice to meet you, Cesaria. I've heard a lot about you."

An electric hum ran up Chess's arm when she shook Lauren's hand. She ignored it. Ignored too the way Lauren clearly wanted her to ask what she'd heard, or make some kind of joke. It wasn't her job to jump through hoops, and she didn't like this one bit.

She'd done some work with the Black Squad before, a few little side jobs, but this was different. This time she wasn't being brought into a group and given a quick briefing; she wasn't meeting a gang of lower Squad members. Lauren's power, her air of command, told Chess more clearly than anything else could have that this woman was a higher-up. Very high. In fact . . .

"Abrams," she said. "Any relation to the Grand Elder?"

Lauren gave a light, soft laugh. "He's my father."

If Chess hadn't already been sitting down she might have stumbled. No fucking way. They were sending her on a case—there had to be a case here, either that or they were busting her, and she somehow suspected that if that's what was going on they would have done it already—with the fucking Grand Elder's daughter?

"Oh," she said finally, since everyone was looking at her as if they expected her to respond. "Okay."

Lauren sat down in Dana's empty chair, crossed her legs with a whisper of nylon. "I bet you're wondering what's going on."

Chess shrugged.

"We have . . . an offer for you. An investigation we think you could really help us with. Interested?"

"What is it?"

Lauren opened her mouth, but before she could speak Elder Thompson cleared his throat and leaned forward, his heavy brows drawn together in a solid line. His eyebrows fascinated Chess; they seemed to grow wilder and thicker every time she saw him, while the hair on his head grew lighter and thinner, like some sort of migration process. Someday she imagined the brows would simply fall over his eyes in a wiry curtain.

Lauren glanced at him, nodded, glanced back at Chess. "It's a very . . . sensitive case."

"All my cases are sensitive." What the hell was this?

Why were they looking at her like they expected her to explode? "I don't gossip, if that's what you're implying."

"Oh, no, no, that's not it. It's just— I'm not explaining this very well." Lauren looked helplessly at Elder Griffin, biting her lipstick-coated lower lip.

Great. One of *those* women: tough and authoritative when it suited her, acting like a simpering poor-me baby when it didn't. So they wanted to bring her in on a case with the Grand Elder's pampered little daughter, who would expect Chess to do all the work while she batted her eyelashes and took all the credit? Ugh. No, thank you.

But then . . . how much money was in it? She fully expected she'd have to start paying for her own supplies again, once the bag she had ran out and she had to tell Lex she wasn't going to sleep with him anymore. So it wasn't like extra money wouldn't come in handy. The payout on her last case would have been huge, but she'd been forced to give it up to save her own skin, so . . . she was broke. As usual.

"Cesaria, the problem isn't that we do not trust you," Elder Griffin said. "It's that the sensitivity of this case, the subject of it, makes explaining a little difficult."

Elder Thompson folded his arms. "We can't tell you what it's about. Not until you agree to take it."

"What? I don't—"

"And it will require a Binding Oath."

Her mouth fell open. A Binding Oath? They had to be kidding. No. No way. They wanted her to take a case so serious it required an oath of secrecy—a form of magical control over her actions—and they weren't even going to tell her what it was about first? Not even a hint?

Lex would surely front her. If he was going to stop giving her what she needed for free, she knew he would at least front her until she got a real case, one where she'd get a bonus. It wouldn't be long, it never—

"The case comes with a bonus before you begin, simply for agreeing and accepting the Bind," Elder Griffin said. "Thirty thousand dollars. You will be given a thousand dollars a week on top of your salary for the duration of the case—we anticipate a resolution within two weeks, however—and an additional fifty thousand when it ends."

Her protest died in her throat. Eighty-two thousand dollars. Eighty thousand dollars minimum. That was a fuck of a lot of money.

That would buy her a fuck of a lot of oblivion. And the way things were going these days, oblivion was even more important than usual.

And she still needed a new car.

"I assume," she said, pushing the words out through a throat gone gummy, "that it's a dangerous case?"

Lauren Abrams rearranged her legs with another nylon hiss; Elder Thompson and Elder Griffin both watched her like they thought she might get up and run screaming from the room. None of them replied.

She'd just watched two people die. Her hand throbbed where she'd sliced it. Her thigh ached. She wanted a cigarette, and she wanted her pills. And she wanted eighty thousand dollars.

No matter what the case was.

"I'll do it," she said, and hoped it would be worth it.

Chapter Three

> And we honor those first Elders above all others, for they were the Founders of our Church and thus the saviors of mankind.
>
> —*The Book of Truth,* Origins, Article 1256

Elder Griffin stood up. Light from the candles on the floor spilled across his face, cast jutting shadows over one eye. For a moment he looked alien, almost scary; then he turned farther to his left and was himself again.

Chess's heart pounded in her chest. It's just a bit of magic, she told herself. Just an oath, no different from the ones she'd taken when she started her training, certainly no different from the ones she'd taken when she completed that training and became a full Church employee at the age of twenty-one.

It didn't work, though. This was different, and she knew it. And she didn't like it. Nor did she like the energy rising in the room, sly and intrusive, or the peculiar smile on Lauren Abrams's face as she watched the Elders set up the altar.

Chess stood in the center of the room with her hands clasped behind her. Dried blood had settled into the fabric of her plain ceremonial dress, making her stomach protest a little when she thought about it. She didn't worry about the executioner and Elder Murray; what few blood- or fluid-borne diseases had survived the Church's strict quarantine and eradication policies, Church employees had been vaccinated against.

But Madame Lupita . . . disease aside, who the hell knew what sort of bacterial stew had simmered in her plaque-clotted veins? Realistically, Chess knew the risk was gone now that the blood had dried, but that didn't stop her from wanting to get the damned dress off as fast as she possibly could.

But of course she didn't have much choice. And the sooner she took the damned Oath, the sooner she'd get a nice fat check. She could slip it in the night deposit on her way home.

Movement to her left brought her back into the room, back into the ceremony. The Elders had started laying out a salt line, murmuring words of power as they moved solemnly clockwise. Lauren stood against the wall, outside the circle, watching them with her arms folded and her ankles crossed. Irritation prickled Chess's skin.

It wasn't that it was so unusual for her to dislike people right off the bat. That was pretty much the way she felt about everyone. But she wasn't usually forced to *work* with people she disliked right off the bat. She felt . . . intruded upon.

But then, nobody was forcing her to take the case. No, not forcing. Bribing. And she was taking the bribe, because she needed the money.

Behind the Elders the salt line erupted into shining deep purple, hissing faintly as it rose in thick lines and cast colored light across everything. Their white stockings glowed, their faces glowed; Elder Griffin's pale hair surrounded his head in a corona of blazing violet that made Chess's eyes sting.

Not just her eyes, either. The energy buzzed and twirled around her, battered her skin. She was caught in it, a vortex of power swirling around her, catching her in it and twisting her inside out. She didn't know where to look, what to focus on; she couldn't bear to close her eyes.

So she looked down, focused on the dusty, blood-specked toes of her once-shiny black heels. It wasn't a good compromise. Her head swam; her feet looked vertiginously far away. But it was better than watching the Elders move—setting up their bowls and setting fire to their herbs—inside the sparkling, viciously bright dome.

The only good thing was that Lauren Abrams could no longer see her. The circle would block her view. It was some relief.

Smoke filled the circle, thick, choking smoke the same purple as the circle, the same color as the fire burning in a large firedish opposite her. She didn't want to breathe it in. Breathing it in was part of the Oath, part of the Binding. Even she didn't know what some of those herbs were, but when they entered her lungs they would enter her bloodstream, locking every cell of her body into the magical oath she was about to take.

Powerful binding herbs, too. The calamus herbs, vetiver, and sweet flag, combined with the deep, throbbing energy of licorice root. She could feel them spreading through her, finding every empty place, drawing her own magic and mixing with it. She was naked, open to them; they swept through her without caring, without feeling, winding from her feet to her head and forcing her to bend to their power.

This wasn't like the oaths she'd taken when she was initiated, not like the ones when she began her training. This was . . . this was heavy, dark magic, trapping her, squeezing her with so much pressure that she thought she might implode. Like nothing she'd ever experienced before. This wasn't right, it couldn't be right . . .

Dimly she heard the Elders speaking, saw vague movement as they added more herbs to the glowing purple fire in the north end of the circle. Myrrh and cedar, bergamot and dragon's blood. Her vision blurred. Shapes formed in the smoke, open mouths, staring eyes. Someone moaned. She wasn't sure if it was her.

Elder Thompson started chanting, low and slow, his voice thick with smoke and power and the spine-tingling thrust of command. She moved without intending to, bound by him. Bound by his commands. Somewhere deep down she fought against it.

She didn't want to do this anymore. She'd changed her mind. Her heart slammed around in her chest like a pinball caught between the paddles, trying frantically to escape. Her mind fought against the Elder, against what he wanted her to do, but she was caught. Trapped. Her hands rose at his words, turned so her pale wrists, veins blue-purple beneath the thin skin, faced the top of the dome.

Elder Griffin's hand on her arm. Desperately she swam through the smoke before her eyes, fought to see him. Fought the spell that slid hard hands up her legs, curled over her shoulders, caressed her stomach and breasts and stroked her neck. Everywhere.

Phantom hands, unfamiliar hands, all over her body. *No.* No, she'd sworn she wouldn't ever—wouldn't lie there, she wasn't a child anymore, she didn't have to do this. Didn't have to let them do this, she could fight, she was powerful. She was a witch, a fucking *Church witch;* she was grown up and she had the power now. She did not have to let them—not anymore—she didn't want this anymore, no . . .

"Stop." Her voice didn't work; her dry lips ached around the word. She couldn't do this, didn't want to be controlled anymore, couldn't give up her power. Couldn't give up her autonomy. Her independence. The strength she'd fought so fucking hard for, the right to keep her own thoughts and her own body, not to be forced to let other people use her like a fucking toy, to ignore her until they took her out of her box to play with her some more and cast her aside when they'd had their fun.

"Stop!" she tried again, but all that came out was a gurgle. Panic overtook her. She couldn't see, couldn't hear, couldn't feel her hands or feet. Elder Thompson's voice grew louder, thundering in her ears; his power forced itself into her, over her. Fighting with her to keep her still.

Her feet moved, like wading through half-dried cement. She had to get out. Had to. Fuck the money. It wasn't worth it, wasn't worth this, wasn't worth being trapped by heavy black hands and forced to give up everything she'd fought all her life to gain.

Elder Thompson was shouting now. His words slammed into her, beat her like fists. She pushed harder, aiming for the thick purple wall. Get out, she had to get out, had to—

Another hand on her, squeezing her arm. She tried to swing, to bat him away, but he caught her. "Cesaria. Cesaria. Cesaria."

Elder Griffin. Elder Griffin speaking to her, his voice quiet but still somehow audible over Elder Thompson's roar. He repeated her name again and again, and the tiny piece of her able to focus grabbed him, grabbed the sound of her name in his voice, and clung to it.

"Cesaria. I am here with you, Cesaria. Give in. Let go and have trust in me. You know me, Cesaria. I know you. You will not be hurt here, no one will hurt you. I promise it will end when you relax, and you will come to no harm. I promise you—let go and it will end, stop fighting it, no one will hurt you. No one will hurt you, Cesaria, I promise . . ."

She didn't want to. Her head flew back and forth, denying it, refusing.

He kept speaking, the same soft litany over and over. Tears ran down her cheeks. She could feel them, taste them, salty and flavored with calamus and cayenne from the herbs invading her body.

Somewhere—she had no idea how long it took, how many times he repeated her name or urged her to give in and let Elder Thompson take control of her—she relaxed. Elder Griffin would not let anything happen to her. She knew he wouldn't. She trusted him as much as she trusted anyone, trusted him more than anyone except— She trusted him, and he wouldn't let her get hurt, and gradually she felt the energy around her change, heard Elder Thompson's voice quiet. With a sigh she reached into herself; with a sigh she gave in to her trust.

The energy changed. Instantly, like a puzzle piece snapping into place. Not scary anymore, not dangerous. She was in this. She was resigned to it. She'd agreed to it and she was doing it, and suddenly she didn't care. In fact . . .

It filled her, sent her floating. Better than her pills. Better than a knob of Dream. Every cell in her body was pure power, pure thick sweetness, light and full of joy. She had no choices to make, no battles to fight. No memories to deal with, no shame, no misery. She wasn't herself anymore. She was someone else, someone who *belonged* to someone, and that someone would make all the decisions and let her float . . .

It switched again, and she slammed back into herself. Her eyes opened.

The light had changed. Still purple, still glowing, but colored with shooting stars of black and red, streaking across the bright screen of energy. Her blood raced through her veins, through her brain, faster and faster, her tattoos screamed and tingled and writhed on her skin, searing through muscle and bone, setting off alarms in her soul.

Around the perimeter of the circle stood the ghosts, their clothing so familiar, their faces ones she'd seen before in paintings. The First Elders. The founders of the Church.

Controlled by herbs, neutered by magic, they stared at her with eyes that were nothing but blank white spaces. Their hands were clasped before them, their feet planted on the floor. They would witness her oath. They would bind her.

They would punish her if she broke the Oath.

Holy *shit*.

Elder Thompson's voice boomed through the silence, an edge of hoarseness ruining the thick slide of it.

"Cesaria Putnam, this night we Bind you. Bind you in loyalty to your Church, to Truth and Fact, to the power of the Church and the power of the earth. Do you accept this Binding?"

Elder Griffin whispered something in her ear. She repeated it with a mouth that felt alien and strange, a voice rusty with nerves. "I request the parameters of the Binding."

"The parameters of the Binding are these: That you will not speak of your purpose to anyone but those authorized to know it. That you will not act with disloyalty against the Church. That what you hear of your purpose after the words of Binding are spoken, and until they are retracted, will not be repeated by you to anyone but those authorized. That you will repeat them to those authorized when told to do so. Do you accept those parameters?"

Another whisper from Elder Griffin. "Who are those authorized?"

"Those authorized are Elder Thompson. Elder Griffin. The Grand Elder. Lauren Abrams, Third Inquisitor of the Black Squad. Those authorized will also be those names given to you by the aforementioned. Do you accept those parameters?"

"What are the penalties of breaking the Binding?"

"The Binding is unbreakable."

"No Binding is unbreakable."

"If this Binding is broken the penalty is thus: That the spirits of the First Elders will punish you. That the First Elders will remove you from your body and discard it. That you will be taken to the spirit prisons and left there until the First Elders shall determine you have been punished enough."

She shivered. They weren't fucking around. But then she hadn't imagined they would be.

"Cesaria Putnam, do you accept these parameters?"

Purple swirled before her eyes; purple flames, purple energy. The First Elders, standing in silent disapproval around her, were translucent, purple glowing through them. Elder Thompson was simply a hulking black shape, barely visible in the vibrant light.

"Cesaria Putnam, do you accept these parameters?"

She licked her lips. "I do accept them."

Elder Thompson muttered something; her arms lifted again. Her breath rattled in her chest, she knew what was coming and she didn't want to look, didn't want to see, but she couldn't help it that her eyes wouldn't close—

Bright violet shrieked off the edge of the blade, just before Elder Griffin brought it down over her wrists in a quick, decisive slice.

Her nerves vibrated. Dimly she felt the pain, a cold prickle beneath the skin, but the magical control holding her kept the worst of it at bay.

She saw it though. Saw her blood burble up from the wounds like purple-black ink, like oil bubbling from a fault in the surface of the earth, and fall on the smoking pile of herbs at her feet. She hadn't seen either of the Elders move it but there it was, the purple flames flashing red when her blood hit it.

"Cesaria Putnam, you are Bound. Bound to obey the strictures of this agreement. From this moment forward you will not speak of what you are told. Say you are Bound."

"I am Bound." The words felt sick and slimy in her mouth.

The First Elders came forward. One of them carried a blade, a real one not a spectral one, shining purple. Her tattoos screamed; her soul screamed.

The blade rose. The ghost—how did that work; she didn't know—he'd sliced their wrists. Each of the ghosts had a wound, a gaping mouth dribbling whitish ectoplasm. Dripping it into her similar wounds. It stung and burned, it raced into her bloodstream, ran through her body, a blast of power and fear and icy death that chilled her even as it set her afire.

"Cesaria Putnam, you are Bound. Bound to obey the commands of those aforementioned in speaking of what you are about to hear. Say you are Bound."

"I am Bound."

Dizziness swam up through her stomach, to her chest, to her head. The First Elders continued to invade her. Her blood continued to flow from her wounds, sizzling onto the fire below them like fat drippings onto firecans in the Market. She smelled it, blood mixed with the herbs, changing the scent into something like cinnamon and copper.

The fire rose, blinding purple. Rose at her feet and rose inside her. Sweat poured down her forehead and neck, between her breasts. Her bangs clung to her forehead.

"Cesaria Putnam, kneel."

Her knees gave way. She didn't feel them hit the floor but knew they had.

"*Richtaru bessiden amacha.*" Elder Thompson's voice rose, thick and strong above the roaring in her ears, the rasping desperation of her breath in her lungs. Smoke curled around her, pressed against her power, twined with it, wrapped around her like a hot, heavy wet blanket.

"By my power you are Bound. By your power you are Bound. By your blood and bones you are Bound. By the power of the Church, by the power of the Truth, by the power of the First Elders and the earth you are Bound."

Flames danced before her eyes, blurred with tears and stinging sweat. Too hot, it was too hot in there, she was losing too much blood . . .

"Let the Binding be sealed!"

The flames leapt, scorching her face. Something poured over her wrists, it seared her skin, stank of herbs. She looked at her arms, watched the thick reddish water pour over her, felt it enter her bloodstream and burn its way up her arms, to her chest, to her brain.

Her throat ached. She was screaming. Screaming so loud and so long she barely felt the Binding lock into place when her wounds healed over. Barely felt something snap in her skull, in her body.

Barely. But she still felt it.

The fire died. Elder Thompson said something else, too quietly for her to hear. The energy lifted; the First Elders disappeared, leaving only the purple circle glowing around them.

Elder Griffin's hands on her shoulder urged her to lean back, to rest against his chest. Her breath hitched; she didn't want to cry, didn't mean to, but she couldn't help it, couldn't stop it. Thirty thousand dollars didn't seem like enough for what she'd just given up. Even her faith in the Church, her trust in it, seemed to fade in light of what she'd lost.

The circle disappeared; fresh air flowed into where it had been, dispersing the smoke. Through the last purplish tendrils of it she saw Lauren Abrams reappear, smiling slightly, looking down at Chess on the floor like that was just the right place for her.

That was enough for Chess. She shrugged Elder Griffin's hands away, pushed herself to a stand on legs that threatened to give out on her. She couldn't do anything about the tears she'd already shed, about her sweat-soaked dress clinging to her body or wet hair clinging to her skull. But she could damn well face Lauren on her feet.

Lauren smiled slightly, looked her up and down. "You did well."

"She fought me." Elder Thompson sank into a chair, pulled out a handkerchief and mopped his heavy brow. "She almost broke out of the circle."

Lauren's eyebrows lifted; she looked at Chess with new interest. "Really."

"Cesaria is very strong," Elder Griffin said, and Chess had to fight not to look at him. Not to go to him and let him hold her again. She'd never—never had someone do that, not like that. Had never heard anyone talk about her with such pride in his voice.

That wasn't exactly true. One other person had done both of those things. But he never would again.

"Well." Lauren dusted her hands together, as though she needed to wash them of Elder Griffin's kind words. "Now that it's done, we have some things to discuss, don't we?"

Chapter Four

> Be proud of the wrinkles and lines that life has given you! They're a symbol of the promises you've made to your family and of your achievements. All important events leave scars.
>
> —*Mrs. Increase's Advice for Ladies* by Mrs. Increase

The picture slid across the polished wooden table, the image's horror barely contained by the thin white edges of the paper. Chess looked at it, swallowed hard. Looked again.

"He was found three days ago. Well . . . that much of him was. We expect an ID any moment." Lauren's crisp, cool tones cut through Chess's anger, the overwhelming pity she felt, looking at the ruined body in the photograph. It was an effort not to leap across the table and smack her. How could she do that? How could she look at that—that *thing,* that lump of flesh and goo that had once been a human being, and just move on with her pat little speech?

"Down by the docks. I believe you're familiar with the area?"

Chess nodded without thinking of it and reached out a tentative hand for the picture. Her dress was still wet; it clung coldly to her body. But that was not why she shivered.

Another picture slid over, knocked into the first one before Chess could touch it. "Yesterday this turned up, farther south. Fifty-fifth and Brand. Several different victims this time, but not their whole bodies. Just what you see."

The slick photographic paper threatened to slice her fingers when she picked it up, angled it so she could get a better look. Not that she wanted to. But Lauren and the Elders watched her too closely, sat too silently and stiffly in their chairs. There had to be something they wanted her to see—to notice—and she wanted to know what it was.

Her gaze skittered over the picture, trying to take it in pieces, quadrants, to shield herself from the full horror of it. Across the top first, then down, the lower right corner, the—

Raised black scars interrupted her wrists. Thick and straight, like railroad ties crossing her forearms. Sprouting from them were curving veins of dark purple in a lacy pattern up to her elbows, down over her palms.

Elder Griffin caught her look. "They'll disappear when the Binding Oath is lifted," he said. "They remain simply as a reminder."

Yeah. Like she could fucking forget.

But she just nodded and continued, steeling herself for the full image, until finally she saw what they wanted her to see. It was barely visible, only a linear shadow in the darkness of the black-and-white gore. But it was there, and Chess's blood ran even colder than it had.

Fuck, she needed her pills. "The Lamaru."

When no one responded she looked up. "Right? The Lamaru are back. That's what this is. Who did this."

Lauren nodded. "We believe so, yes."

She reached down, lifted a thick file from her lap and plunked it onto the table. "We've received information that they've re-formed themselves and are operating somewhere in the area known as Downside. Where you live, is that correct?"

"Yeah."

"Excellent. So you'll be an even bigger help than we thought. When shall I come down? Tonight? Are you free?"

"What?" What the fuck? She was sticky with sweat, she'd practically had a fucking breakdown, she'd watched two Church employees die—and now Lauren Abrams, who hadn't been through any of that, thought Chess was going to invite her out to wander the streets of Downside? At night? And not even her own neighborhood, where she was relatively safe?

"I asked if you're free tonight, Cesaria. Every minute we sit here is another minute the Lamaru could be working against us, you know. I think it's best we start right away." Her eyelashes fluttered. "Unless you're tired, of course."

Yeah, Chess was tired. Tired of being poked at by this irritating woman.

Tired physically? Another question entirely. She was exhausted. She was also holding. A couple of Nips, a nice fat line . . . She had enough pharmaceuticals and botanicals in her pillbox and back at her apartment to keep her wide awake for a week. Ha. The glories of modern living.

"I'm not tired at all," she said.

"Good." Lauren spun the file; it skittered across the table and slammed into Chess's arms. The impact sent the tendrils of purple shifting and sliding, rearranging themselves. Her stomach gave a little twist. Quickly she flipped the file open, shoved the photos inside. She didn't want to feel them looking at her anymore, and she sure as fuck didn't want to watch the physical manifestation of the heavy magic in her system wiggle around below her skin like ringworms. Or worse.

The entire file buzzed with energy. Chess couldn't imagine what kind of shit lurked between those innocuous manila covers. Didn't want to imagine it.

And lucky her, she didn't have to, because she was

going to become intimately familiar with every page, every word, every smear of darkness, every foul deed.

Just what she needed. More filth in her soul. Someday, maybe, she would explode from it; someday, maybe, every rotten thing that had ever been done to her and every rotten thing she'd ever done would erupt from her in a fountain of sewage and sorrow, all those secrets she kept even from herself spilling out and adding to the muck she could never wash off no matter how hard she tried.

She'd never been bound by magic to keep those secrets. Just by her own shame.

"Okay." Lauren rose from her seat, her right hand smoothing her skirt behind her. "Shall we take my car, or—"

"No." Oops, that came out a little too fast; Lauren's eyebrows rose. Chess could practically see her nose pinch in, her mouth opening—probably to remind Chess that as a Third Inquisitor she was Chess's superior in rank, though not directly in department. "I mean, I need my car, and I need to change out of this and take a shower. I have blood all over me." And some pills to take in private, but she didn't mention that. Her palms were starting to tingle, and she seriously needed some breathing room.

"I'll follow you."

Oh, shit. Lauren in her apartment, Lauren poking around in her stuff? No way.

"Actually, Lauren, you should probably change, too. The area we're looking at isn't really the safest part of town—"

"I'm a member of the Black Squad, Cesaria. I think I can handle a few catcalls."

Oh, shit, again. Is that all the woman thought they were in for? A couple of street toughs grabbing their crotches and making kissy noises?

Seeing those pictures, finding out they were dealing with the Lamaru—scary enough in and of itself, without the vendetta she had no doubt they were carrying against her personally for extra fun—was bad. Realizing, as she looked into Lauren's determined, arrogant face, that she was also dealing with a woman who had no concept of what they were about to get into—that was another thing entirely.

And there wasn't much Chess could say about it, because if she gave them too much information about Downside, they might rescind her permission to live there. And that didn't even bear thinking about.

"I think it's probably best if you wear better shoes for walking," she said finally. "And jeans. Something more casual, you know? We don't want to attract attention if we can help it."

Lauren considered it for a minute. "Fine. I'll go home and change. You do the same, and I'll meet you at your house in forty-five minutes."

It wasn't great, but it was better than nothing. "Do you need my address?"

"It's in your file."

"Oh. Right."

Lauren smirked and swung herself up from her seat. "Be outside, if you don't mind. I'd rather not have to waste time coming up to get you."

That remark, and several others, were still stewing in Chess's head when Lauren pulled her sports car—cherry red, the perfect little princess vehicle for the Grand Elder's perfect little daughter—up onto the curb at the corner of Fifty-fifth and Brand. "That lot, there," she said. "That's where they took the second picture."

Chess nodded and got out, taking a deep breath. The air stank, a vile, rotting scent from the slaughterhouse four blocks or so away. When the wind hit the deathhouse right all of Downside smelled like a burned-out plague pit in the summertime. And lucky her, this was one of those times.

She had to admit, though, it did have a few advantages over the cloying fragrance of perfume and bitch that filled Lauren's tricked-out coupe. Like not having to sit right next to Lauren. Or not having to listen to Lauren talk. Or especially not having to listen to Lauren's music.

Decaying carcasses were infinitely preferable to that, she thought, then regretted it—a little—when she remembered why they were there. Her stomach, already a touch uneasy under its load of four Cepts and a couple of Nips, gave a slight protest; she popped the top of the Coke can she'd grabbed for just that reason and poured some down her throat.

"You know, caffeine can mess with your energy," Lauren said. "It's best to stay away from artificial stimulants."

It was probably the funniest thing anyone had said to her in weeks. "I'll keep that in mind."

"I'm just saying, if you want to advance in the Church you should use every advantage, and one of them is keeping your power as sharp as possible. You don't want to—"

"Yeah, thanks. So where did they find—them?"

Lauren's raised eyebrows told Chess exactly what she thought of the change of subject, but she accepted it. "There. Come on."

Together they crossed the street, the heels of Chess's boots as silent as she could make them on the broken slabs of cement. The road itself looked like a patchwork quilt: squares of dirt, sections filled with dirty gravel, here and there a foot or two of blacktop.

It looked empty, and every alarm bell in Chess's head started ringing faintly. Downside streets were never empty, especially not at night. Like tall grass concealing a predator, it was when they were still and silent that they were at their most dangerous. Ready to strike. She knew there had to be at least a dozen pairs of eyes on her back at that very moment, at least a dozen hands reaching into pockets and belts and hairdos in search of weapons.

Lauren's car was probably loaded with wards, safe as it would be inside the Church itself, but the women's tattoos were designed to protect them from ghosts and magic, not from Downsiders out to make their illegal livings.

She hadn't worried about that stuff in a while. Usually if she was out at night she was with Terrible, and nobody dared fuck with Terrible; hell, nobody dared even look at Terrible for more than a few respectful seconds. Even if she wasn't with him physically, everybody knew who she was, or rather, they knew who she was with; everyone knew Downside's Churchwitch worked for Bump.

But Terrible hated her, and she had no idea if Bump knew what she'd done. What she'd been doing. "Stupid" was one word for people who thought they could get away with betraying Bump. The other word was "dead."

She had a funny feeling both those words would end up being accurate if they didn't get out of there quickly. The whole area felt off, even with the speed turning her blood into river rapids in her veins. Speed tended to mask her reactions to ghosts, but not usually to magic in general, and this corner vibed like a just-struck bell.

"You feeling anything?" she asked softly as they hit the patchy grass at the edge of the lot.

"Hmm. A little." Lauren didn't bother to lower her own voice; it sounded like the first bird chirping at dawn. Chess cringed, tried to glance around without being too obvious about it. Still nothing, no movement. This was not good.

Dead grass whispered warnings against their shoes as

they trod across it, heading for the inside corner. Rickety buildings leaned over it, ready to topple; they formed a ramshackle archway, a frame of sorts. Chess knew without being told that this was where the body—the body parts—had been found.

Still the presence of magic set her head buzzing, a little high that she would have enjoyed if she hadn't been half-numb with fear. This wasn't her neighborhood. She didn't know it. Inside those buildings could live a few families scratching out livings working the pipe rooms or at the slaughterhouse or crematorium, or picking pockets in better parts of town. People who kept themselves to themselves.

Or they could be half-mad hallucinating Nipheads with dead nerves and deader eyes. Or worse. No way to tell until they were right on top of her, and then it would be too late.

She shook her head, watched Lauren trot into the shadows in the corner with barely a pause. Either the Black Squad were a bunch of crazy-tough motherfuckers, or Lauren Abrams was dumb as dirt. Chess knew which theory she preferred.

"It was here." Lauren made a circle with her hand, waving it over an area about a foot square. Well, that was all the space that had been needed. It hadn't been laid-out corpses in those photos. More of a . . . pile, really.

Lauren pulled a heavy silver flashlight out of the backpack slung over her shoulder and switched it on. The patch of ground flew into colorless focus, cast spiky shadows against the crooked boards of the wall behind.

Shit. Chess had two choices. Go stick her hand in what was certain to be a raging pool of nasty energy floating above the lit-up spot, or look like a total pussy. And given those options, touching horrible death energy sounded positively appealing.

Tingles ran up her hands, slipping over the new scars on her wrists. In the stark light from the flash the patterns beneath her skin were black; they shifted and curled with the spot's energy, and she felt it like fingernails tickling her.

Darkness lurked there too, a slow chuckle beneath the surface. But not like she would have expected, not at all. This didn't feel like death magic, or even really like serious black magic. It felt like the kind of curse Church students tried out on one another: forgetfulness or clumsiness spells, charms to temporarily confuse the tongue so the bespelled victim couldn't speak clearly. Spells that wore off in ten or fifteen minutes. Harmless shit.

But piles of bloody body parts, carved with Lamaru symbols . . . That was not harmless. Nothing the Lamaru did was harmless.

So what the fuck was going on?

Lauren seemed to feel it too, the wrongness of it. "That doesn't make any sense," she said. "Even if they committed the murder elsewhere and just left the parts here, the energy would be darker."

"Are you sure it was here that they found it?"

"This is where they told me. It's in the pictures too, so it's got to—"

Every hair on Chess's body jumped to attention. She'd just started to spin around when red light splashed across them, across the walls, turning Lauren's hair into a river of blood around her face.

The circle stood in the middle of the intersection, deep red fire, swirled with icy-hot black energy. Chess's stomach jerked. It was darkness in that circle, darkness and misery and despair, and whatever was inside would deliver more of it the second it was unleashed. She knew it. Knew it even before the squealing started.

A pig. Not from the slaughterhouse, but closer, right on top of them, right across the street.

The Lamaru had been waiting for them. How the fuck had they known?

Lauren's eyes widened; the whites gleamed red around black pupils the size of BBs. Chess only caught a glimpse of them, of the other woman's terrified face, before she dropped to her knees and ripped her bag open. Running to the car and getting the fuck out of there was tempting, but she couldn't consider it. Didn't consider it. There were people in those empty building shells, people hiding and watching, and if she was right about what was going on behind that wall of evil, she'd be condemning every one of them to a messy death, and she had more than enough on her miserable conscience as it was without adding that.

She also had graveyard dirt. Good. Wolfsbane, she always had that, and for the last few months she'd carried melidia as well. Iron filings she'd picked up to replenish her supply—excellent. She glanced at Lauren and unwilling respect tickled in her chest. The other woman was in motion, setting up a small firedish, lighting a long wooden match off a striking strip on her shoe. Clever, that.

"Lauren! Lauren, what have you got?" She had to yell; the squealing had intensified. Not just one pig—one sow, if she was right, oh shit please let her not be right. More than one.

Lauren opened her right hand; three brownish leaves rested in her palm, next to a sprig of mistletoe. Spiritweed. Excellent. They'd need all the help they could get.

Chanting male voices rolled across the lot, slithered along Chess's skin and set her tattoos tingling and itching. She grabbed her chalk, sketched a couple of protection sigils on her forehead; they burned the second she finished them.

Her skull she grabbed last, then hesitated. They couldn't cast a circle, not unless they wanted to close the blaze inside it, and that would take too long and bring them too close. But without one, the psychopomps could escape, and that would be almost as bad as whatever was about to burst out of that fire ring; a psychopomp without control would snatch the first soul it found, and that was murder.

Lauren's eyes met hers. Clearly she'd had the same thought. "I guess we'll just have to wing it."

Chess started to reply, but a wave of energy tore the words from her mouth, tore the ground from beneath her feet. Her elbow slammed into the dirt; her shout was lost in the wild crescendo of squeals, the final triumphant shout of the men. Thick, pulsing darkness throbbed around her, so heavy her ears popped from the pressure.

Silence fell. Dead silence, a vacuum. She flipped over, started to push herself to her feet, her eyes full of the circle before her. Wind pushed her hair off her shoulders and face; her entire body waited, like standing on the edge of a cliff and taking the first step off. The relentless beat of her heart thundered in her ears; her body throbbed, a drumbeat in her soul against the reverberating emptiness around her.

Wraiths exploded from the ring of fire.

Chapter Five

> The soul should not leave the body until the moment of death. To do otherwise is to court disaster.
>
> —*The Book of Truth,* Laws, Article 449

With their filmy black bodies came the return of sound. The moment of hesitation was gone. Chess had a sick feeling it was the last semi-peaceful moment she'd be experiencing for some time.

Wraiths. A witch's freed living soul, joined with one of the restless undead. A ghost cranked on living energy, strengthened by magic, its living partner giving it the ability to do what astrally projected spirits could do: fly.

She'd never even seen one, much less fought one. The secret of their creation was closely guarded, the rituals needed—like the sacrifice of black sows—extremely difficult to perform. It was worse than she'd imagined. They swooped and dove above her, absorbing the red light, their slim bodies fluttering in the breeze their flight created.

Beside her Lauren moved. Chess glanced over and saw her on her knees, pulling a wad of silk from her bag. Inert silk, the type used to hold psychopomp skulls. But why? Unlike regular ghosts—unlike psychopomps—wraiths weren't earthbound; they'd have to touch the ground for a psychopomp dog to be useful, and Chess wasn't entirely sure what good it would do anyway. What would happen to the living souls when the dead ones were taken to the City? Would they die?

Not that she gave a shit. She just didn't know.

The wraiths circled closer now, their eyes glowing red in their shadowy faces. Snakelike arms waved and flowed from their ragged bodies. The air temperature dropped. Such cold, such awful cold . . .

And what the fuck was she doing standing there? Quickly she knelt, opened her bags of herbs. Lauren already had the fire going, so Chess dumped wolfsbane on it, grabbed the melidia. As far as she was concerned the spirit prisons were too good for these fuckers, but it was better than nothing—

Her fingers brushed the bag of iron filings, and she stopped. Glanced at the wraiths again, then back. The filings were quite small, more like dust. If there was a way to get them into the air . . . Astrally projected spirits weren't harmed by iron the way the dead were. Could she separate them somehow? Turn the wraiths into regular ghosts that she and Lauren could dispatch?

Only one way to find out, and she was about to get her chance. Her fingers scrabbled in her bag, found her Ectoplasmarker and shoved it into her pocket just as the wraiths dove.

Lauren screamed and ducked, her gun in one hand. It went off. The bullet shattered the dusty wood behind them and shot splinters at Chess's head.

She didn't have time to think about it or to rub the stinging places on her cheek. A wraith was there in front of her, black lips curling back from the even darker blackness, the emptiness, of its mouth. Its wide-open mouth, stretching, jaw falling farther and farther, her skin screaming at her—

She threw herself to the side, rolled. Shoved her hand

into the bag of filings and grabbed some, whipped her hand back around and flung them at the shadowy form. "*Arkrandia bellarum dishager!*"

The wraith twisted out of the way of the full load, but wavered. Beside her Lauren screamed.

That wasn't enough. Wasn't good enough. It would take forever at that rate—time they didn't have.

Smoke billowed around them from the firedish and stung her eyes, filled her lungs. An explosion was what she needed, something to fill the air around them with iron. To create a barrier.

"Lauren! Give me your gun. Give me your gun!"

It flew at her; she caught it one-handed, pulled it sideways. Gunpowder? There would be some in the bullets, right, enough to make a small explosion? Shit, she didn't know. Had no idea, really, but it was the best chance she had.

Lauren was covered in wraiths, all but one of them dancing around her, clinging to her while she writhed on the ground. Chess opened the clip with shaking fingers, pushed bullets out with her thumb. No time to try and open them. Throw them on the firedish, that's what she would do.

Six bullets, small and cold in her hand. Hopefully that would be enough. She tucked the gun into the waistband of her jeans—not the safest place for it, but she couldn't chance one of the wraiths grabbing hold of it. It would all be over if they did that. Without weapons they couldn't do more than steal a little energy. With weapons they could steal lives.

With her left hand she grabbed more filings, then held both hands over the firedish. No time to count, no time to think about how this probably wouldn't work. The horrible, cold, sucking energy of the wraiths surrounded her, muddled her thoughts, made her stomach heave and lurch and her brain buzz.

She emptied her hands onto the fire and threw herself to the ground.

Nothing.

Lauren screamed again and flipped onto her stomach, raised herself on all fours. One of the wraiths reached for the firedish, probably to use it as a weapon—

The firedish exploded. The force of it knocked Chess down. She sucked in a burning lungful of smoke and iron. Flipped over onto her back, pushed herself up in time to see the wraiths separate, the ghosts fall to the ground.

It had worked. She had no fucking idea how and she didn't give a damn. It had worked.

Tires squealed. The red light disappeared. Men shouted. The commotion drew her eyes; she looked away from the wraiths, away from Lauren as her lips started moving, and saw the black sow corpses in a pool of blood in the street, visible now the circle had disappeared. Saw a black muscle car thrust itself into the vacant lot in a cloud of dust, and before her mind even registered it her heart lurched into her throat.

Her legs shook beneath her but there was no time to think of that, no time to stop. The ghosts were stunned. This was the time to get them, now, while Lauren's voice rose, calling her psychopomp.

For the second time that night Chess found herself inventing passports for ghosts with no time to think or plan. She scrawled circles on each of them and finished just as Lauren's psychopomp came into being.

Psychopomps, plural. Ravens, sleek and black. What the hell . . . ? Birds weren't used in Church ritual. They were too unpredictable. So why was a Church employee—a Black Squad member, no less, Church law enforcement—using them?

Soft wings brushed against her face. The air behind Lauren wavered, giving Chess a glimpse of lit torches, of black shapes shifting and turning on their journeys to the City. The birds fluttered around, silent death for the dead, picking at the ghosts who fought them.

A car door slammed. Her head snapped to the side.

Terrible strode toward them. Even in the darkness she could see the set of his jaw, the narrow slits of his eyes. Could feel the fury pouring off him in waves.

Fury aimed at her. For a split second she started to wonder what he was doing there, but she knew. Of course she knew. Bump must own one of the nearby buildings, must have people there. If something went down around Bump's property, they knew who to call.

She took an involuntary step back, ghosts, psychopomps, and Lauren forgotten. Dimly she felt the opening between the worlds snap shut, but she didn't pay attention. Couldn't look away, because her eyes simply refused no matter how hard she might have wanted to. They traveled up the enormous length of him, all the way to the scarred, harsh-boned face. Once she'd thought he was ugly; he still was ugly, she supposed. She just didn't give a shit. He was who he was, and her heart fluttered in her chest and wouldn't stop.

So much for hoping she'd started to get over him. Or that she'd only imagined what she was feeling, only wanted him because she couldn't have him. No. She had to squeeze the board behind her, let splinters drive themselves into her skin, to keep from running up and throwing her arms around him. Begging him to forgive her. To kiss her. Shit, what a pussy she was.

"What the fuck you doin here?"

Not the greeting she'd been hoping for, especially not shouted like that.

"I—"

"Church business," Lauren interrupted, stepping forward. She shoved her sleeve up, exposing the curling black snake. Oh, fuck. Oh, no.

Oh, yes. Terrible's eyes narrowed; he gave Chess the

kind of look most people reserved for ax murderers. Ax murderers who killed children. And kittens. She shivered.

"What is your name?" Lauren continued, leaning down and snatching a pad and pen from her backpack. "And your address? What are you doing here?"

Terrible stared at her. His big arms moved, folding across his chest and straining the long sleeves of his work-shirt. The pose made him look even bigger; the iciness of his expression made him look even deadlier. Chess wondered how he was feeling, whether his wounds had healed. If he was glad to be alive, glad she'd saved him. Wondered if he even knew she'd saved him. Or cared.

"I asked for your name."

He spun around without another word and headed back toward his black '69 Chevelle, still growling at an idle in the middle of the lot.

"Excuse me! You need to—" Lauren reached for Chess, started scrabbling at Chess's shirt. What the—oh. The gun. Oh, shit, the gun. "Stop right there, buddy, or I will shoot you."

"Lauren, you can't—" She tried to twist away but Lauren found the gun butt and yanked it from her waist-band, spun toward the car with the weapon lifted.

The trigger clicked. Empty. The clip still lay on the ground by Chess's feet.

Lauren bent down, grabbed it, but she was too late. Terrible stabbed the gas and spun the wheel, sending the Chevelle roaring in an arc and spraying them with dirt. Its fat tires squealed on the pavement; he swerved around the pig corpses in the middle of the street and disappeared, leaving bloody tracks in his wake.

Chess hit the ground, hard. Her legs simply refused to support her. Without thinking she reached for her bag, shoved her hand in. She wanted her pills. Wanted to throw whatever she had into her mouth and swallow it, wanted—needed—to float away from this whole bloody scene and dull the pain in her heart. How he'd looked at her—worse than before. So much worse.

"Who was that?"

Oh, right. The pillbox fell back into her bag. Lauren was there. Probably not a good idea to pill herself into oblivion with a fellow Church employee—one who outranked her and was the Grand Elder's daughter to boot—standing right there watching. Damn it.

"I don't know."

Lauren's eyes narrowed. She still held the gun; for a second Chess thought the woman was actually going to raise it again.

Then it passed. "It looked like he knew you."

Chess shrugged. The less said the better. Deny everything—the first rule of survival.

"So that's it. You don't know who he is or why he was here."

"No."

Movement in the intersection drew both their eyes; Chess silently thanked whatever luck had finally decided to pat her on the head. One of the witches, still alive after Terrible had bolted through the circle and apparently run them down. Must have been interesting, being forced from wraith form back into one's body and then plowed into by several tons of BT steel. Well, good. She hoped the bastard suffered.

Her legs felt rubbery beneath her as she followed Lauren to the fallen body. What a mess. Blood ran everywhere from the sacrificed sows. Black ones, illegal to breed or own. The blood of a black sow—that was some heavy dark magic indeed. As they'd just witnessed.

Charmarks outlined where the circle had been. The inside was full of blood, tacky under their feet. Menace vibrated up her legs. She stepped over the bodies of two other witches, barely glancing at them. This could be a trick. With her right hand she touched the handle of her knife, tucked into her pocket. Lauren would probably freak if she realized Chess was armed, but better that than dead.

The witch moaned again, writhing in his blood-soaked robe. His robe with the Lamaru symbol on the front.

"They must have been watching," Lauren said. She tugged a bright pink cell phone out of her backpack. "Waiting for us to show up."

Gee, you think so? Chess thought, but said nothing. Lauren had handled herself pretty well during the attack; even if she hadn't, and if she didn't outrank Chess, there was the little matter of pretending she didn't know Terrible or why he was there. Best not to bring Lauren's thoughts back onto her, not when there was a convenient injured Lamaru witch right there to take the weight.

Lauren nudged him with her toe, pressed a button on the phone. "We need a wagon. Yes. Yes. Corner of Fifty-fifth and Brand. Yes, Downside. Yes, you will. What do you want me to do, put him in my car? Get your ass down here."

She snapped the phone shut. "They'll be here soon. Meanwhile . . ." She nudged him with her toe again. "Hey. Hey, you. What did you think you were doing down here?"

The Lamaru witch moaned again. Lauren's mouth twisted. "I asked you a question."

"Lauren, maybe he's not—"

Lauren glared at her. "He'll talk."

"Why don't we see if he has ID or something first? You know, what we can find out on our own?"

Chess didn't want to touch him. Didn't want to dig her hands into his bloody pockets, to make contact with the evil hovering over him like a cloud of locusts.

But she did. The sigil on her forehead blazed on her skin, the wards in her tattoos ringing like fire alarms. She jerked away. "He's Hosting."

"What?"

"Look." She forced herself to touch him again, ignoring the stinging sensation, and tilted his head so Lauren could see the silvery cast of his one open eye. Blood clung to her hands, made it hard to breathe.

Lauren loomed over her, leaning to peer down at him. "How the hell did his Bindmate escape my psychopomps? Shit. Let me call them back and let them know."

"Sure, I can Bind him down on my own," Chess muttered. Luckily the supplies she'd grabbed earlier were still within easy reach in her bag; she dusted the broken Lamaru with asafetida and graveyard dirt, added a little salt and power to keep whatever he had inside him until it could be Banished at the Church. Squatting in pig blood next to an evil piece of shit—and Lauren, too—was bad enough without having to summon her psychopomp and take care of it herself.

Lazy, sure, but then given the type of investigation this was, the Church would probably want to get a look at the thing themselves anyway.

She had to move him to get into his pockets; he shrieked when she did. His right arm flailed, narrowly missed her face.

Lauren grabbed it and slammed it to the ground, eliciting another shriek, while Chess opened the slimy wallet.

ERIK VANHELM said the driver's license. Below that was an address in Cross Town. Erik was awfully far from home—if he actually lived at that address—but then he would be. Nobody would try to pull shit like this in one of the decent parts of town, where the Black Squad actually patrolled and the neighbors actually cared.

She pulled out her notebook and scribbled the information down. Never hurt to keep your own notes, especially not when working with the Squad. Or with anyone, for that matter. One of the reasons Chess chose Debunking was so she could work alone.

Lauren held her hand out for the wallet; Chess slapped it into her palm, aware again that they were being watched. Aware too that she had to get home. He was going to show up, she knew it. If she was right about Bump owning something near here, which she had to be . . . yeah. Arriving with a member of the Black Squad and poking around was not going to win her any points in the Bump's-best-pal contest.

Would he talk to her when he came to get her?

She wasn't sure she wanted to find out. She was sure she wouldn't have a choice.

Chapter Six

> Be aware that when you work for the Church you belong to the Church, body and soul. You cannot serve two masters.
> —*Careers in the Church: A Guide for Teens,* by Praxis Turpin

Pace, pace, pace. Her body still buzzed, woozy from speed; she desperately wanted to take something to come down but didn't dare. Couldn't fall asleep. Needed to be sharp when he got there.

Lit another cigarette. It made her queasy on top of everything else, but what was she supposed to do? She'd rushed through her second shower of the night, dried her hair, put on makeup and a red top she knew he liked, even as the little voice in her head told her there was no point. She took another couple of Cepts to drown it out and kept pacing.

Tried to read; the words swam on the page. Tried to watch TV; the people wandered around, saying and doing insipid things—well, that wasn't just nerves and drugs, that was TV no matter what—until she wanted to throw her knife through the screen. She'd snapped it off and the silence blasted her from her chair. None of her CDs sounded right, were what she wanted to hear. She finally shoved in Radio Birdman just to fill the apartment with sound. Just so her misery had some company.

Where was he? It was after three. Surely he hadn't

just . . . forgotten about her? Did he hate her so much he didn't even care what she'd been doing there?

Maybe he didn't need to know. Maybe he was just going to kill her. She glanced at the stained-glass window that made up one wall of her apartment. Her building had been a Catholic church once, back before Haunted Week and the rise of the Church of Truth. Most churches had been razed during that week when the dead walked the earth and took millions of souls with them—and in its aftermath—but the Church had decided her building had some historical significance and was aesthetically pleasing, so it had been allowed to stand.

There were buildings across the street. Their windows looked into hers. Was he over there with a gun? Just waiting to—

From the street came the low rumble of a car. Of one particular car. Her heart stopped; she ran to the window, looked down in time to see Terrible walk up the steps.

One last pat of her dyed-black Bettie Page hair; one last slick of lipstick over her too-dry mouth. She couldn't do anything about the rest of it. She was pale and shaky, her entire body clammy with nerves.

When his heavy knuckles hit her door she was ready, standing beside it. Her hand flew to the knob, but she caught herself before she turned it. Bad enough that she'd made an ass out of herself the last time she'd seen him. He didn't need to know she'd been hovering here by the door, waiting.

The makeup was a mistake. So was the top, and the high-heeled boots. It was all a mistake. What did she think this was, a fucking date? How much more obvious did she want to make it? Maybe when she opened the door she could fall to her knees and start crying, too, just to complete the pitiful picture.

Another heavy knock. Okay. Deep breath time. She twisted the knob, stepped back, and pulled.

Nobody filled a doorway like Terrible.

Her mouth opened. What should she say here? Hi? How are you? Come to bed with me? Yeah, that would work. Fuck! What was she—

His eyes met hers. For one second she saw something in them. Something like what she used to see, a ghost of what had been.

Then it was gone. He jerked his head to the side in a short "Come on" gesture, turned, and walked back down the hall. No need to say anything; they both knew why he was there, where he was taking her.

Her heart fell into her shoes. It was no more than she expected. No more than she deserved. But it still hurt; fissures inside her she'd thought were starting to heal cracked back open and pumped deep-blue misery through her veins.

Breathing past the lump in her throat, she grabbed her bag and followed him, pausing only to lock and set the wards on her front door. Her arms felt awkward, her hands too big; she shoved them into her pockets, took them back out, folded and unfolded her arms as she tried to keep up with his long stride. Down the stairs, across the wide lobby and through the huge double doors, out into the cold early spring wind.

Out of habit she paused by the passenger door, waiting for him to open it, but he didn't. Right. She grabbed the icy handle herself, felt it bite her palm as she lifted it and let herself into the dark, smoke-and-leather-scented interior. Other scents lurked there as well: bourbon and beer. He'd been drinking. She didn't blame him. She could have used a drink herself just then. Would have been smart to grab a beer from the fridge.

The driver's side sank when he lowered himself onto the seat. Keys jangled.

They didn't move.

Her water bottle was in her bag. She fumbled for it, concentrating on it so she wouldn't have to feel him next to her. To smell his skin. To look at his bumpy, craggy profile, black DA haircut swooped up and back and glistening with Murray's pomade. It didn't work. She was acutely aware of all those things, and of her sadness spilling over all of it. She . . . she missed him. He was her friend. No matter how much she wanted him to be more, no matter how much she'd blown her chance at it . . . all that shit aside, he'd been her friend, and she missed that so much it hurt.

"What'd you do to me?"

The bottle slipped from her fingers; she managed to catch it before it spilled. "What?"

His right hand circled over his chest. Oh, right.

"Oh. It's a sigil, it . . . binds your soul to your body."

Images of that night swirled from her memory, played in front of her again. The way they had so many times since. His body, motionless . . . the hawk swooping down to claim his soul . . . her knife handle cold and hard in her hand, carving the sigil into his chest, the blood seeping from the design like it was responding to her summons.

He gave a short nod, barely more than a dip of his chin. Still refused to look at her. "Why?"

"You don't remember? Didn't anyone tell you?"

"Ain't nobody gave me the rundown. Nobody there, you recall, ceptin yon boyfriend, he people."

"He's not my boyfriend. I'm not . . . I'm not seeing him anymore."

If she thought that would get a response—and she had—she was wrong. His face didn't move. Nothing.

She tried again. "The hospital Goodys must have told you, though. That you almost died. You would have died if I hadn't—"

He turned the key and jumped the Chevelle off the curb. Warm air blasted from the vents; Johnny Thunders blasted from the speakers. Born to lose, no shit. One of her favorite albums, but not the message she needed at that moment.

Words kept coming to her tongue and disappearing before she could give them form. He wouldn't look at her; she couldn't look away. Through the windows the streets slid past, hookers and customers, Bump's people selling little bags of cheer on the corners, their forms black smudges around blazing firecans. Some kids in a ragged group, dancing jerkily; they zipped by too fast for her to figure out what they were doing, and it didn't matter anyway.

"How's—" She snapped her mouth shut. Asking about Katie would be a mistake, one that could very possibly cost her her life. He would not want to be reminded that she was one of the few people who knew the child existed, that he had a little girl out there with his smile and another man's name.

"How are you feeling?" she asked finally. "I mean, are you okay?"

Now he did glance at her, his eyes glittering in the dashboard light. Cold. Dead like a shark's. Apparently chat time was over.

The words tumbled from her mouth before she had time to think. "Terrible, if you would just let me explain—"

He turned up the volume. All the way. So loud her ears rang and her seat vibrated. So loud she couldn't hear herself screaming in her head. She considered turning it down, but managed to stop herself. No point making him even angrier. If that were possible. She didn't think her insides would ever thaw from that last look.

The Market had slowed down, save the lines waiting to get into the pipe room. Chess looked longingly at them as Terrible got out of the car; it took her a minute to realize he was just standing by the hood. Waiting for her to get out. No open-the-door service for her at either end anymore, it seemed.

Which was just what she deserved. But damn if it didn't hurt, almost more than his silence or his dirty look or the fact that he acted like every word he said to her had to be dragged from his mouth.

But anger was one thing. Anger she expected. The door thing . . . like she wasn't even human anymore. Didn't even deserve to be treated like one. She couldn't even blame that on the fact that he thought she was a junkie whore. Bump ran a lot of junkie whores, and Terrible dealt with them, knew them. She'd never seen him treat any of them like that.

But then, she didn't guess any of them had made out with him and pretended they didn't remember it, then made out with him again, listened to him bare his soul, told him they wanted to be with him, then got caught—ahem—red-handed with his enemy on the ground in a graveyard. So she was pretty fucking unique in that respect. And didn't she feel special because of it.

Shit. She wouldn't have opened the door for herself either. But then again, she never would have. So Terrible had finally found out she wasn't worth a second of his time or thought? If she were honest, she'd admit her only real surprise was that it had taken him that long.

She looked down at her hand; she'd grabbed an Oozer. Fine. Why not. Bump wouldn't have a job for her, she imagined; nothing she'd need to remember later, and she had her notebook anyway if she needed it. All he was going to want was an explanation of what she'd been doing there—oh, fuck.

She couldn't explain. She couldn't tell him what she was investigating, not if she wanted to stay alive. Her fingers went numb. She was about to step into the lion's awful clashing red den, and she had no idea what she could safely say without activating the Binding.

She tossed the pill into her mouth and got out of the car in one movement. Maybe if she was lucky she'd pass out.

Why she expected Bump's place to be different from before she had no idea, but part of her did. So much had changed since the last time she was there. It somehow didn't make sense for everything else to remain the same, for the horrible cacophony of reds to assault her and make her already tight nerves jangle as though she'd wandered into a hell dimension, for the naked women on the walls to eye her seductively.

But they were all the same. And so was Bump, leaning against the shiny black bar, toe ring, gold-topped cane, and all.

Terrible sat down; she turned and started to sit beside him the way she would have done before, but his look stopped her. Right. She scooted down, leaned against the opposite arm.

Still Bump did not move. Both his hands rested on the top of the cane. His head was bowed. Sky-blue silk covered his skinny chest and arms; gaudy bright gold covered his wrists and fingers.

"Ladybird," he drawled. She could feel him watching her out of the corner of his eye. "Hear tell you wanderin round Bump's places, yay? Bringin you fuckin Churchcops along. Bump hear true?"

"Yes." Okay. No First Elders showed up; the room was still clean—figuratively speaking. But then, that wasn't the difficult part, right? Where she'd been wasn't part of the Binding.

"Got a fuckin tell for me?"

Okay. Deep breath time. "It's nothing to do with you, okay? Church business."

The cane switched hands, angled to the side, like Fred Astaire performing some graceful move. But this wasn't a Technicolor musical. And it sure as fuck wasn't a beautiful dance hall. "All business Bump's business down here, Ladybird. *All* business. You want to keep doing Bump's business, yay? Keep getting yon fuckin needs? You chatter it out now."

"I—it's an investigation we're doing. That's all."

Bump's brows turned into an arrow; he spun on her with the kind of speed she knew he possessed but had never seen. "Think we playin a fuckin game here? Ain't fuckin playin, yay? You tell now. Or Terrible get he fuckin fight up. Thinkin you ain't like that one, yay?"

"It's nothing to do with you, Bump, okay? I can't talk about it."

Bump shook his head, his expression sorrowful. Chess didn't buy it for a second.

Then she didn't have a chance to buy it, because her face hit the dusty red carpet and something hard and heavy dug into the small of her back. Terrible's knee.

He'd taken her down. He'd really, genuinely taken her down. Like he'd never talked to her, touched her. Like he'd never bought her dinner or sat next to her on her broken couch. Like she was nothing to him. Just another junkie who owed Bump money, just like all the rest of them.

Her right shoulder rang an alarm; he'd twisted it back, pinned her wrist between her shoulderblades. It didn't hurt, but whether that was because she was so loaded with painkillers she wouldn't have felt it had he amputated her foot or because he was being gentle with her, she didn't know. She suspected the former, hoped for the latter.

"Ain't can believe we here," Bump drawled. "Thought we had us some fuckin trust, yay? You an Bump. Thought we had us some fuckin understanding. Hurts

Bump, this do. An Terrible . . . Dig me, Ladybird, think you putting the fuckin hurt on he, hard. Why ain't you just give me the fuckin tell, yay? An end this, so's we can be fuckin friends again. Ain't you like bein Bump's friend?"

"Black magic," she managed. "The Lama—"

The words turned into a scream, one so loud and long it scared even her, as her wrists caught fire. Agony like she'd never felt before, agony like the worst withdrawals multiplied by a dozen, shot up her arms and into her chest, into her brain, until nothing else existed. Bright red flared behind her squeezed-shut eyelids, searing her retinas; patterns like the ones on her wrist swirled in her brain.

Dimly she felt Terrible leap off her as she writhed on the floor, her body curling and twisting like a salt-covered slug, and felt his big hands lift her. Felt one of them on the side of her face, turning it, patting it. Heard his voice calling her name.

It only lasted a few seconds, maybe ten. They were the longest of her entire life. When she came out of it her cheeks tingled and burned from tears; her entire body shook when she tried to sit up. Terrible's arm was behind her back, trying to help her, but she couldn't do it. Her vision spun and popped in front of her, like she was seeing the room through some crazy funhouse lens. She squeezed her eyes back shut and tried to hold on to the water in her stomach.

His free hand moved, lifting her wrist and exposing the underside of it. The skin there still stung, as if she'd been smacked with a wet towel; an itchy, twitchy sort of sting too tender to scratch. Like a healing sunburn, or the first indications she'd gone too long between pills.

"Fuck, Chess," he said, and she realized she hadn't heard him say her name in weeks. "The fuck you do?"

His heart pounded against her cheek. Against her cheek . . . She was in his lap, her legs draped over one of his brawny arms while her ass rested on his thigh and the warm scent of his skin sent a fresh stab of pain—pain that had nothing to do with the fucking Binding—through her chest.

She opened her eyes and caught his, wide with fear, dark with concern. In that one second it was as if nothing had changed—

And it was over. His face hardened; he looked away. Rather than sit there like an idiot staring at him, so did she.

That's when she saw the blood.

It wasn't much. Just a few trickles, winding their spidery way down her arm, seeping from the horizontal black scars below her wrists. Oh . . . shit. Not just pain, then. Blood. A graphic reminder of her oath seeping into the ends of her sleeves.

Was that how the First Elders would kill her if she talked? Open those magically sealed wounds and let her bleed out?

She did not want to find that out for herself. Didn't even want to think about it, but couldn't stop. The blood—her blood—transfixed her; now that the pain had faded, all she could do was stare as one lone drop fell from her arm to Bump's red shag pile.

Terrible lifted her enough to set her on the couch and got up. She heard drawers opening, paper rustling; he came and sat down next to her with some alcohol pads and a couple of Band-Aids.

She started to fold her arms, then thought better of it. "No."

"Ain't can leave that shit open," he mumbled.

"No, it's not— It won't help." She dared to look at him; he was totally absorbed in playing with the little alcohol wipe packet, and pale around the eyes. She could only imagine what he must have been thinking. Having her freak out like that couldn't have been pleasant. Even

Bump looked shaken, at least as shaken as it was possible for Bump to look. The knuckles he wrapped around the tip of his cane were whiter than usual.

"They're Binding marks." She waited for the shocking pain to come again, braced herself for it. When it didn't come she continued. "They're why I can't talk about what I was doing. I'm Bound from it."

Bump's head tilted back. "You ain't give Bump the tell then, causen them Church ain't give you the fuckin yay."

"Right. I can't. It'll—well, you saw. And that's just a warning."

Silence. Okay, well, they both knew she couldn't talk, and knew why, but she had the distinct feeling the matter wasn't going to drop there. Maybe if she tried something else? A little different wording?

"It's not about you." Another shot of pain raced through her bloodstream, but not so bad this time. Certainly not like what it had been a few minutes before. Okay. She was starting to get a feel for this thing now, and that was good.

"But where you at this night . . . Bump got fuckin business there, yay? Ain't wanting no Churchcops havin a wander-round there."

"They found some—" This time she didn't need the pain. No way was she going to be allowed to let that particular piece of information fly.

Terrible spoke up, glancing at her as he did so with quick little eye-darts, like he was looking at the sun and couldn't do it for too long. Only in her case she doubted he was seeing anything bright. "Figure on it bein them body parts, aye, Bump? Ratchet find em, you recall, two days past. That it?"

"You know about them?"

His eyebrows cranked up. Right. Of course he did. What went on in Downside that Bump and Terrible didn't know about?

"You know who found them?"

Another dead look.

"No, seriously. I need to talk to him—her. Whoever. I don't know if their name's in the fi—"

Okay, this was starting to piss her off. On the one hand it was good to get some kind of calibration going, to find out exactly how far she could go. Pushing boundaries had always been one of her hobbies. But she could have done with an easier way to figure out where those boundaries were.

Plastic rustled: Bump's pillbag. Probably the same one he'd offered her months ago, when she first got involved with him—well, involved more than the usual buying-selling game they'd been playing for a few years. She'd taken an Oozer before they came in but it wasn't kicking in. And even if it had been, why the hell not?

She grabbed two more and chased them with water. The little hand on the clock had sneaked past four; she was crashing hard from the Nips and thought of her bed with the kind of yearning she normally felt for . . . well, for the pills she'd just swallowed.

Bump tapped his cane against the floor, setting the gold band around the bottom flashing.

"So . . . Sound like Bump got some fuckin knowledge you need right, yay? Like I do some fuckin help for you. Ain't have they Churchcops all down Bump's fuckin business, dig, ain't have it noways. Think we make us a deal, Ladybird, yay? Fine deal Bump got for you."

Her sigh felt dragged from the depths of her soul. Great. Working for Bump again.

Chapter Seven

> Don't be afraid to admit to yourself what results you're looking for, or to ask your friends for help.
>
> —*You Can Do This! A Guide for Beginners,* by Molly Brooks-Cahill

"I can't do that," she said again, and just as he had before, Bump waved an imperious hand as if her objections were lowly servants to be dismissed.

"Ain't sayin take Terrible when she fuckin Churchcop along, dig. But after. You ain't can say you knowledge, yay, but he fuckin can. Bump gots what he needs, so you gets you fuckin needs. Real simple, Ladybird. Ain't it clean?"

"I'll die, Bump. This isn't something to fuck around with, I took a blood oath—"

"An you ain't breakin it, dig. Just doin you some side work, yay? Takin you some protection where you go. Give Bump the listen-down, here, Ladybird. All business Bump's business, you recall. They black magic shit goes down, Bump's business. They ain't got a sweet spot for Bump, guessing, after Bump's men done give them the crack-up out Chester. Danger for Bump, danger for all, if you dig. Bump gotta get he Churchwitch in it, yay? Ain't gotta run it up again, do I?"

No. He didn't. They'd been through this before; only a few weeks before, no matter that it felt as if a lifetime had passed. Bump ran Downside, and without Bump in control things could get even worse than they were already, hard as that was to believe. Nor was he wrong in assuming the Lamaru's return put Terrible and Bump in at least as much danger as it put her.

And there was more to it, much as she hated to admit it. If Bump wanted to bring her in on this, it meant Terrible hadn't told him about her and Lex. And if Terrible hadn't told him—despite the reason he'd given her for keeping his mouth shut, about not wanting Bump to know how he'd failed, how he'd convinced Bump she was trustworthy and had been wrong—maybe there was a chance.

And working with him? Would give her an opening to find out. Maybe to prove herself again.

Just thinking of it all made her want to dive under a blanket of Dream and stay there until her bones dissolved, to suck that thick yellowish smoke deep into her lungs until she forgot him. Forgot everything and became nothing more than another loose-limbed body draped on a velvet couch, another tiny spark of consciousness fluttering in the ecstatic drugged-out breeze.

Bump seemed to take her silence as the need for more convincing, instead of simply a few minutes' wallow in her own pitiful bog. "Terrible know them streets, dig. Be a fuckin help, he do. You take he 'long, Ladybird, see if Bump ain't right. Bet we get you all in the good lights with you bossmen, yay? They Elders. Like you right, them will, you catch they black magic witches."

The words were out of her mouth before she could stop herself with something ridiculous like common sense or dignity. "Okay. I'll try."

The leering grin split his face like a knife through a half-rotted peach. "That's good, yay, real fuckin good. You get you started on the morrow, yay. Bump takin he off to he fuckin bed now, ain't keep Bump's ladies on the wait longer, dig." He reached into the bag, took out a handful and held them out to her. "You take them. For friendship."

The room spun a little around her when she reached out, let the pills fill her hand. Not too many of them; he was being generous, sure, but generous for Bump was awfully stingy, especially considering all the work she'd done for him. But hey, what was she going to do, turn them down? Free drugs were free drugs, and she wasn't stupid.

At least not about that.

About other things . . . yeah, totally stupid. As she followed Terrible back out into the predawn chill she had plenty of time to think about how stupid. Despite that second or two of connection he still hated her, wasn't likely to forgive her. All she was doing was signing herself up for more heartbreak.

Not to mention the great chance of being killed by the First Elders if she stuck a toe—or said a word—out of place.

Cold seeped through her jeans from the leather seats. Wings of exhaustion fluttered behind her eyes; she could barely keep them open. Even "One Track Mind" wasn't helping. The Nips were well and truly gone. She felt like someone had filled her skin with chilly sawdust, too burned out for the Oozers to do much good.

The drive back to her place seemed to take no time at all. Before she knew it he'd pulled up in front of the steps; she had a sneaking suspicion that she'd fallen asleep.

"So I guess I'll see you tomorrow," she said to Terrible's profile. "Do you want me to meet you, or what?"

He shrugged. "Whatany you want."

A million thoughts ran through her mind, none of which would do any good to verbalize. So she said, "Okay, why don't you pick me up at noon? I have to meet Lauren—she's the girl from earlier—I have to meet her at five."

Pause. "Meet me. Up Edsel's booth, aye? You wanna say midday, no problem."

"I thought you said— Never mind. Yeah, that's fine. I'll meet you there."

Nod.

Whatever. She still got to shove the heavy door open all by herself, and she'd trudged halfway up the stairs before she realized he was right behind her, his boots silent on the cement. One of his talents, that was, the ability to move so soundlessly. But then it was part of his job. Most people didn't line up to get beaten down. They had to be found, snuck up on, snatched off the street, and broken before they knew what hit them. And nobody broke people better than Terrible did.

She should know.

"What are you doing?"

He shrugged. "Ain't can say."

Okay, so not tired anymore. Was he . . . Shit! She hated this. *Hated* this.

Her jumbled thoughts must have been clear on her face; his dark eyes narrowed. "Bump say me come up. Ain't my choosing."

"Oh."

"Shit. Don't you get no ideas, dig. Ain't wanting this. An ain't givin you shit to play pass-on with."

They'd reached the inside staircase now; her voice echoed in the cavernous lobby. "I'm not playing pass-on with anything. I told you, I'm not seeing him anymore."

"Ain't give a fuck who you see."

"Then why are you so fucking mad about it?"

Redness crept up his neck; he glared at her, then shoved past her to continue up the stairs. She'd gotten him with that one. A hollow victory, but she'd take just about anything she could get at this point.

Her turn to push past him, opening her front door, stepping into the dingy little apartment. She made a beeline for the freezer and yanked out the half-full bottle of vodka she'd bought a couple of days before.

The cabinet beside it contained her pitiful collection of mismatched plastic cups and plates. She pulled down two cups and unscrewed the cap on the vodka. "Want a drink?"

He moved behind her; she heard a faint rustle, and the closing of the door. She turned around.

He was gone.

So was the Lamaru file she'd been given earlier.

She couldn't remember the last time she'd seen a sky that blue, and despite everything, it lifted her spirits. So she was about to meet someone who hated her; so she was betraying the Church and walking a razor-thin tightrope over a pit of messy death; so later on she was going to have to meet a woman she already disliked and investigate an illegal black magic group who wanted her dead.

So the sky was blue, and three Cepts calmed her down and insulated her just enough from the buzzing crowds at the Market and the still-cold breeze to make her feel like she could handle all the shit. So that was good. The sun felt great on her face and hands, raised blue lights in her dyed hair. A month before it had been snowing. Now it was almost spring.

Edsel's booth must have been particularly busy that morning; when Chess stopped walking in front of the shabby-velvet-covered counter he was restocking runebones and little hand-sewn bags. Made sense, though. News of his wife's pregnancy had spread.

"How's Galena?" she asked, reaching out to finger one of the runes. A little shiver ran up her arm. "Good, I guess. I can feel it."

Edsel smiled. His teeth were the same color as his skin and ice-white hair; his black sunglasses didn't hide the kind of happiness she'd rarely seen from him. "She right, baby. Still tired, aye, but she doctor say oughta pass up soon and she be bouncin again. She— Damn, what you got there?"

He picked up her hand; when she'd reached for the magical items, infused with the extra energy of pregnancy, he'd caught sight of her Binding scars.

"It's nothing." She tried to pull it back.

"Ain't *nothing,* baby. Know them marks when I see em, aye. Been Bound, you have." He dropped her hand; his deep smoke voice lowered. "Bet you lookin for them Lamaru again, aye?"

"How—" Ouch. Shit. "You know—you've heard—damn it!"

Edsel nodded. "Been hearin them rumors, if you dig. Know some people, them know people. Say big trouble on the way down, them gearin up right."

"Why didn't you tell me?"

"Ain't seen you much, aye? And you ain't look like you up for it, baby. Lookin tired. Lookin mighty down. Guessing maybe got aught doing with why Terrible been rippin it up like him dog dead. Aye?"

Fuck. She did not want to discuss that. Not with him. Not with anyone. Edsel may have been the closest thing she had to a friend—at least, he used to be, and she guessed he was again—but some things were just . . . private. Most things were private.

Of course, she couldn't deny being a little interested in that last line anyway. So Terrible looked upset, did he?

Then again, why wouldn't he?

"Who do you know? I mean, you said you knew people who knew people. Do any of them have any information?"

He hesitated. "I ain't got names, you dig. Need to make some calls."

"No problem. Just, anything you could find out would be a help. Really. Bump's got his fingers in it too, so it's not just me you're helping, you know?"

Edsel looked down, dug his cell phone out of his pocket. The sun glowed off his pigmentless hair. "Gotta hang me a couple days on this one, baby. They folk ain't the kind always answer them phones."

"Sure. Thanks, really. Oh, and here—" She dug her notebook and pen out of her bag, leaned forward to scribble a list. "This is a long shot, I know, but if anybody buys any of this stuff—anybody you don't know—could you let me know? Try to find out who they are, if you can."

Her list wasn't long; the Lamaru would have their own suppliers anyway. But things like corpse water or tormentil were pretty strictly regulated by the Church, and had a big enough customer base outside of it that they might chance buying it off someone. So why not Edsel?

He took the torn-off sheet of paper, nodded. "Hold out, now. Lemme try, while you here."

He punched a couple of buttons on the phone, took a step back into the shadows at the back of the booth. He usually lurked there, out of the sun, looking more like a wax statue or a corpse than a man. Caught a lot of thieves that way, too.

She took a discreet step away, distracting herself by gathering up a few things to buy. Thirty K in her bank account felt really fucking good, and she could use some things, right?

In the center of the counter she made a little pile: one of the bags Galena made, a couple of hare bones, a little vial of goat's blood. That might come in handy if she was dealing with black witches. Oh, and some protective items, too, she'd need those.

In a wicker basket fairly vibrating with power, plastic-wrapped snake segments rested in among lodestones and black cat paws. She grabbed a paw and two bags of snake to add to the pile, too, and tossed a chunk of black mirror on top. She could make a hell of a hex with those, and she might need it later.

What else . . . mandrake might be useful, grab a piece of that . . . She opened her mouth to ask how much spiderweb he had, when he held up a hand.

"Got me a message left. Ain't no guarantees, baby, you know, but we see what we got. You keep touchin me, aye? An I touch back iffen I hear, or sell that list somebody I ain't know."

"Thanks."

"Aye, well. Bump getting involved this one, maybe he willin to kick in some lashers, aye? Babies got needs, you dig."

"Yeah, I'll ask him, okay? I . . ."

He definitely looked paler, she thought, seeing Terrible push through the crowd. Last night she hadn't noticed it, not even at Bump's place; all that red gave everything a low-key sort of glow. But in the sunshine she saw it. He looked a little tired, a little pale. She wondered if his wounds still hurt. She wished she could turn her greedy eyes away.

"Might wanta get yon mouth closed, baby," Edsel murmured.

Chess did, snapping her teeth together so hard it hurt and wishing desperately she'd paid better attention to casting glamours in training. She could have wiped the stupid blush off her face.

Instead she focused on the grinning skulls dancing down the wide stripes on the front of his bowling shirt. It was easy to do so, considering he stood about a foot taller than her own five feet six.

"Edsel," he said. "You right?"

"Right up. Been telling Chessie here, maybe I got some knowledge be useful. You thinkin Bump might kick in, be the case?"

"Aye, he lash you back. No problem."

"Cool. Chessie gonna keep touchin me, I keep her up, aye? She pass it on."

Terrible's gaze fell on her. His chin jerked; it could have been a nod, she guessed.

"Hey." She fumbled in her bag for some money and thrust it at Edsel. "Do you have the file—"

"Aye."

"Where is it? I really need it back, you shouldn't have just—"

"Car."

Deep breath. "Um, I wanted to grab something to eat first, okay?"

Shrug.

Okay, this was bullshit.

The food booths were at the far end; Edsel had set up in the middle, where he usually tried to find a spot. The center was the best, away from the hot smoke of the firecans and the meats cooked over them, far from the clucking chickens and the occasional goat, where the sawdust spread over the cement wasn't soaked with blood.

But she wanted food, anything she could find, despite knowing it would deaden her high. Like he wasn't doing a fine job of that all on his own.

She took her purchases from Edsel and shoved them into her bag, her scuffed boots shuffling on the cement as she headed for the food. The noodle lady was there, but she didn't . . . yes. One of the vendors had a set of bamboo skewers turning over a fire; on the skewers were chunks of what appeared to be chicken. That's what she was going to assume, anyway. They looked good and they smelled good, and if the meat was something unnamable she didn't want to know about it.

Terrible loomed behind her while she made her purchase, barely concealing his impatience, until finally she swung around on him with her stick in hand.

"Look. You want to be mad at me, that's fine. You want to not give me a chance to explain, I can't do anything about that either. But we have to work together. So the least you can do is not treat me like I'm carrying some kind of fucking communicable disease, okay? Be pissed at me on your own time, because I can't work like this."

"Depends the kinda work you doin, aye?"

Oh, man, that hurt. Not showing it, though? Now that was easy. She'd had a lifetime of practice at pretending not to be hurt.

So she pegged him with her eyes, folded her arms across her chest. "Fuck. You."

"Ain't thinkin I got the price."

"No? Then—"

The horn cut her off, loud and rough in the bright clear day. A vinyl record, she realized; the telltale pops and crackles came through the speakers. What the . . .

She turned, along with most of the crowd around her. Street performers weren't entirely unusual in the Market; not common, because most Downsiders mistrusted outsiders almost as much as they liked to stab them and steal their money. But every once in a while some singers would set up, or a couple of acrobats.

This was different.

At the far end, by the crumbled remains of what had once been a wall, a stage had been set up; it appeared to be a layer of wooden crates with wide boards laid across them. Pillars rose at the four corners, draped in orange fabric, and across the top of those stretched more orange strips, the color glowing against that aquamarine sky.

A sign hung down from the top: ARTHUR MAGUINNESS'S POTENT POTIONS.

Okay, this should be interesting.

Chapter Eight

> Only through penitence and pain is forgiveness possible.
> —*The Book of Truth,* Veraxis, Article 72

The trumpet record continued playing, a musical backdrop for the gathering crowd. Chess didn't particularly want to go see—what was the point, really?—but she wasn't eager to get into Terrible's car and fight with him some more either, and she wanted to finish her food.

Plus he appeared to want to check it out, which made sense. Bump didn't generally allow such shows on his front porch. If "Arthur Maguinness" hadn't gotten the okay first, or if his potent potions contained something that might affect Bump's business . . . Terrible would need to know about it.

So she followed his broad shoulders through the crowd, tearing bits of what she was almost certain was indeed chicken off her skewer. It was good, too; when had she last had hot food? She couldn't remember. The hospital, she guessed. They'd brought the stuff to her whether she wanted it or not, and made her take at least a few bites so they could write it on their little charts. It had been made clear that she wasn't getting out of there unless she ate, so she had.

Since getting out, though? Sure, she'd eaten, but nothing more than a couple of sandwiches or something. Hot food wasn't much of a priority for her. Not when there were so many better things she could put in her stomach, and she needed them so much more.

Which reminded her. Thanks to Bump's little gift the night before she wouldn't need to call Lex yet, but she probably should. She hadn't seen him since she left the hospital.

That wasn't a conversation to look forward to, not at all. No, she wasn't seeing him anymore—well, what they'd been doing together wasn't really "seeing," not unless the sentence finished with "each other naked. A lot."

The problem was, he didn't know that.

Sure, he probably had some idea. Seeing her go hysterical—which was a bit of an understatement, really—when Terrible almost died, and commit a capital offense to save him, probably gave Lex some indication that their days together were numbered. Luckily he'd missed most of the horrible scene in the graveyard; well, luckily for her, anyway, as it spared her some embarrassment. Not so luckily for Lex, who'd been out cold on the frozen ground with a broken jaw after Terrible caught them together and expressed his feelings on the subject.

Anyway. She wasn't going to be able to put it off much longer. Thanks to the wired-shut jaw, he hadn't hit on her much while she was still in the hospital, but now she was out . . . he'd be expecting to see her, and he'd be expecting to see her the way he usually did, which was in his bed. After he'd given her drugs.

Technically the drugs and the bed didn't have anything to do with each other. The drugs were payment for the destruction of Chester Airport; it had been haunted, and Bump had wanted her to banish the ghosts so he could run drugs into it. She hadn't been able to, and the airport was no more, and that was good for Lex.

The bed . . . that was just a bit of fun. Had been a bit of fun, until she'd realized two things: One, that accepting free drugs from someone with whom she was sleeping felt and looked way too much like whoring for drugs; and two . . . Two was standing at her side with the air of a man who'd prefer inserting knives into his own throat to being anywhere near her.

The sudden cut-off of the music drew her back to the ramshackle stage before her, silence hovering for a second over the crowd before they started murmuring.

A man walked onto the stage.

At least she thought it was a man. He was tall, even taller than Terrible, she thought, but that could have been just the stage adding height.

Any resemblance to Terrible stopped there, though. Where Terrible was broad and packed with muscle, this man was a rake, his striped waistcoat and drainpipe trousers hanging off his bones. The sleeves of his dingy, inexpertly mended white shirt ended a couple of inches above his knobby wrists; the ragged hems of his trousers exposed ashy-pale ankles over mismatched shoes. And black hair, torrents of it, sprouted from his head and fell in a tangled curtain down his back, over his face, meeting up with a scraggly beard that reached his stomach.

"Good morrow, kind ladies and sirs!" His heavily accented voice rang deep and clear over the waiting crowd. "May the Truth keep you all safe in its arms! For today you are about to see Truth the likes of which you have never seen before!"

Another figure walked onto the stage; this one tiny, in a flowered all-in-one suit with feet. Not a child, though. A little person like Goody Vanderpeet, one of the kitchen Goodys.

But nothing at all like Goody Vanderpeet, aside from stature. This person had bright purple hair, standing straight up in a stiff, elaborate curlicue unaffected by the wind. His face was painted green, as were the palms of his hands.

"My assistant LeRue will open the case, and I will show you wonders the likes of which you have never seen. I come in Truth, good people, and in Truth you shall discover today the miracles of my potions, for I am Arthur Maguinness and my name is known far and wide!"

Chess rolled her eyes and glanced around the crowd. Most of them wore the same yeah-right expression as herself, but not all; she caught a few open mouths and wide eyes.

With a flourish LeRue opened a green-and-purple-striped trunk squatting on the far end of the stage. The lid stood almost as tall as he did; that was one big-ass trunk. As the lid rose, shelves did as well, covered with oddly shaped bottles and flagons. The potent potions, she assumed.

"One touch, one taste, of my potions will change your life, and I guarantee it! In those bottles lives the result of centuries of knowledge, passed down from generation to generation, by the finest masters in history! Men to whom even the Church bowed, begging for the information they possessed!"

Chess jerked at that, a little. Bullshit. Standard bullshit, yes, but still irritating. Legitimate businesses weren't allowed to make such claims, but Maguinness up there looked so far removed from the word "legitimate" she was amazed his name shared a few of the same letters.

Unaware that he was being given the narrow-eye by a Churchwitch, Maguinness bent his long frame like a folding ruler and held up one of the bottles, a fancy cut-glass item of the type usually found on the sideboards of social climbers. This one was dusty and smudged; the liquid inside was a noxious shade of orange.

Her arms itched. She scratched them absently while Maguinness began describing, in florid detail, the benefits of that particular concoction, but it didn't seem to help. The itch remained just below the surface of her skin.

That wasn't right. She'd dosed up just before she left the house, so she wasn't withdrawing. Something was wrong. It was magic, yes, and given that there were potions not far away that undoubtedly had magical ingredients, it wasn't so strange for her to feel it. But this didn't feel . . . normal. Like the magic she used, or was used to.

Instinctively she looked at Terrible fidgeting beside her, with his arms folded and his weight shifted away from her. That wasn't right, either. Well, leaning away from her was, at least these days. But the way his fingers twiddled with the fabric of his sleeve, the way he kept swallowing . . . not right at all.

"Terrible," she whispered, leaning closer. "Are you okay?"

He didn't hear her. Or maybe he was just ignoring her. She tried again, reaching out to touch his arm. "Terrible, are—"

He jerked away with a violence that made her heart stop and glared at her before turning and starting to push through the crowd. "Right. 'Sgo."

She'd thought a few times in the past—more than a few times, really—that he had some magic skill of his own. Not enough to work for the Church; only slightly more than the average person. But more nonetheless. Had he felt it too, the odd tingle given off by Maguinness?

Nobody else seemed to, or if they did they were hiding it well.

So it was affecting her, and it was affecting him . . . The thought finished itself before she could stop it.

Had she done something to him, when she'd carved that sigil into his chest?

The sigil itself was illegal. It had been used in the early days of the Church as protection for their employees in case of ghost attacks, Binding their souls to their bodies until medical help could arrive. A student had modified it with horrifying results, though, turned the person he marked with it into a wide-open receptacle for spirit possession.

She hadn't used the modified version. It should have been safe.

But then, she should have grown up being well taken care of by loving foster families, and that sure as hell hadn't been the case. Not unless you considered "well taken care of" to mean "fucked and beaten" and "loving foster families" to mean "child-raping, drug-running, money-grubbing pieces of shit."

So much for "should have."

Once inside the car he thrust the file into her hands and shot the car off the curb in a maelstrom of squealing rubber. She looked at him sharply, her back tensing in anticipation of an argument.

She'd fucked him over hardcore. She'd betrayed him and she'd lied to him, and she knew that as far as he was concerned she'd led him on and used him as well, had consorted with people who wanted to see him dead and given them information to help them make him so. Most of all, she'd hurt him. And if the pain in her chest was anything close to what he'd felt, she was more than willing to admit he deserved to get his own back. Was willing to do more than admit it; was willing to take it, in the hopes he'd eventually decide she'd been punished enough and they could maybe move on.

But at that moment they were on their way to interview the man—Ratchet—who'd found the body parts in the vacant lot. She needed to have her wits about her, not to be waiting for the next verbal barb or dirty look. He could slash at her with knife-sharp words later; maybe if he did it enough her blood would finally flow clean.

Somehow she doubted it ever would.

But he didn't speak at all. He'd flipped on his sunglasses

so she couldn't see his eyes, but the set of his heavy jaw and lowering brow, the tension in his arms and the way his lips pressed together . . .

"Are you okay? I mean," she added quickly, "do you *feel* okay. That guy back there, I don't know about you, but he made me feel kind of twitchy. He had some power and I felt it. So I just wondered if maybe you did, too."

"Ain't no witch."

"Yeah, I know, but you look like— He was creepy and I just wondered if you'd felt it, too, is all."

When he didn't respond, she tried again. "That sigil in your chest, have you been feeling—"

"I'm right."

"I'd really want to help—"

"Said I'm *right,* dig?"

She bit her lip and turned to the file. Thanks to his sneaky thief act the night before she hadn't even had a chance to look through it, only to skim it before trotting outside like a good little doggie to wait for Lauren.

And she hadn't missed much. At least she hoped she hadn't; but no, they wouldn't have stolen anything. Copied it, sure, she had no doubt. But not stolen.

Sun glinted off the heavy chain around Terrible's right wrist and stung her eyes, and for once she had her sunglasses. She was digging around for them when he pulled the car up in front of an empty-eyed building with dead weeds poking out of the ground floor windows, its walls dark with remembered flames. A squat.

She grabbed her notebook and pen, secured the edges of the file with a rubber band, and stuffed it into the depths of her bag.

He didn't ask if she was okay, but opened his trunk while she climbed out of the car and stood on the patch of crumbled cement that had once been a small parking lot. Ahead of her, dried blood crusted the street; she could still see the tire tracks he'd left when he'd peeled away the night before.

The pig carcasses were gone, of course. And now that she thought about it— Yes, the air carried the faint fragrance of roasting pork. She couldn't imagine the glee that little bit of magic must have left in the hearts and stomachs of the neighborhood, most of whom had probably never seen that much meat in their lives. Didn't want to imagine if any of those lives had been lost in the battle over who got to eat it, either. None of her concern.

She tried to shrug off the heavy stares she knew the two of them were getting, and headed for the empty doorway when she heard the trunk slam shut.

The entire bottom floor was choked with weeds as high as her chest, long spiky stalks of ivory-colored grass gone to seed, spindly bushes. A thin trail had been worn through them into a darker space in the corner. The stairs. Terrible slid in front of her without touching her and pushed his way along the path; the dead plants tried in vain to grab his arms as he passed.

Soft sounds drifted down the stairs when they hit the bottom. Chess paused, took a deep breath. Something rang in the building, so faint it was more of an implication than an actual fact, but there nonetheless. Magic. The slow, deep slither of magic, inching up her legs and along her arms, curling into her stomach.

Not just average magic, either. Almost everyone did some; there was an entire successful industry in spellbooks and items designed for the average person who had little or no skill or natural ability. Most of them didn't really work. They relied more on the practitioner's belief that it would be effective than any actual results.

She was familiar enough with how those spells and charms felt. She'd encountered enough of them in the homes of her subjects: dream safes designed to ward away nightmares, charm bags for wealth or safety, or occasionally sex spells planted in bedrooms. Those tended to be the most effective—and thus the most irritating for Chess, who did not like sex magic—simply because sex was the most accessible type of energy for most people. Any idiot could get turned on.

But this didn't have the blunt edge of amateur magic, not at all. Too subtle; too well hidden.

She didn't realize she was staring at the landing above them until Terrible's low voice broke her reverie. "Any wrong?"

"Feels like magic in here," she said, echoing his quiet tone.

"Some do, aye? Them with them luck spells or aught."

"Not like this, though. Spells like that—spells done by people who really aren't talented—they don't feel . . . finished, if you know what I mean. They're not well formed, they're just like little blobs of weak energy. This isn't—" She stopped, suddenly aware that they were having a conversation. A normal conversation.

One that wouldn't last if she even considered pointing that out. Oops. "This isn't like that. Whoever's been casting in here knows what they're doing. And they've tried to hide it. The magic, I mean. They're trying to hide what they're doing."

"All Bump's here, dig. Them to keep the eye out. Ain't should be doin up that shit here."

"All of them? They're all Bump's people?"

He shrugged. "What they ought, aye."

"I guess we should go see, huh?"

Another small shrug, like he couldn't really be bothered to complete the movement, and he preceded her up the cement staircase. The floor had once been covered in linoleum; curled edges of it remained like bookends where the stairs joined the walls.

The smell hit her nose at the same moment her feet hit

the landing. Terrible stopped short; she would have run right into him if she hadn't done the same. He turned to her, and in that moment she wasn't thinking about what she'd done or what he'd done or what she wished they could do. She was thinking about the scent of death and how it raised the hairs on her arms, and she was thinking things had just gotten a fuck of a lot worse. For everyone.

Chapter Nine

> Remember the power inherent in blood. I recommend burning anything it touches. This may seem like an extreme measure, but better safe than sorry!
>
> —*Mrs. Increase's Advice for Ladies,* by Mrs. Increase

They both ran. Up the stairs, through the open doorway to the left of the empty landing, where Chess's stomach gave a great heave and barely managed to hold its contents.

It wasn't a murder. Wasn't a multiple murder. It was a slaughter; there was no other word for it, no other way it could be described.

Blood covered everything so thickly and thoroughly she thought for a moment she was seeing through a lens. Only the dirty plaster peeking through the spatter on the upper walls convinced her it was blood and not red paint coating them, still dripping slowly down. The scrap of threadbare carpet on the floor was soaked with it; the heaped garbage bags in a corner were slick with it; a couple of ragged blankets slumped sodden against the wall.

It took her a second to find the bodies in that sea of blood, but they were there. At least . . . the parts were. They were scattered across the floor as if some careless child had been playing with them and grew tired of the amusement; a leg here, an arm there, a torso, a head . . .

Her stomach lurched again. Desperately she swallowed,

hard, forcing down the saliva that suddenly filled her mouth. Too much, this was too much, everywhere she looked she saw an empty staring eye or a horrible sharp piece of white bone protruding from shriveling flesh—

Terrible's hand, hard and warm on the back of her neck, wrestled her out onto the landing. An open window there, a blank hole in the smoke-colored wall; he thrust her head through it, forced her into the cool fresh air. She filled her lungs, heard them like bellows in her chest. Blinked furiously, trying to clear her vision of the spots obscuring it.

Slowly she came back to herself. At least enough to realize they weren't alone on the landing. Muffled sounds, like someone speaking in another room, floated through the stillness and became audible as her breathing slowed.

She spun around. No one there. But Terrible had evidently heard it too; his cautious gaze scanned every inch of the landing while she checked the ceiling. He barely looked better than she felt, and she wondered if he'd hustled her to the window purely for her benefit or because it provided him with a good excuse to get some air himself.

To the right of the stairs, across from the blood-filled deathchamber, another entrance loomed. There, sheets of newspaper covered the windows and blocked the light, rattled ominously in the breeze.

Still the voice. Wordless. Muffled. She realized what it was and jumped forward, only to be caught by his hard arm across her chest. He shook his head. So he realized it too, then. Knew what was in that room. Knew they'd found either a survivor or a murderer.

She watched him poke his head cautiously into the gloom and look both ways. He motioned her forward with a quick twitch of his fingers.

No blood in that room. Graffiti covered the walls instead; fuzzy shapes dotted the floor.

One of them moved.

Chess jerked back. Kind of a stupid thing to do, really; she could see what it was—who it was—even as her feet moved without her. But the tension in the air crawled all over her body, the memory of that blood-filled room refused to leave her head, and she could still feel the weight of Terrible's hand on the back of her neck.

"Right, now, little one." Terrible held his left hand up by his shoulder, palm facing the huddled figure on the floor. His right sneaked behind his back; Chess watched it wrap around the handle of his knife. Just in case. "Ain't nobody hurt you, aye? Whyn't you get on up, we—"

The person—the woman—raised her eyes. Chess looked into them and saw what Terrible couldn't possibly see: the dark glee of black magic. Felt its aura slam into her like a freight train, felt her skin grow hot and her brain expand in her head.

Two other shapes materialized, grew from what looked like bundles of cloth on the floor into people. Two men, two witches. Two murderers, interrupted before they finished whatever they were planning to do with all that blood and energy in the next room.

The woman on the floor ripped the tape off her mouth and leapt to her feet in one smooth, too-fast movement. A fetish dangled from her hand; Chess saw it and screamed.

Terrible spun toward the wall, trying, Chess assumed, to get his back against it. Along the way he grabbed her arm and practically wrenched it out of its socket attempting to force her behind him.

She wouldn't go. Couldn't go. Because the thing that woman held carried death worse than whatever had happened across the hall, and Chess had to stop it.

Fuck. If she told Terrible what the real worry was it would only make the woman start her spell faster. If she didn't tell him he wouldn't know and the spell would go off, anyway.

Her arm ached where he'd yanked it. She gritted her

teeth and lifted it, taking advantage of the split second before the fight started to grab his hand and squeeze.

His gaze darted to her; she dipped her head toward the fetish, squeezed his hand again. Begged him with her eyes to understand. If he didn't . . . Shit, if he didn't, they would just go ahead and die here. She didn't doubt for a second that he could beat the two male witches—the two Lamaru, she assumed—standing in lame-ass martial-arts-movie fighting poses in front of them. There was no reason to doubt; even if she didn't have the confidence she had in him, the look on their faces made it very clear they hadn't bargained for quite what they were getting, and those looks of worry deepened when he drew his knife and pulled a length of thick dull chain from his pocket.

But the fetish—the desiccated toad clutched in the woman's fist, its body stuffed with all manner of—

She'd bought a bunch of stuff from Edsel, it was in her bag. Get it now, yank the zipper open and find the rustly plastic. Go for the mandrake first, and the mirror . . . Her hands shook.

The woman started speaking. Words of power, tinged with seeping, kicking misery, in the kind of voice that made cats scream on fences in the middle of the night. It hammered into Chess's skull; she fell to her knees, her fingers curling into claws to try to protect her ears from it.

The fight started in earnest, that second of hesitation over. Terrible's chain flew through the air and the Lamaru jumped to the side. A hand tangled in her hair and yanked her away from the fight. She scratched at it, wishing she had longer nails, wanting nothing more than to draw blood from that fucker's sensitive inner arm.

Blood. All that blood in the room across the hall, the blood of murder victims. All that power, the fear and pain, just waiting to be activated. Don't forget it, don't let the fetish taste blood—

The woman screamed in the middle of her chant. Chess

managed to look at her in time to see the chain wrapped around her wrist and Terrible yanking it up, forcing the woman's arm over her head. The fetish fell at the same time as his fist slammed into the woman's face. At the same time the other witch thrust a dagger forward: a fake-out while his free hand skimmed the floor.

Shit, what was she doing? Her attacker's crotch was just at the right level; Chess clasped her hands together and drove them home. He groaned and collapsed, taking a chunk of her hair with him as he fell. She barely felt it. Get her bag. *Get her bag.*

Terrible kicked back the blade-wielding witch and dropped the unconscious woman. Blood ran down his arm. He reached for the fetish, still there at his feet.

She couldn't breathe. Couldn't get the word out of her mouth fast enough. His blood would activate it, she didn't know if the woman had actually finished the chant before he got her, but whether she had or not, if his blood touched that thing—

He heard her. Stopped. Her own hand closed around the fetish. Violent, raw power tore up her arm and through her body until she couldn't see, couldn't feel anything but its unthinking, unfeeling greed. It wanted all of her, her death, her pain, anything it could get; it was pure destruction racing through her body and battering at her skin, looking for escape.

She would not let it. Her stomach writhed inside her as though it had developed its own mind as she scuttled back to the wall, away from the male witches now back on their feet.

She couldn't hold on anymore. Too much, the blood and the misery and the evil pouring through her system. She pressed her head against the pitted wall and threw up, barely conscious, clutching the hideous toad to her chest with every bit of strength she had.

Clawed fingers closed around her arm. The woman,

her face covered in blood. Chess kicked feebly at her, every movement a struggle through mud and the roaring hate in her body.

The woman's voice creaked out of her mouth, crawled over Chess's skin, searching for the fetish in her arms. Chess kicked again, tried to scream past the horrible taste in her mouth and the horrible power suffocating her.

The woman's head jerked back. A quick movement like the flash of a hummingbird's wings, and blood gushed from her throat. The light in her eyes died, a bulb stuttering out. She fell to the floor in an ungraceful heap.

Silence fell with her, broken only by Chess's heart hammering. Through the haze over her vision she saw Terrible bend down, reaching for her. She pushed herself farther into the corner, away from his hands.

"No. No, don't touch me, don't touch me, it's all over me, you can't touch me—"

"Aye, Chess. Aye. No touching, aye? Give me the knowledge what to do. What you need?"

Fresh tears stung her eyes; she shook her head, both to deny them and to try to clear the lowering clouds in it. The spell's pressure had lessened when the caster died, but the fetish itself still choked her, still felt as though slippery black tentacles were slithering into her body and hooking into her organs. Into her soul. The image—not to mention the feeling itself—made her stomach lurch again. Fuck, it was awful.

"Got time, Chess. No problem. You say when ready, aye? 'Sall cool here."

What did she need? "My bag. I need my bag."

The blood—blood from the three dead witches now littering the floor around her, blood from the victims in the next room—called to her, sung to her so sweetly she had to push her forehead against the wall again, hard, to fight it. The fetish in her arms writhed with power. It wanted the blood. The blood wanted it.

The bag thunked to the cement beside her, half-open, but her fingers refused to let go of the fetish.

She tried to speak; swallowed and tried again when the words tangled into a wiry ball in her throat. "Get, um, there should be some gloves in there."

It was a little late for gloves at that point, but she had the horrible feeling that every second she touched the fetish was another second it sank its awful teeth into her, another second it sucked out her energy like a mosquito.

He opened the bag wide, poked his hand in. Even through the haze of power she felt his discomfort.

After a few seconds the gloves waved before her; she managed to use her knees to hold the toad while she slipped one on, then switched her grip. The power lessened. Still there, still awful, but definitely better. Her lungs actually filled when she took a breath; when she spoke again her voice came clearer than it had.

"In my pick case there's an iron blade, a black one. Can you get it out?"

In the opposite corner an expanse of floor stood bare, as clean as it was possible to be. When Terrible handed her the short knife she stood up on legs that barely felt attached and headed for it.

Newspaper still covered the window there. She set the fetish down and tugged at it, tearing it away.

In the bright afternoon sunshine the thing was an abomination. Black stitches ran in a crooked line up its stomach, bulging with whatever lay inside. She held it steady with her gloved left hand, used the iron blade to break the stitches.

Oh, shit. The stench pouring from it burned her nose and eyes, made her cough. That wasn't natural, not all of it. Something chemical lurked in there too, mixed with the odor of dead toad and sour milk and what appeared to be a rotting bird's heart.

That was unusual. Really unusual. Bird hearts weren't typical in hexes; hell, they weren't typical in any magic she knew of. She used the tip of the blade to wedge the thing out and deposit it on the floor, along with a wad of tight hair and—yuck, an eyeball.

Not human, thankfully; after what had happened a few weeks before she didn't think she'd be able to take even the faint suggestion that human eyeballs had anything to do with this particular case. No, not human. Animal. Goat, perhaps? Or dog. Stray cats and dogs were plentiful in Downside. It could have been from a fox or something, she guessed, if they'd gotten a supplier. Another possibility to ask Edsel about.

Terrible's lighter clicked to her left, a lazy curl of smoke drifted toward her. Once he'd always offered, always lit one for her, too. She thrust the thought back into her still-churning stomach and focused on removing the rest of the toad's stuffing. With every item she pulled out the power lessened.

More hair. Some blood-soaked cloth. Pretty standard for cursing, really. A . . . a finger, a small one. Pinky? Not so standard. She shuddered. A dead cockroach with a pin through it, a tiny rodent head, some black cotton wadding and some herbs. Their fragrance was killed by the other items, but she recognized one of them. Her lips turned down.

"What you finding?"

"Mistletoe." She glanced up at him; he was standing at the window, smoking. Not looking at her. "It's used for a lot of things, but mostly for regulating ghost travel. Summoning and Banishing, but not like what we do. It's . . . it's more like opening the doors to the City, if you know what I mean. A guardian instead of something that actually has power over the ghosts itself."

"Figure maybe they giving the City a try-on again?"

"I guess. Shit." She was going to have to tell Lauren

about this, damn it. Somewhere in the back of her mind had lurked the vague hope that they wouldn't discover anything of use. No such luck. Instead she was going to have to come up with some kind of lie to explain how she came to possess the fetish.

Whatever. She'd deal with that when the time came. Her gloved hand poked around inside the now-empty corpse, grateful she could breathe again. The thing was, for all intents and purposes, disarmed. She dumped salt over it all to make sure, almost sighed when the energy dissipated completely.

Terrible stayed where he was, smoke twisting into the air around him, while she hunted around in her bag. Inside it she kept inert plastic bags; she grabbed a handful—almost her entire supply—and began carefully sealing up the fetish's ingredients, shaking them clean of salt before dropping them in the bags. Normally something like that would be thrown into running water or, if it was small enough, washed down a sink. But this was part of a Church investigation. She'd need to hand it over to Lauren, let the Black Squad have a look at it and see what if anything they made of it.

She took a quick glance around the room, more out of nerves than anything else, and noticed what she hadn't before. Some of those lumps on the floor—dogs. Dead ones, unmarked but unmistakably deceased.

"Those belong here?"

He followed her gaze, shrugged. "Dogs everywhere."

She stood up, snapped the glove off and dropped it on the floor. Beyond the landing the death room loomed; another thing she'd have to tell Lauren about, she supposed.

But right now she was looking at the dogs. Two of them, heaped in the corner. When she got closer she saw they were not, in fact, unmarked; one of them had a long slice down its back. She bent over. "What the hell?"

"Looks like they takin the skin." He stood close enough to see, but not close to her, she noticed.

"Yeah, but—"

"Maybe for eating. Or keepin warm, dig."

He could be right. Probably was, disgusting as the idea might have been. Most people didn't eat dogs or cats, but "most" didn't mean "all," especially not in Downside. And really, dining on innocent pets seemed like something the Lamaru would take particular pleasure in.

But then, lots of people took pleasure in destroying innocent things. In that the Lamaru were no different from anyone else.

Assuming they'd killed the animals. And that they hadn't done it just to shut the things up, which was just as likely.

"Who all lived here?"

"People Bump payin, dig. Watch the place."

"He does business in this building?"

No answer, unless she counted the darting, suspicious glance, the faint disbelief on his face.

Right. "I just meant—"

"Bump an me take care of it. Ain't yon business."

"If this is related to the Church invest—ouch!" Shit. She'd actually managed to forget that fucking Binding for a few minutes.

"Nobody say shit to them Church pilgrims, dig. Nobody here. They find what they find, but this ain't them business neither."

"But—" His glare cut her off. Fine. He was probably right anyway. Ratchet hadn't been in the files; the Church didn't even know he existed. And she couldn't bring them in here without admitting she'd been working on the case with someone who had absolutely no business being involved.

Ratchet's death would be avenged, she reminded herself. Ratchet and whoever else was now nothing more than a few parts lying around—including the dogs. Whether the Church caught the murderers or Bump and Terrible did, there was a place warming up for them in the spirit prisons.

It comforted her, as much as that was possible.

She tossed the deconstructed fetish into her bag and followed him down the stairs and back out into the sunshine, grabbing her pillbox as she did. Might as well try to relax. She had a feeling Lauren wasn't going to let her do much of that.

Chapter Ten

> They performed all manner of experiments on both living and dead flesh, for they did not know the Truth.
> —*A History of the Old Government, Volume VI: 1975–1997*

She was right about that one, at least mostly. Lauren called her cell phone just as Terrible dumped her off on the steps of her building and peeled away: Chess should meet her at Church instead because she had too much to do to drive in to Downside. They were apparently going to check out Erik Vanhelm's place anyway, and the Church lay between Chess's apartment and Cross Town. Great. So instead of having time to relax a little, she had just enough time for a quick salt-scrub shower to wash off the remnants of sick magic clinging to her.

Too bad salt scrub couldn't do anything about the other stuff. The memory of his hand on the back of her neck, of the moment when he'd spoken to her as she huddled in the corner with twisting evil eating her insides, so gently. How it had felt safe. The way he always used to make her feel. And how fucking stupid she'd been. Fresh pain throbbed through her veins; it dulled a little when she sent four Cepts in after it, but did not disappear.

Her stomach still felt heavy and too warm when she parked outside the Church and plodded up to the tall front doors. For once they gave her no peace. Nor did the inside, the soaring entryway with high carvings on the walls and tender blue light glowing from the ceiling.

The building bustled and hummed with people; Church employees, Debunkers like her who nodded or said hello as they passed her on their way to the enormous library upstairs, or Liaisers, quiet with the secrets of the dead, on their way to the elevator and from there to the City below the earth.

Where she would have to go, she remembered with a shudder. In four days they would all go, to perform the Dedication ceremony for the executioner and Elder Murray.

In four days she would have to stand with her fellow employees, all of whom would smile and talk about how peaceful it was, how beautiful, and how pleased they were that the Elder and the executioner had found their eternal bliss, and she would have to smile and pretend she felt the same way. Pretend the City didn't terrify her, didn't look to her like the literal interpretation of the emptiness and misery she carried with her every day. Pretend she didn't want to scream and tear the skin off her body with her fingers for just being there.

Pretend she was just like the rest of them. The way she did every day. Normal. Happy. Clean.

"Hey, Chessie. Are you okay?" Dana Wright came down the stairs, her slim arms loaded with books. "You look kind of upset about something."

"Huh? Oh, I'm fine, I just . . . I was just thinking about Elder Murray."

"Oh." Dana bit her lip. "I know, it's so sad, isn't it?"

"I—"

"I mean, I know it isn't, I know he's going to be so happy now." Dana glanced around them, eyeing the little crowd of Goodys at the far end of the hall. Her next words were spoken in their direction. "I'm just being selfish. I know this is a good thing for him."

The Goodys didn't seem to be paying attention, but you never could tell. The acoustics in the hall were funny sometimes. Chess figured a total change of subject was the best idea. "What are you working on?"

"Trying to determine who Madame Lupita was Hosting and how it got into her. It's really something the Squad is handling, but since I was in the room . . . Here. I have the list of people who came to visit her before her execution." Dana shuffled the load in her arms, came up with a thin sheet of paper clasped between two of her fingers, draping over her hand. "Do you recognize any of the names? Just because you were the one who actually went in, we thought you might."

Chess plucked the paper off Dana's hand and scanned it. "I didn't really get any names, I mean, not the kind they'd sign officially. But . . ."

"But what? Chessie?"

Her voice dragged Chess back to reality, away from the name glaring up at her in spiky copperplate. "What? Oh, sorry. I kind of drifted for a second. Hey, can I make a copy of this? Some of the names might come back to me, you know?"

"Sure. They told me to show it to you, so I can't imagine they'd have a problem with it."

Lining the wall to her right were low, long, dark wooden benches. On Thursdays they'd be full of people, family members of the dead come to consult with the Liaisers. Family members with full pockets; talking to the dead didn't come cheap.

Nothing did with the Church. Most people didn't have to pay more than tithing taxes, but for special services . . . Liaising, weddings, childhood indoctrinations and blessings . . . It all had a price.

Chess didn't begrudge the price, oh, no. That was what paid her meager salary. More to the point it was where her bonuses came from. That thirty grand in her bank account represented the toil and sweat of a thousand or so taxpayers, and she appreciated it. She'd appreciate it even more later, when she got to take some of it to the pipe room and suck back some forgetfulness.

But that was later. This was now, and she knelt before the bench and rested her notepad on it to copy the list.

All of the names, all eleven of them. Best to copy them all. Best not to make Dana suspicious by simply copying ARTHUR MAGUINNESS on her pad, along with the address he'd given at Ninetieth and Mercer. In Downside.

The address might have been real, but the name wasn't. She searched every database she could think of in the Church mainframe, where birth and death records were kept since the end of Haunted Week and the Church's installation as the ruling body. Granted, even with the Church's control it was possible for people to slip through the cracks, but the lack of any information on Maguinness still disturbed her.

He was clearly old enough to have been born BT. He would have had a birth certificate, filled out and filed in whatever state he'd been born and entered into the database; an entire full-time staff had done nothing but copy that information in. And if that accent of his indicated he'd been born elsewhere in the world? There still should have been a certificate to be entered.

So his name couldn't have actually been Maguinness, because out of the hundred and forty Maguinnesses she found in the system, none of them could possibly have been the one she was interested in. Shit!

But how had he gotten in to visit Lupita without a real name? Visitors had to produce some kind of identification; their identities were checked. Hell, they were fingerprinted. It wasn't unusual for blood to be drawn and checked against the DNA database for some prisoners.

Lupita probably didn't qualify for that kind of security, but still . . .

She made a note to check with the prison and see if any of the guards remembered Maguinness. Not all the guards were witches; some were people with lesser skill. More than the average person, but not enough to qualify them for employment in any of the upper levels. It was entirely possible that Maguinness could somehow have bespelled one of them.

But Lupita had been convicted of a magical crime; wouldn't her guards have been witches?

She sighed and wrote that down as well. This really wasn't what she should have been focusing on. Maguinness was a side project, a bit of mild curiosity. She was supposed to be investigating the Lamaru, figuring out who they'd killed and why.

Speaking of which . . .

The file they'd given her the night before still sat in her bag, bound with a rubber band; a quick stop in Elder Griffin's office had given her a few additional pages. Hard to get used to, that was. Debunkers didn't keep their files, having to hand everything over to Goody Tremmell to be stored in the enormous cabinets in her little office. But the Squad kept their own reports, and for this case Chess got to do the same.

She pushed the plastic-covered fetish parts aside and pulled out the manila folder and the new pages, then paused. The Church library wasn't full, but it wasn't empty either; a couple of Debunkers-in-training studied at one of the tables at the far end, casting glances at her every few minutes or so; various other Church employees, including two junior Inquisitors, wandered between the shelves.

Goody Glass let her into the Restricted Room. Much better. There she could be alone, without worrying someone might see the file over her shoulder.

Hmm. Okay. The new reports confirmed an identity, and what a nice fucking bingo that was. At last, proof of Lamaru involvement beyond a stupid symbol any idiot could have carved; the dead body in the lot by the docks had once been Garret Denby, whose records had a nice big Lamaru stamp on them in red. *Ding ding ding.*

Or at least, it would have been a *ding ding ding* if that hadn't opened up a whole new can of confusion. She'd been brought into this thing to investigate Lamaru crimes, not Lamaru deaths.

Not that they weren't fully capable of killing their own. Even if their reputation hadn't preceded them, Chess would never forget the fear in Randy Duncan's voice when she'd realized he was the Church employee working with the Lamaru several months back. Couldn't forget the sheer terror on his face at the prospect of failing the Lamaru and what they would do to him.

So had Garret been killed because he was trying to leave the Lamaru, or because he'd failed them? Either was entirely possible. They were in that respect like any terrorist organization; there was no retiring, and failure meant death.

Which meant checking out his place would be well worth it, at least after Lauren finally got tired of playing Precious Daughter and decided to do some actual work.

But didn't it seem odd that he'd been left in a pile of useless parts in one lot, while another pile of parts was left in another lot with Lamaru marks on them?

Speaking of those other parts . . . No ID on the bodies Ratchet had reported to Bump; those were the reports she'd glanced at earlier in Terrible's car. Whoever had been killed, they hadn't been in any of the DNA databases, and there were no fingerprints . . . no fingers to print. Ugh. She made a note to double-check the lack of DNA results; not all the parts had been tested before she was brought into the case, so ID might still be possible. Only a few of the parts were DNA matches with one another, which meant she was looking at images of three dead bodies, or rather, various parts from three bodies.

No organs. No heads. No fingers. Hell, not even feet. In other words, the parts found in the lot were leftovers, items of no or very little magical value. She supposed that could account for the lack of malevolent energy around them, at least in part.

She skipped the chart of each DNA string—the Black Squad might be able to understand it, but she couldn't—and headed for the summaries.

"*. . . genetic anomaly in parts two, six, and seven does not match anomaly in three and four. Three and four do not match one, five, eight, and nine. All contain communal genetic markers.*"

Okay, so . . . what? She looked again, checked the pictures. That was no help so she read the second summary, wondering if perhaps she was either a little too high or just stupid.

Or maybe the case was simply more fucked-up than she'd thought. If she understood correctly—she'd have to double-check with Lauren but she thought she was right—each of the three dead people had possessed genetic anomalies; had been chromosomally imperfect. Not in a recorded and common way, but in ways that at least the two Seekers who'd done the analysis had never heard of or seen before. And the people whose parts they were had been related to each other in some way.

Were the Lamaru doing experiments with people? Altering their— No, she didn't think it was possible to alter the DNA of living people. But in utero, before fertilization . . . That in itself was a major crime.

But not one she'd put past the Lamaru. She wouldn't put anything past the Lamaru.

Shit, though. How long had they been planning this? Those body parts did not belong to infants or small children; their size alone indicated that couldn't be the case.

The entire report was full of thick scientific analytical language she didn't really understand; Debunkers didn't generally get involved in investigations of that sort. Why hadn't Lauren told her about this the night before? Sure, she'd probably imagined Chess would read it for herself, but wouldn't this be the sort of thing she might mention upfront? "By the way, it seems the Lamaru are breeding genetically imperfect humans and killing them?" Wouldn't that have made sense to mention?

Probably a test of some kind. What a pain in the ass. If Lauren was going to play games with her, this whole thing was going to be— Well, hell, it could take as long as it wanted, right? Chess was getting a grand a week. She could use the money.

Still, she'd ask about it. Being kept in the dark didn't make her happy; having her work double-checked by means of some sneaky let's-see-if-she-mentions-this made her even less so.

One last thing to check, as long as she was in the Restricted Room anyway. Most of the books concerned advanced spells and research materials, things the Church didn't want just any training witches to be able to get their hands on. Among them were a few volumes on human-ghost spells, Hostings, and Bindings. Might be some information in there about how Maguinness—if it had been Maguinness—had smuggled a ghost in to Lupita, how she'd managed to keep it hidden while in custody. She thought she'd seen something in one of them a few years before, in one of her first solo Debunking cases when the family had been trying to claim that a ghost had possessed their daughter.

A little shiver ran up her spine when she thought again about her last Debunking case, about the sigil on Terrible's chest. The sigil had turned a promising Church student named Kemp into a sick, ghost-possessed toy for any clever spirit who had a use for him. And one certainly had; Kemp had played battery and human slave to a murdered prostitute who wanted to stay in business forever. And Kemp had liked it enough to attempt to kill those who wanted to stop him.

Later. She'd worry about that later; it wasn't like there was anything she could do about it anyway, when Terrible wouldn't talk to her. What was she supposed to do, wrestle his enormous frame to the ground and make him? Take him down to the City and let him loose to see if any ghosts invaded his body? Sure. He'd be eager to do either of those things with her, to do anything at all with her.

She scanned the index of the oldest of the books she'd grabbed. Yes, this was the one. Okay. She grabbed her pen and copied:

It is possible in some cases to bond with a spirit so completely that it becomes part of the living body itself. This is achieved through the use of black magics so dark I hesitate to describe them here. See Baldarel.

Baldarel? What was . . . ah. Another book. *Uses of Spirits,* by August Baldarel. She pulled the slim volume—little more than a pamphlet, really—off the shelf and started to open it.

"Cesaria! There you are, I've been looking everywhere for you." Lauren stood in the doorway, with her arms folded and a frown twisting her mouth.

Chess ignored it. "I've been doing some research about the case, the—"

"Never mind that. They're about to separate Vanhelm's Bindmate and Banish it. Let's go."

She turned and stalked away without looking back. Gee, working with her was almost as fun as working with Terrible these days. Didn't they both make Chess feel all warm inside.

But she reshelved the book, grabbed her bag, and followed. Lauren had already reached the top of the main staircase; Chess refused to run, but did manage to catch up halfway down the steps.

"Why didn't you—"

The shrieking of the alarm cut into her words, into her thoughts, like a white-hot iron blade. What the fuck? The alarm—the prison.

Lauren's wide eyes told her she was thinking the same thing: The Banishment was taking place there.

They both started running.

Few prisoners were kept in the Church building prison itself; only those awaiting trial or execution, or those who were particularly magically dangerous. On Friday nights the small Reckoning cells filled up, citizens who'd confessed their crimes and wanted to be punished, or those who'd had complaints filed against them. Minor crimes or moral crimes only, though; petty theft, adultery, information crimes like insider trading or hacking below a certain damage level.

But a situation that required the alarms to sound was serious. All-hands-on-deck serious, and as Lauren and Chess reached the back hall they met more Church employees, all with the same white faces and steely eyes.

They were too late, though. Too late to save the guards lying on the cold tile with crimson pools of blood forming around them. Too late to save Gary Anderson, a fellow Debunker, slumped against the wall behind a still-smoking firedish, his unmarked face and bloody lips and the odd bluish cast of his skin giving mute testimony as to how he'd died: His soul had been torn from his living body. Murder by psychopomp.

Chapter Eleven

> We all know there's safety in numbers. But what about fun? An apartment in Cuesta Verde guarantees you a lovely modern home, friendly neighbors who share your interests, and proximity to the Church!
>
> —*Advertising pamphlet for Cuesta Verde Apartment Homes*

For the first time Chess could remember, the Grand Elder looked shaken. He stood at the head of the table, almost as pale as the ice-blue walls around him, sniffling nervously and flipping with one long-fingered hand through a thin sheaf of notes on the table.

Lauren sat to his left, watching him as though he'd just turned lead into gold through sheer force of will. The rest of the Church staff didn't seem quite as cheerful; most of her fellow Debunkers, in fact, looked positively terrified. Dana Wright sat beside Agnew Doyle with one hand frankly clinging to his sleeve. Interesting. How long had that been going on? Not that Chess gave a shit. She just hoped Dana didn't either.

"Good morrow," the Grand Elder said finally, in a creaky, insecure voice Chess had never heard him use before. He didn't wait for the chorus of replies to die down before continuing. "You are all aware of the incident that occurred earlier in the prison. The Elders and I are here to offer our reassurance. There is nothing to fear."

Nothing to fear? For the second time in two days a psychopomp had not been what it was supposed to be. At least so Chess assumed; no one knew for sure whether the psychopomp that killed Gary had been rogue or if Gary had made a mistake.

Mistakes happened. One had happened to Chess; almost every one of her coworkers had a story to share about the Time the Psychopomp Almost Got Them.

Somehow Chess had a hard time believing that that was the case here. But what did she know? Only that by the time she got there the carnage had ended; only that Vanhelm had escaped and she'd wanted to question him, and that time was getting on and she was certain he was out there, disappearing into Triumph City. Laughing at her, at all of them. Her fingernails dug into her palms.

"To begin with," the Grand Elder continued, "we believe the executioner involved in yesterday's contretemps was performing experiments on his own. Several of our Inquisitors"—he nodded at Lauren—"have examined his home, and that is their conclusion."

The sigh rolling around the table stopped at Chess. Despite the reassuring words, something in the Grand Elder's demeanor didn't sit right with her. She'd seen him blow off the concerns or problems brought to him by others before; just a few months before, in fact, when she'd hidden on a staircase and watched him treat Bruce Wickman—a Liaiser who spent most of his days in the City among the dead—like a wedding-night virgin because Bruce noticed the dead's unease and asked the Elders to investigate. It hadn't exactly inspired confidence.

Neither did watching Lauren preen herself in her chair. The Grand Elder had raised *that*. Despite the respect and affection Chess had for the Church, she couldn't help wondering what the mere fact of Lauren and her utter and complete pain-in-the-assiness meant about what sort of man the Grand Elder really was.

Which wasn't entirely fair. The Church had internal politics, just like everything else. Charles Abrams had had the power and the connections to rise to his position, to sit at the head of the continent's Church branch. That didn't make him a genius, and it certainly didn't make him some kind of god; there were no gods. Being Grand Elder didn't mean he had no weaknesses, and it wasn't fair for Chess to expect him not to. Especially not for her, of all people.

"We are likewise convinced this is an isolated incident. The security tapes are currently being prepared for Inquisitor review. The moment this task has been completed notification will be sent to you. Remember," he said, and fixed them all with a much more familiar steely gaze, "only Facts are Truth. Conjecture is just that. Coincidences do happen."

Sure they did. But what were the odds of psychopomp trouble happening while a Lamaru member was around, and that being a coincidence?

Given that the Lamaru had learned some Church tricks from Randy Duncan, Chess supposed there was a chance Vanhelm had somehow figured out how to set the psychopomp against Anderson. There were ways to do it, to steal control.

But how would Vanhelm have been able to do it tied up in a prison cell without any equipment?

The Grand Elder nodded at the end of the table. "Elder Shepherd, thou mayst speak."

Elder Shepherd stood up, his skin dark around the eyes. Chess could certainly imagine why. As head of the Psychopomp Divison of the Materials Department, he must have been imagining his head on the chopping block should the error turn out to have been his. Literally on the chopping block, too; if malice could be proven, he'd be convicted of treason.

"Every one of your psychopomps has been created and trained by myself, or my staff under my supervision. Be calm. There is no cause for alarm."

This seemed to reassure the others. But for perhaps the

first time since she'd entered training, it was not enough to reassure Chess. If there was no cause for alarm, why were they having this meeting? Something kept tapping inside her brain, some snippet of memory she couldn't quite pin down.

What she did know, though, was that she'd been placed under a Binding Oath which forbade her from discussing her case. Which forbade her from telling anyone else that the Lamaru had resumed their fun little murder games in the city.

And that meant her fellow employees, now shuffling to their feet with satisfied looks on their faces, had no idea the Lamaru were wandering around, cooking up another plot to destroy the Church. Had no idea they were all in danger, that the Lamaru were even at that moment plotting the death of every one of them.

And Chess had no doubt she was high on their list.

"Don't be ridiculous, Cesaria. I was at the executioner's house. He was experimenting. There is no connection between him and whatever happened in the prison today."

The car door closing cut off Lauren's words, but luckily for Chess—luckily, anyway, if she'd been the sort of person who enjoyed being lectured by a snippy, stuck-up bitch—Lauren was still talking when Chess got out of the car herself.

"He was clearly acting on his own. No evidence of Lamaru involvement. No evidence of any kind of involvement by anyone else."

"But where would he have learned how to create—" Chess began for what felt like the dozenth time, but Lauren cut her off. Also for what felt like the dozenth time.

"I don't know and I don't care. We have other Inquisitors looking into that. Maybe he hung around the Materials Department. Maybe he was buddies with somebody there. Maybe he found some books on them somewhere. It's not our business."

"Come on, Lauren. You don't think it's even remotely suspicious that we've had two psychopomp incidents in two days, just as the Lamaru show up again?"

"No. I don't. I think what's-his-name today must have made a mistake, which—"

"His name," Chess snapped, "was Gary. Gary Anderson. And he—"

"Fine. So *Gary* made a mistake. And the executioner—whose name, by the way, was Louis Reynolds—also made a mistake, messing around with things he had no business messing with. Accidents happen. You know that."

"We're investigating—"

"The Lamaru. And *only* the Lamaru. Remember them? The ones who've been dumping body parts all over the district? Let's stay focused here."

She gave the building to their right a significant glance; Vanhelm's building, or at least the address on his ID. Pale walls, open walkways with iron railings. Suburban generic, right down to the coffee shop sharing the parking lot, so the yuppies could have their frothy caffeine fixes before they even left the property.

Funny how addiction was socially acceptable—even a status symbol—when it made people extroverts rather than introverts. Whatever. Like she cared about social acceptance. Especially not if the people she was expected to pal around with were like Lauren. "Sure. Focused. Let's totally ignore any possible other avenues and just tunnel-vision our way along. Maybe we'll get lucky and blunder into a Lamaru hangout, right?"

Lauren folded her arms, boredom all over her face. "Psychopomps do not slice their victims up and leave them in piles. Psychopomps are *animals*. If you can tell me a way that a psychopomp could have used a knife—"

"The Lamaru could have cut the bodies up to hide the cause of death. None of the magically important parts were in that alley, I didn't see that the Seekers even tried to determine—"

"Do you normally ignore the subjects of your investigations to go interfering in cases that don't involve you?"

This. This was why Chess worked alone. Arguing with Lauren was like trying to persuade Bump to be less self-involved: impossible and exhausting. "Do you normally ignore every other option in your cases and refuse to open your mind for even a second?"

Lauren tilted her head. Her hair flowed over her shoulder almost to the elbow, a solid, swinging mass. "I really don't think that attitude is necessary."

Oh, for fuck's sake. She had to work with Lauren; she had no choice in that—at least, she had no choice that wouldn't leave her totally broke again. But she did not have to put up with this. Lauren outranked her, yes, but she wasn't her superior, and Chess might not be the Grand Elder's daughter, but her file looked pretty fucking good just the same.

"I'm not giving you any attitude you're not giving me. And I'm really not interested in comparing dick sizes here. But this is my investigation, too, and I deserve a say in how we handle it."

Lauren's eyes narrowed. For a second Chess thought of what she might do if she had to give the money back; surely there would be another case soon? False hauntings usually spiked at the end of March when annual tithing taxes were due. Something would come in soon.

So she met that measuring green gaze with her own. If Lauren fired her from the case, she fired her from the case, but she was not going to be spoken to like that anymore. She wasn't a fucking lackey.

Then Lauren burst into laughter. She was very pretty when she laughed, Chess noticed unwillingly.

"Okay." Lauren nodded, nodded again. "Okay. What about asking his neighbors, what do you think?"

"I don't think we'll get anything from it, but it's worth a try, sure."

The building was one of those places that called itself a "community," as if a group of random rent payers constituted anything like one. It gave Chess the shivers. All those assembly-line apartments, with the exact same floorplan and the exact same imitation-wood, glass-topped furniture and the exact same oat-colored carpet and oat-colored appliances. All those people living identical lives.

She found herself being surprised every time a door opened and a different person greeted them. She found herself again very grateful that the Church let her live in Downside instead of forcing her into sardine-can sameness in the employee cabins behind the main Church building.

They started at the top and worked their way down, interrupting dinner most of the time. Oh, well. Wasn't like anyone was going to complain, not when the Black Squad stood on their doorstep. It was a little like questioning Downsiders with Terrible, except the residents here weren't quite as scared of the Squad as Downsiders were of Terrible; she doubted parents here told stories about the Squad to their children to make them behave.

Over and over the same questions and answers, until she could have recited them by rote. No, nobody knew Erik. No, he'd kept to himself. Seemed pretty quiet. The serial-killer checklist, basically, and they ran it down with every person behind every door.

Until they reached the apartment at the end of his hall.

Barking dogs answered their knock, so many barks that both women took a cautious step back. Big dogs, sounded like. And no matter how many times besotted pet owners claimed their dogs were perfectly nice or well trained or whatever the fuck they wanted to say, the fact was that dogs were pack animals. Pack animals who behaved like pack animals; all it took was for one to lose its head and they all followed suit.

So it was with some apprehension that they watched the doorknob turn, listening to the muffled cries of "Down! Down! Go lie down! Go lie *down*!" that were the standard doorside pregreeting of any dog owner. Lauren's hand moved to her side, beneath her tailored black jacket.

She dropped it when the barking quieted and the door opened, though.

He was one of the most nondescript men Chess had ever seen. Just . . . *basic*, was the only word she could come up with. Medium brown hair, medium build, medium yuppie-after-work clothes: khaki pants, khaki plaid shirt. He matched the slice of room visible behind him; she wondered if people entering his apartment had to pause for a minute and hunt around for him, he blended in that perfectly.

Lauren introduced them both. "We were wondering if you could tell us anything about your neighbor there, Erik Vanhelm? Maybe you talked to him or knew him?"

Khaki Guy rubbed his chin. "I didn't talk to him a lot or anything, just to say hi, you know? I had some friends over once to watch a game and he came and had a couple of beers with us. He was really good with my dogs."

"Did he talk about friends? Did he say anything about himself?"

"I don't think so. Just, he was just my neighbor. We weren't, like, buddies or anything. I think he said something about the slaughterhouse, like he did something there. Management, I think. He said something about interviews, about interviewing some people?"

Chess and Lauren exchanged glances; Lauren's eyes gleamed with the same curiosity Chess knew was in her own. Most Lamaru didn't have jobs, at least not ones like management, and the thin file they had on Vanhelm didn't indicate a place of employment. Were they talking about the same man? Or had the Lamaru just picked some poor slob and stolen his address?

It was worth checking out, anyway. They thanked the man—Chess had already forgotten his name—and headed for Vanhelm's apartment.

The inside was pretty bare. But not totally. Chess figured it was possible for a man to live there with so few possessions; hell, she didn't own a lot of stuff herself. And it wasn't like she'd spent a lot of time putting personal touches all over her place, either. Most of her stuff came from thrift stores. Who was she to judge how other people kept their homes?

But even to her this seemed like subsistence living, like a front. It reminded her of the bedroom one of her foster parents had claimed was hers; everything in its place, but the layer of dust and general air of neglect, the stale musty odor permeating the walls, the unmarked, stiff couch cushions, told another story.

But the neighbor, what's-his-name, had seen Erik. Had invited him over for football and beer. So what had he done in here?

Not cooked. The fridge was full of moldy takeout containers. Maybe he slept; the bed was neatly made but at least looked as though it might have been used. He'd kept a few changes of clothing in the closet.

Chess glanced at Lauren, who was digging through the almost empty drawers in the pressboard dresser against the wall. Either the clothes in there had a different purpose, or Lauren didn't notice it; but Chess did. The closet smelled of herbs—the kind of herbs she'd found in that horrible fetish earlier.

For the fourth or fifth time she tried to think of a way to tell Lauren what had happened, and for the fourth or fifth time she discarded the idea. There was no way, especially not after the We-do-this-the-way-I-say-and-that's-final-so-shut-the-hell-up discussion they'd had outside.

Not that "discussion" was really the word for it, but the point was the same. Lauren didn't know who Ratchet or the other dead people were, or that they existed; Chess had no reasonable explanation for why she hadn't contacted Lauren immediately to share the information. Besides, Lauren already knew the Lamaru were around and planning something.

The only new clue Chess really had for her was the fetish, and she could surely think of another way to introduce that. In fact, it went against every instinct she had, every last smattering of integrity, but for a moment she wished she hadn't bagged and salted the thing so carefully. Vanhelm's apartment would be the perfect place to plant it. Technically it wasn't even planting evidence; it was real evidence, she'd just be fudging the location and circumstances a bit.

But no, she couldn't. She'd have to find some other way. So she glanced back at Lauren again, now moving into the small bathroom, and started poking around in the pockets of the hanging clothes.

She'd reached the last shirt when her fingers closed around something small and stiff, a square piece of card about two inches on each side. Its edges rasped against the fabric as she pulled it out of its pocket.

Oh, shit. The room darkened around her; for a moment she thought she was falling, tumbling into a black tunnel so deep she'd never hit bottom.

Then the world righted itself. What was she, surprised? She'd known the Lamaru knew who she was, known they were after her.

But the superstitious shiver running up and down her spine didn't stop until she'd tucked the picture into her own pocket. *Her* picture—her official Church employee portrait, updated yearly and kept—supposedly—in her confidential Church file.

Erik Vanhelm had been carrying it over his heart.

Chapter Twelve

> Of course, no home is complete without a copy of *The Book of Truth,* and the Church provides these in colors to match any décor.
>
> —*Your Home, Your Sanctuary,* by Delilah Ross

Randy Duncan could have given him the picture before he died. Chess had never seen her confidential file; she supposed she could ask Elder Griffin about it—if she wanted him to panic and order her back on the grounds. Hell, she could ask Lauren. The Black Squad could access any fucking thing they wanted.

If only Lauren weren't so damned offputting. Not a surprise, really; most of the Squad members Chess had worked with were fairly irritating, in an anal, law-abiding kind of way. But Lauren had in addition the arrogance of birth and her father's position, which took her beyond annoying. Bottom line: Chess didn't trust her. Couldn't bring herself to trust her. They were opposites, natural enemies. The haves versus the have-nots.

And again, it didn't matter anyway. The Lamaru knew who she was, so what. They had for months. Of course, without Terrible's protection . . . yeah, that sucked. Funny how she hadn't realized how much she depended on that until it was gone—how much she depended on *him* until he was gone.

But she'd been over that ground too many times lately, and she had other things to focus on at the moment.

Like the fact that what she was doing right now could get her fired. Well, a lot of what she did could get her fired, but this was different.

She hid in the shadows behind the executioner's house, with her lube syringe and her lockpicks, and prepared to use them.

It wasn't violating a direct order. Lauren hadn't forbidden her to search the place. Nor had Elder Griffin or any of the other Elders. But as Lauren kept reminding her, it wasn't technically part of her investigation. Which meant that what it was, technically, was trespassing. Trespassing in a dead man's house. If she got caught, and if they wanted to be hard on her, they could call it looting and she could do time for it.

But she wasn't going to get caught. She'd parked two blocks away. She'd watched the house for almost three hours, while the neighbors returned to spend their cookie-cutter evenings in their cookie-cutter homes. Not a soul had moved on the street for the last hour, and windows were starting to darken, lights popping off like spent bullets.

The executioner's house was dark, and had been dark. Empty. No family, no friends. Time to go.

She tossed another couple of Cepts into her mouth and crept toward the door. A quick squeeze of the syringe plunger—she used to use a spray, but after a major leak in her bag she'd switched to the syringe, which she'd discovered one night had the additional advantage of being an excellent murder weapon—and a few seconds with her lockpick, and the door swung silently open.

Enough light seeped through the half-open blinds and the open door to let her see. Her flashlight rested in her hand, warm from her body heat, but using it might alert the neighbors. Best to wait until she really needed it.

The back door brought her into the kitchen. Debunker

protocol demanded she search all the cabinets, left to right, then the fridge and freezer and other electronics, but technically this wasn't a Debunking case. And even if it was, it wasn't hers. And even if it was, the kitchen was a veritable soup of gross bits of food and empty containers and grime on every surface. Even with gloves on, plunging into the mess didn't appeal.

So instead she shut the door behind her and wandered around for a few minutes, avoiding furniture and stacks of porn magazines and dirty clothes, opening her senses. If he'd been making psychopomps in there he would have left traces of magic. Hell, the Psychopomp Division in the Church building set every hair on her body on edge when she just walked near it. So surely experiments like creating wolf psychopomps would leave traces.

But she felt nothing.

Okay, then, shit. Start searching, just as she'd been trained to do. Under the furniture, along the shelves on the wall. Plow through miscellaneous papers, most of which related to various dating services and not to magic of any kind. Pity twinged in her chest, pity and shame. The first because lonely people deserved pity; the second because she'd become one of them, hadn't she?

Into the kitchen, placing her feet carefully on the tile floor. Unused cleaning supplies under the sink, canned food in the cupboards, vodka in the freezer. His possessions told her nothing.

But what he did not possess interested her as well. No bare marks in the dust indicated anything had been removed. Clearly he kept his supplies elsewhere.

The stairs didn't protest as she crept up them. Here the sour, unused smell of the house grew stronger; here the light from the windows did not penetrate. Her gloves skittered along the banister, sticking intermittently; she switched the flashlight on just long enough to see the staircase walls were bare.

Nothing in the bedroom. Nothing in the spare room. Frustration rose in her chest, almost stronger than her high just starting to set in.

No empty spaces. No herb-scented drawers or cabinets. No animal fur, no traces of blood. She supposed the Squad might have removed such things, but given the outrageous mess, how would she know?

What a waste of time. The idea that the executioner was innocent, that the Lamaru were involved up to their slimy necks in whatever was happening with the psychopomps, still throbbed in the back of her head, but no proof awaited her in this house. Fuck. Much as she hated on principle to believe Lauren, maybe she'd have to. Working with the Squad wouldn't give her access to their evidence rooms or files unrelated to her own case; the house was her only hope. So much for hope. Like she didn't know that already.

She'd just managed to shove the door of an overstuffed closet closed when a man's voice drifted up the stairwell.

"This place is disgusting."

Something about it—aside from the mere fact of it—stopped her in her tracks. Familiar, but not overly so.

Someone else spoke—a woman. "Yes, but it's practically the only place in the city we can guarantee no one will be looking for you. You have too many neighbors."

"Anywhere in Downside—"

"Anywhere in Downside one of that creepy bastard's horde could find you. They see everything. We've been over this again and again. Besides, it's not up to me. Or you."

Fuck! How the hell was she going to get out of this one? She could take the stairs in a leap and run for it. But the front door was double-locked, and flipping the bolts would cost her a few precious seconds. The kitchen wasn't that big. They'd be on her before she managed to hit the street.

"I don't know why we can't just kill him. After what he did to—"

"You can find him, you can kill him."

"He's easy to find. He puts on those silly shows to sell his stupid potions that don't even work. It's—"

The woman interrupted him again, but Chess wasn't listening. Maguinness. They were talking about Maguinness.

What the hell? Who were these people, that man with his fucking familiar voice and the woman? Had Maguinness known the executioner?

Damn. She'd missed something. They'd stopped discussing Maguinness, at least so she assumed.

"Just trust him. He knows what he's doing," the woman said. "Hasn't he already proven that? We just do what he says, and keep him informed, and we'll—"

"I don't want to be here long."

"And you won't be. One night, Erik. Maybe two."

Erik? Erik Vanhelm? Chess hesitated, then took a chance and peeked down the stairs into the kitchen.

Yes. Erik Vanhelm, talking to a woman whose back was to Chess. Long hair fell to just past her shoulders; where the moonlight caught it, it gleamed silvery. Dark blond, maybe, or light brown? Whatever. Figuring it out didn't feel worth getting caught for, so Chess slipped back into the darkness.

"Why don't you stay here with me?"

"You know why. I have to go, and you need to get some sleep."

Vanhelm sighed. "I know, I know. But tomorrow—"

"I'll see you there, yes. And after you can spend the night."

Fabric rubbed against fabric; a faint change in the

atmosphere told Chess the pair's mouths were busy with other things for the moment.

She could duck down the staircase, hide in the living room until Vanhelm went upstairs. *If* he went upstairs, and didn't decide to watch TV or crash on the couch. TV was probably out; they wouldn't want to chance a neighbor noticing the telltale light, but who knew for sure with the Lamaru?

Or she could make her way back upstairs, assuming Vanhelm would take the master bedroom. Once he fell asleep she could sneak out. She had her Hand of Glory with her.

She needed to make a decision, and she needed to make it immediately. Up or down? Up or down? Fuck!

Up. Probably the wrong choice, but a choice at least. Better to be stuck there until Vanhelm slept and have a shot at escaping than to try to duck into the living room and be discovered by both of them.

The smaller front bedroom was probably the better place to hide. Its closet had some room available, at least. Or . . .

Not just a closet. A side window, dingy curtains hanging limp over it. The executioner's house wasn't new, so it didn't have the soaring ceilings and lofty heights of newer buildings, and the window sat low in the wall; she figured from the sill to the ground below couldn't be more then ten feet or so. She'd dropped larger distances than that before.

No sounds rose from the kitchen below. Either they were still kissing, or they'd started disrobing and just weren't making any noise. Wow. Exciting.

Either way, they probably wouldn't notice if she slid the window open and dropped out of it. Assuming the window opened, and that it didn't squeak as it did so.

But it wouldn't open. She pushed as long as she dared, until their voices rose in farewell and the back door opened. No escape, then. Not for a while, assuming it was possible at all. She tucked herself into the closet and listened to Vanhelm's heavy footsteps on the stairs.

Her legs ached from crouching when she made it back to her car an hour later. Vanhelm had finally fallen into the deep sleep of the wicked after about half an hour, and she'd waited another fifteen minutes or so just to be sure. It was after midnight, and she was more lost than ever.

Maguinness and Lupita had known each other. Maguinness and the Lamaru were involved in something, some kind of war. But Maguinness obviously made them nervous. She'd never heard of anyone making the Lamaru nervous, so her feeling about his power was correct.

But why hide that power? Especially when doing a job like his. He could have forced the residents of Downside to empty their pockets for him with a few well-chosen spells; why not do so?

The idea that honesty prevented him from doing it never even entered her mind. Honesty was for those who could afford it, like heating or electricity or a conscience. To be honest in Downside was to be a victim in Downside.

At least having overheard what she'd overheard gave her something else to do, some other place to go, although her welcome wouldn't be remotely welcoming. She circled Trickster's, then headed for Chuck's, looking for the Chevelle. If he wasn't at one of those places she'd try the Market, or his apartment. No point in calling. He wouldn't answer if he saw it was her, as she well knew. Even working this together at Bump's behest probably wouldn't change that, and she didn't want to give him any warning she was looking for him.

The Chevelle sat in its usual place across the street from Chuck's; she slid into a spot another block down and headed for the bar, shivering in the chilly air. At least, that's why she told herself she was shivering.

Muggy heat blasted her face when she passed through the dingy entrance—heat, and Richard Hell's "Blank Generation." It took her tired eyes a second to adjust; when they did she saw him at the back of the room, caught his scowl as he turned and headed for the rear exit. Shit.

Luckily for her, midnight in Downside counted as early so the place hadn't filled up yet, but she still had to practically shove a gang of drunken teenagers out of her way in order to catch up with him. Her hand brushed his arm; he yanked it away.

"I need to talk to you. About work."

His cold stare turned her into a smudge on the floor, something filthy and worthless. Which she pretty much was. "What?"

Several interested people watched them. Chess glanced at them, looked back at Terrible. "Outside, okay?"

For a second she thought he would say no, and then she'd really be fucked. Going to Bump to tell him Terrible was refusing to help wasn't even close to an option; even if she didn't know that snitching on him would infuriate him further, she wouldn't consider it. If he said no she'd have to figure out some way to get the information. Maybe she could go talk to Maguinness himself, but something told her he wouldn't be any more pleased to find her on his doorstep than Terrible was, and he had no reason at all to talk to her even if she could tell him why she was there.

But Terrible nodded and pushed his way out the exit. Chess managed to catch the door before it hit her and followed him into the narrow alley. Someone had left a lamp burning on the second floor of the building behind; it cast a square of pale light across broken crates and rolls of chicken wire leaning against the rusty fence. Rotted leaves mixed with dirty bits of paper and garbage on the cracked cement. The bottoms of her boots made faint sucking noises when she lifted them.

"What," he said again.

Right. Obviously he didn't plan to make this any easier on her. She couldn't really blame him. "That guy, Maguinness. The potion guy we saw today. Did—"

"Ain't—"

"No, just listen. Did he get permission from Bump to set up in the Market? Did he talk to him, I mean?"

His head tilted; his gaze didn't leave her as he lifted the beer in his hand and took a long swallow, emptying it. The scrapes decorating his knuckles hadn't been there when she'd left him that afternoon.

She waited. Waited, and forced herself not to think. Not to speak.

"Why you askin?"

"I think he's connected. To them. I heard—ow!—I just need to know what you know about him. If he's doing any other business besides the potions, or if he said anything to you or Bump about—"

"Oh, aye. I dig. Figure we got knowledge we ain't sharin with you. Figure we got whoever-the-fuck workin for us, and ain't gave you the tell."

"No! I don't mean it that way. I just need to know what you know about him, that's all. Maybe he said something and you didn't think anything about it at the time, or whatever."

"Too stupid to know what to pass on, what not to?"

"Damn it, will you stop? I don't think you're too stupid to know what to pass on, and I don't think you're hiding anything—"

"Good, causen I ain't the one who lies, aye?"

The venom in his voice almost made her jump, and not

just because it hurt her feelings or scared her. It didn't sound like him. How many beers had he emptied before she got there? She'd never seen him drunk, not really, and fear settled cold in her stomach. He had a target on his back most of the time; sure, in general people were too scared to go after him, but all it took was one pissed-off speedfreak with a gun. And he knew it. She'd seen his caution, his awareness of his surroundings; they'd even talked about it once at his place—the only place he said he really relaxed—before she passed out on his couch.

No point in asking, and no point worrying about it. That road didn't lead anywhere good, and she had more than enough to worry about already. Instead she lit a cigarette to give herself something to do and tried again. "I need to know what you know about him, for the case. I'd appreciate it if you'd tell me."

His own lighter clicked; the alley glowed for a second before he snapped it off, shutting down the six-inch flame. "Aye," he said finally. "Came and talked to Bump. Bout three, maybe four weeks past, I were still in the hospital. Been here longer'n that, though. Said he'd been."

"Did he say what he was doing? Any businesses aside from the potions?"

"Ain't talked to him myself, dig. Only know what Bump gave me."

"But if he was doing something else, you'd know, right? You would have heard."

His eyebrows rose a fraction, like he was trying to figure out if she was using cheap flattery or not. "Ain't heard shit on him. Got a family, he say. Guessin a big one. Sells whatany he sells to feed em. But nobody say me ought else."

Damn. That didn't give her much of anything, did it?

"His potions. He might be selling them to— Did Bump try them? Did Maguinness give him any of them, like, as a sample or something before Bump said okay?"

"Aye. Bump said ain't done shit for him. Say tasted some nasty, too."

"That might not have been one of his real potions, though. Not one of the ones . . ." Shit. She couldn't finish that sentence, even if she thought she was right, which she didn't. The Lamaru had had some involvement with Maguinness. Maybe it was about his potions, maybe it wasn't.

Terrible shifted position, his face a deeper shadow. "Got other asks, or can I get gone?"

She wanted to ask him more questions. She wanted to let him go. Figuring out if it hurt more to have him run away or to stay and talk to her like she barely existed didn't really appeal. Of course, she'd spent most of her life feeling like she barely existed, but never around him. Not before, anyway.

"Got shit to do. We done here?" He gripped the door handle to head back into the bar.

"I guess— No, wait. Can you talk to Maguinness? Or ask Bump to talk to him? Ask him about this, you know? And if I could be there when you do, that would really help."

A pause, a curt nod. The door opened, and he was gone.

Chapter Thirteen

[The Church has a hand in every aspect of your daily life, from food production to education to transportation. It watches you, so you can relax and live a safe and happy life.
—*The Church Guides You,* a pamphlet by Elder Warren]

Her choices after that conversation were easy. Break into the slaughterhouse in the middle of the night, hunt for Maguinness, or go home, take everything she could manage to shove down her throat, and pass out. Not a hard decision, but she regretted it a bit as she walked across the slaughterhouse parking lot the next afternoon with the stench making her stomach dance and Lauren's voice pounding into her skull like a screeching, whiny jackhammer. Three Cepts helped; when they got inside she'd duck into the bathroom and take another one.

"I don't appreciate getting such a late start, Cesaria. You said yesterday you'd be ready by noon, and here it is almost two—"

"Sorry." Another sunny day, too. The day before it had thrilled her; today she would have given her left hand for some fucking cloud cover. Or some speed. Or both.

"I don't mean to be a bitch, I really don't, but I've been waiting here—"

"I said I was sorry." Damn it, the bitch actually had a point there. Chess *had* agreed to meet Lauren at noon, and she couldn't really blame her for being pissed; hey, she could get in fucking line, right? The long, long line of People Chess Let Down or Fucked Over or whatever.

She just wished Lauren would shut the hell up about it.

"My father says the Elders speak very highly of you, and that's why I think you should know that behavior like this—"

"I know, Lauren. I am *sorry*. Okay? Can we stop talking about it now?"

Lauren did stop, to Chess's surprise. The sun glinted off her hair so bright and sharp that it was painful even through the dark lenses of Chess's sunglasses; two days in a row she'd remembered them, which had to be some sort of record.

Lauren gave a half-shrug. "Fine. Just don't be late again, please. This is a horrible place to wait. It stinks and it's dirty and noisy. How can you live here? How do you sleep?"

With lots of chemical aid, was generally how Chess slept, but she wasn't about to say it. Nor was she about to point out that she didn't actually live that close to the slaughterhouse, so the smell and the noise weren't as bad, or that she'd happily deal with both as long as it meant she had easy access to the afore-unmentioned chemicals. Instead she just shrugged. "You get used to it."

"Ugh." Lauren adjusted her jacket and started walking toward the building. "I feel like I need a shower just being here."

"Wait till we get inside," Chess muttered, but Lauren didn't hear her. Chess assumed she didn't, anyway, since she didn't turn around or make a snotty reply.

The slaughterhouse waited for them, a dark gray stone hulk with tiny windows and spiky smokestacks like weapons raised toward the sky. Death hovered over it; now Lauren had finally gone quiet the sounds of animals drifted across the parking lot, growing louder with every step. Chess pictured them, long lines of them trapped in curving mazes, each step taking them closer to their messy end.

A security guard, visible through the glass double doors of the entrance, buzzed them in, and called the plant manager when they explained why they were there.

"Mr. Carlyle be here in a minute," he said, settling himself back down in his chair. "Usually Mr. Hunt deals with you guys, but he ain't showed up in weeks."

"Mr. Hunt?"

The guard nodded. "Assistant manager."

Chess glanced at Lauren, already dangling Vanhelm's picture from her manicured fingers. "Is this Mr. Hunt?"

"Yeah, that's him. Why? He do something?"

"We're just establishing his employment," Lauren lied. "How well did you know him?"

"Didn't. Not much. He didn't talk to me 'cept hi in the morning and 'bye at night. Mr. Carlyle be the one to ask."

"Was there anyone he did talk to?" Chess asked.

"Wouldn't know. I just sits here at the desk."

A door opened off to the left; the animal sounds that had been muffled by it blared through the open frame before quieting again when the door snapped into place.

Chess didn't know what she'd expected the manager of a slaughterhouse to look like; she supposed if she thought about it she'd have imagined some sort of burly lumberjack with dried blood under his fingernails. But Mr. Carlyle—"Call me Ben, please"—stood barely taller than she did, with wispy brownish hair, watery blue eyes, and so many nervous tics she almost wanted to offer him a Panda to calm him down.

"Erik Hunt?" he said, after leading them back into his office. The nervous tics made more sense after that walk; if Chess had to hear all that noise, feel that fear and death and panic slamming against her skin for hours on end every day, she'd be a wreck too. Not that she wasn't already, but damn, that place was awful.

"He'd been with us for six months or so. Nice guy. Good manager. I mean, the employees liked him, and I liked him. I can't imagine why he would just stop coming to work, he was so dedicated. Always coming in early, staying late, all of that."

The words were accompanied by various cuff tuggings, nose rubbings, and hand wringings.

"And he showed you photo ID when you hired him?" Lauren asked.

"Of course! Of course he did." Carlyle turned to the row of filing cabinets behind him, the same industrial tan as the files kept in the Church library. "We conform to all Church rules here, in hiring and in practices. Here."

Chess reached for the file folder he set on top of his paper-strewn desk, but Lauren beat her to it and began flipping through the papers inside.

Okay. Chess had some questions anyway. "What Church practices? Aside from hiring, I mean."

Carlyle shrugged and played with his earlobe. "We follow Church rules in our slaughtering practices, of course, and maintain a Ritual Room for Haunted Week meats and dogs, and—"

"Dogs? What do you mean?"

Lauren glanced at her; Chess caught the frown but ignored it.

"Well, Miss—Putnam?—all slaughterhouses are required to keep our own psychopomps as well as providing hallowed space for their creation should it be necessary. We only handle a few a year, but of course for Haunted Week—"

"Right, you have a special room. And you have psychopomps in that room?" Her head spun.

"Of course. I guess this isn't your department, but we're not permitted to do any slaughtering during that week without a psychopomp present—"

"Who oversaw them? The psychopomps, I mean. Was it Va—Hunt? Or do you have someone else?"

Lauren opened her mouth, but Carlyle spoke before she could. "Yes, it was one of his responsibilities."

"This is all in order," Lauren interrupted, handing the employment file back to Carlyle. Chess hadn't had a chance to look at it, but Lauren didn't seem to care and frankly neither did she. Who gave a fuck what ID Vanhelm had provided? He'd handled psychopomps here. He'd been in charge of them. He knew about them, in other words.

So she ignored Lauren's glare. "Can we see that room?"

"Of course."

It took a minute for Carlyle to find his key—apparently he was as absentminded as he was jittery, although Chess couldn't help wondering if perhaps some of his nerves were due to their presence—and lead them along an iron walkway above the slaughterhouse floor to the Ritual Room.

By the time they reached it her ears were ringing and her entire body felt sticky and cold. Not just from the fear and death and pain, either; actually, if she were honest, she'd have to admit the floor wasn't as bad as she'd thought it would be. Loud, yes, but not horrible.

Something else lurked beneath it all, though, something she didn't have time to stop and think about but that she was aware of, slow and sinuous in the air. Something wrong.

It didn't feel like Lamaru; didn't have the same dark, almost maniacal edge to it, the same feeling of evil lurking beneath it.

But something was there, and she didn't know what it was, although it tingled just out of reach in her memory.

"This is it," he said, pushing the thick, heavy-looking iron door open and ushering them inside.

The energy hit her harder there, locked in—she

assumed—by iron-lined walls. Snippets of information came back to her, hazy memories of lessons she hadn't paid much attention to since she'd known from the beginning she wouldn't be working in Compliance or any of the Government-related Church jobs. Slaughterhouses were required to have ritual rooms, just as hospitals were required to have iron-walled wards for terminal patients. Death of any kind posed a double threat during Haunted Week, and no chances could be taken.

The room she stood in appeared to be in total compliance: locked, clean, empty save for a naked lightbulb high overhead. Faint brownish stains lurked on the concrete floor, but that was to be expected. The scent of bleach tickled her nose.

"Erik started working for us just before last Haunted Week." Carlyle scratched his neck. "He oversaw production in this room during the week, and the cleanup after."

Chess inched her way along the walls, scanning the floor. "And that included psychopomps?"

Behind her Lauren sighed, but who gave a fuck what she thought.

Carlyle nodded. "We have Elders in the room, of course, for the summoning, but Erik was in charge of the team."

The closer Chess looked at the room, the less convinced she became that it hadn't been used in months. She supposed the bleach smell could remain in the air as strongly as it had, with the door locked. She supposed the energy could stay as heavy, too, given the iron in the walls. Determining the age of a spell or a particular energy usually didn't pose much of a problem, but with iron walls . . .

It didn't matter, anyway. Lauren said her name, loud enough to cut through her thoughts; she looked up to see Lauren and Carlyle outside the room again, Lauren with that raised-eyebrow look that made Chess want to hit her. Want to hit her *more*.

"Will you call me if you hear from him?" Lauren

handed Carlyle something that could only be a business card. La-de-da. Chess didn't have business cards.

Carlyle nodded and smiled, and made all the right responses, but Chess blocked him out. He didn't have anything to do with the case; she'd known that the minute she shook his hand. He had about as much magical ability as Lex, which meant none at all.

But that room, and Vanhelm . . .

"Vanhelm handled psychopomps," she said as they left. Intellectually she knew the parking lot didn't smell any better than the interior had, but it still felt amazing to be outside again.

"So?"

"So? Lauren, come on. Vanhelm handled psychopomps here. He manipulated a psychopomp at Church yesterday. You can't tell me—"

"He didn't 'handle' them, he might have seen them once or twice. And you don't know that he manipulated that psychopomp. And even if you did, that's not our—"

"It *is* our investigation. The Lamaru are our investigation, and if they're doing something with psychopomps, we—"

Lauren sighed. "Okay, Cesaria. Fine. Let's say for the sake of argument you're right. How do we prove that? How do we find out what their plan is?"

"We—" Oops.

"What?"

"Nothing." She'd been about to mention Maguinness, and the possibility of finding and questioning him. Had been about to mention the toad fetish. Damn it. She had real information, information that could have made a difference to Lauren, but she couldn't share any of it. Instead she had to let it fester in her mind, had to spend hours turning it over and over again to find some way to introduce it.

"Fine." Lauren pulled her keys out of her little purse.

"Look, Cesaria. I appreciate you think you're right about this. I don't agree. But even if I did, spending hours in useless conjecture does us no good. We need to work with the facts, and the facts we have are that the Lamaru are murdering people with real physical weapons."

"This could be a lead—"

"And so could the bodies. You know, the actual evidence we have. Let's focus on that, okay?"

The worst part was that as much as she wanted to, Chess really couldn't fault Lauren. Given the information they had—the information they were *supposed* to have—Chess might very well have thought the same way.

Oh, who the fuck was she kidding. No, she wouldn't have, at least she hoped she wouldn't have. But she couldn't totally fault Lauren, which pissed her off.

"Fine," she said, because Lauren seemed to want her to say something.

"Good. Now why don't you meet me at the Church in, say, three hours. We should have some new reports by then. And we can head over to the docks and check out the place where the Lamaru body was found, what was his name?"

"Denby," Chess said. "Why three hours? Why not head over now?"

"I have a meeting with Daddy." Lauren frowned and checked her watch, while Chess just managed to restrain her eye roll. "In fact, I'm late. Have you finished studying the file? You said yesterday you were looking into that genetic anomaly—did you finish?"

"I haven't had time, since—"

"Well, you have time now."

Chess gritted her teeth. *Mustn't smack the Grand Elder's daughter. Mustn't smack the Grand Elder's daughter.* "Yes, I guess I do."

Lauren plunked herself down into her car. "Good. You can fill me in later. See you then."

She didn't wait for a reply. Chess hadn't expected her to. Instead she watched the car speed out of the lot, and thought about what to do next. Yes, she could head over to the Church and sit for hours in the Restricted Room. She probably should do that. But what the hell did it matter? The case wouldn't be solved by figuring out what the genetic problems of the victims were. The case would be solved when they caught the fucking Lamaru and figured out what the hell they were doing with psychopomps, and what that had to *do* with people with genetic problems.

She had her psychopomp with her, in her bag. For the first time ever she thought of it with unease, picturing the skull as something that could erupt into being without warning and attack her. In her years as a Debunker she'd gone through four or five of them; they were tools, something to be controlled. More than that, they were part and parcel of the Church, a symbol of its sovereignty, and as such represented her own power and independence. Her freedom, such as it was.

The Lamaru had attempted to destroy the Church before. Had been attempting to destroy it almost since it had taken over. But they'd never struck at its heart like that, turned its own magic against it in such a direct fashion.

Lauren could say all she wanted that the Lamaru and the psychopomps had nothing to do with each other. Lauren was also welcome to say the earth was flat. Neither happened to be true, and Chess knew it.

Fuck the Restricted Room. Chess had real evidence. And real drugs. She already knew how to use the latter; she had years of practice at it. Now she just had to figure out how to use the former, and she wanted to do both immediately.

She hopped back into her car and headed for the Market.

Chapter Fourteen

[Family is the most important thing there is, and you should encourage your beloved spouse to be close to your children.
—*Mrs. Increase's Advice for Ladies,* by Mrs. Increase]

Yes, fine, she'd been hoping to see Terrible, and yes, fine, her heart sank a little when she scanned the crowd and didn't spot him. But at least that wasn't the only reason she'd come there, even if it was the only reason she'd taken four Cepts instead of three before leaving her car.

Nor did she see Maguinness anywhere, which really sucked. She'd been certain he'd be giving his flowery speeches from his makeshift stage. He had to know something. *Had* to. Why else would the Lamaru be scared of him?

Of course, getting involved with someone who scared even the Lamaru didn't exactly appeal, but she didn't have a choice. Her thoughts during the short drive from slaughterhouse to Market had continued along the same lines as her thoughts in the parking lot: she couldn't stop picturing the skull in her bag suddenly erupting into a thoughtless, emotionless deathbringer.

If she could be made to fear Church magic, what the fuck was left to her?

Well, okay. She knew the answer to that. What was left to her were the pills hiding in their ornate silver box in her bag, the pipe room off to her left. She took solace from them, wrapped them around her. She still believed in them.

She could believe in her own talent, too. As a person she was pretty much useless, but as a witch . . . That had value.

And she still believed in the man who hated her. Shame that all those things—except her magic—were equally bad for her; was it less self-destructive to ride the knife edge of slow suicide, or to spend most of her time wanting someone who wished she'd just go ahead and slip on that edge?

But she still had things to believe in, things to trust, and she needed to keep that firmly in mind if she wanted to keep her fucking sanity during this mess.

The bright weather had brought Downsiders out in droves; they lounged on crumbling steps and sidewalks with their sleeves pushed up to catch the sun, stood in ragged clumps on the corners, and flooded the Market. Chess pushed her way through the crowds, felt them watching her.

Erik Vanhelm had her picture. Any one of the crush of semi-humanity around her could be Lamaru. Did eyes follow her because she was Bump's Churchwitch? Because everyone had seen her with Terrible all the time and that had obviously stopped? Or because they planned to grab her, drag her into an alley, and slice her to ribbons?

She gripped her knife handle in her pocket and kept walking. They hadn't come after her yet, she reminded herself. When she'd tangled with them before, they hadn't waited long to break into her apartment and attack her.

She wasn't sure if that thought made her feel better or worse.

Seeing Edsel definitely cheered her up, though, despite having to ignore the concern in his eyes. Did she look that bad?

"Chess." He smiled and finished taping a price note

to a basket of beeswax chunks on the counter. "You right?"

"Right up," she answered automatically. He'd set up closer to the meat booths, where the background noise hummed louder. Good. It gave her an excuse to lean in tight. "I wanted to ask you about something."

"Ain't chattered with Terrible on you, baby."

She raised her eyebrows. "That's not what I wanted to ask."

"Just givin you the tell, is all."

"I don't— Whatever. Do you know anything about that potion guy, the one from yesterday? Maguinness."

"The hairy dude? Give me the creeps, he do."

"Yeah, him. Have you seen him before, have you heard anything about him?"

Edsel's head tilted; a ray of sun soaked into his hair. "Ain't can say as I have. Been here a while's all the knowledge I got. Sells he potions an magic. Never buy from me, though."

"Do you know where he gets his supplies?"

"Figure he makin em heself, dig. Ain't been told he buyin elsewhere."

Shit. She'd hoped— Wait. "Wouldn't that cost a lot, or need a lot of space?"

"Guessing him got a big place, aye. Way up. Could be him uses the market there."

"Shit." She'd never visited the market closest to the address Maguinness gave when he signed in to the prison.

Wait a minute. If there was a market near his address, why had he started selling out of this one?

Granted, he'd need Bump's permission to set up his stage there, too. Hell, he'd need Bump's permission to set up a booth—or rather, if Bump or Terrible or one of Bump's other people noticed a vendor selling anything they shouldn't, they'd be shut down. And probably beaten down, too, to make sure the message sank in.

But if he'd been in Downside for a while and had suddenly changed his methods, didn't that suggest he needed money, and fast?

Unless he'd just decided to branch out, to expand. She saw again those pale, grimy ankles below his too-short pants, the way his shirt hung off his bony frame. No. It may have been safer to pretend to be poor, especially in Downside, but most people couldn't resist the chance to show off. Especially when trying to convince others of their power and skill. In order to impress, one first had to look impressive.

Appearances were deceiving, sure. But it was elementary psychology, or had been back when psychology was legal. Chess had done enough late-night reading in the Archives to know that, even if a lifetime spent watching empty-pocket shitbags being treated like kings simply because they looked the part hadn't taught her already.

It was possible Maguinness was rich. He could be richer than Bump for all she knew. But she just didn't think so. Bump would have known if he was. How much was Bump charging him to work the Market?

Wait. Hadn't Terrible said Maguinness had a big family to feed, and that's why he'd asked to work the Market in the first place?

"What's in yon thoughts?" Edsel watched her from behind his black shades. "Trouble up with he?"

She shook her head. "I don't know. Just, could you ask around for me? Anything you hear about him would be a help."

"Aye, coursen I will."

"Thanks. Hey, do you know anything about psychopomps?"

"Sure I ain't know more'n you on that one."

"No, I mean— Here." Suppressing a shudder, she pulled the fetish parts in their plastic shrouds from her bag, laid them out on the fabric-covered counter. "I figure they used this to make psychopomps, but it's also a destruction spell."

"Aye. Seein the finger there." Edsel gave one of the bags a tentative poke, yanked his hand back and shook it like he was trying to fling off droplets of evil. "Some serious trouble you got with that, baby. Tear the energy around it good, be a bomb with the right words behind it."

"Right. That's what I figured. But I've never seen a destruction spell with these other ingredients. They look like the kind of thing the Trainers use to make psychopomps, I mean, when they first start summoning them before they release the skulls to the supply room, you know?"

"That one part I ain't got much knowledge of."

"But you know the kind of ingredients that go in psychopomp spells. So why add something like the finger?"

"Guessin they either tryin to destroy them some psychopomps, or make them some psychopomps destroy other else. Come to think on it . . . been hearing some chatter lately on dogs. In the deathhouse, dig. Galena got she a brother up that way, say them ain't sleeping so well with barking."

The thrill running up her spine had nothing to do with the goat horn she'd brushed with her hand. "Dogs? At the slaughterhouse?"

"What Galena's brother tell she, aye."

Vanhelm in the slaughterhouse. What had Carlyle said? That Vanhelm had been a very dedicated employee, coming in early, staying late after everyone else had left.

Spending lots of time alone there. Alone in a building with its very own psychopomp creation room.

Lauren would have to listen to her now, right?

As soon as the thought formed she knew the answer: No. No, Lauren would not have to listen to her now. She'd tap her pointy little foot and say of course dogs barked in the slaughterhouse; dogs lived there, guarding the building. Dogs lived inside, too, or at least they lived until they walked down their own chutes.

Not all dogs became psychopomps. The skulls of the ones who didn't were destroyed, but dog bones and fur had other magical uses, as did their blood and eyes and organs and just about everything else. It would all be gathered there and handed over to the Church, or sent to dealers like Edsel.

Not to mention that a thriving little black market existed for their meat, although she didn't think Lauren would even know about that. The point was, the fact that dogs barked at night at the slaughterhouse wouldn't make one bit of difference to Lauren.

"Okay," she said finally, scooping up the bagged fetish parts and dumping them back into her bag. "Thanks. That might help. If you—if you see Terrible, tell him what you just told me, okay? And that I told you to tell him."

"Oughta give he the knowledge you own self, baby. No good playing pass-on, ain't solve nothing."

For once that damned Binding came in handy. She lifted her wrist. "Actually, I probably can't tell him myself. So will you just do it, please?"

His lips pressed together in a thin line, but he nodded. "Aye. I give it over, on the soon-as."

"Thanks."

They chatted for a few more minutes, mostly about Galena and the pregnancy, before Chess moved on. Walking might clear her head, and she could certainly use a little clear-headedness at this point. Maybe she should go home. She still had two hours or so before she had to meet Lauren for another round of Bitch Games. If she went home she could sit down and go through the file again. She could make notes. She'd be safe there, too.

Okay. Snack, then home. She made her way to the row of permanent booths against the fence, not hungry but figuring at least eating was something to do. Not to mention that it could be hours before she got to eat anything; she had a sneaking suspicion that Lauren wouldn't let her go until well after dark.

She should ask Elder Griffin about her file and see if the picture was still in it. See if duplicates were made, too.

Should she tell him why she wanted to know? Good question. Redundant question, since she'd been turning it over and over in her mind since the moment she'd done that exact thing with the photo in her hands, but still—

Instinct brought her hand down to her pocket when someone bumped into her. Instinct made her grab her bag in time to catch the child trying to sneak its grubby hand into it.

The second her skin touched its—his? hers? she couldn't tell—energy shot up her arm. Creepy, oozy energy; she staggered under the weight of it in her head.

But she didn't let go, although the child struggled and wriggled so hard she barely managed to hold on, and still couldn't even make out its features. A shaggy mop of black hair obscured its eyes; its face below the hair was a reddish blur with a gaping, semi-toothless mouth. And its energy felt like the dirty whispers of a pervert in a dark room.

Chess dug her short fingernails into the delicate skin of the child's inner wrist and held on.

The child shrieked. Chess didn't give a shit. Neither did anybody else. If every Downside pickpocket and cutpurse drew crowds, nobody would ever get anything done.

The energy grew stronger, felt worse, as Chess dragged the child out of the noodle line and toward Bump's place. Not because she wanted to go to Bump's place, but because nobody stood outside his front door; she could have a little privacy there, and it would be harder for the child to escape.

A child shouldn't have energy like that. Chess's tattoos

itched and stung; no living thing should make her feel that way.

"Lemme go!"

A sharp foot slammed into Chess's calf. The kid was tougher than she—closer inspection made Chess fairly certain it was a girl—looked.

"I'm not fucking letting you go. I'm going to find Terrible. See how he likes thieves in the Market."

"Weren't stealing!" The girl slapped at Chess's hand, tried to twist her arm away.

"Were too. You were trying to get into my bag."

"Weren't *stealing*!" With every movement the girl made, a fresh wave of that horrible energy slid up Chess's arm; with every movement she made, a fresh wave of her horrible stench assaulted Chess's nose. The girl stank of sweat and animals and filth, like she'd been sleeping in the sty at the slaught—

"Where do you live?"

The girl must have sensed Chess's anger turning into curiosity. Her struggles quieted. "Ain't got no tells for you. Lemme go."

"What were you trying to get out of my bag?"

The girl glared at her. Up close Chess could see the child's eyes, squinty and strangely unfocused, too small and too close set. Her nose didn't fit properly either; it looked more like a fat earlobe, just a knob of flesh rising above her tiny upper lip. Her features crowded too close to the center, leaving wide, pale cheeks and a prominent chin floating around the edges. She looked like a computer simulation of a human rather than an actual one.

And she felt like something that shouldn't be breathing at all.

"What were you trying to take from my bag?" Chess repeated, daring to take her eyes off the girl for a second to hunt for Terrible in the crowd.

Mistake. Sharp pain exploded in her forearm; the

child had bitten her, sinking those crooked, needlelike teeth into her skin.

"Fuck!" She dug her fingers deeper into the girl's wrist, but that made the girl bite harder. They wobbled for a second in front of Bump's black door, Chess's bag slipping from her shoulders, before she tangled her free hand in the girl's hair and twisted it.

The girl howled and let go of Chess's arm. Her hair felt like a bird's nest full of motor oil, but Chess twisted harder, pushing down as she did so. Yes, it was just a child, and Chess didn't want to hurt a child, but the little bitch had tried to turn her arm into lunch.

And now the little bitch had a knife. Sun caught the blade and sparked into Chess's eyes; she barely managed to avoid having it sunk into her stomach.

Her fist was still tangled in the girl's hair. The girl fell backward, twisting Chess's wrist and forcing her to lose her grip.

Chess stumbled. So did the child, but she had the advantage of not having a bleeding bite wound on her arm to distract her. She hopped up and started running across the Market, toward the animal vendors.

Another exit stood right behind those vendors. Another exit, and beyond it the Downside streets full of alleys and squats and other hiding places for a little girl to sneak into. No fucking way was that kid hitting that exit. If she did, Chess would never find her.

So Chess followed. The girl ducked and dove between people; Chess had to shove them out of the way. Her heart pounded. Blood dripped from her arm onto the dirty ground; Chess sure as fuck hoped nobody knew what kind of power resided in that blood or what its uses were, because if some enterprising shithead decided to scoop up the dirt on which it fell they'd have a lovely little spell ingredient or the means to build a curse against her.

No time to worry about that. She leapt over a couple of chickens, her eyes still pinned on the child's thin, dingy gray shirt and too-big jeans with fat rolls at the ankles.

The child ducked through the exit and turned left. Chess followed. She almost had her, just another few inches and she could grab that awful hair and pull her back—

The girl spun around. Her knife flashed in the air again. This time Chess tripped over an empty beer bottle and fell, slamming her knees onto the broken sidewalk. Pain shot up her legs.

She got up anyway, refusing to let some kid get the better of her, but it was too late. The girl ducked sideways into an alley; something clanked, louder than the fast-receding sound of the girl's footsteps.

By the time Chess reached the narrow space she was gone. Or at least, she was almost gone. Movement caught Chess's eye at the end, where the alley opened onto Fifty-third; two figures disappearing into the sun-drenched crowds. One second she saw them. The next they were gone.

But she had seen them. The girl's shaggy head was easy to recognize. Almost as easy to recognize was the much shaggier head of Arthur Maguinness beside it, as he scooped the child up and carried her away.

Chapter Fifteen

[Their roads are marvels of technology, which the Church has only improved upon over time.
—*A History of the Old Government, Volume V: 1930–1974*]

Maguinness needed money. Maguinness sent some kid to steal from her. From her specifically? Or just to steal from someone, and she looked like an easy target?

But she didn't look like an easy target—at least she didn't think she did. Trouble lurked around every corner in Downside and hung over crowds like layers of smoke, but not only was Chess careful, not only was Chess Church, Chess worked for Bump. Since that had become common knowledge she hadn't had any trouble.

And why would Maguinness start trouble with her? He had no idea what she was investigating. Right? And even if he did, if the Lamaru were scared of him or in some kind of fight with him, he'd be glad she was investigating them, right?

Shit. Why was it that every time she so much as breathed in the Lamaru's direction, everything in her life went totally fucking haywire?

No, the business with Terrible had nothing to do with the Lamaru, but at that particular moment, as she pulled into the Church parking lot, it felt like it did. After all, if the Lamaru hadn't been pulling their shit at Chester

Airport she never would have gotten involved with Terrible, or Lex, right? So this was their fault.

The lie totally felt like a lie, but whatever. She wanted to blame the Lamaru, so she did. What were they going to do, attack her? They'd do that anyway. Scum-sucking shits.

And speaking of shits . . . Lauren stood outside the huge double doors at the Church entrance, tapping her foot. Chess glanced at the digital clock lurking beneath a thin layer of dust on her dashboard. Five minutes to six. She was early. So what was Lauren's problem?

Lauren's problem was simply that Chess existed, it seemed. With a sigh Chess got out of the car and trudged over, discarding as she went her loose plan to tell Lauren about the pickpocket attempt and connect it to Maguinness as someone the Lamaru might possibly deal with. Lauren wouldn't listen anyway, not when all Chess had to go by was an overheard conversation she couldn't share and an attempted crime that happened dozens of times every day.

"I'm not late. It's only five till."

Lauren's lips thinned. "Did I say you were late?"

"No, but you look irritated."

"Not everything is about you, Cesaria."

Chess treated that comment with the dignity it deserved—none at all—and plunged on. "I had another look at the file. I was thinking maybe we could start hunting for the kind of equipment someone would need to create embryos, or implant them, or whatever. There's got to be a black market for that stuff, maybe the Squad would know something."

Lauren considered it. "I think if we knew something, we'd have busted them, but it's worth a try, I guess. Let me call— Shit!"

Chess started to reach for her, wondering what exactly

the problem was, but Lauren's gaze was fixed on a spot behind her. Chess turned, Lauren's ghost-white face making only the faintest, most fleeting impression on her before all the blood drained out of her own.

Erik Vanhelm stood not twenty feet away, on the lawn near the stocks.

For the space of a heartbeat he stared at them. They stared back. Chess noticed every detail, the way the bluish dusk light darkened his hair, the flaring of his nostrils, the blurry faint movement of branches in a tree behind him.

Then he took off for the parking lot.

"The car," Chess said, already making her way toward Lauren's egomobile. "Come on, he's—"

"No, he's probably running somewhere—"

"He's getting in his car, why wouldn't he?" Chess grabbed the door handle and yanked it. Locked. Her pulse throbbed beneath the thin, decorated skin of her wrists. "Come on, he's going to get away!"

"I think he's still here!"

"Yeah, but he's not going to be for much—"

"No, we need to follow on foot."

"Follow where? He has a car, he has to, and—"

A door slammed. An engine started.

Chess didn't even have time to say "Told you so"; Lauren could move that little-rich-girl ass when the situation called for it, she had to give her that. They were both inside and the powerful engine was turning over before the black sedan roared past them with Vanhelm at the wheel.

They spun out of the lot right behind, blew two red lights up the street. "He's heading for the highway," Lauren said, laying on the horn as they sped past an oblivious pedestrian.

"Yeah." Chess had a feeling she knew where he was

headed, too. Where else would he go but Downside, where he could get lost in a crowd or down an alley with a hidden entrance or . . . wherever?

Especially not when he probably had a cell phone on him as well. Which meant he could have a happy little Lamaru welcome party waiting for them when he finally decided to dock that boat he was steering.

She'd just *come* from Downside, damn it. She could have stayed home.

She said as much to Lauren—except for the part about staying home—and Lauren nodded. "What have you got on you, anything?"

"Um . . . yeah, actually. I've got some mandrake and a couple of chunks of snake, and some frankincense I think. Graveyard dirt. Melidia. Asafetida. Iron filings, but not much, I forgot to refill them this morning."

"Good kit." Lauren swerved around a convertible full of hip young things and grabbed Vanhelm's ass again. She wasn't a bad driver, Chess noted. Not bad at all. Not as good as some, but she was certainly holding her own. "I have some filings, so that's taken care of, and I have some wolfsbane and blood salt. Oh, and some ajenjible, and a set of hare bones. Well, not a whole set, but some."

They were on the highway, zipping along in the fast lane. Before Chess had a chance to suggest it Lauren fell back a little, trying to trick Vanhelm into thinking they couldn't keep up.

"You guys carry that stuff all the time?"

Lauren smiled. "I could ask you the same thing."

"I just believe in being prepared."

"Me, too."

The car jolted back; some idiot cut them off. Lauren cursed and buzzed around him.

"Well, aren't we a couple of Girl Apprentices," Chess murmured. "Hey, do you know how to place a track? That's something you guys do, right?"

"Yes . . ."

"What?"

"I've never done it in a moving car. I mean, usually you sneak up and set it while it's parked or get close and set it on them."

Chess raised an eyebrow. "You don't think you can handle it?"

"Oh, fuck off." Lauren thought for a second, sped up a tad. Vanhelm's car was a good five lengths ahead now. Damn it, there was no way he was going to think he'd lost them, not while they rode in the automotive equivalent of a pair of five-inch fuck-me pumps. "I have to get close, and either you'll have to take the wheel or I'll have to talk you through it."

"Great choices."

"You don't think you can handle it?"

Chess acknowledged the joke and unbuckled her seatbelt. "Just tell me what to do."

"Get my bag."

Unlike Chess, Lauren carried her work supplies separately. She had a petite Coach purse on the backseat and a larger black nylon and suede bag on the floor behind Chess. It was heavy and awkward to lift; the edge of her seat dug into her empty stomach, and the cars and scenery whirling past in that position made her feel, for a moment, disoriented, like she'd been hanging upside down. Add to that the jolt of energy from Lauren's supplies and she got a nice queasy little headrush right when she didn't need it.

The black bag was covered in designer initials woven into the fabric. Chess wasn't sure if it was a lack of taste or an excess of it that made her find the thing ugly.

Still, it was well stocked. She pulled out the tracking reader and a couple of sensors; they came with minute blobs of sticky goo, like chewing gum, at the corners.

Okay, here's the problem with bravado, Chess thought.

They were currently running at about seventy miles per hour, but they were just tailing Vanhelm now, taking a leisurely little cruise along what the newspapers called "the 300 Corridor." Once they got close to him he was going to start evading, and she was not looking forward to being the center of a rubber-and-steel sandwich at probably double their current speed.

Erik's car could probably handle it. Those BT big-blocks could run it out—as she well knew, after months of listening to Terrible extol the virtues of heavy pre-Church muscle—and Lauren's car, despite Chess's initial assumption that it was nothing more than a fancy lawn mower, had plenty of room left on the tach and wasn't even breaking a sweat.

Unlike certain Churchwitches she knew. Namely herself. She could think of a fuck of a lot of things she'd rather be doing than getting ready to lean out the window of one speeding car to get friendly with another.

Lauren glanced at her. "Ready?"

"No. But let's do it."

She kept the window up while Lauren gunned it, closing the space between themselves and Erik. Chess's stomach sank with every foot they gained.

Erik noticed them coming and sped up. Lauren followed. Chess gritted her teeth. Her palms felt sticky and dirty; she rubbed them on her knees and wished she hadn't agreed to do this. Who cared if Lauren thought she was a pussy? Was it really worth the arm she was pretty sure she was about to lose?

Another car jumped into the passing lane ahead of Erik, who slammed on his brakes, forcing Lauren to do the same.

"Hold on." Chess's throat was dry; she grabbed her water and took a few gulps. "He's going to know what we're doing. We need a distraction."

"I'll shoot at him."

"Are you fucking— No! No shooting. You might hit *me*. How about— *Shit!*"

Vanhelm swerved, almost hit them—would have, had Lauren not been quick at the wheel.

"Do it now," she said. "He's coming again, look—"

Chess caught a glimpse of Vanhelm's profile, saw his hands jerk the wheel as if in slow motion. She grabbed the sensor. Leaned out the window.

Nothing between her and bloody highway death on the gray pavement beneath her but the rim of the car door. Her hair completely obscured her view, stung when it snapped against her face. She couldn't breathe, couldn't see. Her hand stretched out with the sensor and she gritted her teeth, waiting for the crunch of bone, the tearing of flesh.

The sensor hit the car. The car swerved toward her again; for one horrifying second she lost her balance and fell forward. She was about to be crushed, the black quarterpanel of Vanhelm's car loomed before her like a brick wall she was speeding into—

Fingers tucked into the waistband of her jeans yanked her back into the car. Her head hit the top of the door with a painful thud. Vanhelm's car narrowly missed Lauren's; Lauren slammed on the brakes, Vanhelm jumped ahead, and Chess just managed to avoid throwing up.

Erik swerved to the right, cutting across all four lanes. Heading for the off-ramp at Mercer. Downside. Damn, they'd covered those miles fast. Time flew when she was certain she was going to die.

She'd been right about his destination, at least. And they'd be able to step back a little, now they could track his car.

Which, it occurred to her suddenly, was a little useless. Sure, they could track the car, and that might be handy, but once he got out of it he'd be lost. Untraceable. Just another no-hoper hunting oblivion on the Downside streets—just like her.

Lauren wasn't about to let her prey go; she twisted the wheel and followed, leaving screeching tires and honking horns in her wake.

Red lights barred the end of the road, but Erik wasn't much of a law-abider. He fishtailed into the intersection and headed right, Lauren dogging behind.

They tore across Mercer at speeds that made Chess, even as used as she was to Terrible's lead foot, cower in her seat. Lauren's car was a hell of a lot smaller and less solid, and Lauren was a good driver but not as good as he was. Her hand started to ache; she'd been clutching the tracking device hard enough to form grooves in her palm. The thing should have gone back into Lauren's bag, but just in case . . . she slipped the strap around her wrist, kept the sensors in her palm. Erik was a slippery son of a bitch, but if she got close enough she might have a chance to plant another one on him.

If her trigger-happy pal there didn't just shoot the guy. She still felt Lauren's hands on her bare stomach, reaching for the gun as Terrible strode away.

Erik made a sudden left down an alley; they emerged onto Ace just in time to see him leap out of the moving car and start running.

The sedan bumped into a wall and bounced off. Lauren wasn't as careless with her coupe. The tires squealed so loud that Chess barely heard Lauren cursing.

She shoved her door open before the car stopped moving and thrust herself out of it. Not the smartest move in the world—ow, her knee—but effective enough. She caught sight of the heel of Erik's shoe disappearing around a corner and pushed off running as hard as she could.

Without thinking she followed him, ignoring the

alarm ringing in the back of her head. She didn't know the neighborhood and he probably did. That was a stupid situation to put herself into, even with Lauren right behind her. Or maybe *especially* with Lauren right behind her. All she knew was that sweat poured down her face and the damned tracker kept bouncing on its strap and throwing her off her stride; her knee was killing her, her head and bitten arm still hurt, her bag slapped her thigh, and the sunlight disappeared as they moved into another alley, narrower than the first.

He stumbled on a trash can and hit the pavement. Chess leapt on him, already congratulating herself for keeping the sensor in her hand. The slap of it against his back was immeasurably satisfying.

Satisfaction that didn't last. Lauren yelled something, probably "Freeze!" or some other dramatic TV-Squad sort of dialogue, but Vanhelm brought his heel up with savage speed and kicked Chess in her already sore knee.

"Fucking hell!" He leapt up and took off again before she'd even finished the obscenity. Oh, it was so tempting just to lie there on the concrete, even with dirty water seeping through her jeans. Let Lauren do it. Just go home. This wasn't her neighborhood, but it wasn't that far, she could—

Gunshots. Shit, Lauren. Was the woman trying to rack up a kill count, or was she just reckless or stupid? Considering they had no idea where Vanhelm was leading them—or to whom—wasting bullets was not a great idea.

She was up and running again before the shots stopped echoing. Wood crashed. Lauren ducked through a hole in a wall. Chess followed, and almost ran into her.

Dead end. The room they stood in measured about fifteen by fifteen; just a blank square, empty save for a couple of rickety shelves. They wasted a minute banging on the walls, checking for hollow spaces or hidden doors, and found none.

"Are you sure he turned in here?" Chess stomped her foot, just in case, but the floor sounded and felt solid enough.

"It looked like he did. He just . . . disappeared into the wall. *Damn* it!"

"Maybe there's another—"

They heard the engine roar into life at the same time, tore out of the room in time to see the rear end of Vanhelm's sedan burn rubber out of the alley.

He'd slashed Lauren's tires before he left.

Chapter Sixteen

[Laws are made for our safety and should be followed. Don't think that just because you want to do something, you should. Leave complicated magic to the Church.
—*You Can Do This! A Guide for Beginners,*
by Molly Brooks-Cahill]

At least working with the Grand Elder's daughter had one advantage. A gang of low-level Church employees from the Maintenance Department showed up within about half an hour to replace the slashed tires. Chess tried not to look at the loose flaps of rubber as the tires collapsed in pitiful heaps by the side of the car, their shape gone. Useless and empty.

And fast as those Maintenance employees were, it was still almost eight by the time they were done. Lauren's impatience revealed itself more clearly by the minute through jiggling, watch checking, pacing, and casting ever more annoyed looks at Chess as she leaned against a wall and smoked.

Lauren could be annoyed all she fucking wanted. Chess just wished she'd do it somewhere else. Lauren's irritation assaulted her, rubbing up and down her spine and making her palms tingle like early withdrawals.

Fuck, that might actually *be* early withdrawals, now that she thought about it. Not quite five hours . . . a little early. But she'd been stepping on it for a while, hadn't she? More pills, more often . . .

Blah. Something to worry about later. At the moment

the issue of actually taking the pills was far more important.

As was the tracker in her hand. She'd been fiddling with it while they waited, trying to figure out how to zero in on one of the sensors she'd placed on Vanhelm and not the handful still sitting in Lauren's bag. Tricky little bastard. Each sensor seemed to have a code, but the buttons were tiny and stiff, the menu impossible to decipher in the dark.

She waited for Lauren to snatch it from her hands again—and fail to make it work again—but she didn't. Instead she watched while Chess hit button after button.

The machine lit up. Chess almost dropped her smoke.

A map grid appeared on the screen, a map grid with a single flashing green light. Carefully Chess turned the little knob next to the screen. It rewarded her by zooming in.

Was this the track she'd placed on his car, or on his shirt? He knew about the one on his car—at least, Chess assumed he did. Whether he was aware of the one on his shirt she had no idea.

And it didn't matter anyway, because the screen zoomed in and Chess read the address, and her heart slammed into her throat. "Lauren!"

"You got something?"

Her triumphant grin refused to hide as she showed Lauren the screen. "He's at the slaughterhouse."

Feeling triumphant about being right and feeling glad about being right were two different things. On the one hand, Chess was thrilled, in a take-that-bitch sort of way. On the other . . .

On the other, her palms still buzzed and dizziness crept around the edges of her mind, as she crouched in the bushes beside the darkened slaughterhouse, a hulking beast with only a sliver of moon to illuminate it. If she never crouched in another bush it would be too soon.

"There has to be a back door," she whispered to Lauren. Maybe she could get Lauren to go one way while she went another. All she needed was a minute. Just one, with Lauren not around, so she could crack her pillbox.

To her surprise, Lauren nodded. "Let's go around the side. I think I saw a door there earlier."

Fuck. What else could she do but nod and follow Lauren through the shrubbery to the granite corner of the building? Church protocol for Squad members meant working in teams and staying together. Hell, Church protocol for Debunkers on the very rare occasions they worked together said the same. Once inside, getting away from Lauren would be extremely difficult.

And extremely necessary. The itching wasn't bad yet, but it distracted her, and she didn't need any distractions. Not when she faced at least one Lamaru and probably more.

Lauren stood too close to her while she eased her picks in and out of the lock. Chess's shoulders twitched. The only person whose breath she didn't mind feeling on her neck was . . . well, enough about that.

The lock gave with a tiny click. Chess started to grab the knob, thought better of it, and squeezed her lube syringe over the hinges. Too late, probably, but worth a shot anyway. Lauren twisted the knob, and they slipped into the darkened slaughterhouse.

It stank. They stood in some sort of pen; Chess's boots scuffed through a thin layer of damp ammoniac straw and warm animal bodies blocked her way, surrounded her. She had to force her lungs to keep working; claustrophobia and cow shit didn't really aid her breathing, wouldn't have even if her chest hadn't started tightening for other reasons.

For a second she stood in total darkness before her

eyes adjusted. It *was* a pen. The cows slept all around her, and Lauren's dainty hand pinched her own dainty nose. When she saw Chess looking at her she gestured forward. Right. They wouldn't find anything here. Even if there was something here they probably wouldn't find it. Chess was committed to her job and all, but she was not going to start playing around in manure just in case some Lamaru had dropped something. Not unless it became absolutely necessary.

She dug a pair of latex gloves from her bag—her hand brushed her pillbox, oh, damn, she just needed a minute alone—and slipped them on. Again, just in case. If manure squeezing did end up being on the menu, she'd be prepared.

Besides, with the Lamaru in there, who knew what else she might end up touching?

And they were there all right. She could feel them. Their darkness crawled over her skin, rolled up her spine to buzz in her head. The cows around her looked like black monsters, threatening her, as her mind swam and her body tingled.

She needed to find the Lamaru. She needed her pills.

Together she and Lauren wound their way among the sleeping cows like worms through an intestine. Chess concentrated on breathing and not slipping, on placing one careful foot in front of the other and steadying herself before the next step.

Voices murmured just out of range. Voices and soft whimpers. Dogs.

Chess moved faster, ducking around the cows. She didn't see a door, but there had to be one. With every step the voices grew louder. She glanced at Lauren, whose face tilted up. Listening. Good.

Finally they hit a door. Locked. Chess grabbed her picks, only to stop when Lauren touched her arm. What now?

Lauren leaned in close again, too close. "Cesaria, you were right."

"What?"

"You were right. About the psychopomps. I'm sorry I didn't listen."

How was she supposed to respond to that? What did it say about her that she couldn't even trust Lauren's apology? It sounded sincere enough. "Yeah, that's okay."

Lauren hadn't let go of her arm; now she gave it a little squeeze and dropped her hand. "Thanks."

Okay, whatever. Not really the time to worry about Lauren's motives, and she couldn't really bring herself to care that much anyway. So she picked the lock by feel and they found themselves in another space, empty save for winding steel walls stretching halfway to the ceiling. The chutes. The trails the animals walked down to their deaths.

Only the faintest moonlight shone on them through the windows high on the walls. They stood gleaming in it, silent and cold and watchful.

Animals entered at one end, were drawn blindly from one sharp turn to the next, not knowing where they were going or that they'd been led into a death trap from which they'd never escape. From which they'd never had a chance of escaping from the moment they set foot in the building, made the commitment to take those first steps forward.

Chess shivered.

The room ended in a grille, the kind stores pulled over their windows at closing time. Beyond that were flames, their glow making Chess and Lauren duck.

The Lamaru were there. She saw their black forms against the flames, heard their voices rising louder than before. Heard the dogs whine and smelled their fear acid-sharp in the still air. Smelled their blood. Their urgency infected her, cranked her heart.

So did the urgency of her body's demands. If she didn't find a little privacy soon, she'd have a real problem. Fighting the Lamaru would require all her strength, and she couldn't give it in this condition, not when her brow was damp and her palms were starting to burn.

They had two choices. The grille didn't reach the floor; it descended just over halfway down, ending right above Chess's knees. They could slide under.

But another door stood at the far end, with one of those staircase symbols of a stick person walking down beside it.

"There's that walkway upstairs," Chess whispered. "We could see what they're doing. We'll split up, you go to the left and I'll go right."

Even in the dark she saw Lauren's nostrils flare with annoyance, but who gave a fuck. The horrible thick energy of Lamaru magic, the slithery whisper of psychopomp magic, choked her, and she just wanted it to stop. Their chant had a rhythm, a heavy beat, that cut into her soul and made her blood pump in time.

"I don't think that's such a good idea. They're right there."

"Call for backup. We can't handle them all with just us."

Lauren didn't sigh, exactly, but she made a faint huffy sound in her throat. "You want me to light my phone up with them right there?"

A dog howled. Energy thundered across the floor, blasted into Chess. The Lamaru had done it. They'd made a psychopomp. Probably one of many. Oh, fuck. She didn't think she'd ever been so pissed off about being right.

On the other hand . . . here was her chance. "Get into the stairwell and call. I'll stay here and watch."

Her hand already clasped her pillbox.

"I don't think we should separate."

For fuck's sake. Chess grabbed Lauren by the arm and

practically shoved her into the stairwell, realizing too late that the door's hinges weren't oiled. They made an unholy squeal, cutting through even the howling dogs and the Lamaru's chanting.

The chanting stopped. *Fuck*.

The heavy steel door of the stairwell slammed shut behind them. To get out the way they'd come in would take too long, would be too difficult. The screech and the silence had awakened the animals, or broken whatever spell they'd been under—a Hand of Glory, probably, and likely more than one. Even through the thick walls Chess heard them barking and howling, mooing and squealing and bleating. Too loud in her oversensitive ears.

"Great job, Cesaria." Lauren grabbed her arm and started dragging her up the stairs—not that it was necessary. Chess was already moving. She thought she remembered seeing a stairway door across from the offices where they'd been earlier; from there they had a straight shot down the hall and out the front entrance.

A straight shot with at least two locked doors between them and freedom. *Fuck*.

"Call for backup, damn it!" She yanked her arm from Lauren's grasp and started digging in her bag. Not easy while running balls-out up a flight of stairs in the pitch-dark, but she'd do her best. She had those chunks of snake, the black mirror, the goat's blood . . .

Light exploded in her eyes. Lauren's phone. "No signal."

It didn't matter. They'd reached the top of the stairs. The door resisted but gave, and they spilled out onto the slick tiles outside the offices.

The Lamaru lunged. More followed behind, racing up the central staircase that led to the office hall and the walkway she'd taken with Lauren to get to the psychopomp room earlier. Hard hands grabbed Chess's arms, her waist and neck. She managed to fit the tips of her fingers into her pocket where her knife waited, but more hands caught her, held her fast. Her feet slipped on the floor.

Lauren screamed. Through the crush of bodies and chaos of shouts and laughter Chess glimpsed her being dragged off down the hall.

Dragged in the opposite direction. Chess and her captors passed out of the dim light of the offices and to the bottom of the three steps leading to the psychopomp room. She fought harder. Her muscles ached, sweat dampened her brow and her heart threatened to explode out of her chest. Still they held her, pressing her forward, their arms tight around her stomach and legs. Their harsh laughter echoed in her head.

That room had solid iron walls. No exits. A small barred window. It wasn't a room, it was a deathchamber, a deathchamber in a deathhouse, and she was being dragged right into it.

And Erik Vanhelm waited for her there. The arms around her disappeared.

He was on her before she had a chance to react, his heavy fist catching her across the jaw. Pain exploded in her face; her brain caught fire with it, throbbed with it, as though it had suddenly swollen three sizes. She hit the floor, her shoulder taking most of her weight.

No time to feel it, or think about it. Get up, run, back to the hall. They'd catch her again, they were right there, but her hands were free, she could get her knife—

He grabbed her hair, yanked her back. She heard Lauren scream.

"Lauren!" she managed, her jaw creaking and throbbing, before her ass thumped to the cement. Vanhelm over her, grinning at her. He glanced up and nodded; she heard the door close behind them. That could not be good.

"Cesaria Putnam," he said, and the sound of her name

in his voice made her want to scream. Ugly power crawled over the words like roaches. "I've wondered what you look like."

What the fuck did he think this was, some kind of spy movie? Did he want to get into a clever little dialogue with her or something?

Fuck that. She dug her shoulders into the floor and jerked her legs up hard; her knee connected with the side of his face with a satisfying—if painful—thump.

His grip on her hair loosened. She rolled away, tried to get up. Not fast enough. His arms closed around her, trapped her. His weight pinned her to the floor. She inhaled a mouthful of foul-smelling dust that tasted of raw meat and sand and gritted her tongue. The floor had been clean earlier. What was going on in there?

Lauren screamed again, barely audible through the thick door. Heavy footsteps thundered past in the hall. A harsh voice: "Erik?"

"Five minutes." Vanhelm's breath heated her ear, her neck. His arm pressed hard on the back of her neck, shoving her face farther into the filthy floor. Not just dirt or dust; blood seeped across the cement toward her, blood from the dead animals in the corner.

A chuckle from the doorway. "Make it fast, we don't have time."

She barely heard it. Her stomach lurched. Only her desperate swallows, the realization that if she threw up she'd have to lie there with her face in the puddle, kept her from losing the little bit of water she'd had in the car. The germs on that floor, in that blood, the dirt on her body, the hands holding her down, so dirty, so filthy . . . She couldn't breathe, couldn't think, couldn't move, she was trapped, she was too small, too weak, and she deserved it. Shit, why hadn't she managed to grab her pills when she was in the stairwell? She needed them, she couldn't think without them. . . .

Vanhelm's free hand beneath her stomach, finding the button of her jeans. Undoing it.

She broke. The dizzy haze of very early withdrawal, the paralyzing fear, the memories of lectures in a horrible sonorous voice about germs and the germs filthy little girls carried—they snapped, set her free, disappeared from her mind, and all that was left was mindless, red-haze rage.

He meant to rape her. Had waited up there, lurked up there, punched her, shoved her into filth, and now the scumsucking motherfucker actually thought he was going to get his sick fucking rocks off, use her without her permission?

Nobody was ever, *ever* going to do that to her again. Never.

She went limp, germs and bugs and the horrible-tasting dust forgotten; something cold and watchful replaced them in her mind. Let him think she'd given in. She forced a few whimpering sounds out of her throat. Fucker was about to die, she'd feel his blood pour over her hands . . .

Her zipper went down. No fear. Just waiting. Only one of them was in danger here and it sure as fuck wasn't her. His arm still pressing the back of her neck. She felt it like a brand, felt him behind her like a movie she was watching. Every cell in her body, every cell in her brain was focused on him, nothing else existed.

"Erik?"

"I'll be right there," he shouted.

"No, Erik, *shit*—"

"Five minutes!"

Her knife was in the pocket of her jeans. She'd have to reach it fast. When was the best time? If she moved too soon he wouldn't be vulnerable enough. He'd still be focused on her entire body instead of the parts he wanted. She had to time it right, just right . . .

A gunshot, incredibly loud. Lauren screamed—she must have found her gun. Male voices shouting. Lauren still alive. That's what mattered.

Her pants down now, cold floor against her soft skin. His arm lifted her, pulled her to her knees, cold metal against her throat. Not her knife. "Don't move."

He had no idea what mistake he'd just made. No idea at all.

The sound of his robe shifting behind her, so loud. So slow. Her knees trapped by her jeans. The blade in his right hand, pressed to her right side. Roll away from it. A smell in the air, one she should know but couldn't identify, she was too focused on the moment, on waiting for the right moment.

His other hand lifted from her body. Positioning himself. Now. *Now!*

She spun to her left, dropping her elbow, flinging her right arm behind her. Her shoulders knocked his knife out of the way; her arm missed him but her legs, carried along with the force of her spin, did not. She knocked him on his side, her legs over his chest. Not enough, not bad enough.

His blade sliced her thigh. No time to scream, but fuck that hurt, oh, shit, she needed her fucking pills and he was keeping them from her, it was his fault.

Good thing she still had her gloves on. Her left hand shot out, grabbed him where it would hurt the most, squeezed as hard as she could. His scream broke the air around them into vicious shards, brought more footsteps, coming back. She didn't have time—the smell was stronger, her heart pounded, her body knew what it was even if her mind refused to accept it, and the Lamaru were shouting outside and banging on the door.

Her knife's handle leapt into her hand; she flicked it open, lifted it, ready to bring it down right into the center of his evil, foul little chest—

Something hit her, sent thick black vibrations through her body. A curse bag, energy so vile that tears sprang to her eyes, like the fetish she'd found earlier. Exactly like it, in fact. Another toad fell to the floor at her knees. She wavered, unsteady, trying to catch her breath. Blood trickled down her leg from the wound on her thigh. She scrambled away, not wanting her blood anywhere near it, kicked it away from the blood already there. Another bell in her head. Her back slammed into the cold cement wall, so hard she thought she felt it shake behind her. Hard enough to echo in her head like a gunshot.

They grabbed Vanhelm, dragged him from the room. She took one faltering footstep, then another, pressing herself against the wall to try to get as much distance as she could from the thing; it radiated evil like a dead fish throwing off stink, and she couldn't seem to drag her gaze from it. But her knife was still in her hand and she was ready to go, ready to move, she could catch them. Catch them fast, slice their throats, and take her pills.

She turned to do just that and stopped short in the doorway. Sure, early withdrawals were one thing, but this hallucination was beyond anything she'd ever experienced. Was this— Fuck, what the fuck happened?

Instead of the slaughterhouse she stood in the doorway of a hell dimension, a fiery cavern of smoke and noise and heat blasting her face and body, making her throat even drier. Flames rose almost to the ceiling, half-engulfing one of the iron walkways crossing the length of the building.

Something clicked in her head. The building snapped back into focus and she saw it all. For one dizzying, horrible moment she just stared, rooted to her spot in the doorway as men's shouts mixed with the frantic screams of the animals and crackling of flames. Through a hole in the thick, oily smoke she saw the Lamaru's firedishes, the ones they'd been using in their ritual, turned over.

But more flames crawled along the pens, far from the dishes. What the—

Blue flames exploded at the far wall. The building shook; the ceiling's groan was audible even over the rest of the noise. Holy shit. The first explosion she'd thought was Lauren's gun. The second—when her back had hit the wall. Not *that* hard. An actual explosion. A bomb going off.

The closest exit was probably through the offices. Fuck picking the locks, she'd smash the glass doors, she'd find something heavy to use, run to the right and get the fuck out—

Vanhelm appeared again, his face twisted in something that could have been a smile, could have been a grimace. She had no idea and didn't give a fuck anyway. All she could do was raise her hands, try to get past him, but his fist slammed into her face again, knocking her down, and the door of the psychopomp room slammed back into place. And locked.

She was trapped.

Chapter Seventeen

> The dead never cease in their quest to harm; the Church never ceases its vigilance against the dead.
>
> —*The Book of Truth,* Veraxis, Article 77

Okay. First things first. She had to get the hell out of that room before it turned into an iron-bound oven. Already her shirt clung to her body and her bangs stuck to her forehead in an itchy clump.

No, wait. *Really* first things first, she needed her pills. Her hands shook as she popped the catch on her pillbox, grabbed three Cepts, and crunched them into a bitter, chalky mess. In her haste to wash them down she spilled water on her shirt. Whatever. Probably not a bad thing, considering she was trapped in a fucking inferno.

And even if she hadn't been she didn't give a damn. The water got her pills down her throat, and chewing them up had given her a small dose, and that was all that really mattered. *Almost* all that really mattered. The fog in her head lifted a little, she could think again, focus again.

Now to get out of the room. Her palm practically sizzled when she placed it against the door. How could the flames spread that fast?

Another explosion answered that question. Her heart jerked in her chest like an insect caught in a spiderweb. That's what she was, a trapped insect, struggling to stay alive even though she would probably fail.

She skirted the toad-thing on the floor again to check the window. The bars didn't want to give under her hand but—there appeared to be a fire escape. Not directly outside the window, but close enough. If she could get out she could probably reach it.

Not like she had much choice, right? She'd take her chances leaping for the fire escape rather than be roasted slowly in a sealed room.

Except— Damn it! Damn it fuck damn it! Lauren. Where was Lauren?

And did she really care?

No. No, she didn't.

But Lauren didn't deserve to burn to death in a stinking, shrieking slaughterhouse. And how the hell would Chess explain to the Grand Elder that she'd saved her own ass without having any idea what had happened to his daughter?

She had to at least try to look. She had to at least try to get the door open—if they investigated, which they would, they'd know if she'd gotten out of the room or not, and that she should have been able to. She wanted—needed—to be able to say she'd tried, and to say it clean.

Her lube syringe was almost empty, but not quite. One small piece of luck, at least. It only took a couple of seconds to pick the lock, even with her none-too-steady hands.

Deep breath. She tugged her sleeve down over her palm, ignoring the don't-open-the-hot-door-you-dumbass warnings ringing in her head, and yanked the knob.

The month before, she'd had to visit one of the spirit prisons beneath the Church, a horrible fire-bright cave of misery.

This was worse.

The noise had not abated. Smoke stung her eyes, burned her throat. Black smoke, gray smoke dimmed the painful sharp light of the flames. Animals still screamed. The stench of burning hair and roasted flesh filled the air, it tasted of death and ashes and made her gag. Half the building was given to the fire. She could hardly see from the screaming orange blaze and the sweat running into her eyes and blurring them.

But even the fire and the noise and the smell she could have dealt with. Would deal with. What chilled her blood despite the heat were the ghosts.

The Lamaru—at least some of them—had been Hosting. She knew that, or would have known if she'd thought about it. What she hadn't thought about was that when they died, a psychopomp would come for them—but the ghosts to which they were bound didn't "register." No psychopomps. No one to summon the slaughterhouse's psychopomps. And she sure as fuck wasn't going near whatever the Lamaru had made, even if she could find them on the main floor.

Ghosts milled about down there, flickering out of existence when they passed through the hot flames, reappearing moments later when the heat energy abated and they were able to take form again. A clump of them struggled up the stairs, their horrible faces turned to her, their hollow eyes focused on her with hateful intensity.

In their hands they clutched knives and chunks of cement. Armed ghosts. Deadly ghosts, coming right at her.

In the psychopomp room she'd be safe from them. They wouldn't be able to get through the iron walls and door. She could turn right around, work on the bars in the window, get it open and reach the escape . . . and leave Lauren to die.

"Lauren! Lauren!" Why *not* scream? Wasn't like she could hide her presence, not with the ghosts staring right at her. In fact, this could be better. Get them watching her mouth, make them pay attention to her face so they wouldn't see her slip her hand into her bag.

"Cesaria!" It hardly sounded like Lauren's voice; thin

and high with an edge of panic. Still, it was Lauren, and that—plus the asafetida in her fist—was a relief.

What wasn't a relief was that Lauren's voice seemed to be coming from the offices at the opposite end of the walkway. The main stairs, the one the ghosts climbed, stood between herself and Lauren. She'd have to go through them.

She chanced a quick look in that direction, taking her focus off the ghosts. The offices on this level had solid walls—perhaps they too were iron-bound—but narrow horizontal windows interrupted them just below the ceiling. Cracks stretched across one of them; as Chess looked, something hit it, pushed the glass a few inches farther out. Yes. Lauren was in there.

The ghosts had reached the top of the stairs. Beneath the sweat now coating her entire body, her tattoos itched and burned.

But beneath that was the sweet soothe of her pills, an entirely different kind of warmth spreading through her, chasing the worst of the darkness and giving her some strength in return. They were just a couple of fucking ghosts—she did this shit for a living, didn't she?

She sure as fuck did. Okay. Her fist tightened around the asafetida as she eyeballed the luminescent dead advancing on her. Seen through them, the flames looked dimmed. Shadows formed behind them like bruises on their nonexistent skin. The black holes of their mouths opened.

She flung the asafetida, twisting her upper body and giving it to them right in the eyes—where the eyes would have been, anyway. *"Arkrandia bellarum dishager!"*

The generic Banishing words made them flicker a bit. She hadn't expected the words to actually work, not without any other ritual tools or anything to give her control over them. But the asafetida bound them in place. It wouldn't last long, but for now they were frozen, and the ones behind weren't at the top of the stairs yet. This was her shot.

The strap of her bag dug into her sweat-slicked skin as she pushed past them, through them. Damn, she never would have thought the frigid, bone-deep chill of a ghost's body would be a relief, but it was. If she hadn't been so desperate to get out of that place—and if she hadn't been at least halfway sane—she might have been tempted to hang out there for a minute or two.

But she *was* at least halfway sane, and more than that she was at least somewhat intelligent, and she reached the door of the office before the ghosts re-formed themselves. "Lauren!"

The door rattled in its frame. "Stand back!"

Stand back? Those ghosts would come at her again any second, and she was almost out of asafetida, and Lauren wanted her to—

The bullet sent wood chips in all directions, took a chunk out of the wall three inches to Chess's left. On instinct she threw herself to the floor in the opposite direction, then regretted it when her cheek hit the sizzling metal.

Another shot. Lauren flung the door open and practically yanked Chess's arm out of its socket pulling her up.

Shit, what the fuck had happened to her? Everything in the building glowed like the inside of a furnace already—hell, it wasn't *like* the inside of a furnace, it *was* the inside of a furnace—but Lauren resembled a madwoman. A madwoman with a bruised face and a wig made of blood-soaked cotton wool. Her torn clothing stood in mute testimony to what at least might have occurred; the rage in her eyes almost made Chess drop back to the floor.

She'd seen eyes like those before, usually right before a fist made contact with her face or a boot with her ribs.

It didn't seem to be directed at her this time, though,

and Chess couldn't blame her. If she hadn't been delightfully insulated from those horrible emotions—which meant *all* of her emotions, all of the time, really—she'd probably have had the same sort of look on her face.

But that wasn't important at the moment. "You have a gun."

Lauren, holding said gun out before her like a divining rod, gave Chess a narrow glance. "You know I have a gun."

"Yeah, but—you have a fucking gun. Why didn't you blast out of there before? Why the hell did I have to risk my life to come get—"

"Fire escape." Lauren wrapped her sticky, sweaty hand around Chess's and dragged her to the window. "I had a fire escape."

Broken glass crunched underfoot; Chess felt it but couldn't hear it over the general din. "What do you mean, you *had*— Oh."

No chance of any more escapes out of that window. A few scraps of twisted metal, rough-edged and pitiful, still clung to the sheer stone wall; fifty feet below, the rest of the ladder lay in a crumpled heap, dust still swirling around it.

Beyond the wreckage of their hope for a quick, simple escape the parking lot teemed with life, illuminated by flames. A few animals had managed to save themselves: a couple of cows, a gaggle of pigs and sheep, a number of dogs—how many had there been? Too many.

Whatever. Chess couldn't bring herself to worry about the Lamaru plan at that moment. Save her ass first, then think about the Lamaru. Or rather, then think about the Lamaru in some manner other than how much she'd like to wring each and every one of their necks personally for this. Especially Erik Vanhelm's.

She knew nothing about the escaped dogs, whether they were just generic Labs or hounds like those the

Church used, or wolves like the executioner's had been, or worse. Hell, they could have been magic-cranked pit bulls for all it mattered. No matter how tough or bloodthirsty they were, she gave them ten minutes at the outside before they met their deaths. If the black sow had been an unexpected treat, this was the sort of event that became Downside legend: The night that food walked right past, practically begging to be killed and eaten.

Lamaru still ran around, shouting, their tattered robes flapping behind them. A few of them argued and fought, wrestling with one another— No, wait. They weren't wrestling with one another. Who the hell were *those* people?

"The door to the hall—the one we came through earlier—is blocked off. I started to climb down the escape and another bomb, or whatever, went off at the foot of it. I barely made it back inside." Lauren held up her hands. Patches of raw skin crisscrossed them.

"I called the rest of the Squad, and the fire department. They're on their way. Did you have a fire escape? Where were you?"

"In the psychopomp room. There's an escape there—shit, they might bomb that one, too. We need to go."

Damn. They needed to fight the ghosts first. Chess saw them over Lauren's shoulder, seeping through the walls. They'd had to leave their weapons outside, of course, but it wasn't like they couldn't find more. "Shit!"

She dug in her bag for the rest of the asafetida, for her graveyard dirt and what little supply of iron filings she had. If the Lamaru bombed the other fire escape, too, they'd have no way out of there, not if the office door was truly blocked. Sure, Lauren had called the fire department. The possibility even existed that one of the slaughterhouse's neighbors had called them, although they were probably too busy killing the escaped animals or planning a looting.

But Downside didn't have a fire station; what was the point? It would take at least fifteen minutes for an engine to arrive, and by the time it did, it wouldn't matter. The fire was eating the slaughterhouse, crawling along every inch of wood and plaster like a starving, handless beast. Already smoke drifted through the office wall. They had five minutes, ten at the outside, if they hoped to avoid the City.

Less than that, of course, if they couldn't do something about the five ghosts taking full form between them and the door.

Lauren ducked, yanked her raven skulls from her bag and set them on the floor. Her already bleeding hands touched each one, lightly, leaving a faint smear.

Chess fought down the panic rising in her chest at the sight of them and dug out her plastic bag of salt. Psychopomps probably weren't a great idea, but they didn't have much choice, did they? Just because there'd been a couple of accidents, just because she'd been right about the Lamaru's plans, didn't mean Lauren couldn't control her ravens.

Of course, technically she shouldn't have been able to control the ravens anyway—but whatever.

And standing there gaping like a moron wouldn't do anybody any good. Chess found her Ectoplasmarker and popped the cap, tapping Lauren's shoulder with the other hand. Power zinged up her arm; for the first time she could remember, the feeling bothered her. Too much stress, too much rage and fear slithered along the underside of that power. Whatever had happened to Lauren in this room, it hadn't been good.

But Lauren's eyes didn't reflect much of those emotions. She glanced down and nodded; she'd made a pile of herbs on the tile. While Chess watched she lit them, then filled her hand with more.

"Go!"

The ghosts leapt forward at the same time Chess did, which was exactly what she wanted them to do. She jumped to the side, letting salt from her Baggie pour onto the floor. If she could just keep them focused, keep them watching her eyes—

Icy cold sliced through her brain. One of the ghosts' hands. For that second she was blind; agony ripped through her skull. Instinct and Church training kept her focused. She ducked, ready for the next freezing swipe and better able to ignore it when it came.

Behind them now. Constant cold as their hands passed through her, tried to grab her, hit her. Their rage infected her, made her already speeding pulse race faster, until it felt like she'd taken a bagful of Nips and a heart attack was waiting to pounce.

But she'd almost finished the circle.

Lauren's voice rose behind her, behind the ghosts. Shit, why was she starting her summoning, the circle wasn't finished yet—

Glass shattered. Pain lit her nerve endings like thousands of white lights as tiny shards of it embedded themselves in her skin. The windows high up on the walls. They'd exploded from the heat. Smoke poured in through the empty spaces.

Shit. And double shit, because not all the bits of glass were so small. A particularly large and sharp piece caught the light as one of the ghosts lifted it; she tried to jump out of the way but didn't quite make it. A slice on the back of her right arm reminded her—as if she needed it—of the penalties for poor reflexes.

Hey, blood would help set the circle, right? Yes. Look on the bright side. Bright-side Chess, always sure in the knowledge that things would turn out just fine.

She flung herself onto the desk, dropping salt along the way. The beginning of her circle lay on the floor at

Lauren's left hand; all she had to do now was close it so the ghosts were subdued and mark them.

"I call you!" Lauren shouted. Chess, stunned, tumbled to the floor with a painful thud she hardly noticed. What was one more bruise? Far more important were the rising skulls, the bodies forming in the air covered with sleek black feathers. Her entire body went cold, colder than it had even moments ago when she was playing keep-away with the dead.

"What the fuck, Lauren? The circle isn't—"

Too late.

The ravens rose into the air, screeching their death cries and drowning out Chess's voice. The circle wasn't finished. The ghosts weren't marked. The psychopomps were free to latch on to any soul in the room.

Huge heavy wings stirred the smoke. Chess's eyes watered and stung. She didn't want to cough, didn't want to draw their attention, but she couldn't help it. Flames ate into the ceiling of the office.

"Benchitak! Benchitak!" Lauren shouted, words of power Chess didn't know but that sent more of Lauren's ugly, strong power rippling over her skin. Could she control the ravens that way, just with her power?

Two of the ghosts disappeared into the ragged hole between the worlds Lauren's ritual had opened; the remaining ravens flapped around the other three, their wings punishing the air. The ghosts tried to flee back through the walls but the salt line, incomplete though it was, held them long enough for the ravens to catch them, sharing the extra ghost between them.

Chess's muscles relaxed. She hadn't realized how tense she was, how much she'd expected the ravens to grab her, to drag her off.

Church magic. She could still believe in Church magic. It felt good.

What didn't feel good, of course, was the volcano heat she stood in, or the rawness of her throat, or her dry, itchy eyes and her hair sticking to her forehead and cheeks. Time to get the hell out of this place before it collapsed around them—on top of them.

She'd been standing close to the wall—too close. Any second that thing was going to burst into flames like a Haunted Week effigy, and it would take her with it.

Lauren still stared at her psychopomps, watching them disappear through the opening between the worlds so intently that Chess wondered for a moment if the woman didn't have some sort of psychic connection with them. She'd done that once herself with birds, the month before. The night Terrible—

No. No fucking way. The last thing she needed to do at that moment was to start having those thoughts again. Not when her own death was so close that she could smell its hot smoky breath and only her fear of the City—and her absolute refusal to let the Lamaru beat her, those sleazy fuckheads—kept her from simply collapsing on the floor and letting it have its way with her.

That thought, more than anything else, galvanized her. She grabbed Lauren's wet sleeve—she wasn't the only one soaked in sweat—and pulled.

"We need to get out of here. Come on, I haven't heard another explosion."

"Just let me get my . . ."

"What?" Chess looked down. Looked down, and saw the empty floor at Lauren's feet. The smoke hadn't reached the lower half of the room yet; she could not blame what she saw—what she *didn't* see—on blurred vision or optical illusion or anything else.

Oh, fuck.

The skulls weren't there. The ravens still had form.

They'd gone to the City and taken their skulls, and they still had form, still had physical bodies. They'd disobeyed

Lauren, disobeyed their training and instinct and just about every rule of magic Chess knew.

Her head refused to turn; she didn't want to check to see if the hole between the worlds had closed behind the ravens the way it should have. The longer she didn't look, the longer she could lie to herself—always an important skill to cultivate, and she was an expert at it—and pretend the hole had closed, that she couldn't still sense it there, feel its faint chill on her slick skin.

She forced her neck to work, and turned toward the hole just in time to see the ravens burst through it and head straight for her.

Chapter Eighteen

[The creation of a psychopomp is a complex process, one only designated Church employees may perform. It is to them we entrust the safety of all humanity.
—*Careers in the Church: A Guide for Teens,* by Praxis Turpin]

Death came for her on thunderous black wings, in sleek black bodies way too large for the room. The ravens stole the air from her lungs, the thoughts from her head. They were coming, and she could not escape. How the hell did someone escape from a psychopomp?

Getting out of the fucking office might be a good start. Lauren's sleeve almost slipped from her fingers as she flung them both to the floor just in time to avoid swooping claws like the spikes that carried dead cows in the slaughterhouse below.

One thing about Lauren, she could think fast. She usually thought wrong, but fast still had its virtues. Her gun was already in her hand; they'd barely hit the tile before she took aim and shot, an action that made Chess scream inside.

But not out loud. Instead she slammed her own fist into her leg, hard, to give herself something else to focus on. They didn't have time. Didn't have—

Mistletoe. She had mistletoe, taken from that hideous totem in her bag. It wouldn't beat the ravens, at least she didn't think so, but it might buy them a few seconds, and that was all they needed. Just enough time to get out the door.

Fire crawled across the ceiling above them. The ravens outlined against it looked larger than they had before, hollow outlines in the ever-moving ocean of flame.

Lauren shot again. The skull of the bird closest to them exploded in a cloud of bone fragments and dust, mingling with the smoke. No blood. No brains.

Chess had never known if psychopomps actually came back to life, if they were for the brief time of their use breathing creatures with pumping hearts. Seemed they weren't. They weren't animals at all, just reanimated corpses, empty shells full of instinct and magic.

Another shot. One of the ravens lost part of a wing. Feathers and bone flew, tiny scraps of desiccated skin hit the flames above and disappeared.

Yet another shot. A miss. No wonder—the smoke thickening the air made it harder and harder to see.

Chess stopped trying. Her fingers shook as they struggled with the plastic bag holding the mistletoe, finally yanking it open and pulling the leaves out.

No need to light a fire, at least. Lauren's little pile of herbs still smoked a few feet away. Chess could have tossed them into the air, let them be devoured by the inferno hovering above them, but the mistletoe would have burned too fast. Instead she dug out her lighter and, holding the leaves by the stems, lit them.

"By this—" The words ended in a coughing fit. She struggled to swallow, dipped lower to try to breathe some fresh air—as fresh as it could be, anyway—and tried again. This time she managed to finish, dropping the leaves onto Lauren's fire as she spoke.

"By this power I command the escorts of the dead. By my power I command the escorts of the dead. Hear me, escorts. I Bind you. *Ornithramii mordreus,* I Bind you."

Shit. Not enough power. Maybe not enough power in the mistletoe; being used in a fetish bomb and then doused with salt probably didn't do much for its effectiveness. Definitely not enough power in herself. She couldn't seem to get grounded, to feel the energy flowing through her. Instead she felt the heat, the fire getting closer, the constant streaming ache in her eyes and the pounding in her head as her brain cried for more oxygen. They were running out of time. She didn't want to die here, not this way. . . .

Taking her eyes off the ravens and blocking out the deafening gunshots terrified her, but she had no choice. She closed her eyes, took a deep breath. Reached inside herself as far as she could, past the filth and slime and fear, past the boiling pit of rage, and found the spark of power hidden there.

And set it free.

"Escorts, I command you! I Bind you! *Ornithramii mordreus,* I Bind you!"

The shock of her energy as it combined with the mistletoe and hit the birds reverberated through her. It hadn't worked completely. The mistletoe was too tainted, was connected to whatever had made the ravens murder weapons instead of servants.

But some of it was there. A tiny germ of mistletoe's true power still lurked beneath the filth, and it combined with hers. Unfortunately, so did the filth. Her stomach lurched, her mouth filled with saliva. Not good. Not good energy. Foul, sick, twisted energy, inside her now.

It wasn't permanent, she knew; when she let go of the ravens it would leave her, just like any other spell. But it was there for the moment, and that was bad enough.

The ravens fell silent, landed on the desk not two feet away. Their bodies were still but Chess felt them struggling. The Bind already slipped and thinned.

"We have to get out of here now, it won't hold them for long."

Lauren tried to speak but coughed instead. Together they slipped under the back of the desk and crawled to the door. Staying low was their only hope if they wanted to keep breathing. Which Chess pretty much did.

Her wet sleeve offered no protection at all from the doorknob's heat, but she turned it anyway, steeling herself against a sight that nothing could possibly prepare her for.

How did the roof still stand? How had the metal walkway not collapsed? They stood in the middle of a nightmare, silent now save for the hungry, eerie susurration of the flames.

Ghosts still wove themselves in and out between the columns of burning wood and softened steel. They didn't seem to have noticed Lauren or her yet; she imagined the intense heat masked them and the minor energy their bodies radiated. For now, at least. It wouldn't be long before they were spotted, and not all of the spirits wandered on the lower floors. It could be a trap, a chute of fire just like the metal livestock chutes below. She shuddered at the thought and forced her heavy feet to move.

Her lungs burned. Every breath was an effort. The thin dry air didn't seem to provide any oxygen at all. She expected to burst into flame at any second; the heat ravaged her, made her feel like dust herself, like an empty, hollow body—a psychopomp.

But she wasn't heading for the City. At least she hoped to hell she wasn't.

With Lauren at her side she led the way back toward the psychopomp room and the fire escape she hoped still existed. If it didn't . . . if it didn't, they would die. She almost didn't care; at least the City was cool and dim.

No, not cool and dim. Cold and dark. She would not

go there. Not today. Hell, when she finally went she'd probably end up in the spirit prisons herself; just because she worked for the Church didn't mean she was a good person.

And she couldn't bring herself to give a shit just then, either. She and Lauren clung to each other; Chess didn't know who was helping whom. Every breath turned into a cough, every desperate swallow into sand rubbing her tonsils.

Walking caused its own set of problems. Smoke so thick she could cut it with her knife clouded her vision, forced her to feel the floor ahead with a careful toe before putting her weight on it. Lauren slumped against her; Chess didn't know which bothered her more, the extra weight or the forced intimacy. Maybe Lauren wasn't so bad—at least she'd shot down one of the psychopomps, had summoned them to begin with and saved both their asses—but that didn't mean Chess wanted to snuggle with the woman.

The walkway hadn't collapsed yet, but she had the uncomfortable feeling that it was only a matter of time. It jolted and shifted under their feet, their steps loud and somehow inappropriate against the hungry whisper of the blaze. She wanted to say something to Lauren, to push her off, but it didn't seem worth the trouble.

Instead she coughed, her chest aching, and dragged her feet along the walkway. A dead Lamaru blocked the way, his face a mess of charred flesh.

And behind him, his ghost.

Chess whipped her head around, checking one last time for another exit. Nope. Instead, there were more ghosts. They'd been spotted, and two spirits had almost reached the top of the stairs by the office.

Oh, for fuck's sake, were they ever going to get out of this place? Couldn't something, sometime, just be straightforward and easy?

Right. Stupid question.

Lauren saw it too. They stopped short a few steps from the Lamaru. Through his spirit's translucent form the door to the psychopomp room beckoned. Hell, it practically fucking glowed at them, promising all manner of seductive escapes, like a very expensive Downside hooker.

Those were promises Chess intended to see that it kept, ghosts be damned.

The last of her asafetida barely filled her palm. She had more graveyard dirt, she could— No. Hold on.

"When I say go," she muttered to Lauren, "run for the door. But *stay down,* okay? Low to the ground."

Lauren's skin had a grayish cast to it. Any doubts Chess had about the dangerous, half-assed plan forming in her head were dispelled by the sight. She still didn't like Lauren, still wouldn't trust her with anything more important than a piece of lint. But they were in this together, and that little flash of the Grand Elder's face, of her career being sidetracked into Debunking cases like ghostly mice in an abandoned barn, tipped the scales.

She'd been trying to ignore the heavy illness from the fetish still riding in her gut. Now she reached for it, felt the ravens and their fury, felt their utter ruthlessness. Creatures without soul, whose only purpose on the earth was to constantly seek what they did not possess.

She let them go.

Lamaru energy ripped through her; their revenge, the spell's backlash, the effects of ten minutes of solid smoke inhalation combined with fear and stress and sadness and Cepts made her retch. Good thing her stomach was empty. There was never a good time to puke, but this moment had to be in the top ten worst moments.

"Go!" she shouted, as the ravens swooped out of the office and around the corner.

They hit the ghosts at the top of the stairs. One raven

grabbed one ghost. The other two ravens kept on coming.

Well, shit. So much for that half-assed plan.

The ghost grabbed for her and Lauren as they neared him. Too late, Chess saw what she had not before: He held a jagged shred of steel.

He swiped at them as they ran past. Chess managed to shift to the side, narrowly avoiding a slice in the throat. Lauren wasn't quite so lucky. The metal missed her throat as well but caught her shoulder.

Lauren screamed. Drops of blood showed purplish against the smoke. The ghost tried to scoop them up and absorb their power.

Whether the ravens saw it too, Chess didn't know. All she knew was the sensation of talons scraping at her head but failing to find purchase. The tip of a wing slammed into her back and knocked her forward through the doorway of the psychopomp room.

The ravens shrieked their fury. The ghost made no sound but obviously shared their feeling. The remaining two ghosts pushed their way past him, reaching for Lauren, reaching for Chess as she scrambled to her feet and grasped the door so hard rust gritted into her palm. The ravens swooped around in a half-circle and came in for another dive.

They all appeared framed by the doorway: three dead men, their faces studies in frustrated anger and thoughtless greed. Two ravens pitch-black against the rippling red-orange wall behind them, getting closer every second.

Chess slammed the iron door.

Had she thought the psychopomp room felt like an oven earlier? Ha. That had been nothing more than a warm summer day. Her concerns about the iron-cored walls and floor had been absolutely correct. It didn't seem possible that the room could actually be hotter than the fire outside, and intellectually she knew it wasn't, but it sure as hell felt like it.

But it didn't matter. Didn't matter one bit, because they'd be out of there in a few seconds.

Lauren slumped against the wall while Chess leapt over the fetish to the window. Barred, yes, but her small victory over the ghosts and psychopomps outside gave her another burst of adrenaline; she felt capable of ripping the bars out of the window with her bare hands.

So much for feelings. No. No way could she pull that off. But it did feel like the bars shifted a little.

"Lauren!"

Lauren's muffled reply sounded vaguely like "Mphgr." Or maybe "Fuck off." Or a combination of the two. Who cared? Not Chess.

"Lauren, get over here."

This time Lauren obeyed, keeping her distance from the fetish still on the floor. Its horrible body had shriveled from the heat. "What?"

Shit, she really looked sick. Maybe this wasn't the greatest idea. Well, of course it wasn't. Did she have a choice?

No. "Get on the floor, on your hands and knees. I need to stand on you."

"Are you kidding?"

Ah, Lauren was back to normal. Sort of.

"No. I need to get these bars off the window, and I need better leverage."

For the first time since the ordeal had started she let herself really think about Terrible. He could have pulled those bars out of the window with one sharp tug. A wave of longing, of misery, washed over her so intensely that for a moment she was actually grateful for the heat and dryness. If even a few molecules of water still existed in her body she probably would have started to cry. And she definitely didn't want to do that.

But she kept him in her head. Before she'd betrayed him—okay, before he'd found out she was betraying him—he would have reassured her. Would have reminded her that she could do anything. He'd believed that once.

So she could believe it now.

She grabbed the bars and stepped onto Lauren's back, planting her right foot at the base of the other woman's spine. Her left settled between Lauren's shoulder blades.

The fire escape still existed. Thank the gods who didn't exist, the fire escape hadn't been destroyed.

Not for lack of trying, though—at least so she assumed. The Lamaru simply hadn't had the chance to do it, caught up as they were in their fistfight below. Not so many as there had been—she checked her watch—just under ten minutes before, when she'd looked out the window in the office. Had that little time really passed?

Yeah. Less than ten minutes, and the Lamaru were still fighting whoever it was they were fighting.

Wait a minute. Vanhelm and the woman he'd been with, the blonde. She'd said if Vanhelm entered Downside, Maguinness would find him, hadn't she?

Looked like she'd been right. Now that she knew what she was looking for she saw, at the very edge of the circle of illumination from the single streetlight in the center of the slaughterhouse parking lot, the fluorescent glow of Maguinness's assistant's tall purple hairdo.

Maguinness's men were there. Not only were they there, she realized as one of them lit something and tossed it into the blazing building that they'd set the fire. She and Lauren had walked right into an ambush intended for someone else.

"Cesaria, are you done?"

Oh, right. "Almost."

But she wasn't. The bars moved a little, and left welts and bits of rust in her palms, but they refused to give.

Exhaustion dragged at her limbs and clouded her mind. Too hot in that room. She was being cooked.

One last try. Her palms burned, it took every bit of will she had not to let go. Her feet lifted off Lauren's back and braced against the wall. She leaned back, putting all of her weight behind it, all the strength she had.

The bars shifted, so fast Chess lost her balance and let go, landing on her side on the hot floor. Pain jolted through her upper arm, her shoulder and hip, but it didn't matter. The bars had come loose. They would get out.

And would walk right into a Lamaru/whatever-he-was battle at the bottom of the fire escape. Shit. She didn't see any possible way they could get through that unharmed or unnoticed; the Lamaru would be looking to kill them because they'd caught on to the Lamaru plot, if not just on general principles, and the Maguinness crowd—well, they'd probably want to kill her just for fun. They needed help.

So, while Lauren finished pulling the bars off the window and smashed the glass, Chess grabbed her phone and dialed the one person whose help she really wanted—the one person she thought could actually help—and the one person she knew wanted to talk to her less than anyone else.

But he would come. He wouldn't let her die, no matter how angry he was. Right? He wouldn't just let her *die*.

"The number you have dialed is no longer in service. Please check the number and dial again. Facts are Truth."

What? That couldn't be right. Okay. Don't panic.

She scrolled though old texts until she found one from him, hit reply, and quickly tapped out a help-I'm-in-the-slaughterhouse-and-need-you-here-it's-on-fire message. He probably knew about the fire—well, no "probably" about it, of course he knew—and she'd be willing to bet he was in the area. Bump had a pipe room not far away, and they wouldn't chance the fire spreading to it.

"Your message could not be delivered."

"Cesaria! Come on, we need to get out!"

Chess barely heard. The bright screen of the phone hurt her eyes, mocked her. He'd changed his number. He hated her so much that he didn't even want her to have his number anymore. Even with them working on this together.

Fingers like the raven's talons earlier gripped her arm and yanked her off the floor. "Cesaria, come on!"

Semi-clean Downside air swirled through the now open window to caress her face. She almost fell down again, it felt so fucking good. Not good enough to heal the ache in her chest—nothing could feel good enough to heal that, she didn't think—but good. Her lungs practically danced with relief when she sucked it in. She grabbed the rough edge of the window frame and hoisted herself up.

Leaning too far out gave her vertigo; in her mind she saw ghostly hands poised right behind her—hell, she saw *Lauren* right behind her—ready to give her that one solid shove that would end all her problems. In her mind she saw herself stepping over the edge of the window. He'd changed his number, it didn't make a difference, all her stupid hopes about getting him to forgive her, to talk to her again . . . She could just let go. Just fall, and make the pain in her chest stop.

Then she saw the City, and gripped the window frame harder. Nope. Not today. The fire escape waited for her, just barely out of reach.

One more deep breath, cool and sweet despite still being tinged with smoke. Her muscles tensed, her eyes narrowed, and she jumped.

Landing on the rickety steel made a horrible clattering sound. Fuck! They had to have heard that. No matter. Keep going. She was out, she'd gotten out, and if she'd done that she could do almost anything.

The steep steps shook and groaned beneath her, rusted railings bit her palms slick with sweat.

Carefully she started down. From this vantage point on the side of the building she saw how close the place was to complete destruction. Smoke and fire poured out of every window, climbed the outside walls. They didn't have much time.

Lauren came down after her. The ladder gave a mighty creak, the balcony above broke free of the wall and hung crazily over them. Shit. Go faster. Faster.

Her hands slipped on the rails, her fingers stiff and aching. With every step down it got harder to let go; her legs ached, her head went light.

The ladder boiled and shifted beneath them. Down, and down; she'd been doing this forever, all her life had been spent on this fire escape, with orange light taunting them and the sky a hazy dull gray above them.

Flames danced along the wall and found her right leg; her jeans caught fire. Without meaning to, without thinking, she screamed. Her right hand left the rail, batted at the fire, and she fell.

Chapter Nineteen

> Don't forget the Church. They're always willing to help, and should be the first place you turn when there's trouble, whether it's ghosts or fights with your beloved husband.
> —*Mrs. Increase's Advice for Ladies*, by Mrs. Increase

Death waited at the bottom, she knew it. She'd been up too high, there was no way she could survive the fall—

Her back slammed into the pavement. She was dead. She must be dead. It didn't hurt. It didn't hurt that bad, her leg screamed but she was—

She wasn't breathing.

For one long, agonizing moment she stared at the sky while her lungs refused to inflate. Flames poured from the window above her, bits of ash dancing on the wind. She saw it in slow motion, the fire escape black, Lauren's body a denim spider inching down the ladder at the end. She could not breathe. She could not breathe, this was it . . . Her psychopomp would come for her, she waited for it, watched the nightbirds circling overhead and wondered which one it was, hoped the horrible ravens hadn't escaped from the building but knew they might, if they didn't burn up . . .

Something gave in her chest, a gear finally snapped into place. Her lungs inflated. Her eyes stung, her mouth opened.

She rolled over, thinking she was going to be sick, but nothing happened. Nothing but the world coming back into focus, the feel of her blood racing through her body and the agony of her burned and cut leg and sore hands and her throat raw from smoke and screams.

Lauren hit the pavement beside her—on her feet, a much more graceful landing than Chess had managed.

Oh, shit. She was lying there ruminating while beside her a burning building was about to collapse and the parking lot was full of Lamaru.

She didn't need Lauren's rough hand to get her up. She did need it to hold her steady; for a moment the world veered crazily around her.

She was moving before it righted itself, a hesitant, stumbling run that jarred her knees. Out of the corner of her eye she saw the crowd breaking up, turning toward her and Lauren.

Her ears were ringing. At first she thought it was from her fall, but as hands brushed her arms she realized it wasn't ringing, it was sirens, and her body flooded with relief as red lights swirled against the surrounding buildings and caught Lauren in their strobe effect.

The fire trucks had arrived.

The Lamaru—and Maguinness's people—shouted and ran around her, ignoring her now in their haste to escape. Firemen were Church employees, and they never traveled into Downside alone—well, they hardly ever traveled into Downside, period, but when they did they brought with them a full Squad. Clearly the Lamaru didn't want to stick around to tell the Squad how someone had interrupted their illegal psychopomp party.

Behind her, steel groaned, the sound tearing the air and shooting straight up her spine. Every step was agony. Everything hurt. Her chest felt ready to explode, her smoke-choked lungs wanted to die. But if she didn't haul her ass out of there immediately it was going to burn right off, and she hadn't escaped from that fucking building just to be crushed by it when it collapsed.

They hit the bushes and turned, heading for the main gates. No need for stealth now, and they needed to wave down the arriving Squad members and inform them of the ghosts and the three psychopomps still in the building.

On the other side of the fence—the street side—Chess caught a glimpse of a tall, shaggy form that could only be Maguinness, strolling along with his hands in his pockets like an innocent freak just out for a casual jaunt. She'd been right, then. It had been him; *was* him.

Bastard. She didn't give a fuck about him trying to kill the Lamaru; hell, she'd give him a hand if she could—and if he wasn't such a bizarre ball of criminal awful.

But he'd bombed that building with her inside it, just as she was about to catch the Lamaru and earn herself fifty grand. Fifty grand and the chance to be done with Lauren for good. So fuck him.

As if he felt her eyes on him, read her thoughts, Maguinness stopped and turned around. Even at that distance she could see him smiling.

"I just don't get it," Lauren said again. Her sports car, dusty but none the worse for wear, idled on the street outside Chess's building. Dirty baby wipes filled the interior; between them they'd used almost a whole pack trying to tidy themselves up.

Chess shook her water bottle over her open mouth, desperate for the last drops. Her throat felt like she'd been sucking tailpipes and she did not want to talk. Not now. Not tonight. She wanted to go upstairs and swallow her entire pillbox, wanted to trudge to the corner store and buy a tub of ice cream and eat it on her couch while watching mindless television. Oliver Fletcher, the bastard, had sent her an entire box of his intellectually vacant TV shows on disk; she hadn't done more than glance at it, but tonight she couldn't imagine anything better.

Well, no. That wasn't entirely true. She could imagine

a few things better, but only one of them was feasible, and even she didn't think the pipe room was a good idea with her throat the way it was. Damn it, she'd been looking forward to that all day.

"I don't either," she managed. Her voice creaked. "But what difference does it make? Either they somehow got into your bag—when they slashed your tires, maybe—or they've managed to cast some kind of spell over— No, wait. They had some kind of fetish, in the psychopomp room. Maybe it infected your ravens."

"I can't see how they'd be able to make anything that powerful. But then I guess they are pretty . . . pretty strong . . ." Lauren sighed. Sighed again.

And again. Chess glanced at her, her thoughts running fairly solidly along what-the-fuck lines, and then she saw with horror that Lauren was crying.

Oh, shit. What was she supposed to do?

She reached a hesitant hand over, rested it lightly on Lauren's shoulder. "Hey . . . um, are you . . ."

Stupid question. People didn't cry because they were okay. Even Chess knew that. Hell, she knew that better than anyone, didn't she?

"How did you get over it?"

"What?"

Lauren looked at her, her eyes gleaming in her sooty face. "How did you get over it? Having them—having them do things to you?"

Oh, fuck. Sore throat or not, she was getting her ass to the pipe room the second she managed to extricate herself from the car. She knew what Lauren was talking about. Knew she'd been right when she wondered if Lauren had managed to fight off her own attackers. Knew she hadn't.

And apparently—obviously—Lauren knew things, too. Things about her. The bitch, the total fucking— She'd read Chess's file. Not just her regular file, her *confidential* file. The one with the results of her medical tests, the ones that showed how she didn't need the birth control implant given to female Church employees in active jobs because her body was as barren and inhospitable as the world around her.

The file that said why that was the case. The results of the single discussion she'd had about it with Elder Banks years ago.

Elder Griffin . . . He'd probably read it, too. That's how he knew, the night before in that horrible purple circle. That's how he'd known how to help her.

And he'd never told her. No one had ever told her. Did they all know? Did they all watch her walk past and see dirty fingerprints on her body? Did they see it in her eyes, hear it in her voice?

Her head throbbed, fury boiling up her throat and into her brain, loaded with bile from her stomach twisting and leaping in her belly. They all knew, *they all knew* . . .

"You just do," she said finally. Gave Lauren the lie, because she couldn't bear giving her the truth. Because she didn't think Lauren needed the truth. "You just move on, and you stop thinking about it because you don't let yourself think about it."

"I can't stop." No wonder Lauren's nails were so short; while Chess watched she ripped a hangnail so viciously with her teeth that blood welled from the cuticle, a perfect red teardrop on her pale skin. "I can't stop thinking about it."

"Yeah, it just happened, I mean . . . Why don't you talk to someone, you know, maybe your father or someone can—"

"I thought I *was* talking to someone. You."

"But I'm not—I'm not really, I mean, I don't think you'll be really comfortable talking about this with me, right?"

Lauren was a pretty girl—a pretty woman. She didn't

look it now, with her jaw set and her eyes narrowed and her skin dark and still smudgy. Jagged streaks of pale ran down from her eyes. "I think you're the one who isn't comfortable with it, Cesaria."

What the fuck did she want? Some kind of fucking encounter group or something? Empowering chants by candlelight? She could get that shit somewhere else. Chess only lit candles when bright light was too much for her narced-out pupils.

Lauren was imposing on her. Maybe it was wrong to feel that way, not supportive or whatever, but that's how it felt: as though Lauren was pressing sticky little hands all over her, trying to pull off bits of her skin and see what was beneath it.

And despite the other woman's tears, which seemed real enough, Chess couldn't get past the idea that Lauren's eyes were fixed on her, that she was being viewed through a microscope. Whether that was because Lauren thought she'd somehow Triumphed Over Her Past or because she wanted to make Chess uncomfortable or simply because she was at heart a creepy fuck, Chess had no idea, and at that point it wouldn't have been possible for her to care less. All she wanted to do was go home, clean and dress her wounds, change her smoke-stinking clothes, and get high. Sobriety was not a fucking option.

"I'm not uncomfortable," she said. A cough fought to free itself from her throat, but she refused to let it. She didn't need to show any sign of weakness. "I just don't think I'll be very good at helping you. I think there are people better qualified than me. It happened a long time ago. I don't remember it very well, I mean, I don't think about it anymore. That's all. I just think if you go— You should go to the hospital, right? Let them do their tests, and they'll set you up with someone. You know the program."

"Right. And let everyone I work with know what happened. That I couldn't defend myself."

"There were like a dozen of them, you couldn't—"

"You did."

"I only had one of them there. You could have beaten one of them, too." At least so she assumed. She had no idea if she was right about how many men had attacked Lauren, but Lauren didn't contradict her, so she wasn't going to worry about it.

"Whatever."

Okay . . . was that enough? Could she go now, or—No. Damn it. "Look," she said, and put her hand back on Lauren's shoulder. "You have two choices now, right? You can let this eat at you because you're too ashamed or scared or whatever to get help—if that's what you need—or you can try to move past it on your own. And that's different for everybody. What worked for me might not work for you, and that's why I can't really advise you, okay? Just . . . I'd go to the hospital if I were you. That's what I would do."

That was *such* a fucking lie.

"But you have to do what you think is best. It's not like, if you don't do something about it right this second, you'll never have the chance, you know?"

Shit, had she really said that? That actually sounded kind of wise. Or maybe not. How the hell would she know?

But it was amazing what kind of motivator it was, knowing that all she had to do was get rid of this woman—this woman with whom she felt she'd spent years at this point—and she could be alone. Blessedly alone, and blessedly close to unconsciousness.

Lauren nodded. *Yes!* "Yeah. Yeah, I guess you're right. I just feel, I don't know . . . so dirty. Like it was my fault. Like I did something to make them want to do it, like I should have been able to defend myself."

Just like that, Chess's triumph evaporated. Fuck. She was never going to get out of that car, and to make matters worse she felt that wound, all those old wounds, rip back open at Lauren's words.

"There is no 'should have.' " For the first time since this conversation had begun, she knew exactly what she was talking about. "There just isn't. What happened happened. You can't change it now; it's done and you can't ever go back. So now you just have to move on. However you can."

It seemed to strike a chord with Lauren; Chess wasn't sure if she was glad of that or not. Her freedom from that car was worth just about any price, but she hadn't counted on having to pay with truth. That sucked.

"Thanks, Cesaria. Thanks."

"No problem."

They made tentative plans for the next day; as it was two days before Elder Murray's Dedication, neither could be certain what it might bring and how much time they might have. The entire discussion had lasted much longer than Chess would have liked, but then, the entire endless day had lasted much longer than she would have liked, so what was a few more minutes?

She finally bounded out of the car. Her wounded leg reminded her not to run but fuck, it was tempting. She unlocked the tall wooden door, crossed the tiled lobby that had once been the nave. Pushed herself up the stairs as fast as she could, her keys in one hand, her pillbox already in the other. The second she got inside and closed that door behind her—

Or not.

Lex waited outside her apartment, his long lean frame slouched negligently against the doorjamb. "Hey, Tulip," he said. "Where you been at?"

Chapter Twenty

> A promise to the Church is far more important than any other promise. Not just because the Church protects you, but because the Church is always watching you.
>
> —*The Book of Truth,* Veraxis, Article 1340

The swelling in his face had gone down; he looked like himself again, with only a slight tension in his jaw letting her know he was still wired up inside.

Shit, was she actually glad to see him?

Yeah. Yeah, she kind of was. Despite the conversation she knew they were about to have, despite her resolution not to do the things that seeing him immediately brought to mind . . . she was, in fact, glad to see him.

And it wasn't even because she knew that in the inside pocket of his leather jacket he had a bag of pills just for her.

Not entirely.

"Hey." It came out a little breathlessly; the trot up the stairs had strained her abused lungs more than she'd realized. And of course she was surprised. And probably looked like utter hell, dirty and torn, stinking like a barbecue pit.

He noticed it, of course. "Damn, girl. Know I ain't seen you in a while, but ain't had the thought of you going rabid on me."

"Ha-ha. I was in a fire."

"Oh, aye? Figured you was doing some witchy shit at you Church."

"No." He smelled of soap and leather; she caught a whisper of it when she pushed past him, avoiding his attempted kiss, to unlock her front door and release the wards on it.

"So where this fire at, then?"

"Why do you want to know?"

She wanted to get her jeans off—needed to get them off, so she could take care of the burn. But something told her it wasn't a good idea to start disrobing just yet. Well, no, not *something*. *Everything* in her knew that wasn't a good idea.

She'd made a resolution. No more. No matter how good it was, she was not going to sleep with Lex anymore. Part of her penance, part of her attempt to convince a man who no longer gave a shit about her that she wanted to be with him.

Stupid. Really stupid. She'd almost died, and she had to admit she was a little freaked out about it. Not to mention her heart still running double-time and her mind still swirling like a nasty stew over her little chat with Lauren.

So why not? Wasn't like Lex was going to say no. Wasn't like Terrible would ever know or care. And she needed it. Needed to forget, needed to lose herself, needed to put it all behind her.

She toed off her boots carefully, trying to avoid rubbing her injured thigh against the denim still half-covering it. Her hands went to the button of her jeans.

And stopped there.

No, Terrible wouldn't know, and he might not care—hell, no "might" about it, he *wouldn't* care. But *she* would know. If the subject ever came up she wanted to be able to tell the truth: that the last time she'd been with Lex was two nights before Terrible caught them in the cemetery. Wasn't the best timing in the world, considering that had been the night when Terrible told her how he felt about her. How he *had* felt about her; how he *used to* feel about her.

But it was true, and it was clean, and she wanted to keep it that way.

Conscious of Lex's gaze, she padded across the cold linoleum to the fridge and opened it, grabbed two beers and gave him one. "How's your jaw?"

He took the beer from her but didn't drink it. Instead he watched her, his head tilted slightly to the side. When he spoke his voice was soft. Almost tender. "You giving me the gillwheep, Tulip?"

Shit. "Lex . . ."

"Aw, c'mon now. Ain't like I ain't figured on this coming, me. Just ain't figured on it bein now."

"It's not . . . It's not you, I mean, I know that sounds—"

"Aw, nay, ain't needing the explains. Dig the picture, I do." He pushed himself off the wall, strolled to the couch and dropped himself into it, with his Fear T-shirt riding up and his Chucks propped on her rickety coffee table. "Funny, though. Got some discussin to do, you and me, on the elsewheres."

That was it? She'd just broken up with him—well, sort of, it wasn't like they were dating or anything, but still—and that was his entire response?

Not that she cared. No, it was much better to have him shrug and get over it. She hadn't really expected anything else. But she had to admit, at least a small part of her felt a little . . . let down. Had their this-doesn't-mean-anything-to-either-of-us affair meant *nothing* to him?

"Discussing on what?"

"Why you witches been taking the sight-sees in my tunnels? Thought you ain't like the downs."

"What?"

His eyes narrowed, and a chill ran right up her spine. Oh. Right. He wasn't taking anything easily. He thought she was up to something, and that ending their whatever-it-was had something to do with it. Thought she'd been working with Bump and Terrible to take over the tunnels under the city. Bump ran most of Downside, sure. *Above* ground. Only Slobag and his men used the tunnels.

For a second the impulse to laugh bubbled crazily up from her stomach. He actually thought Terrible was speaking to her?

Then again, he was. Sort of. As long as he didn't have to take her calls.

"Witches down my tunnels, Tulip. Finding all kindsa shit down there, aye, all kinds. Frogs an fingers and shit, like that dead hand you carry? What you got on the action down there?"

Frogs and fingers. The fetish. Maguinness. The Lamaru. Her mouth went completely dry; she drank half her beer, aware that she couldn't have looked guiltier if she'd plastered a sign across her forehead that read I DID IT.

"No use putting the stall on. Ain't never figured we'd be playin this rundown game, but you want—"

"It's not me, Lex."

"C'mon now, ain't—"

"It's not me, Lex. It's not. It's the Lama— *Aah!*"

Fuck! She'd forgotten. Forgotten the Binding, forgotten the shriveling pain of it. An entire evening spent with Lauren, talking freely, an entire evening of stress and fire and near-death fun had completely wiped her mind of that particular complication.

Now she was on the floor in a puddle of beer, with blood seeping from her wrists and her thigh shrieking from the impact.

To his credit and her surprise, Lex came and helped her up. "The fuck is that?"

"I'm Bound. They're Binding marks. I can't talk

about— All I can say is it's not me. It's not the Church or anything, it's nothing to do with Bump or anybody."

She had to lean on him to get to the couch; her muscles felt like they'd been microwaved. What were they doing in the tunnels? For that matter, how had they learned about the tunnels? She'd thought they were a myth before; so did everyone but Slobag and his gang, as far as she knew. "What were they doing down there? You said toads and fingers—what else was there? Did you see it? Where was it?"

"Hush now." He pulled the magic little bag from his jacket pocket and dug around in it, then opened his palm. Two Cepts and two Oozers; lady's choice.

She shouldn't. She needed her wits about her. Her Cepts wouldn't put her too far under; she could take enough notes that she wouldn't miss anything important. But the Oozers . . . she couldn't write on those. Couldn't do much of anything.

Fuck, that sounded good.

"Them cuts, they achy?"

"Don't they look achy?"

"Look kinda sexy, seein as you asked." But his smile was bland enough, as he held his flat palm out for her to make her decision.

Fuck it. She emptied his palm and tossed the entire contents into her mouth, washed them down with beer. She'd have to switch to water; one beer wasn't going to do much to her, even on top of the Oozers, but it probably wasn't a good idea to keep drinking. "Thanks."

He nodded. "So, them Lamaru back, aye?"

The purple marks under her skin moved. A warning? They moved anyway, but were they moving faster? It'd be awfully nice to find a warning system that didn't hurt. Yes, it was obvious, don't talk about the case. But she needed to if she wanted to stay alive.

"Ain't can give me the knowledge, aye?"

She just looked at him, raised her wrist so he could see the ridged black cuts.

"What was the happening with that leg you got? Jeans all torn to fuck there." His gentle hand moved over her thigh. "Oughta get you cleaned up, Tulip. Ain't looking to me like something can be left on its own."

"Yeah." He was right. She should. But she didn't want to get up. The pills hadn't hit yet, but they would soon; fifteen minutes, maybe twenty tops. Her stomach was empty.

"Lemme give you the help, aye? Stay you there."

She waited, staring at the watermarks on the ceiling. Tomorrow she would think about it all. She'd sit down and try to figure out what it all meant. They were making cursed fetishes and they were using them to create psychopomps or alter them, or both. And they were doing it underground, at least part of the time. Obviously the slaughterhouse was off the menu as far as a ritual space went.

Why underground? Why were they leaving magic items in the tunnels? "Hey, Lex."

"Aye?" Something clattered in the bathroom; she sighed. He was probably making an enormous mess.

"Will you show me where you found the stuff in the tunnels?"

Another noise; plastic falling on the tile floor, she thought. It had that particular hollow sound, like an off-beat bongo drum. "Why you gotta see?"

She blinked. It hadn't occurred to her he wouldn't— Well, why would he? She'd just dumped his ass, and he knew why. He had no reason at all to believe she had any loyalty to him at this point; for all he knew, she was going to map the damned things out for Terrible and Bump.

And the sad thing was, she might, if she thought it would make Terrible change his mind.

How the hell did people do this, this emotion-and-forgiveness thing? How did they stand these feelings? She could barely handle it and she had lovely, necessary, reason-for-living drugs to smooth over the rough spots. How did people do this shit sober?

Lex walked back into the tiny living room and sat beside her, his arms loaded with first-aid supplies. It looked like he'd brought everything she owned. "Already gave you the knowledge what they found."

"Yeah, but I need to— If I could feel the energy there, it might really help."

"Take them jeans off."

Oh, right. She'd have to, wouldn't she? Shit. Well, maybe taking her jeans off would make him more inclined to say she could check out his tunnels.

Of course, he was pretty much *guaranteed* to say yes if she let him check out *her* tunnel again, but . . . no.

"Lex."

He unraveled a long strip of gauze, laid it across his lap. "Aye?"

"Terrible . . . he isn't talking to me. He doesn't really want anything to do with me. He called me a— He said some things. So it's not like I'm trying to spy for him, or he asked me to get information for him or anything. I swear. I need to see where you found that stuff for work. It could be really important."

By the time she finished, her face felt as hot as the raw skin on her thigh. And for once—for pretty much the first time since she'd met him—he was tactful enough not to look at her, to examine her discomfort and tease her about it.

"Aye, then."

"Wh— Really?"

He shrugged. "Aye, take you down, I will. But Tulip . . . you and me, we ain't never had the troubles before, over that slicktongue and he fist-man, aye? Ain't figuring we start now. You dig me?"

Relief flooded her limbs; relief, a little apprehension, and the first warm swirls of her pills. "Yeah. Yeah, I got it. We're not starting any trouble there."

"Aye. Now get them jeans—"

They both stopped. Her bag was beeping.

Stupidly, she felt in her pockets. Was that her phone? Her phone didn't beep. What the— Oh, shit. Her bag had been on the floor in the psychopomp room, had the Lamaru planted something in it?

No, dumbass. Who planted things in the bags of people they were about to kill? The Lamaru had certainly thought she was about to die when they locked her in the psychopomp room and left her there in the burning building like Romans throwing Christians into the lion pit. So why the hell would they have put some kind of electronic device into her bag first?

The thought made her grin. Oh, yeah. The Oozers were definitely kicking in. Her stomach started to lift, her blood to warm and thicken, running slow and smooth through her veins.

"Tulip?"

"Yeah?"

"You gonna see what the beeping is?"

"Huh? Oh, yeah. Okay."

Her leg hardly hurt at all now. She could feel the ragged edges of her torn jeans touching the wound, but it wasn't painful. Nice.

Of course, it also made her feel a bit like she was walking on legs that didn't actually exist. Like floating. Floating was nice, too. She felt graceful, moving smoothly through the dense, gentle air around her to her bag, bringing it back to the couch before opening it simply because that seemed like the right thing to do.

But what was that thing? It looked vaguely familiar. More than vaguely. If it hadn't been for the Oozers she would have twigged faster, but as it was she held the chunky black box with its greenish LED-grid screen in her hand and forgot why she was looking at it in the first place.

"What you got there?"

"Huh? Oh. Um . . . oh! It's Lauren's tracker."

That didn't seem to clear it up for him; he sat beside her with his arms folded and his eyebrows raised, waiting for her to continue.

"It's a tracking device, you know? For, um, tracking people. You plant the sensor on something, like their car or whatever, and it gives you their . . . their coordinates. Where they . . . where they are." Was she making sense?

"Oh, aye." He took it from her, turned it over in his hands. The thick silver ring he wore flashed in the weak light; it was hypnotic.

Or maybe it was simply that she was really starting to drift. Glorious lethargy spread over her like . . . well, like something warm and runny, she had no idea what and she didn't care. All she knew was the room kept fluttering around her as she struggled to keep her eyes open and she didn't seem to have bones in her body anymore; it was utterly delightful.

Lex had to ask the question three times before she heard him. "Who you got the track on?"

"Oh. One of—um." Yeah, her leg didn't hurt. But she'd felt that, the twinge in her wrists. Apparently magically induced pain was impervious to narcotics. Oh goody. There went the loosely formed semi-plan to get herself good and doped up and speak more freely.

"One of them Lamaru, aye?" He turned the thing in his hands, pressed the buttons. "How'd you get it on him?"

She smiled. Her hair was very soft, at least the parts

that weren't tangled and dirty. It slid coolly between her fingers. "I tackled him. Hurt my knee."

"So why it giving them beeps? Ah, dig it. Giving you the warning it's been on too long."

"Uh-huh." Air swirled around her legs; her jeans fell in a dirty heap on the floor and she stepped out of them. It took a while. Lex helped her back onto the couch.

"C'mon. You look ready to fall down, let's us clean up that leg you got."

As she watched him clean her wound and bandage it with impersonal fingers, only one thought really penetrated the delicious calm in which she floated, one thought she quickly pushed away because nothing ruined a good high faster than mortal terror.

If the Lamaru had taken control of all the psychopomps, the Church couldn't use them anymore. And if the Church couldn't use psychopomps anymore . . . how would they defeat the ghosts?

Chapter Twenty-one

> Remember you are known not simply by what you say, but by what you do. The Church requires Truth; your fellow man requires no less.
>
> —*The Church and You,* a pamphlet by Elder Barrett

And what would happen in a world where the Church couldn't defeat ghosts?

She surfaced from sleep to the kind of dull pewter light that told her it was either raining or about to. So much for the glorious early spring of the day before.

She didn't pay attention, only noticed it, just as she didn't pay attention to the vague memory of Lex throwing her tattered blanket over her before he left. Her thigh ached; her jaw ached where Vanhelm had hit her, but not as bad as she expected.

Not as bad as the pain in her mind and chest. If the Church couldn't control ghosts, couldn't Banish them, they'd lose everything. It would be Haunted Week all over again, only worse. Worse because there would truly be no hope, or worse because the Lamaru would step in, and the thought of a world where the Lamaru were in charge made her reach for her pills even faster than usual.

She stumbled to the kitchen and grabbed a bottle of water from the fridge. Her throat burned and ached from smoke inhalation; her entire body felt gummy and dirty, although part of that was because she hadn't gotten those pills down yet.

And it was Thursday. She'd have to visit the City in two days. Ugh. Didn't even want to think about that. Or about the look on Lex's face when he'd realized she was ending their relationship, such as it was. Or about how she was going to have to visit the tunnels with him.

Or especially about whether she—of all people—would actually have the willpower to keep from falling back into his bed at some point, especially in the face of Terrible's . . . He'd changed his number. And he'd done it recently; the last time she'd tried to call had been, what, ten days before? Nine?

Now the Lamaru posed a real threat. Psychopomp magic was the basis of the Church's power, the reason they existed. They'd done something to Lauren's ravens; who knew if any psychopomps were safe? Her paranoia the day before about the skull in her bag hadn't been so far off the mark after all, and that was pretty fucking scary, wasn't it?

No Church. No protection for humanity. No job for her—probably no life for her, because she had little doubt the Lamaru's first act after taking over would be to kill every Church employee they could get their hands on. A world of darkness more complete than the one she lived in now.

And how had Maguinness gotten involved in all of this? He was fighting the Lamaru, great. But why hadn't he come forward to the Church? Why had he gone to visit Madame Lupita, for that matter?

Shit. None of it appealed to her as a topic for contemplation, so she shoved a few pills down her throat and whiled away the time before they hit by playing with the tracker.

She switched it on, fumbled through a few of the menus. Maps . . . intensity settings . . . sensors. Two lights blinked, one for each of the sensors she'd used the day before.

But neither of them was at the slaughterhouse.

Vanhelm had escaped, that she knew. But neither of the sensors was moving, either. Had he discovered the sensor on his shirt and discarded it? Or was he resting somewhere, hiding out?

It probably didn't matter. The odds that Vanhelm was still wearing the clothing he'd worn the night before, and that the sensor was still attached to that clothing, were pretty slim. That his car might be there was a little more reasonable, though the car wouldn't tell her much at all. But it was something to check out, anyway; at the very least she might find some more information about where the Lamaru were setting up now that the slaughterhouse was gone, and hopefully retrieve the sensor itself to give back to Lauren.

Her Cepts had just started kicking in when someone knocked on her door. Shit. She was only half-dressed, and she was filthy. Not really up for greeting people.

Not just people, either. Terrible.

"Just a minute," she called through the door, with that particular lilting voice of people trying to pretend they're wide awake and ready to start their day, while in reality they've just fallen off the couch in their underwear.

Shit. Her face was dirty, her teeth not brushed. Okay, first order of business: throw some water on her face, some mouthwash into her mouth, and some jeans on her legs. For some reason she didn't care to analyze, she didn't want him to see her injured leg, or rather, her bandaged leg. Lex had made a rather neat job of that. She'd have to thank him when he took her into the tunnels.

She hurried as much as she could, and threw the door open with fresh breath and clean clothes, binding her hair with a ponytail holder so it at least looked tidy if not clean.

"Hey."

He nodded and stepped inside with his hands in his pockets, his gaze focused anywhere but on her. She was getting used to it now.

"Why did you change your number?" was on the tip of her tongue. She bit down on it with effort and instead made herself say, "What's up?"

He shrugged. "Figured on seein what else we dig up. You had the meet-up with that dame last night, aye? Get any knowledge?"

She didn't need the warning of her wrists. "I can't talk about it."

He walked past her into her tiny living room, sat down, and took out a cigarette. "Got notes? Ain't you write shit down?"

"Yeah, sometimes, but I didn't get much chance to last night."

She thought he might ask why, ask what had happened to make her look like she'd gotten into a fistfight with a fireplace. He didn't. Instead he picked up the tracker, turned it over in his hands much the same way Lex had. Well, fine. He didn't even want to know what had happened? Didn't even ask? Fuck him, then.

"I'm going to take a shower."

He grunted.

For a second she considered taking her shower, then wandering naked into the living room. He'd definitely notice that. But no. While such a move was certainly effective, she knew—she'd tried it more than once with different men when she was tired of waiting for them to get things started—it wasn't the right thing to do here. She didn't want casual sex. Didn't want him to get dressed and go home after, the way she usually wanted them to do.

How did people handle this? There had to be some way, right?

Yes, there was. And that way usually started with not fucking over the person you wanted to be with. Too late for that one.

He glanced at her; she realized she'd been standing there staring at the back of his head. "You showering up or what? Ain't got all day."

"Oh. Yeah," she managed, and fled before she made things even worse.

"Turn right."

They were in Terrible's Chevelle, a couple of blocks away from the wreckage of the slaughterhouse, zeroing in on the tracker's signal. It had to have been dumped somewhere; it hadn't moved all morning. She couldn't imagine Vanhelm would be just sitting somewhere in last night's clothes, waiting for her to show up and bust him.

Of course, it could be his car. The sensors were numbered, and the tracker identified the signals by number, but she hadn't paid attention to which number went where.

"Okay . . . here, can you see this?"

He braked in the middle of the lane and took the device from her. Chess glanced behind them; another car idled in the road, waiting for him to move on. No horn sounded, no impatient motion could be seen through the windshield. Terrible stopped wherever Terrible damn well pleased, and nobody challenged him unless they had a death wish.

"Right up there, aye?"

She nodded. He stabbed the gas and pulled into a spot half a block up, in front of a Stop Shop like the one by her place. This one was in even worse shape than hers; the plastic signs out front were broken and long silvery *X*s of tape covered one of the windows.

Terrible cut the engine, interrupting Them in midsong, and studied the tracker. "Ain't make sense."

"What?"

"Look to me like he inside there. But who sit in a store all day? He work there?"

"No, he—ow! He . . ." What a pain in the ass this was. Okay, time for Plan B. She did have a note about Erik's employment at the slaughterhouse; she grabbed her notebook and held it, hoping he'd take the hint.

He did. He snatched it from her hand—taking care not to touch her, she noticed—and read it over while she stared out the window and ignored the twinges in her wrists.

"Work at the deathhouse, aye. Only burned up last night."

She nodded, saw him glance at her with a little more interest, making the connection. But he still didn't ask. Didn't care enough to ask.

"Hey," she said finally. "Did you manage to set something up with Maguinness?"

His head shake looked more like an involuntary flinch.

"He's— Remember the night I got poisoned?"

Oh. Maybe that wasn't such a good thing to mention. The look he gave her was like an ice pick to her head.

Well, what did he expect? She couldn't change the fact that they'd spent time with each other, had talked and hung out. Couldn't change the way the ghosts of their past friendship hovered everywhere she looked, shades of them together on every corner, filling the city with memories. She swallowed and continued. "Maguinness visited the woman we busted that night. I think he might have smuggled a ghost in to her. And he's up to something, he's fighting with— I need to talk to him."

He didn't reply. Instead, cool air swirled into the car as he got out. She reached for her own handle, wondering if perhaps she should follow, but it didn't seem to be necessary; he disappeared into the Stop Shop and came out a minute later with a Coke in his hand.

"Maguinness gave an address near here," she continued, trying to pretend nothing had happened when he got back in and lit a cigarette. "I thought maybe after we find the sensor, we can stop in and talk to him."

"Nobody in that store lessin they got some room hidin or ought like that. Only the dame workin the counter."

Okay, apparently he was not interested in checking out Maguinness with her. Once he would have been; he'd liked helping her with her work, she thought. Had been interested, asked questions, had been one of the only people—no, not one of, he'd been the *only* person—whose opinions she'd wanted to hear, had trusted.

"If they have a hidden room, though, how would we— Oh! Maybe they have something under there, like in the—" Her mouth snapped shut. Could she tell him about what Lex had said?

She had to, didn't she? If she could, anyway; if the Binding marks would let her. She couldn't very well just claim she'd heard a rumor about the tunnels, he'd know that wasn't true; he was one of the few people on this side of town who knew the tunnels existed at all, though he had no idea how extensive they were.

But she wasn't exactly eager to bring Lex's name into the conversation. She'd rather yank out her tongue with pliers.

"Aye? Gonna finish up?"

She sucked back some water, stalling. Okay. She had to say something. Especially because the more she thought about it, the more she thought she was right. Vanhelm had left something in the tunnels; the Lamaru were using them, and maybe—she couldn't decide if it would be luck or the exact opposite—Vanhelm had left his clothes with the scanner attached in their little headquarters room, maybe they'd created some sort of hellish burrow below the earth.

Why would they be underground, though? She

couldn't imagine black magic witches wanted to be underground any more than regular witches. Sure, it was close to the slaughterhouse, but so were lots of other places. Above-ground places.

She drained half her water bottle trying to decide what to say; her stomach felt uncomfortably full. "The tunnels under the city, you know? I heard . . . I heard that somebody found some stuff in there. Like the fetish and everything, remember?"

He folded his arms over his chest; both eyebrows went up this time. "Aye? Where you hearing that?"

"I just—" No. He already knew. She could see it in his eyes, in the tight set of his lips. He already thought—already *knew*—she was a liar; no point letting him catch her in another one. "Lex told me."

"But you ain't see him no more, ain't that what you tell me?" Icy sarcasm so thick she imagined she could chew it dripped off the words. Shit.

"I'm not. I mean, not like that. I'm not. But he came by when they found the things in the tunnels, he thought maybe it was me doing it, so—"

"Thought you ain't do that shit. Curses and shit. Thought you ain't that kinda witch. But guessing *Lex* got better knowledge of you than me, aye? Knows better what you might do?"

Color started creeping up his neck; Chess scrunched herself back into her seat without thinking. Once his anger hadn't scared her. Things had changed. She knew that look in his eye well enough, and all bets were off as far as how he might choose to express it.

That wasn't entirely fair. She still didn't believe, deep down, that he really would hit her. But he might decide to hit something else, and she didn't want to see it. Didn't want to know he was imagining it was her. Wishing it was.

"Maybe you just ain't wanted to do it against he. Or

maybe Bump ain't offer you enough to do it, aye? Maybe he gave you *all* your needs free, you do anything he say? Maybe— Fuck."

He got out of the car, slammed the heavy door so hard the entire vehicle shook. Through the driver's-side window she saw him lean against the door, watched his arm raise and lower while he smoked one furious cigarette after another.

She shouldn't go into the tunnels without Lex. She knew that. He'd told her he would take her, and she should wait.

But how much waiting was she supposed to do? Sit here and wait for Terrible to calm down, or to decide he was still pissed and get back in the car to really yell at her?

He wasn't interested in looking for Maguinness. Fine. But she wasn't going to sit there all fucking afternoon and do nothing, either. She had other, better things she could be doing, and he was wasting her time. Being pissed at her was one thing. She said she'd take that and she would. But now he was fucking with her job, and the only way to deal with the ache in her chest at that moment was to get pissed off about it, so that's exactly what she was going to do. Fuck him.

She got out of the car, grabbing the tracker and her bag. "I'm going to take a look," she told his back. "Come along if you want."

Chapter Twenty-two

[They ordered the underground spaces be filled, for venturing beneath the surface of the earth can only lead to danger and destruction. There the dead have more strength; there does energy increase.

—*The Book of Truth,* Origins, Article 355]

Of course, she didn't know where the tunnel entrance was, but it had to be around somewhere. Most of the other ones were hidden back off the streets; they tended to be short rusted doors, with traces of faded gray paint in splotchy patterns and the occasional street tag or "Fuck you" scratched into them.

They were triple locked, heavy and hard to open, too, but she wasn't worried about that. Enough furious energy coursed through her at that moment she figured she could lift a car if she needed to.

Her leg started to sting as she stomped up the road, so she grabbed another couple of Cepts and washed them down while she moved. Okay, no doors here . . . but she'd learned through experience that there were usually doors every five hundred feet or so along each tunnel. And if she was right about a tunnel being there—which she had to be—there had to be a door of some kind. The tracker said the sensor was there, and machines didn't . . . Hmm.

The tracker had maps programmed into it. Lots of maps.

Technically the tunnels belonged to the Church, just

like everything else. But they'd originally belonged to the city and been part of some sort of transportation or municipal system or something; might some record of those systems still exist? The Black Squad had access to a lot of information, information other Church branches didn't have.

Worth a shot, anyway.

A shot that paid off. After ten minutes or so of fiddling she managed to bring up the maps menu. None existed for the tunnels, but there was one for utilities, and on that map she noticed some little doorlike lines at set intervals. In fact, one of them was at Forty-ninth and Cross—right around the corner from her place. That was the tunnel Lex used to get to her. She'd found the right map.

From there it was a simple matter of scrolling up until she found the address of the Stop Shop and then moving the cursor around until she found the closest tunnel entrance, which appeared to be at the end of the block. Yes! She'd been right.

The little triumph was enough to make her forgetful; she turned, smiling, back toward the car to see Terrible heading in her direction.

"I found it," she started, then saw his second of hesitation. Right. He wasn't going to share her happiness in this, was he? Wasn't going to tell her how smart she was or act impressed. Her smile fell.

"There's an entrance up here. Eightieth and Foster."

He took the tracker from her, checked it himself. Did he think she was lying about that, too? "See, it's that line there—"

He jerked away from her. "Aye. Let's us go then."

With no choice but to follow, she did; down to the corner and then, when they didn't find the door, around it.

Still no door.

He raised his eyebrows.

"It's on the map," she said, a little defensively. "Maybe it's in the building? What is this building, anyway?"

The structure at the corner was one of those most rare of Downside creatures: a building with its windows and doors intact, or rather, windows and doors still mostly boarded over. The boards looked fresh, too. New, or at least newer; they hadn't warped completely yet. Her practiced eye told her they'd been up three, maybe four months tops.

Terrible must have been thinking the same thing. "In there, aye?"

"Worth a try, I guess."

It took him only a minute to rip the boards off one of the back windows, while Chess waited a few feet away in the alley. The breeze was picking up, bringing with it the fresh, slightly ozone scent of impending rain; the air around her was heavy with it. She shivered. Going underground, into the tunnels . . . not the way she wanted to spend an afternoon. Going into the tunnels with someone who hated her? Yeah, that didn't exactly make it more appealing.

But her Cepts were kicking in nice and slow, and if she was lucky they might actually find something useful. Not that she expected to get lucky, but thinking about it was at least a diversion. She didn't want to watch him in action—well, she didn't, but she couldn't help sneaking glances, watching the muscles in his arms bulge, remembering how they'd felt around her.

She hadn't let herself think about that, not once. It was better that way.

He hoisted himself over the sill easily, was halfway across the floor by the time she reached the window.

Luckily he had a flashlight. As she made her own careful way over the ledge the first few drops of rain fell, fat heavy drops that splattered cold on her bare hands and scalp, and the clouds overhead grew even darker.

Inside the building all was black, save for the circle brightened by the flashlight. It swept over the bare, clean floor, over the walls innocent of paint. In the corner hung a rickety shelf; it was the only thing in the room that could even remotely be considered decoration.

But the energy was there. The second her foot touched down inside the building she felt it. Subdued, hidden by whatever they were using to mask it, but there nonetheless. The energy of death and ice-cold hearts and slithery things; it sneaked up her legs, circled her waist, tried to pull her down into its secrets.

She shuddered. Oh, no. The last thing she needed was to have that shit forced on her, on top of everything else.

Her chalk was in her bag, as always. She scrawled a sigil across her forehead and on the back of her left hand, then paused for a minute. Was it worth it to switch her shoes onto the wrong feet? No. The floor had been swept, and recently; not even the finest coating of dust covered the bare cement.

"Come here," she said, interrupting his slow flashlight sweep. "They've—ow—there's definitely been some magic here. You should have some protection."

He shook his head.

"Terrible . . . come on. Especially if we're going to go underground, you really should let me do this, okay?"

The light kept playing over the ceiling, the walls and floor. He waited just long enough for her to open her mouth again, then sauntered over to her, letting her know by the way he moved that he gave his consent with great reluctance. Like she didn't already know that.

Quickly she drew a protective sigil like hers on his forehead, another on his temple. He refused to admit he'd felt anything when they'd seen Maguinness, and she knew he wouldn't admit it if he felt anything there, but she was worried enough to think he needed something extra.

She licked her lips, focused her gaze over his right shoulder. Looking him in the eyes probably wasn't a good idea. Not after what had happened the last time she'd marked him, after what he'd said to her then. "Hey, seriously. Have you felt any different or anything since—since the hospital? That sigil might have some kind of weird—"

"Ain't talkin this shit with you, dig? Why the fuck you keep askin?"

"Because I want to help you. If—"

"Don't need your fuckin help."

"You needed it that night." Her eyes stung. She hadn't meant to do this, hadn't intended to start this conversation, but now that they were there, alone in the big empty room while rain thundered down outside and made a low rumble against the walls, she couldn't stop herself. The words tumbled out, backed by every lonely, miserable thought she'd had since the night he'd caught her in the graveyard; she couldn't seem to stop them. "You would have died if I hadn't— I saved your life. Can't you just—"

"Aye? An I recall savin yours once or twice myself. Maybe makes us even. Ain't make us aught else."

"I never meant to hurt you. I didn't, that's not what I wanted, not ever. I was going to end things with Lex, but we were at the graveyard and that sex magic they'd been doing—"

"Aw, shit. Ain't fuckin believe this. We here to work, or chatter? Got better things I could be doin."

"I just want to talk to you. To explain to you—"

"Talk?" He shook his head; she saw his profile in the dull glow of the flashlight's beam, his eyes closed. "Why? Got more lies to give me?"

"I didn't lie! Not about wanting—"

"Ain't chatterin on this no more. Let's just get this done, I can get you back. Makin me . . . makin me sick just bein in the same room as you. Dig?"

Yeah. Yeah, she dug. It was over. Really, really over; she'd never heard him talk to her that way before, that flat, cold detachment. Every hope she'd had, every stupid, naïve, idiotic little hope that one day he would forgive her, that there was still some kind of future there, that she hadn't fucked everything up, died. Just . . . died, there in the empty cement-gray room.

All those years she'd been alone, and she'd never felt loneliness like that, a fist in her chest.

She cleared her throat, loud in the heavy silence. Cleared it again, hoped that when she spoke her voice had some strength in it, that he couldn't hear how close she was to losing it completely. "Okay, then. Let's look for that door."

There was a door, a low one back in the far corner of the building. They walked through it, into the tunnels, the tracker emitting quiet little beeps; the farther they walked, the closer together the beeps came. The farther they walked, the harder the restless energy beat against her skin.

Their feet sloshed through a grayish stream, barely half an inch deep. It disappeared about a hundred feet along the way through a hole in the floor. They peered down into it; magic breathed up from the dark space below. Chess figured they were right before the Stop Shop then; whatever the tracker had found, it was down there.

"Ain't look too far down, pretty straight bottom." Terrible crouched by the opening, angled the light farther. "You go first, aye?"

"I— Oh. Sure." He'd rather dangle her down than catch her at the bottom. Of course. Less physical contact that way.

His hands gripped hers tightly; she set her feet on the edge and swung down.

For a second she hung there in the darkness, with the warm breath of the room swirling over her skin; her shirt rode up, exposing her stomach. Completely vulnerable. She had no idea how far down it was. No idea what she would land on. All she could do was trust him, and he hated her.

He let go.

She hit the cement with a knee-creaking thud, fell to the side, and landed on her injured thigh.

Whether her scream brought him down so fast or whether he'd planned on following her immediately she didn't know. She was too busy trying not to cry after her initial, helpless shriek. Oh, that hurt, that really fucking hurt; like the fire had started again, the knife slashed through her skin again.

"Chess! You right? What's got you?"

"I'm fine," she managed, but the light hit her in the face, and she didn't manage to turn away quickly enough to hide the tears on her cheeks.

"Aw, shit. I drop you on somethin? Ain't seen aught down here, dig, ain't meant to—"

"Don't." She lifted her right hand from her leg and held it in front of her face, trying to block the light. Her entire body trembled from the shock of the sudden, intense pain. It was too much, on top of everything else. The slight energy she'd felt upstairs was stronger here; they must have done their rituals in this room. It didn't feel old, either. They'd been there recently. Her skin buzzed with it. The tracker beeped faster in her bag.

It probably meant something, but at that moment she was too tired and in too much pain to care.

"Aye." Metal scraped on cement; he propped the flashlight off to the side. "Ain't in the eyes now, aye? What'd you do? I ain't meant to—"

"Fuck, just . . . don't, okay?" Shit, she was pitiful. "Please don't do that. Please."

"Aye, right. Ain't doing nothing, aye? Just sittin here, you just take—"

"Would you fucking stop it?" She buried her flaming face in her knees. Couldn't look at him while she spoke, the words rolling out like the tears down her cheeks. "Don't—don't talk to me like you care about me, okay? I can't—I can't take it, please, just don't."

Silence. Shit. He probably didn't even have contempt left to feel for her now. Didn't even have hatred left.

And her leg hurt like a motherfucker, too. She gave it an experimental stretch; it blazed in response. The bandage felt loose, the skin beneath it sticky; she was bleeding again.

Okay. She needed to pull herself together. Bad enough she'd made a fool of herself up in the building; bad enough she'd let fly with her Downside's-most-pitiful line a few seconds before. She could not give in, could not allow herself to start crying now, because if she started she wouldn't stop.

"Ain't meant to drop you on somethin," he mumbled again. "True thing."

"You didn't." That wasn't too bad. At least she didn't have that awful warbly tone in her voice, that hovering-on-the-edge-of-tears thing. "I was in a fire last night and— Aaah!" Damn it! Now her wrists joined the fun. Was there some other part of her body that would like to erupt in pain? Maybe something from the ceiling could fall and smash her toes. "My leg got burned. Could you turn around, please?"

"At the slaughterhouse? Them Lamaru got you there?"

Was he *trying* to hurt her? Oh, right. Yeah, he probably was. "Could you turn around, please? I need to check my leg."

She caught only a glimpse of his face, pale in the weak light, before he gave her his back.

Her hands shook a little as she slipped off her jacket—she didn't want the sleeves getting in the way—then unzipped her jeans and carefully slid them down her legs; they caught on her boots. Duh. Nothing more fun than planting her ass against the cold, damp cement wall behind her while she pushed them off her feet, followed them with her jeans, and her socks when they tangled in the jeans and she didn't feel like fighting them. The room's energy skittered over her skin, an uncomfortable feeling like dry wrinkled fingers stroking her.

Yeah, the bandage had come loose, and yeah, she was bleeding again. Luckily, she'd thrown some things into her bag; unluckily, Terrible had moved it aside when he landed, and it was now just beyond him.

Shit. "Could you hand me my bag, please?"

"Aye, got it—"

She hadn't thought he would turn around to hand it to her; she hadn't thought to grab her jeans and hold them in front of her. His eyes traveled up and down her bare legs, stopped on her wounded thigh.

"Ain't just look like a burn," he said. Was it her imagination, or did he sound a little strained?

Best to ignore it. "One of them had a knife and— Ow, dammit!"

"He ain't got you, aye?"

"Ha, no. I got him, though. He . . ." She stopped. Stopped, because he wasn't listening to her anyway. She knew that look. Had seen it on other men's faces before, had seen it on *his* face before.

But he wasn't moving; she wasn't even sure he was breathing. Only his gaze kept in constant motion, up and down her legs, lingering on her breasts; she didn't have to look down to know her nipples were poking at her T-shirt through her thin cotton bra.

Her tongue felt swollen three or four sizes too big. Should she say something? But what? She didn't want to speak, didn't want to break the spell.

But just because he was there, and looking at her, didn't mean anything. Just because he'd shoved his left hand into his pocket and his right shook slightly as he held her bag, that didn't mean anything either.

They were stuck there, staring, while the air around them waited and the tracker gave the occasional beep. And she had a choice. She could walk up to him, press herself against him, and hope he wouldn't turn away—hope he didn't shove her away, which would be so humiliating she didn't think she could ever get over it—or she could try to talk to him. Really talk to him.

Neither seemed like the right thing to do, but then when had she ever done the right thing?

"They—Lex, I mean—kidnapped me, right after that first night you took me to Chester."

Chapter Twenty-three

> We must not simply atone for our sins, our crimes against Truth, with words. We must atone for them physically as well.
>
> —*The Book of Truth,* Laws, Article 323

True to form, wrong thing. His face darkened; he stepped away. "Ain't—"

"He told me if I let Bump use the airport they would kill me. And I believed them, I mean, they kidnapped me from my apartment building. And maybe I should have come to you—I should have, I know that now—but I didn't know you then, not like I did later. Not like I do now. And by the time I did it was too late. So I agreed. I didn't want to but I agreed, and they gave me—they gave me stuff for free. That's all it was."

"Ain't looked like—"

"And yeah, eventually I—I started seeing him." Her mouth was so dry. She needed a drink, but was afraid to stop. He was listening; he wasn't happy about it but he was listening, and she was not going to let him out of this—this whatever it was, it wasn't a tunnel, it was some kind of room—without hearing the rest of the story. She had to tell it to him, couldn't stand having it sit in her stomach like a lump of coal anymore.

"But what happened at the airport didn't happen because of him, honest. It was all I could do, the only way to beat the thief. And I never told him anything about you, or about Bump, or anything, and I didn't— He was just a friend, really. I never cared about him like I— It wasn't serious. It wasn't like that, it wasn't about that, it was just—"

He spun around. His eyes were slits in his angry face; his fury stretched between them, oozed sticky and dark over her already tender skin. Her heart hammered in her chest. "Why the fuck you givin me this? Think this supposed to, to fuckin make all better? You—"

"Because it's the truth, and I want to tell you the truth, okay? I didn't lie to you on the bridge that night, I was going to end it with Lex, I wanted to be—"

"Fuck this." He snatched up the flashlight, stormed away from her. "Fuck this, fuck you. You—"

"Go ahead, run away from me. Pussy."

"What?" Oh, shit. If she'd thought he was angry before . . .

She wasn't backing down, though. No way. She was sick of this game, sick of paying the price; weariness weighed on her, dragged her down behind the ever-strengthening rush of the room's energy and her own anger and the slick, aching tickle of desire that had started the second his eyes found her bare legs. "You heard me, you fucking pussy. What's the matter, Terrible? You afraid of me, afraid of some *girl*? Afraid to stand there and listen? What do you think I'm going to say, why can't you just listen to me?"

"Wastin my fuckin time, is—"

"No! That's bullshit and you know it. Come on. Listen to me—look at me, you're not even looking at me, why? Why are you afraid to—"

"Shut the fuck up, Chess."

"Make me." The damp wall behind her was cool under her palms; she pressed them against it, braced herself. Her entire body shook. She was about to do something that would either get her what she wanted or get her killed, and at that particular moment she wasn't sure she cared which. She couldn't do this anymore, was all she knew. She missed him, and she wanted him, and she was so fucking guilty and she hated herself for hurting him, and she couldn't let this sit between them anymore. One way or another it was ending. She needed him to end it. Needed him to do something, anything, to end it.

He blinked. "What?"

"You heard me. Make me. Come on. Make me shut up."

He gave his head a shake, started to walk away. Farther into the big dark room; she couldn't see the walls very well, but water glistened in a crooked stream down one of them. And still magic whispered against her skin, probed her with delicate fingers. Tried to get in.

She pushed off the wall; the cold uneven cement scraped her bare feet as she headed toward him. "What got you so mad, anyway? That I was fucking Lex? Or that I wasn't fucking *you*?"

"Fuck off."

"Make me!" She splashed through the narrow, shallow stream zigzagging down the center of the floor; the water was icy but she barely noticed it. He was only a few feet away. "Make me, Terrible. Come on. You want to hit me? You want to make me pay for what I did? Why don't you, then? Make me pay, come on."

No reply.

"Come on!" She pushed him. Hard, putting all her strength behind it, suddenly furious. Not just determined, not just angry, but furious. Who the fuck was he to judge her? To ignore her? To tell her he cared about her, wanted her, and then to turn on her because of one mistake? She was only human, only herself. She'd never had anyone to advise her, to pat her back and hold her hand through life. She'd had to make her own mistakes.

And she'd made them. And lying to him was one of them.

But he'd lied too. He'd lied, because he'd told her—not in those words, but he'd told her—that he'd seen something special in her. He'd made her believe, for that one moment, those two short days between the time he'd made his little speech and that horrible night in the graveyard, that there *was* something special in her. Something good.

And there wasn't. And she'd hurt him, and she hated herself so much, *so much* for that, for making that mistake, for doing that to him, so much she couldn't stand it another second, and he could make it stop. He could forgive her or he could punish her; somehow in the twisted magic-thick confusion of her mind he became the only one who could. He became the one who could punish her for *everything,* every pill and drink and powder and every lousy thing she'd ever done, Brain and Randy and the dead hookers she hadn't saved and all of it—

So she pushed him, with every bit of strength she had, and was rewarded when he took an involuntary step forward.

"Fuckin stop it." It was more than a warning, it was a growl from the depths of his throat; the sound of a wolf about to defend itself.

She ignored it. Pushed him again. "Why don't you make me? I lied to you, right? I fucked somebody else, right? A lot! I fucked him a *lot,* Terrible, all over the place, all different positions." Another push. "Doesn't that piss you off? Why don't you fucking do something about it? Why are you so scared to—"

"Shut the fuck up, I ain't—"

"I hurt you, right? So why don't you hurt me? You want to hurt me, Terrible? Hurt me back?" Another shove, harder. She was getting into it, getting lost in it; energy raced up her body, rage and pain and lust, swirling around her, making her vision blur, and she couldn't get rid of it. Couldn't make it go away. Couldn't stop even if she wanted to. Her voice echoed in her ears, echoed against the walls around them; she heard the edge of panic in it, felt tears slide down her cheeks.

"Come on, Terrible! Hurt me. Hit me. You want to? Make me pay. Please, Terrible, just—just—"

One more shove, her entire body behind it. He spun around, his face almost unrecognizable; one arm raised, ready to strike.

"Fuckin warning you—"

"Don't fucking warn me, hit me! Hit me, you pussy! You fucking—you asshole, you fucking—"

Her swing was clumsy, her vision too blurred for accuracy. It hit him, though, caught him—somewhere, the jaw she thought—with a resounding crack that sent pain streaking up her arm. Glorious pain, her entire body was tight with the anticipation of more, she needed it and she needed him to give it to her.

"Fuck!" His hand started to move up to his cheek, but she couldn't back off. Couldn't stop hitting him, shoving him. Power thundered through her blood, through her body; incoherent thoughts tumbled through her brain like kaleidoscope images.

"Hit me! Hit me back, why won't you punish me? Please, please you fucking shithead bastard just do it, hit me, please . . ."

She swung again, connected again, his upper arm she thought. Good, but not enough, not enough, he wasn't hitting her, what was wrong with him why wasn't he hitting her, couldn't he see how bad she needed it, why wouldn't he punish her just fucking make her—

She fell backward without realizing it, her brain stupidly refusing to see him in front of her, to understand what was happening. She could barely see, couldn't hear anything but the blood rushing in her ears.

But she could feel.

Feel his lips on hers, giving her the punishment she'd craved, hard and bruising and demanding. Felt his body above hers, felt his arm beneath her check their fall then snake up so his fingers could twist in her hair and crank her head back.

Her already racing heart leapt so hard she thought for sure he could feel it. His free hand shoved itself under her shirt, yanked her bra cup out of the way, found her nipple; she cried out into the darkness, into him.

"Fuck you, Chess," he mumbled into her throat, and she didn't know if he was cursing her or making a promise and she didn't think it mattered either way. "Fuck you."

Her right leg was free; she wrapped it around his waist, pulled him closer to her. Her back scraped against the damp cement and she didn't care. All she cared about, all she wanted, was to feel his bare skin against hers; all she cared about was that he wouldn't stop, that he wouldn't come to his senses and leave her there alone on the cold ground.

Her fingers shook as she fumbled with the buttons of his shirt, moving as quickly as she could despite the distraction of his mouth on hers again. His tongue danced against hers, his fingers curled around the back of her neck. Every bit of fury, of energy, of fear and pain and misery and hatred she'd felt a second ago remained, channeled into something else, into need so desperate and consuming she thought it might kill her and she couldn't bring herself to care one bit.

She gave up on the buttons, reached under the shirt instead, under the T-shirt he wore beneath it, finding warm skin and hard muscles. His heart pounded beneath her palms; she slid them across his chest and felt the thick hair and the odd scar on the left side. The scar she'd made.

"Chess," he said again, a gasp into her mouth as his

lips devoured hers. "So . . . so fuckin bad, want you so fuckin bad . . . shit so *fucking* bad . . ." Cool air hit her stomach, her chest; he'd bunched her shirt up out of the way. His teeth scraped the skin of her throat, over her collarbones, down farther until he caught her nipple in his mouth and pulled it hard. Heat exploded through her body; his hot, wet tongue teasing her, his teeth almost, but not quite, digging into her skin.

Her voice echoed again off the walls; no words this time. She didn't think she knew any. Couldn't think of any, save perhaps "please." And then she realized that was what she'd said, that she was still saying it. Realized her right hand was tangled in his hair and her back had arched up off the cement and her left hand clutched at his shoulder so hard it hurt.

"Please, please, Terrible, please . . ." She couldn't stop; she dragged his head up, his mouth back to hers. Yanked his shirt up so she could feel his skin against her, so she could run her hands over it, then slid them farther down, over his ass, lifted her hips and pulled him even closer so his erection ground against her. His belt buckle gave with a sharp tug, his buttons with another one; he gasped against her lips when she pushed her hand into his open fly, gripped the heavy solid length of his cock through his boxers. It jerked against her palm and her insides went liquid.

"Shit, Chessie . . . oh fuck . . ." He kissed her harder, his hips moving against her hand, until her ears were ringing and everything in the room disappeared. She didn't even know where they were anymore. All she knew was that he was there, and for that moment he was hers, and she'd waited too long, wanted him for too long, and she couldn't wait another minute. All that mattered were his hands all over her body, caressing her uninjured thigh, her stomach, her breasts, her face, like he was trying to touch her everywhere at once.

Her panties disappeared with an audible protest she paid not the slightest attention to, especially not when they were almost immediately replaced by something much better. His hand found her smooth bare skin, hesitated; then pressed forward, exploring her, and she had a second to be almost embarrassed by how wet she was, by how badly she wanted him and how he knew it, until she pulled his boxers out of the way and found she wasn't the only one.

He was hard and hot, swollen and slick with his own desire; she closed her fingers around the thick shaft and twisted gently, played the heel of her hand over the blunt head. He gasped her name again as his hips pressed forward and their kiss, their long, shared kiss, became something even more; like she was breathing him in, like he was feeding her. She wanted to look down, to see him, but she couldn't pull away from that kiss. Couldn't bear to end it.

She fumbled at the waistband of his jeans, trying to push them down but unable to ignore his two thick fingers working inside her and the way her inner muscles clamped down on them, unable to ignore that he'd found exactly the right spot with his thumb and was stroking it in exactly the right way.

"Shit, yes . . . please don't stop, Terrible, please don't stop, fuck, please—"

"Ain't fuckin stopping," he growled. And he didn't, and she finally pulled her mouth away from his because she needed air, because all of her blood had left her head and was congregating farther south, and she clutched at him and her eyes squeezed shut and she exploded.

He didn't wait, didn't give her a chance to come down before his fingers disappeared and he thrust into her, all of him at once stretching her, sending her back over the edge. Still he didn't stop. His hips pounded against hers, punishing her. Giving her what she'd begged for, what she still wanted. She felt his teeth sink into her neck and screamed into the darkness, shoved her hands up under his shirt and dug what little fingernails she had into the soft skin there.

He groaned and pushed her harder still, his body shaking. Forcing her to keep up his furious pace, forcing her to accept every bit of him. His thumb slipped back between her legs, teased her again, and this time she couldn't find words to scream but screamed just the same.

"Aye, Chessie . . . fuck, aye . . ." This was too much; his voice in her ears and his body inside hers and his anger and lust, the raging desire, the energy of the room around them increasing with every second. His rhythm changed, grew even more frantic; the slight twist of his hips disappeared and he swelled inside her.

She grabbed his head, pulled his mouth down to hers, taking control as much as she could with her trembling hands. His breath came in short, rough gasps, his fingers called bruises from her skin, he was damp with sweat and so was she.

He shuddered, shaking even harder than he had before. His muscles tightened under her hands. She held him closer, pulling him deeper into her, onto her, relishing his weight above her for one last second before his fingers convulsed, his entire body convulsed; she felt him throb inside her, heard her name on his lips as one long, low moan before he fell still.

Chapter Twenty-four

> A Church employee does not get distracted. Does not lose sight of the goal. Does not waver in his or her objective, which is to defend the Church and to protect humanity, whatever the cost.
>
> —*The Example Is You,* the guidebook for Church employees

She didn't know how long they stayed there, didn't know how much time passed before cold fear crept into her heart. He hadn't spoken. Hadn't kissed her again. His body was slack above hers.

Finally he rolled away. She'd thought before that it was warm in the little underground space. Now she realized it wasn't at all, and shivered. Her jeans were still across the room by the hatch, along with her jacket. Her panties were a torn heap of pale blue cotton in the middle of the little stream.

Great. So she got to walk bare-assed over to get her jeans? She had a spare pair of panties in her bag, but . . . Something in the quality of his silence told her he wasn't going to make flirty little jokes as she retrieved them.

She adjusted her bra cup, tugged down the hem of her top. Something landed beside her with a soft, muffled sound; Terrible's bowling shirt.

"Thanks." It was short-sleeved, but wide enough that she could wrap it around her waist at least; hell, if she slipped it over her shoulders it would hit her knees, given how it reached the top of his thighs. Nice of him. But further proof of her fears. Nothing had changed.

She'd riled him into it, practically forced him, and now . . . now nothing had changed.

His lighter clicked; the warm glow of the high flame brightened the room for a second. He waved a cigarette at her and she took it.

"Thanks," she said again. Her lips didn't want to work properly. They felt swollen and bruised, like she'd been smacked in the mouth.

Well. This was uncomfortable. She had no idea what to say, and she guessed he didn't either. She knew what she wanted to say, what she wanted to do. She wanted to close the three-foot gap between them and tuck herself under his arm. Wanted to invite him back to her place and climb into bed with him—the bed she'd never let anyone else into—and do that again, slowly. Properly—not that it hadn't been just fine the way it was. She couldn't remember the last time she'd— No. No, she never had. She'd never felt like that before.

And she wanted to say it was worth it, but fuck, as the silence stretched between them like a crack in her heart growing longer and longer . . .

He cleared his throat. "Sorry."

He might as well have stabbed her.

"You didn't do anything I didn't want you to do," she said wearily. She needed her bag, her pills were in there. Lex hadn't brought her just the two Oozers the night before, he'd dropped a couple more in there, and she'd brought one along, thinking it might come in handy. She didn't care about the case just then, about the fucking Lamaru or their fucking psychopomp games or Maguinness. Didn't give a fuck about any of it. She just wanted to go home, get high, and hide, and try to forget the whole thing. She didn't think that last item, at least, would be possible.

"Aye, well. Maybe I ain't want—"

"Yeah. You didn't want to do that. I get it." For a

second she waited for him to disagree, to say that what he hadn't wanted was to do that *there,* or that *way,* or whatever, but he didn't. What a shock. She glanced at his shirt, tried to decide whether she wanted to use it or not; decided she didn't. Let him look. Whatever.

It hadn't seemed like such a great distance when she'd gone after him, from the hatch they'd dropped through to the space where they'd—where they'd ended up. Now it seemed to be miles, to take hours, crossing the chilly floor with her feet bare and her trembling thighs sticky. The faint ache between them would have been incredibly pleasant if the one in her chest wasn't so much worse.

She could smell him everywhere on her.

The panties were in a side pocket; she slipped them on, dug out all of her first-aid stuff, and set to work on her leg. Funny, she hadn't felt the injury at all in those fevered minutes. Clearly she should have, because bits of dirt clung to the edges of the cut, visible even in the very dim light.

She needed the flashlight. But asking him to bring it over . . . Yeah, not really what she wanted to do. So she got it herself, her legs jerky beneath her.

Of course, there was also the problem of holding the damned thing. She tried to stick the end in her mouth but it was too big, too heavy. It didn't work tucked under her arm either. Finally she set it on the floor, started to sit down—

Metal clinked across the room; she glanced up and saw his back, heard his belt buckle clink again before he turned around, his gaze somewhere on the floor. "Lemme give you the help, aye?"

"No, thank you."

"C'mon, Chess. I ain't— Just lemme do this."

Guilt covered his face like five o'clock shadow. Well, good. Maybe it was mean—hell, no maybe about it—but good. About time he got to feel guilty for something. Why should she always be the one?

But she let him hold the flashlight while she used her baby wipes to dab away the little specks of grit and rubbed some antibiotic ointment on the wounds. The burn still didn't look too bad, mostly just red, with a few insignificant blisters. Nothing that would scar, thankfully. She'd hit the pavement fast enough to put it out before it caused any real damage.

But she was acutely aware of his eyes on her, watching her hands. Acutely aware that his breathing was still a bit louder than she was used to; and if she took exaggerated care in gliding her fingers up her thigh, in lifting the entire leg and pointing her toe while pretending to do nothing more than examine herself, she supposed she couldn't be blamed for that, could she? All's fair in love and war; and at that moment she figured one or both of those definitely applied.

She took out a fresh package of gauze and folded it to make a pad big enough to cover the burn. Trouble was she couldn't quite figure out how to hold it in place while taping it— Oh, okay. If she laid the tape sticky side up across her lap she could set the gauze over it.

Would it have killed him to help her? Wasn't it enough that he hated her, did he have to watch her struggle like that—

His hands took the tape from hers. "Hold yon bandage there, aye?"

Had she thought she wanted him to help her? She'd been wrong; it was much worse that way, with his nimble fingers skipping up her thigh, pressing into her. Too soon, it was too soon. Maybe later she would have been able to handle it, but as it was, when she could still feel him inside her, still feel those same fingers digging into her skin, sliding over her ribcage . . .

She gritted her teeth and looked away. His touch was

light, almost impersonal, but as the minutes ticked by she realized the tape was on, the bandage fixed in place. He was just stroking her under the pretense of adjusting the tape and smoothing it out, his palm gliding over the top of her thigh, his fingers coming to rest on the inside dangerously close to where she was starting to throb again.

She jerked away, stood up. "Thanks. I think I'm—I think it's fine now."

"Aye." His head was down; his hair still stood up in tufty spikes.

Slipping her jeans on felt like saying goodbye to the entire episode; fully dressed again, as if it had never happened. Only the awkwardness remained, lingering like indigestion.

Speaking of which . . . Time for her pills. Well, technically it wasn't—it had only been forty minutes or so—but she couldn't have given less of a shit. She took four of them. What the hell. Wasn't like they were going to be doing anything she needed to be alert for. She wasn't sure they were going to be doing anything at all, in fact. Now that her eyes had fully adjusted to the meager light, she saw her initial impression had indeed been correct. The room was empty, totally and completely. Bare walls. Bare floor. Only the energy remained to tell anyone that something had occurred there; energy, the faint smell of herbs, and the beeping of the tracking device.

"Right," she said, shoving her feet back into her boots. "Um, I guess we should—"

"Tunnel keep going on, aye?" He swung the flashlight to the side and she saw, just past her ruined underwear—she'd have to grab those and put them in her bag; the last thing she wanted to do was leave a clothing item that personal and therefore powerful in the hands of the Lamaru—an arched opening leading into a regular tunnel, with another battered steel door guarding it.

It wasn't lit the way Lex's were, and she had a sinking feeling that it wouldn't share any other similarities either. "Yeah, I guess so."

"Guessin we oughta check it. Us bein down here any-road, an yon machine still makin them beeps."

The words should have comforted her. At least he wasn't running out of the room and speeding home to shower with lye and disinfectant or something. Or spitting at her, or even being particularly rude.

But she knew him. Knew him far too well to think the absence of insults meant all was forgiven, or that he'd changed his mind about not wanting anything to do with her. The words encouraged, but the tone, so flat, as if he were talking to a stranger . . . that didn't.

He was there to do a job, and he was going to do it, and that was that. He could stroke her thigh all he wanted but it meant absolutely nothing.

Her eyes stung as she shouldered her bag and scooped up her torn underwear, tucking it into a pocket. "Yeah. Let's go."

The door was locked, but she had her lube syringe and her set of picks, so it only took a few minutes to get it open. It felt like longer. Trying to concentrate with his body next to hers was like trying to save the best drugs for later; she could pretend it wasn't there, but every cell in her body knew it was and would not allow her to forget.

The tracker's beeps sped up almost immediately after they stepped through the low doorway into the cool damp darkness. She pulled it from her bag, held it in front of her, watching the red light flash and cast eerie shadows on the crumbling walls. Her and Terrible's outlines stark against the red, creeping along like gangly insects.

The tracker's beeps sped faster, turned into a continuous high-pitched wail; the sensor lay at her feet, half-buried in a pile of dirt. Damn. She picked it up, pressed the button on the tracker so silence fell just as loud and harsh in her ears as the beeps had been.

His voice startled her. "What we on the look for, aye?"

"Yeah. Shit." She took the flashlight from him—their fingers touched and he jerked his away—and focused it on the little black chip in her hand. It didn't look damaged; there was no sign that it had been attached to Vanhelm at all. Dirt clung to the sticky bit on the back. Was this from his shirt or his car? The tracker told her it was sensor three, but which one was which? "This doesn't tell me anything."

"You expecting it to?"

"Maybe."

He might have made a joke, or said something reassuring. Certainly he would have before. Now he just remained silent, dark eyes examining the tunnel around them as if she wasn't even there.

She sighed. "Okay, let's keep going, huh? If they came this way maybe there's a reason."

Twenty silent minutes later they hit a fork. By Chess's reckoning—her sense of direction was usually pretty good—they'd been heading northeast, but she had no idea how far they'd actually gone.

Time seemed to move differently there; she felt she'd been plodding along beside Terrible for hours. Or maybe it wasn't the tunnels, maybe it was the ache getting stronger with every passing minute, the discomfort growing more intense. The desire to speak, the desire to—She didn't know what. But it was possible they'd only managed to go a half mile or so. Of course it was also possible they'd more than doubled that.

Her mood and the gloomy, scratchy silence weren't the only problems. She'd been right to suspect these tunnels weren't like the ones Lex and the rest of Slobag's men used fairly regularly. Those weren't just lit, they were well kept—as well kept as a tunnel could be, anyway—and clear.

What they were attempting to traverse now was anything but. The walls crumbled on either side of them, thick dirt tumbling down into their path, scented of mold and age. Lichen and moss sprouted from cracks in the cement, stretched like alien fingers over their heads. Stones and chunks of cement littered the path; every step had to be carefully taken, every foot of forward movement hard-fought.

Sweat had collected between her breasts and beaded on her forehead when they hit a fork and the tunnel opened into two. The air stank, like dead things and rotting things and things that only grow in the darkness. Things that would slither along the floor and up her legs, things that would crawl inside her and attack—

She yelped; a rat. An actual scuttling thing, not whatever she was creating in her fevered, overstressed, and overactive imagination. She needed to calm the fuck down. Her pills should have kicked in; they had kicked in, she felt it, but they weren't soothing her the way they should have.

Weren't soothing her, because the pressure and discomfort and fear didn't come from inside her. It came from the air around them. She stopped short, glanced at Terrible; his eyes were narrowed, like he was staring into a strong wind.

"You feeling okay?" She didn't really expect an answer.

She didn't get one. He shrugged.

"The energy in here's getting stronger," she went on, keeping her voice low. "Like we're getting closer to something."

"Which way you figure we take?"

Neither route appealed; they were identical holes in the ground filled with emptiness. She closed her eyes.

"The one on the right feels more powerful."

"So that the one we should—"

"I don't know. Their magic is so masked that it almost seems like it would be wrong to go that way, you know? Because maybe I shouldn't be able to feel it."

She opened her eyes in time to see his gaze leap away from her face. What was— No. The thought of trying to analyze his movements or behavior, trying to read his mind and heart based on the way he stood or talked or grabbed her arm to help her across the rocks or whatever, just exhausted her. She couldn't do it anymore.

At least not just then. "I guess we should go to the right. Maybe they just aren't bothering to clean up after themselves so much."

"Figure they use these?"

"Yeah, I guess so." Damn it. That fucking Binding was really starting to piss her off.

"Guessin you ain't can talk about that fire, aye?"

Now it was her turn to shrug.

He paused, took her elbow roughly to help her over a particularly large dirt slide. "What happen, you chase em there, you and that Churchcop?"

She ducked her head; not a nod, but enough like one that he could see it.

"So they catch you in there, blaze the place up?"

She managed a small shake, a twist of her head to the side; she had to press her lips together, hard, to keep from answering.

"They ain't burned it out? Who done the job?" Then, at the pleading look in her eyes, "Be the potion guy, aye? That how you know he in it?"

"But why would he be trying to kill them?" She spoke before she thought; luckily her wrists kept silent. Apparently speaking hypothetically was acceptable.

"Maybe them buyin his magic shit. Or buy ought else, an ain't paid, or using it against him."

She hadn't thought of that. "I don't know why they'd buy some useless potions, though."

"Maybe a front, an he hiding his real business. Maybe he just ain't like em."

"Yeah, making friends isn't really their strong suit, I guess."

He smiled; shit, he smiled, and it was the first one she'd seen from him in a month and it made her heart twist hard in her chest. "Aye, well, we catch on why he after em, could be we— Aw, shit."

His gaze had jumped to the left while they talked; she followed it now and saw the reason for his darkening expression.

The tunnel ended ten feet or so away from where they stood, in a regular steel door like all the others. Dim light showed beneath it; the street entrance, she assumed. End of the line.

But to the left of it stood another door, surrounded like an exit wound by jagged cement. Magic pulsed from it, from the weathered boards held together with bent nails and half-rotted leather straps; it throbbed faintly before her.

Terrible's eyes narrowed; his head tilted to the side.

"Can you see it?" Lex wouldn't have, she knew; she wasn't sure if Terrible would, or if she hoped he could or couldn't. He'd never had a lot of power; enough to feel uncomfortable in the presence of magic, or to sense a ghost before one appeared, but only a tickle. A fraction of what she felt, or what any other witch would feel.

But all bets could be off at this point, and she'd done that when she'd carved that sigil into his chest, and guilt warred in her mind and heart with the absolute certainty that she would do it again in a second.

"See something. Like a— Look like the wall moving there, dig? Like breathing."

That was something at least. He couldn't see it entirely.

"There's a door there. They broke through the cement, I think. And it's—it's not a good door."

She stepped closer, wrapping her arms around herself. Something was scratched into the wood, a sigil? A . . . No, not a sigil. This was a drawing; skinny curved arms, a bloated potatoesque body . . .

Her breath caught.

"What? What you got?"

"There's a toad scratched into the door. And . . ." She straightened, checked the top of the rough boards. Swallowed. "A fetish. On top of the door. It's a toad's leg."

A toad's leg, tied to a bone with black thread. Herbs poked out of the hole at the top of the leg, the joint where it was once connected to a body.

"Like what them had on yesterday? That thing you take apart, aye?"

"Yeah. This isn't a whole toad, though, it's just a leg."

"What's the tale on it? Toads, meaning. They magic?"

"They're familiars." She stepped back, pulling herself from the sucking darkness of the makeshift door. "They're extremely powerful, magically. I mean, they're illegal, they're so strong. The Church breeds them—they're really useful for a lot of things, or they can be, but yeah, they're used for a lot of black magics. And they're also . . ."

Her voice cracked. She dug around in her bag for her water bottle, but it wasn't dryness that made her throat tight.

"Aye?"

The water tasted like plastic, and like the murky air around them. She grimaced. "They're used to create psychopomps."

Chapter Twenty-five

> There are those who seek to hide from the Church, to keep unsavory secrets. They do not succeed. The Church and Truth see all.
>
> —*The Book of Truth,* Veraxis, Article 728

"What action you want?"

She didn't mention what her first choice would be. "I guess we have to go through it."

He shoved his hands in his pockets, considering. "Got any knowledge where we at?"

"We've been headed northeast is all I know, really. I don't know how far we've gone or anything."

"Guessin ten blocks or so, dig. Put us up Ninetieth, round there."

"Ninetieth and Foster," she said.

"Aye, maybe. You got some knowledge there?"

"Ninetieth and Foster, that's where Maguinness lives. It's the address he gave when he visited Madame Lupita. Remember I mentioned in the car how he saw her before her execution?"

Curt nod. Whether it was from her mentioning the scene in the car or something else, she didn't know, and she wasn't really eager to find out either.

"Anyway. So maybe this is his place, maybe he . . ." No, that wasn't right, though, was it? Well, she guessed it was as good a theory as any, but it still didn't feel right. That sensor in the tunnel, almost like she was being led here. If he was at war with the Lamaru, and they knew she was tracking them . . . She wouldn't put it past those evil fucks to send her into a trap.

He leaned back against the opposite wall of the tunnel, unobtrusively taking another step back from the hellish door. "So iffen he got a fight up with em, and he livin here, he behind all this toad shit, aye? Them yesterday who killed Ratchet an they. Maybe them toads what he selling em."

She hesitated, waiting for pain to streak up her arms. When it didn't, she nodded.

"They need to kill to make them psychopomps? That what they getting on?"

She hadn't really thought of that, that the killing might itself be part of making whatever psychopomps they were making. If the spell was a destruction spell—which it was—she supposed that was possible. "Psychopomps don't usually require death to make, but theirs aren't—ow!—normal. And it's . . . it's a capital crime to kill a wild one, you know. An executable offense."

One she'd committed. For him. She let that memory ride behind her eyes for a minute, hoping he'd know and see, but she had no idea if he did. And she sure as fuck wasn't going to just come out and say it, not now. Not when she knew he'd see it as her trying to force herself on him.

Again.

If he did know what she was alluding to, he ignored it. Just what she'd expected. "So we go in here, could get all solved."

"Yeah."

The answers could be behind that door, sure. The solution to the mystery, the end of—the end of working with Terrible again. For good.

Fuck, she was so sick of herself—herself and her fucking emotional retardation. How did people do this shit all the time, this wanting people, caring about them? How did they stand it, how did they ever get anything done?

She was sick of being lost.

"Yeah, come on. We're here, we might as well."

"Ain't— I gonna be able to—"

"Yeah. It's just a glamour. I'll have to help you through it, though. It's kind of short. Okay?"

She didn't miss the suspicious cut of his glance, but ignored it. "Aye."

"Okay. Hold on a minute."

The door didn't appear to be locked; it was held shut not by a normal bolt or knob but by a metal hook in a loop. A makeshift jamb had been fashioned from a couple of two-by-fours wedged into the dirt just behind the cement hole.

But looking easy to open wasn't the same as being easy to open, and nothing that felt like that door did should be touched without first investigating.

She raised her hand, held it with her palm facing the door. Her tattoos tingled a little, a mild buzzing like touching her tongue to the end of a battery.

The first ward registered as a blip, an empty space near the topmost leather hinge. Okay. Probably something pretty basic; a decent push of power would likely be enough to unlock that.

But that very simplicity bothered her. Nobody who created the kind of energy she felt vibrating off that door would be unable to produce a few good wards or hexes. It felt like a trick to her. Like bait, like the crying child on the sidewalk who enticed passersby into stopping so their parent or master or owner—in Downside you never knew for sure—could clock the innocent, stupid victim over the head and steal their wallet.

So she kept checking. Yes. Another ward, stronger, at the bottom left corner. Black spots appeared before her eyes.

She knelt on the pebbled floor and pressed her hand closer. Along the bottom of the door . . . she'd work her way up, instead of down—the opposite of the way it was normally done, but anyone trying to be sneaky would automatically do it backward in an attempt to create confusion. So she figured, anyway.

A creepy, crawly tickle started at the base of her spine when she hit the center of the door. Okay, that was kind of weird. She followed it, using it as a guide for her hand; when it grew stronger, her arm slowed, when it grew weaker, she moved it back.

The darkest energy came from the fetish on top of the door, as she'd assumed it would. The fetish . . . She'd have to cross that bridge when she came to it. Which unfortunately would be in only a few minutes.

For a second she thought of Terrible. She could have him grab the fetish—guide his hand to it, tell him what to do. But the thought evaporated almost as quickly as it appeared. She couldn't do that to him, not now. Not when she had no idea how it might affect him, not when she had no idea what it might do in general. Toad bones—which she suspected the bone tied to the herb-stuffed leg was—were incredibly versatile. The bone could be a simple ward, or it could be a death curse; it could poison her, or it could bring water rushing from the earth to drown them.

Three more wards sat at intervals up the door, connected by thin lines of energy she felt when she waved her hand over them. And the hook holding it shut . . .

Ha! It was connected to that first ward, to the empty, harmless-feeling space. Like the point of a star it sat diagonally— Shit. Yes. Like the point of a star.

A pentacle, made of dark magic, hanging there over the door. Guarding it.

She rocked back on her heels, stared at it for a minute. Yes, she could see it, now that she looked: vague lines of darker air crisscrossing the seams of the wooden slats.

"What's troubling?"

"Huh? Oh." Her knees creaked a little as she got up. For a minute she'd actually forgotten he stood behind her. "It's hexed. Guarded by a black pentacle—an upside-down one, I mean. They definitely know what they're doing."

"You do, too, aye? You get it broke up—" The words had barely hit the air before his eyes narrowed, stealing from her whatever pleasure his compliment might have given her. He hadn't meant to say it, regretted saying it.

The heavy silence was almost worse than the slimy energy emanating from the hexed door. "I can break it," she said finally. "It's just going to take a couple of minutes."

Good thing she'd stocked up at Edsel's. From her bag she drew the mandrake and the black mirror and set them down before the door. Next came a stub of candle; she sprinkled a few iron filings—damn, she'd forgotten to get more again—over the top, and grabbed a coffin nail from a little pocket.

Tormentil and powdered crow's bone, hopefully to counteract the toad bone at least a bit, some dragon's blood resin and a chunk of snake. She didn't have her stang with her, but she did have a small firetray; that would do, she supposed.

Last she pulled out the little plastic container of blood salt she always carried, and the bottle of water purified by iron rings.

She lit the candle. *"Saratah saratah . . . beshikoth beshikoth."* A few pebbles lay near her knee; she slid them over, used them as a makeshift base to set up the mirror so it faced the door. The trick to breaking a spell like the one she thought they were dealing with was turning its malevolence back on itself, essentially creating a circuit that would burn itself out. It usually worked, anyway.

Next she used her knife to slice off a piece of the mandrake root and set it in the firedish, then piled it with the dragon's blood and tormentil. Lighting it was the next step; she pushed her own magic into it, grabbed a thick pinch of powdered crow's bone, and said, "Power to power, these powers Bind. Let this power, my power, become pure."

Thick smoke rose from the fire; through it she saw the lines of the black pentacle clearly, saw the five points of darkness and the small, seething clump of it in the center. She tossed the powdered bone at it, watched it catch the lines and hold. Good. She needed to see the center, find out what it was, so she could break it. It might be something as simple as a Bindrune, if she were lucky.

Oh, who was she kidding? She wasn't fucking lucky. But hope sprang eternal, for whatever stupid reason.

With her left hand she waved the smoke back, over herself, over Terrible. Power caressed her, slid into her nose and mouth and spread out from her lungs; it hit the energy already there, not just hers but the power of the Binding, and heated and twisted inside her, fighting to get out. Her right hand trembled as she dropped the chunk of snake onto the firedish. "*Sessrika.*"

The fire leapt high and bright pink before her, and so did the energy. She squinted and ducked her head, panting, checking the mirror where reflected flames danced against the black.

The pentacle flared into pinkish focus. Behind her Terrible made a sound, something between a grunt and a gasp, but she didn't turn around. Couldn't turn around, not when power roared through her body like a mad dog chasing blood and her fingers clenched tight and she wanted to fly, and she wanted to make him fly with her. Knew she *could* make him if he would let her.

The Church-designed basic counterhex required her to stand, to spin counterclockwise and build and release the energy that way. Something told her not to; there wasn't much room anyway. Instead she used her left pinky to stir the smoke in ever-decreasing circles, watching it build into a vortex. The slow build: it would work just as well with the amount of power coursing through her system. Fuck, she could probably light up half of Downside at that moment.

She watched the funnel form, its low point touching the flames, the high point stretching to her moving finger. Felt the same funnel form inside her, pulling her power up, twisting it, sucking it from her, leaching it from her internal organs, from her very soul . . .

The black pentacle blazed before her, throbbing, reaching for her. It wanted her, wanted to pull her in, and she'd be safe there, there was no fear, no sadness, no—

Her vision scrambled, she shook and couldn't stop shaking, and she was going to explode. Her hand was just a blur above the pink tornado she'd created and this was it, the sigil appeared in the center of the pentacle and it was so simple, and she pushed the vortex forward with all her might.

"Hrentata vasdaru belarium!"

The pink smoke exploded; the energy exploded from her. The pentacle shrieked, ululating high and sharp in her mind. She popped the cap on the blood salt and flung some at the door, felt it scatter and burn. The coffin nail practically leapt into her left hand, she grabbed her knife with her right and used the handle to hammer the point of the nail into the sigil.

Blowback threw her against the wall. Her firedish flew to the ceiling; so did the black mirror, which shattered. Black-silver glass rained down on her. She ducked her head, raising her hands to try to protect herself. Pink flames mixed with the shards; she clutched at the nearest solid thing she could find and it was Terrible and she couldn't even be embarrassed because everything died around them, the candle and the flames and the pentacle and sigil, and they were plunged into silence with the wooden door hanging open before them.

It was almost a minute before he let her go, edged silently away. Without his arms, without the buzzing rush of power, she felt cold and shaken; it was all she could do not to grab him and yank him back to her.

"Damn," he said, after another pause. "Were . . . damn."

"You okay?"

He nodded. The light returned to normal, the flat unreality of the flashlight's beam. In it his eyes glittered dark, his heavy muttonchops were black slashes against his pale face. "Aye. Right up."

She wasn't. Not at all. But she wasn't going to admit it, any more than he was, so she stood on legs that threatened to rebel and dusted herself off.

It only took a minute to clean up. She couldn't do anything about the mirror shards, and the coffin nail needed to stay in place, but the rest she packed back in her bag, save the iron-ring water. That she opened and took a healthy swig before offering it to him. "Here."

He took it without comment, and she watched him drink before handing it back with a nod.

Every muscle in her body hurt; she forced herself to stand, squared her shoulders before draping her bag's strap over them. Fuck, was this day ever going to end?

Probably. No, definitely. Whether she would still be alive to see it was another question entirely.

And it didn't matter. She *was* alive, and she was stuck in this fucking tunnel, and she had just broken a fuck of a hex ward, and now she was going to have to walk through the toad-door into who-the-fuck-knew-what with someone who touched her only under duress.

Some days it just didn't pay to get out of bed; in that sense at least, this day was no different from any others.

Chapter Twenty-six

> We know anything can be possible through the use of magic. But just because it is possible does not mean it is acceptable; the possible and the moral do not always intersect, and that is Truth.
>
> —*The Book of Truth,* Veraxis, Article 873

He pushed ahead of her, bent over deep. The space surrounding them was a tunnel in the most basic sense of the word: an empty tube cut through dirt, scraped away with shovels and picks and hands, hands she could feel with every crouching step. Hands that wanted to touch her. Hands like snails sliding out of the dirt to grab—

She stopped short. Pressed her own hands into the dirt. Even infused with black magic, it was still dirt, still pure and natural, still a source of strength and power. That power was the Church's wellspring, the source of all its magic and its dominion over the ghosts who wanted to destroy humanity out of simple, unthinking hatred; just touching it, digging her fingers into it, centered her.

But oh, yeah, the grime and darkness were there. Anger and blood and . . . what was—

"You right? Ain't dig spendin all day in here."

She looked up at his whisper and saw him several feet in front of her, half-turned, still bent over. This was uncomfortable for her; it must be awful for him, with his height.

"Yeah, yeah, it just— Something feels wrong."

"Ain't none of this right, aye?"

"But this feels . . . *wrong* wrong, you know what I mean? Not just like black magic or murder or whatever. It feels like, like the people who dug this are *wrong*. Something's wrong with them."

"Like they fucked in them heads?"

"No, it's— Well, yeah, but . . . I don't know. I can't explain it." She pulled her hands back from the dirt, brushed them against each other.

"Wanna head back?"

She looked up sharply. Yes, she wanted to head back; no, she didn't want to admit it. "No. Go on."

He shrugged and kept on; she noticed he carefully avoided touching the hard-packed mud on either side of them, and that when on one occasion his shoulder brushed it, he jerked away from it.

She didn't bother to ask. And honestly she didn't think she could find her voice even if she wanted to. With every step the feeling of *wrong* increased. She caught herself rubbing her arms, trying to calm her goosebumped skin. Trying to still her shivering, trying to soothe the turmoil in her mind.

It was no use. She couldn't seem to calm down. Couldn't seem to focus on anything.

Terrible stopped short; she bumped into him and hardly noticed it. He glanced back at her, gestured for her to look.

The tunnel opened to a cavernous space, a space like nothing she'd ever seen in her life and hoped never to see again.

At first she thought they were back above ground. Bright light dazzled her eyes, made them sting and water; it took a few seconds to realize it wasn't daylight but candlelight she was seeing, that candles climbed the dirt walls in dizzying columns. Stretched across the ceiling were long crisscrossing strands of rope; from the ropes hung bones and skulls, scarves, ratskins, and twisty lines of feathers bound together. The same ropes dangled down the walls, between the candle rows, between shelves of bone and wood, between what looked almost like beds.

Small beds. Narrow beds.

More skulls littered the floor. Some of them were human.

The stench of rotting meat filled her nose; bile and saliva filled her mouth. This wasn't a home, wasn't someone's cavelike hideaway. These were the hidden people, the ones so secret and reviled even Downside spoke their names as curses. This was a charnelhouse, a slaughterhouse.

Not the Lamaru, at least not if what she knew about Downside legend was true. Something much, much worse.

"We have to get out of here," she started, grabbing his arm and starting to turn back. "We have to get out of here now, right now—"

Too late. Something scuttled along the wall behind the ropes; boards in crooked rows created a kind of hall outside the main open space, and something . . . something tiny and misshapen ran behind it, its feet slapping the hard-packed dirt. They'd been seen.

Terrible's hand went to his knife. "We run they follow, aye?"

She nodded, her teeth sinking into her lip so hard she drew blood. They could run—maybe. But their journey to this cave had been rough, a long hard slog over rocks and dirt. She didn't think they could get back much faster, and she had absolutely no doubt that the inhabitants of this little corner of hell could.

More movement over their heads; a small body clambering along the rope like a monkey. A very small body. A child.

"Ain't see another way out."

Her skin prickled everywhere, every gaze that hit her registering like another shock. So many of them, she felt them, their choking sick hunger clouding her thoughts and her vision. The door they'd come through had been hidden by glamour. She bet the exit—if there was one—was hidden as well.

They really didn't have time for this shit, but neither did they have a choice. She fisted her hands, took a deep breath. Found her power, deep inside, let it flare while she scanned the walls. Ignore the movements, the unmistakable fact that more bodies twisted past behind the boards, that harsh dry whispers crossed the bone-littered space, and find the exit. Find the door.

"There." She pointed at it; they didn't have time for her to explain. "There, go, run—"

His big hand wrapped hers, held it tight as he set off across the floor. At the same time the people behind the boards came out, ran for them.

Oh shit they're wrong they're so wrong—

Twisted bodies, handless, deformed. Gaping mouths devoid of teeth, bloody smiles with too many of them. Leering foreheads reflecting the candlelight, tiny eyes set too close over humping crooked noses. Reaching for them, brushing her clothes, her hair—

She stumbled; Terrible yanked her back up, kept running. Around her wails sounded, voices cackling and screaming. Steel glinted as knives were raised.

The door wasn't far now, she saw it, a plain door—a real door—high over steps cut in the dirt. It was a star she reached for as she pulled Terrible to the side and let him draw her along faster than she could go on her own, her lungs threatening to explode from breathlessness and hopelessness and the aching pressure of madness and twisted inhuman humanity.

A figure stepped in front of the door. They were halfway up when she saw it was Maguinness, smiling gently, his arms folded before him.

He raised a pale, long-fingered hand; the noise around them ceased, left only the ringing of her ears.

"I know you." His gaze ran up and down Terrible's body; Terrible's hand tightened almost imperceptibly around hers. "Work for the lord, you do."

"Aye."

Now that beatific smile, horrible in its emptiness, fell on her. "And you work for the other one. Why have you bothered my children?"

She cast her eyes away from him, couldn't keep looking at his waxy visage. Above him toads danced on strings, rows and rows of them. Guarding the door. Guarding the inhabitants of this room. His children?

His *children*. She gagged, tried unsuccessfully to turn it into a cough. The glint in his eye told her she hadn't fooled him.

Terrible spoke. "Looking for aught else, is all."

"Oh, no . . . no, I don't think so. Methinks you wouldn't have entered here by mistake. You, witch. You destroyed my door."

"I'm sorry" was on the tip of her tongue, but she couldn't bring herself to utter it, much as she knew she should. Terrible had calculated their chances pretty well; between the two of them they could handle a lot, but an army of inbreeds—quite probably cannibalistic inbreeds, if the skulls on the floor were anything to go by—was too much. Their odds of fighting their way out of this wouldn't attract even the most desperate lost-cause gambling addict.

"I thought it was connected to something else," she said. "The Church will pay damages if you file a claim."

Not that she expected him to. But perhaps mentioning

the Church would cause him to rethink whatever murder-and-devour plans he was formulating in that rat's-nest head of his.

Of course she didn't really expect that either. But it was worth a try.

He blinked, slowly. Like a toad. "The Church . . . ah. I see. Followed them, you did? The other witches."

The Lamaru? "Is there something you want to tell me about them?"

"I do not believe I do, no."

"But you know who they are. You attacked them last night." And he was smiling, a smile she didn't like at all; it raised nervous prickles up her spine.

"I know many things. I know they have dark plans that should be stopped. I do not know what they are."

"Then why are you—"

"I see them. Bothering me. Bothering my children. You waste our time, witch. Catch them. That you should, I do know."

"Why? What did they do to you?" Shit, she shouldn't be doing this, not now. Not when his horrible "children" licked their lips on the steps below her and she could feel their hungry gazes on her body.

Their hungry gazes . . . his children. Had the Lamaru killed them? Were his children the genetically altered bastards that that report described? If they truly were inbred, the result of years of it . . . ugh. "They bothered your children?"

His eyebrows disappeared into the tangled mass of his hair. "Said it, did I not?"

"How did they bother them? Is that why you did what you did?"

"Not your business."

"I think it is." Bells rang in her head, deafening bells. If the Lamaru had killed Maguinness's children . . . that would be reason enough for revenge, right?

And now he knew who she was. Knew she knew about him, knew she was—however peripherally—involved. Crossfire could be a real bitch. Her skin went colder than it already was.

But he clearly wasn't going to tell her anything, and she didn't have the authority to change that at the moment. Sure, she could ask Terrible to step in, but even if things between them hadn't been totally fucked up she didn't know if he'd be too eager to do the stepping in while a horde of inbred lunatics filed their teeth into points behind them.

And either way, she had to account for the information. She was well within her rights to be out wandering the streets with anyone she chose, and to stumble across Maguinness's hidey-hole in the process, but to actually bring him in for questioning she'd need Lauren. Unless she could get him to talk on his own. To come in on his own.

"We can stop them, you know." She looked him dead in the eyes, wished she hadn't when the contact jolted down her spine. How was he so powerful? "If you tell me what you know, we can—"

"I don't think it's your business," he repeated.

He stood before her; she hadn't seen him move, but there he was, on the next step. Closer than he'd been a moment ago. The stink of him was almost as bad as the realization of what sort of family he was raising; sweat and smoke and greasy, bloody filth.

His eyes were worlds in his face now, swirling orbs of color and darkness. "Yes," he whispered. "Look at me. Let me see . . . let me see into you, little witch."

He grabbed her arm, flipped it over so her wrist was exposed. She gasped. A stab of pain flew up it at his touch, but she couldn't look away, couldn't focus on anything else. Terrible's hand on hers tightened even more; she felt it without it actually registering in her mind, like watching him squeeze someone else's hand.

"Hmm." His fingers crawled spiderlike over the black scar of her Binding while his gaze kept hers trapped. "Interesting."

His hand closed over the scar like a vise. Power shot through it, searing power that stole her voice, stole her thoughts.

"Arteru niska," he whispered. Her arm hummed, her tattoos crawled and itched. She tried to scream but nothing came out; he'd taken her breath along with her will, and her vision went black around the edges.

In that darkness, between the red spots exploding before her eyes, she saw bright white lights form and spread, blotting out everything until all she saw was blinding, hateful white—

Pain slammed into her, exploded from her wrists into her chest and her head, breaking the spell. Her entire body shook; she tried to pull away from him, from his grip wet with her blood, oh, shit, her blood drooling from the Binding wound, dripping out, and his children started screaming.

More light flashed into her eyes: Terrible's knife at Maguinness's throat.

He didn't speak. Didn't need to.

Through the haze of pain and blood she saw Maguinness glance from her to his children and back to Terrible.

"Aye, they might," Terrible said quietly. "Too late for you, though."

"I could help you, little witch," Maguinness said to her. "Could break that Bind and set you free. We could help each other. Yes, we could."

She swallowed. "Tell me why you're fighting them. What you know."

He shrugged, dropped her wrist. The energy receded.

"Do not come here again," he said. "Leave us be. We do not need the Church interfering in our lives."

He stepped to the side.

It took two tries to get her rubbery legs to climb the stairs, but the door opened easily enough when they got to the top. Fresh, damp air—what could be considered fresh in Downside, anyway—flooded her lungs, her face. The rain had stopped.

Before the door closed behind them she took one last look back, and wished desperately that she hadn't.

Maguinness stood there in the shrinking space between the door and the jamb, watching them go.

He was licking her blood off his fingers.

Chapter Twenty-seven

> The Church's blessing did not come without conditions, for nothing ever does, but the condition was thus: That the people know and accept Truth, and live in it, and be guided by the Church.
>
> —*The Book of Truth,* Origins, Article 700

Lauren's red sports car lay in wait across the street from her building, a big shiny reprimand that Chess hadn't called her that day.

And she should have, she really should have. After what Lauren had been through the night before it was really inexcusable; she wasn't exactly a Lauren fan, but she should have called to check on her. Score one major insensitivity point for Chess.

"Shit," she said, breaking the silence. And it had been silent, the entire drive back; with the Supersuckers playing through the speakers, but without a single word exchanged between herself and Terrible. "Just what I— Oh, shit, stop!"

He did, so suddenly and effectively that only the seatbelt kept her from hitting the dash. "What?"

"That's Lauren's— She can't see you. She can't see your car. Quick, back up or something."

He cocked an eyebrow.

"The other night, in the lot. She asked me about you and I told her I didn't know you, she saw your car, if she sees you she'll know I—"

The car raced backward, slid against the curb neatly as a magnet attaching itself to a refrigerator door.

"Thanks. I just—"

"I dig it. Don't want her knowin you know me. Gave her the lie."

"But—" No, he couldn't be thinking that, could he? "Only because I didn't want to drag you into it, I mean, she thought you were involved, you know? Wanted to question you. And I didn't think you'd want that."

He nodded, his eyes fixed straight ahead.

Shit.

"I don't know if you want to call me later or something . . ." She swallowed. "I don't have your number anymore, I guess. I tried to call you last night but you changed your number."

Long pause. "Aye."

She wasn't quite sure what to say; with every passing second she became more and more convinced that she should be sure, that she should say something, but nothing came to mind. Nothing appropriate, anyway.

"Chess."

"Yeah?"

He lit a cigarette, leaned back and blew smoke at the ceiling. Watched it. "Sorry. True thing."

"Sorry—why? I mean, because you changed your number, or—"

"You know why. Shit. I ain't meant to—"

"But you know what? You did. You still *did,* Terrible, you can't sit there and tell me you don't still want—"

"Wanting ain't fuckin trusting, aye?"

"Right. All those months, and now you can't trust me just because of one thing, one thing that—"

"One— You got any fuckin thought what you done to me? Any fuckin thought what seein you under that— Fuck. Trusting you, an you lyin every fuckin day."

"But I didn't! The only thing I lied about was seeing him—"

"*Fucking* him. A *lot,* aye?" His voice dragged sharp icicles across her skin. Her temper roared.

"And who were *you* fucking? How many? Am I supposed to believe—"

"Weren't fuckin nobody wanted to see you dead. Not like you. Weren't playin you a lead-on game, neither, lyin about wanting you, like you lied—"

"But I didn't lie! I just—I couldn't handle it, you know—you *know* this, I told you all this, on the bridge, that I just needed—"

"Ain't needed time with Lex, aye? Months you with him, an—"

"Because I didn't fucking care about him!" Shit. That came out too loud; the car itself seemed to shrink away from her voice. "I didn't and I still don't, he was a friend that's all, that's all it ever was—"

"Oh, aye, you fuck all your friends? Or just the ones look like he—" He snapped his mouth shut, looked away.

Oh. She should have known. And she supposed if she were honest with herself, she had. But she never thought about the way Terrible looked, at least not that way. He hadn't been ugly to her for months; he'd gone from just being a face she was familiar with to being a face she loved to look at, a face that made her . . . happy.

Who gave a shit what anyone else saw when they looked at him, when they saw the crooked, many-times-broken nose, or the scars, or the jutting brow or thick jaw and heavy muttonchops? She knew what she saw, and that was all that mattered. Knew what was behind those hard dark eyes, and wanted it more than anything.

She'd be lying if she said she wasn't aware of his insecurities, the few he had. She knew he was embarrassed by his lack of education, that he was continually and vocally impressed by hers. Knew he thought he wasn't very smart, despite all evidence to the contrary. That he didn't see himself as being good for much more than muscle.

But somehow she'd never thought those insecurities were serious, that they applied to her or that he would think . . . Shit. What a dumbass she was. He'd even told her himself, words whose significance she hadn't seen at the time: *Only reason any dame want a baby off me is money*. The night she'd met his daughter, the night she'd kissed him and he'd told her what he really wanted from her. She hadn't thought much about those words then, but sitting in the car, hearing them in her head again . . .

How would she feel if she were him and saw her with Lex? Handsome Lex with his perfect features and his clever smile and his arrogance? Some smart fucking Churchwitch she was.

"I don't care what he looks like," she said carefully, waiting for another explosion. "I don't care because I lo—I like the way you look, so much more, I—"

"Fuck." He flicked his smoke out the window, lit another. "Don't—ain't even can trust nothing you say, don't know why I even botherin to give you the chatter, wasting my fuckin time. You gave me the lies then, you give me em now, lied for months behind my back, and now—"

"And if you didn't give a shit about me that wouldn't bother you." Her throat felt like someone had rammed a steel pipe down it. She had to get out of the car. Had to get out, immediately, before she said or did something else she would regret—another regret to add to a lifetime full of them.

But the words flowed from her mouth anyway, before she could stop them. "If you really, honestly didn't care about me and didn't still—then it wouldn't bother you, you wouldn't care, you wouldn't be sitting here talking to me. Yeah, I lied and I shouldn't have and it was lousy of me and I'm sorry. I never meant to hurt you, I never wanted that, and I wish so bad I could take it all back, okay? But we both know which one of us is lying now and it's not me. So you call me when you want to actually talk to me and not just yell at me or tell me what a shitty person I am. I already . . . yeah, I already know that, okay?"

She slammed the door on his reply and strode away with her head high, her shoulders set; grateful he could only see her back, that he couldn't see the tears streaking down her face.

She hadn't really had a choice when it came to telling Lauren about Maguinness, not after he'd almost burned them both to death and staged a bar brawl in the slaughterhouse parking lot. Finding out if those body parts did indeed belong to members of Maguinness's family—or rather, confirming that they did—was important. Talking to him was even more important. She hadn't been able to pull rank with Terrible there, but a Squad member made a difference, and they were so fucking close to a solution.

He could find the Lamaru if they ventured into Downside; he obviously had some kind of connection with them. Maybe a connection they could use. Hell, maybe if the Lamaru knew their enemy was working with the Church, they'd back off. Not likely, but possible.

Maguinness was scary powerful; he'd make a terrifying enemy. She'd sure as fuck clear out if he was after her.

At least that's what she wanted to do. What she would have done if she hadn't been who and what she was. Instead she stood at Lauren's side at two in the morning, hidden by the darkness of broken streetlights at the corner of Ninetieth and Foster, getting ready to break into his place and have a look around.

The meeting at the Church earlier had been short and sweet, her worst fears come to pass. No more psychopomps, not until the Lamaru were caught. She was the only Debunker currently working. The others were on indefinite leave until the problem was solved, until every skull in the Church stores had been tested and cleared.

She'd never realized before how much she counted on her psychopomp, how much she counted on her ability to send ghosts to the City. Without it she felt vulnerable, exposed; her belief in the Church and its magic, which she'd once thought unbreakable, lay in shards around her feet. It felt like she was struggling to save a life already gone, and the Lamaru had done that, and hatred burned hot and strong in her chest.

Her Hand of Glory twitched in her palm. Reading her energy, she assumed; she certainly wasn't feeling very calm, despite the four Cepts she'd managed to down in the Stop Shop bathroom.

It wasn't just the rage, or the vague sense that even both of them and their Hands wouldn't be enough to enchant Maguinness and his family to sleep. Wasn't the fear of what he might do to them if he caught them. Lauren had a gun; if it came to trouble, they'd blast their way out of there.

It was the memories of earlier that refused to leave her alone. His skin against hers. His voice in her ear. His hair between her fingers, his body under her palms. Sense memory, so strong she almost gasped, overwhelmed her; her muscles clenched.

"What is wrong with you?" Lauren finished loading a fresh clip into her gun and tucked it into the shoulder holster beneath her jacket. "You look like you're about to pass out."

At least the comment gave all that hot blood somewhere else to go—not that she liked knowing her face was as red as Lauren's hair. "I'm fine. Just . . . I really think we ought to call for some backup or something."

"Why? You said he was a creepy guy with a few creepy kids. Hell, he should be glad we're here, if he's really fighting the Lamaru. We can beat them for him and make sure they leave him alone."

"Yeah, but . . ." Damn, and damn again, and fuck for good measure. She'd had to downplay her encounter with Maguinness in the retelling, not wanting Lauren to know Terrible had been there—so completely leaving out the physical threat stuff—and especially not wanting her to know how Maguinness had read her Binding marks. That he'd read *her,* knew who she was, that the case could be compromised. If they booted her off it, she'd have to give the money back.

It hadn't even come close to occurring to her that Lauren would want to bounce on over to his place that very night without bringing any more of the Squad. Without even calling Elder Griffin first to let him know what was going on. Chess had envisioned a full-on invasion of his disgusting underground charnelhouse, not two women—no matter how skilled or well armed—popping in to ask a few questions.

"But what?"

"I just think it would be a good idea to call someone," Chess finished. "That's all."

"Why, are you scared?"

"Hell, no." Hell, yes. But she'd rather slit her wrists than admit it, especially to Lauren.

"Do you normally call someone when you enter your subjects' homes?"

"No."

"Then we don't need to now. Come on. I want to get something to eat after this."

"We already— Never mind." Apparently Lauren liked to eat a lot. Fine.

Lauren pulled her own Hand out of a little leather case inside her bag and set it on the pavement while she dug out a stub of white candle to place in the palm. Chess already had hers ready to go.

Lauren was being awfully . . . nice, though, wasn't she? After what happened the night before and her insistence that Chess become her counselor and very best friend?

Whatever. Wasn't like Chess could judge how people handled things, especially not while three hundred milligrams of narcotic slid its slow, warm way through her bloodstream and settled false calm over her nerves. Maybe Lauren's response was normal. Chess's certainly wasn't.

They lit their candles in unison, two bright sparks of light on the dark street. *"Algha canador metruan,"* Chess whispered, and heard the words echoed by Lauren.

She hung back and let Lauren pick the lock on the door. If trouble started she was welcome to be first in line for it.

But no trouble came, and when they slid into the cave Chess understood why.

It was empty.

Maguinness's energy still waited there, foul and thick around them. The ceiling ropes still hung with their rows of bizarre decoration; the little bed slats still hugged the walls.

But not a single body slept in them. Not a single living being slept anywhere in the cave, at least not that she could see, and when she opened up to the Hand's magic she found it hadn't touched anything, hadn't found a living person to enchant.

He'd known they were coming. Had to have known, unless he simply liked to be out and about at all hours of the night. Which wouldn't have surprised her, but the idea that he'd taken his entire family with him did.

She knew that wasn't it anyway. The air of neglect already hung over the place, as if Maguinness had taken something vital from the room itself when he left.

But had he left because she'd been there earlier and he

knew she'd be back, or was it because . . . well, because of something else? Because of war with the Lamaru, or whatever?

"Shit." Lauren's shoulders sagged.

Chess tried to hide her relief. Maybe even did a decent job of it. "Come on. We still might find something."

They split, Chess moving off to the right and Lauren the left. Being in the room, deserted though it was, felt lousy; the power she'd felt earlier had dissipated but it hadn't disappeared. And every step she took showed her another little bed, another bone or scrap of garbage, another reminder of what had lived here. And worse, that the family was now out on the streets. Who knew what they were doing?

Tied beneath each slat bed was a little charm, a toad bone wrapped in black thread with a piece of mirror dangling from it. Chess reached for one; her skin started crawling before she even touched it.

She fished in her bag for a glove, glanced at Lauren across the room. "What do you think the charms are?"

"Who knows. Not sleep safes or anything like that. Probably just general protection."

"Yeah, but those are toad bones. Who uses toad bones in general charms? And how did he get so many of them?"

"There are black markets everywhere, Cesaria." Lauren's dismissive tone rankled. Chess was looking at more toad charms, which connected in her head with the toad fetish she'd seen earlier, the ones at the murder scene and the slaughterhouse, and the way they'd practically eaten her soul. As she'd told Terrible, toad magic was serious magic; those charms could be anything, for any purpose, and they were strong enough to sting her even through her narcotic haze.

"Hey, Lauren? Maybe you could stop acting like my

legitimate questions aren't worth your time, do you think? How does it not bother you that someone doing whatever it is he's doing has a supply of toad bones?"

"This isn't our case, Cesaria. We're investigating the Lamaru and their psychopomps. When that's done, maybe we'll look for this guy—and by 'we' I mean the Squad, not you—and find out what he's doing. But we don't need to get distracted, and that's what you're doing. Focus on the case at hand, please."

Chess opened her mouth, shut it again. Lauren was right—well, she wasn't, but it didn't matter. They were only here in hopes of finding some evidence that Chess was correct in thinking the dead bodies had been members of Maguinness's family and that he was thus at war with the Lamaru.

But then, hadn't the people who'd attacked Ratchet, who'd been about to destroy the building with that hideous thing still in her bag, been Lamaru?

Maybe. Probably. But Lauren didn't know about that, and Chess couldn't tell her; further reflection had failed to show her any possible way to explain what she'd been doing in that building.

At least not outright. "I was thinking, though. If the Lamaru are doing something with psychopomps, they might use toads, right? So if this guy has a steady supply of them, maybe they came to him? Maybe he made some illegal magic for them, and they didn't pay him or something, and that's what started the fight?"

Lauren's sigh carried all the way across the room. "And when we catch the Lamaru, we'll ask them, and make a case against them. This isn't one of your Debunking cases, where you can just follow your whimsy wherever it leads. This is a Squad case, and there are protocols to be followed."

Chess's hand closed over the charm and snapped the

thread holding it, quickly so Lauren couldn't see. Maybe harder than she needed to; if she didn't break something she was going to start screaming. "Why the fuck are we here, then, if you don't care about Maguinness or his connection—"

"We're here because you made it sound like he might have witnessed something, or like perhaps he'd been victimized. So I thought we'd come in and see if we could get him to talk while he slept, and if we couldn't we'd wake him up and question him. He's not here. Fine. So we have a quick look around and we leave. Unlike you, I actually want to solve this case. I'm not Bound, remember? I'm not getting an extra grand a week just for keeping my mouth shut."

Even her Cepts were barely enough to help keep her voice calm. "I'm trying to solve the case, Lauren. I want it solved just as much as you do, and you know it."

Lauren shrugged. "Then stop going off on tangents."

"Fine."

Fuck Lauren, and fuck her focus. If she didn't want to listen to Chess, that was her problem, but Chess wasn't about to give up. There was a connection between Maguinness and the Lamaru, and it was more than the Lamaru picking some of his children to kill or him trying—and succeeding, to some extent—to kill them in return. It had started somewhere. They'd found each other somehow. That both were involving themselves in the same type of magic, or at least in connected magics, could not be a coincidence.

Lauren could do whatever the fuck she wanted. Chess was going to solve the case. She turned back toward the wall, ready to finish her search—the room ended only a few feet away—and caught sight of a shadow, a thin vertical line in the smooth dirt.

The edge of a door. It thrummed with power when she touched it, sent vibrations up her arms, but wasn't warded or hexed. Wasn't even locked. Apparently Maguinness felt it was safe enough in his little dwelling.

She'd wondered vaguely why all the beds were so small when Maguinness himself was so tall; here was her answer. His bedroom.

Her Hand twitched a little when she picked it up and used its candle to light her way. The flame danced, sent shadows waving onto the walls. The walls . . .

Covered in skins. Not all of them were animal.

She took a deep breath. Wasn't like that was news. Maguinness was a sick fuck; big shock.

A sick fuck who slept on a mattress stuffed with herbs beneath a wire canopy frame of some kind. She assumed it had once held more skins arranged as draperies, but those were gone. By the side of the bed sat a battered wooden table; its surface was covered with dust-free spots where ornaments or candles had rested.

The only other item in the room was a trunk. Not the one he'd taken onstage with him, but a different one, covered in pink silk faded to dusty salmon and radiating black energy like a revving engine.

She glanced back through the open doorway; Lauren had disappeared around a corner. "Lauren!"

"What?"

"I found his bedroom. He's got a trunk in here you might want to come see."

She expected the other woman to sigh again, or groan, but she didn't. Instead her footsteps sounded on the dirt floor and she appeared in the doorway a moment later.

Her face crinkled into a little moue of disgust. "I can feel that thing all the way over here."

"Yeah, it doesn't improve when you get closer. Come on."

"I really think this is a waste of—"

"I know. But we're here, right? So let's just take a look anyway."

The trunk's lock was a flimsy tin affair; Chess picked it, although she thought one good yank would be enough to break it.

She also thought she must be higher and fuzzier than she felt, because until the lock clicked open it didn't occur to her to wonder what exactly the trunk was doing there. Why had he left it behind?

Only one way to find out. She tugged up the heavy lid.

Power breathed out of it, power and the sick, rancid stench of death. Both women gasped. Chess's tattoos heated; her skin crawled. Not just power, not just magic. Ghosts.

She spun around at the same time Lauren did, her hand already finding the zipper slide of her bag. She had graveyard dirt in there, she had—

Nothing. The room was empty.

What the fuck? Nothing else made her feel that way, it had to be . . . In the trunk.

Not a ghost, though. At the bottom of the trunk, alone and small in the center of the half-rotted boards, lay a thick bundle of what looked like burlap. Chess reached for it with her still-gloved hand, but Lauren was faster.

Her bare skin touched the burlap. Energy flashed through the room, roaring ravenous energy; Chess saw Lauren's face change, her eyes grow wide, and then—Holy shit, what the hell?

It wasn't just Lauren's expression that changed. It was her entire face. Her features. Her hair. For a split second Chess saw another woman beside her, like a double exposure, before Lauren yelped, dropped the bundle from her shaking fingers, and scrambled away from the trunk.

"Are you okay? Your face changed, it—"

"I'm fine." Lauren huddled against the far wall, her arms wrapped around her waist and her knees drawn up. "I'm fine."

"You—" No. *Unlike you, I actually want to solve this case* still rankled, and she doubted Lauren would actually talk to her anyway. More to the point, Chess didn't want her to.

Instead she grabbed another glove and carefully lifted the thing out of the trunk. Energy sped up her arms even through the latex covering her hands; her vision wavered for a second, curved around the edges like looking through a fisheye lens. Lauren gasped behind her.

"Chess, your face!"

"What?" Setting the bundle down felt good. Too bad it wouldn't last; she had to untie the dirty string holding it together.

Or, not untie. She pulled her knife from her pocket and cut the thing.

"Your face—it changed, you looked like someone else."

"So did you, for a second there."

Lauren said something else, but Chess didn't pay attention. The edges of the burlap fell open; her heart sank into her stomach when she saw exactly what she suspected she'd see.

Another toad fetish. But this time she knew what it was for; seeing Lauren's face change, feeling that awful tingling that meant *ghost,* was more than enough to tell her, bizarre as it was, hard as it was to believe.

Bound with ghosts, powered by whatever the hell was stuffed inside it and whatever the hell Maguinness had slaughtered to create that thick miasmic energy making it hard to breathe, what she was looking at was a glamour so powerful she hadn't even realized something like it could exist. A glamour that went beyond illusion and into transformation. This was what Maguinness's daughter had tried to steal back from her, in the Market. Chess had had the parts laid out on Edsel's counter; the child must have seen them, must have recognized them. That's why she said she wasn't stealing. That Lamaru fetish came from Maguinness.

Most glamours only changed the surface; she could see through them, as could any witch. Like the door that led from the Lamaru's tunnels and into Maguinness's place—she'd seen it, and Terrible had known something wasn't right. But this . . . It didn't simply hide things, it changed them. Holy shit. She'd never even heard of such a thing.

Her mind ticked through the possibilities, each one more awful than the next. Soul-powered spells even stronger than the one she'd encountered months before with the Dreamthief. Undetectable Hosts; wraiths inside living bodies, the witch's soul so intimately bound with the ghost that they behaved as one, felt like one entity, and could leave the body at any moment to wander and fly and perform evil.

All right there in front of her. All terrifying. And all the work of a man who might at that moment be anywhere, doing anything, and she couldn't do a thing about it.

Chapter Twenty-eight

The Church provides these psychopomps not because only Church-trained psychopomps can take souls to the City, but because only Church-trained psychopomps are proven safe for ritual use. A wild psychopomp is still a wild animal.

—*Psychopomps: The Key to Church Ritual and Mystery,*
by Elder Brisson

It was almost three o'clock in the afternoon before she managed to stumble into the Market with her mood even darker than her sunglasses. All that work. She'd been the one in danger with Maguinness—and still was—she'd been the one who'd wanted to check out his place, to check out his room. She'd been the one who'd found the fetish.

But Lauren had practically snatched it away from her, and she had not a doubt in her mind that Lauren planned to behave as though finding it had been all her doing.

After all, technically it wasn't connected to Chess's case, right? So Chess got to piddle around running Lauren's errands, and Lauren got to look like the golden girl in front of the Elders—as if she needed more of a boost in their eyes.

Which wasn't really fair. Chess wasn't an Inquisitor, she was a Debunker, and as such all this jockeying-for-position shit wasn't part of her job. She didn't have to worry about promotions or quotas or whatever else the Squad members had to worry about. Debunkers got bonuses, and if she needed help solving a case it looked bad for her, but beyond that she didn't worry much about Church politics or looking impressive. Which was probably a good thing.

But part of the reason she became a Debunker was so she wouldn't have to take orders from somebody else. Wouldn't even have to work with anybody else. So not being in charge on her own investigation, giving up her independence . . . felt like a fucking iron band around her throat.

Edsel smiled when she got closer to him. "Hey, baby. Guessing you got my message, aye?"

"Yeah, what's up?"

The black lenses of his sunglasses shifted to the left, then to the right. Nervous, then. An anticipatory shiver ran up her spine; not that she wanted Edsel to be scared or in danger, but if he had good information for her . . . Hell, if he had really good information, Bump would kick him some cash, and with his wife pregnant he could use every penny, she knew. She'd like to see him get it. Would have given him some herself if there was a way to do it that wouldn't have offended him.

He jerked his head to the right, indicating she should slip behind the counter. Okay, change that "nervous" to "really nervous." She'd never been back there before.

Not that it was all that different. Just everything on the counter looked upside down, and the power from the really valuable objects, the rare things Edsel kept out of public reach, skittered along her exposed skin and under her clothes, a cheery little high she hadn't expected.

"Aye, run this down for you, baby. You ever hear the name Baldarel?"

"I— Yeah. Yeah, actually." Baldarel was the author of the book on ghost magic she'd picked up in the Restricted Room two days before, the one she planned to look through when she went back there after talking to Edsel. "Why?"

"Got a friend got some friends, if you dig. Gave me the

tell them Lamaru, they been talking to the dude. Getting him in some of them work. All letters they been sending, ain't ever seen him for real. Figure maybe the Church got some knowledge where he at, maybe find they like that."

Slim. But something. "Thanks, Edsel. That might come in handy."

"Hear knowledge, too, they gots them an enemy. Whatany they got the gear-up for, they tryin to push causen someone after em. Somebody strong, if you dig. Them figuring they get them plan workin, them win. What tell were gave me, anyroad."

Hmm. Again, not much she didn't know, although the idea that the Lamaru didn't quite have their plan in place, or ready to go yet, reassured her a little. People who rushed things made mistakes. Maybe she could catch them in that mistake? Maybe they'd already made it, by involving Maguinness in whatever fashion they'd involved him—by buying his magic and not paying, probably, as Terrible had suggested.

Still, it was something, and at the moment she was pretty desperate. The Church could hide, pretending there wasn't a problem, for a few weeks. Maybe even a month. But at some point they'd run into a problem. At some point the Lamaru would come forward.

She'd do anything to keep that from happening. And it looked like she'd probably have to.

Unfortunately, figuring out what to do wasn't proving to be easy, and the slight confidence boost the conversation had given her faded as she forced herself to read every title on the lower left section of the Restricted Room shelves again. And again.

No question about it. The Baldarel book was gone. What the fuck? Books weren't supposed to leave the Restricted Room. Not ever. They weren't even supposed to be taken into the library proper.

But it was all based on the honor system. There were no security sensors in the books, no detectors hidden in the walls. Just Goody Glass hunched behind her desk, glaring at everyone and guarding the key like a gold-hoarding dwarf.

Goody Glass hated her. The feeling was mutual. Still . . . the book may or may not have contained information that would help her, but the fact was she couldn't find out now. Not to mention what it could mean if someone had deliberately taken it to keep her from finding it.

So she pushed the door open and approached the desk. "Hey, Goody Glass. Did one of the Elders—"

"Good morrow, Cesaria." Goody Glass stared pointedly at Chess's knees until Chess finally caught on. Shit, she hated that woman.

But she gave her a quick curtsy anyway, wished her good morrow just as if she hadn't already done it not half an hour before when she'd asked for access to the fucking room to begin with. "Did one of the Elders maybe take a book from the Restricted Room?"

"It is not permitted for books to leave the Restricted Room."

"Yeah, I know, but I thought maybe—"

"It is not permitted for books to leave the Restricted Room, Miss Putnam. Art thou implying one of the Elders has committed a crime against order? Has broken the rules, which are laws, which are Truth?"

"No, that's not what I meant, I just thought— There's a book missing."

"Impossible." The Goody half-turned away from Chess, lowered her eyes back to her novel and scratched her hairy chin.

"Forgive me, Goody, but it is possible. The book was there three days ago. Today it's not. I believe that's pretty much the definition of *missing*." She heard the impatience in her voice and didn't care. Yes, she could be disciplined for her rudeness; no, it wasn't a good idea to express her own feelings despite how Goody Glass had never bothered to hide hers since the day she'd discovered the truth about Chess's background.

But she didn't have time to worry about it just then. She was supposed to meet Lex in an hour to take a look in the tunnels, and she wanted to have a chat with Elder Griffin before she left.

Goody Glass slammed her book on the desk with an echoing thud. "Art thou being impertinent?"

"Impertinent" wasn't really the word for what Chess wanted to be at that moment; "violent" would have been more accurate. Or "high," but that was a given.

What she didn't want, though, was to get in trouble or stand there arguing any longer. So she clenched her fists behind her back and lowered her eyes. "I didn't intend to be, Goody. But I need that book, and it's not there. And I thought— You see everything that goes on in here, I mean, you know everything, so maybe you had some ideas."

Her respect for the Goody went up one tiny, unwilling notch when she saw the woman wasn't buying her cheap attempt at flattery one bit.

But at least she answered, stretching her black-cloth-encased arm to the phone on her desk. "It's been a busy few days, Miss Putnam. I'll call someone to help thee search for the book. What was the title?"

Chess told her, and watched her mildly revolted expression switch back to fully revolted. "What need hast thou of that book?"

"It's research for a case."

"What sort of Debunking case involves research of that nature?"

"It's—it's not a Debunking case. I'm working with the Black Squad, and—"

Goody Glass shook her head. "Dangerous. Dangerous and unnecessary. I will call someone to look for it, if thee insist. It may take some time."

Chess opened her mouth to argue, but shut it again. What was the point? She'd go downstairs and tell Elder Griffin instead. He'd help her look, and wouldn't Goody Glass love that. So instead she just forced out a terse "Thank you" and headed for the stairs.

Shit. It was starting to get dark outside, and she didn't have much time before she had to meet Lex. Either way, the book was a wash for the day, and since the Dedication was the next day she couldn't count on having much time then, either.

The ceremony itself would only take a couple of hours, but there was usually a meeting afterward to anoint a new Elder and discuss changes being made or whatever else came up, and those took the better part of a day.

Elder Griffin wouldn't be pleased when he heard the book was missing. And she wanted to show him the fetish. She'd never really worked with him before, not like that; he oversaw all the Debunkers but didn't generally get involved. This was different. It might actually be fun to talk to him about it, to see if he had any theories himself.

With all the work and planning being done, and the shock of what had happened, the hall buzzed with activity. A couple of Elders she'd never seen before whispered past her to disappear around the corner, the Liaisers huddled in a small group against the opposite wall, a few Goodys carried stacks of files up the stairs. All of them with somber expressions and hushed voices. She'd never felt so much tension in the building, so much fear coating her skin. It made her want to hide. Instead she forced herself to knock on Elder Griffin's door. It opened so fast she wondered if he'd been waiting for her.

"Ah, Cesaria. Good morrow. How fare thee?"

The wan smile on his normally peaceful face looked like it hurt. She curtsied and greeted him, forced a smile of her own, and followed him into his office.

He slumped into his chair with less than his usual grace. "Cesaria, how do you think the Lamaru have learned to create these psychopomps, to turn our own against us? Hast thou formulated a theory?"

"I— Yeah, I have. I think I have. Here." She hoisted her bag into her lap and pulled out the bagged fetish parts. "I—I was attacked. I'm fine, it wasn't a big deal. But they had this. I think they got it from this street vendor in Downside, who sells potions. He's been doing toad magic, I know, I—" She dug out the toad bone she'd taken from the bed. "These were all over his place. And he had a fetish that was more like a glamour, it changed my face and Lauren's when we touched it. She took that one."

Against the pallor of his skin the dark smudges around his eyes were pandalike; the wide fear in those eyes was anything but. "Transformational magic. This is how they're controlling our psychopomps."

Chess nodded. "I think so, I— You already know what happened in the slaughterhouse. What they were doing."

"I was informed, yes."

"That guy Maguinness, he was the one who bombed the place. He was trying to wipe out the Lamaru."

"So Lauren said. She seemed to feel that was proof he was on our side, working with us, no matter how wrongfully he chose to do it. I see by thy expression thou dost not feel the same. How do you find working with her?"

She shrugged. "She's okay. I mean, we're not best friends or anything, but she's okay."

"And you feel you're being given an equal voice in the investigation?"

"Mostly." Discretion warred with the need to discuss

her suspicions; suspicions won out. She told him about her little chat with Maguinness—a carefully expurgated version—and about Edsel's information that the Lamaru had an enemy. "Lauren thinks he's only peripherally related, that he has this personal problem with them and we should let somebody else deal with him. I think he's important, that he's the one who started all of this and sold this stuff to the Lamaru to begin with."

"Ah." He sat back, clasping his hands in his lap the way he did when thinking. "You feel he's working with the Lamaru?"

"No, at least not anymore. I think he was, but— Have you heard of this Baldarel person? He wrote a book on ghost magic; it disappeared from the Restricted Room. Someone told me they'd heard the Lamaru were corresponding with him. Maybe he taught Maguinness, too. Maybe that's how they met."

"I have heard of him, yes. At one point he desired to join the Church; this was before I entered training, I believe. A very powerful spellworker, but an unorthodox and unethical one."

"Where is he now? Can we get in touch with him?"

"Hmm. I believe he passed to the City not long ago, or at least so the rumor states."

"So the Liaisers can find him? Can we—"

He shook his head. "I apologize, my dear, but we cannot involve a non-Bound employee in the case. And"—he held up his hand—"I do not believe the Grand Elder will approve another Binding payment. Especially not now, when our very existence hangs by a thread."

Shit. The first thing she'd had in days that looked like it might end in an answer instead of more questions, and she was getting a big fat *no*.

"Can we at least see if we can confirm his death?"

If the Lamaru had been working with Baldarel, they might have killed him. If Maguinness had been working with Baldarel, he might have taken great offense to that killing.

Of course she could still be right about it being related to nonpayment for supplies. Debunking cases were usually solved by following the money; she couldn't help that her first instincts always led her straight into people's wallets. But any new theory was a new chance to solve the case, right?

Elder Griffin smiled. "Indeed. Wait a moment."

She watched as he pulled up a computer screen and started typing, soothed by the clicking sounds his fingers made on the keys but made ever more anxious by the frown darkening his face. "No. No, it appears he has not passed—at least, I find no certificate of such here. And no address."

Rumored dead, but not dead. An address the Lamaru were writing to, but no address listed in the Church system.

Baldarel had disappeared. And Chess knew a damn good place to disappear to.

If Maguinness and Baldarel were the same person, it would answer a lot of questions—how he'd known to find them at the slaughterhouse, for example. It would also create more. The Lamaru were learning from and at war with the same person?

Unless Baldarel had, by letter, advised them to visit "Maguinness." He'd wanted to check them out in person, to see what kind of people he was dealing with, and she guessed he'd found out. And now he was slowly leading them into trap after trap. She almost admired him, but she was more terrified by him. Someone who could use the Lamaru like lapdogs—how appropriate—and get them running scared was definitely someone she didn't want to fuck around with, and that someone knew who she was, had read her.

But hadn't come after her. Why?

The whole thing made her head hurt; or would have, had she been capable of feeling physical pain. As it was she was simply tired, her thoughts running creaky circles in her head like an exhausted treadmill mouse. Baldarel and Maguinness and dogs and toads and Lamaru, rooms and streets crimson with blood . . . Terrible's hands on her skin, his mouth on her throat—

"I have an image here, if thou wouldst look." Elder Griffin turned the slick flat screen of his desktop toward her; a flash from the overhead light turned it momentarily into a blank silver slab, revealing nothing. "Is this the man you encountered?"

The screen cleared. With very little surprise Chess found herself nodding, staring at a picture of a young Arthur Maguinness—a young Baldarel—leering out of a grainy scanned photo.

"Yeah," she said. "Yeah, that's him."

Chapter Twenty-nine

> One who will perform dark magics will stop at nothing else; evil is evil.
>
> —*The Book of Truth,* Veraxis, Article 915

She'd never been in this section of the tunnels before. Well, that wasn't a surprise; she'd never been in a lot of sections of the tunnels before. With the exception of one night, when she'd used them to escape from the train platform outside the City of Eternity, she'd really only ever used them to travel between her place and Lex's. And with the exception of that one night, never alone.

Lex always seemed to know where he was. She generally had some idea, enough to be fairly certain she wouldn't get totally lost down there—and there were exits—but nowhere near the kind of confidence he displayed.

It wasn't just fear of being lost that kept her from feeling entirely comfortable with the idea of wandering around alone down there, though. The night she'd made her escape from the platform—from the Lamaru who'd chased her there—she'd literally stumbled upon some of Slobag's dirty little secrets: dead bodies in the tunnel, executed men rotting away beneath the earth.

It wasn't an experience she cared to repeat.

Add to that memory the antipathy any witch felt to being underground, to the concerns and confusion over what she and Elder Griffin had discovered, and Chess would have been twitchy even without the Nips in her system. Or without the memories that refused to leave, or the jumpy, irrational certainty that Lex could tell when he looked at her that she'd been with Terrible, as though even after a couple of showers and a night of sleep he'd left imprints on her skin.

Outside it was only five-thirty or so. Inside it was eternal fluorescent-bulb night, stark and unnatural, with deep shadows that moved when she wasn't looking and snapped back into place when she turned around. Playing tricks on her, those shadows—the sneaky games of children, of twisted little bodies . . .

Ugh.

Lex must have noticed her shiver. "Be you wanted to come on down here, Tulip. Ain't made you, I ain't."

"I know, I just— How much farther?"

"Ain't much long now. You feelin it?"

She thought for a second. Did she? Beneath the speed twitches and general nerves, the memory of Maguinness's hideous family and . . . everything else . . .

Yes. Something was down there, now that she focused on it. They weren't close enough for her to get a read on it, though.

She told him as much, and he nodded. "Aye, ain't far now. You know what's on the happening, though? Who it be? Ain't like thinking of them Lamaru using my tunnels."

"I'm not sure it's— Ouch!" She folded her arms over her chest, trying to think of another way to put it. "There's this potions guy, set up a booth in the Market? My market, I mean. He's got a cave, or something. Up at Ninetieth and Foster."

"He the one got this, then?"

"I think so, yeah." She thought so; well, no, she knew so. So did Elder Griffin. Hopefully so would Lauren, when Chess finally got in touch with her to tell her; she was out with her father, with their phones off.

It didn't matter much, really. Knowing Maguinness/ Baldarel's true identity was all well and good, but it meant absolutely nothing when they had no idea where the bastard was hiding.

Lex led her to the right, into another, dimmer tunnel. "So more'n one set down here. Ain't likin that, Tulip."

"Yeah. Me either."

His lips moved; the closest he could get to a smile. "Guessing you ain't."

"When do the wires come out?"

He shrugged. "Nother week or so, them tell me. Be good when they do."

"I really am sorry—" The apology ended in a gasp, a choke that bent her double. They were close now, she felt it, energy punching her suddenly like a surprise blow to the gut. The tunnels had a curious dampening effect on magic sometimes, she'd noticed; it didn't dissipate the way it did above ground, becoming something one eased into, felt tingling long before reaching the actual place where it had been performed. Rather it stayed tight, lurking like a pocket of darkness between streetlights.

"Got it now, aye?"

She nodded. Oh, that was awful. Really, really awful. It wasn't just the horrible sensation she remembered from the toad fetish, or the slithering wrongness of Baldarel's family. Something deeper, more shocking clung to it, hung beneath it like slugs on the bottom of a rock. Death magic—death itself. The void a life left behind when it was ripped without mercy from a body.

"Lookin kinda pale, Tulip. You right?"

"Right— No, not really. There's— Let's just hurry up, okay?"

He shrugged. "That's what you're wanting."

His fingers on her arm helped keep her feet steady;

they sped up, feet making muted splashing sounds through the thin stream of . . .

The thin stream of pinkish water, turning ever deeper red with every step they took. Lex noticed it at the same time she did; his muttered oath was like a spur in both of their backs.

They didn't have to go far. The body lay just around another curve. Chess saw the few light strands of hair beneath the sticky dark blood, saw the empty chasm where the chest had been—

Vanhelm had been slaughtered. Not just murdered, no; no clean gunshot wound or slit throat. No death curse finally bringing an agonizing but outwardly unremarkable end to his life by a stroke, a heart attack, the slow shutdown of his internal organs.

He didn't even possess those anymore. He lay there staring at the ceiling with his milky eyes wide, his chest cracked open and plundered.

But the thing that made her shut her eyes, that turned her instinctively to Lex to hide her face in his chest—making her feel like a total pussy for doing it but unable to stop herself—were the teethmarks.

Three deep breaths of the clean detergent-smoke-and-Lex scent of his Blanks 77 shirt was enough to clear her head a bit, at least enough to force the bile in her throat back where it belonged. She shifted away, embarrassed, to see Lex's own face pale above hers; but he lit a cigarette with a smooth movement and tilted his head back to blow out smoke. When he looked at her again his color had returned, his brows raised in the way they did when he was about to be particularly Lex-like.

"That some shit, aye?"

Absurdly, she laughed, a short gasp of laughter like the bark of a yappy dog. Dogs . . .

Chess plucked the cigarette from his fingers and dragged from it herself, taking a step closer to Vanhelm's ruined body. Okay. To say she hadn't been expecting this was an enormous understatement. What the hell was going on? Could the Lamaru . . . ?

Well, yes, they certainly could have. And Vanhelm had been working with dogs; the sorts of dogs who left teethmarks like— Damn, those were some big-ass dogs.

Pulling a pair of gloves from her bag, she crouched by the body to take a closer look. Nothing like a mutilated corpse to get a girl's mind off other things.

Something wasn't quite right. That Vanhelm had been attacked by dogs—that he'd most likely been killed by dogs—seemed plain. The long teethmarks, the way his throat had been—she swallowed hard—ripped open, the claw marks on his cheek.

But while blood still colored the water flowing beneath and around him, growing paler now as he bled out, there were no splotches of it on the dry cement. A dog attacking and killing a human might eat that human's organs; much as the thought made her stomach churn, she could see it happening. But would they have been able to eat an entire intestine without its touching the floor or leaving stains or marks anywhere else?

And peeking into Vanhelm's abdominal cavity showed none of the—well, none of the *mess* she would expect to find had dogs removed those organs. It looked like they'd been cut from him.

So why would someone wait until he'd been mauled to death by dogs, then tidily remove his heart and stomach and . . . yuck, everything else?

Someone must have had excellent control of their dogs. And someone must have needed those parts for a spell. Fuck! Murdered bodies had all sorts of power, power she didn't even want to think about. Not that she had a choice. As with everything else in her life.

Lex leaned over her, peering down. "Dogs ate him all up, aye?"

"I don't think so." She explained her reasoning to him, stumbling a little over the words. Even in her line of work, it wasn't common to utter sentences like "His stomach doesn't appear to have been torn out."

Lex nodded. He'd lit another cigarette; in the stifling air, still thrumming heavy with power, the smoke hung around his face and half-obscured his features. "So somebody cut them parts out, usin them for they witchy business."

"Yeah, but, Lex . . ." She bit her lip. He wasn't going to be happy with what she said next.

His raised eyebrows told her he already had a good idea what was coming. "Aye?"

"I need to report this. I need to tell them about the tunnels. If he's down here, using them for—"

"Oh, nay, nay, Tulip. Ain't havin no Churchcops down here, ain't you even think—"

"Lex, I have to. This man is a susp— Ow! He's a— I have to. I can't just pretend this didn't happen."

"You able to pretend a lot of other shit ain't happen, so I think. No trouble you just add he on the list, aye?"

"I can't."

"Ain't you can do what you like? You ain't never give em the true tale on Chester, recall. Ain't never tell em how you spending your off-days neither, aye?"

She blinked; stood up so fast it made her dizzy. Dizzi*er,* actually, as the power throbbing around her was doing a pretty good job of that all on its own. "Are you—are you threatening me?"

He shrugged. "Just givin you the true."

"But—" She stopped. But what? She wasn't stupid, and she wasn't naïve; and she wasn't sleeping with him anymore. Which meant, as far as he was concerned, all bets were off.

And honestly, even if she had still been sleeping with him, he might very well have drawn the line at this. The

Church wasn't, to her knowledge, even aware that the tunnels existed, or at least that they were so extensive. Those old municipal maps she'd accessed on Lauren's tracker were decades old, from BT.

Certainly the Church had no idea a minor drug lord and his crime family used the tunnels as their own private transportation system and dumping ground for inconvenient bodies. And whatever else.

If they knew, they might be driven to take steps. Fill the tunnels in, most likely. No one was supposed to be underground unless they were visiting the City of Eternity itself.

So this was serious, and she had no doubt Lex took it so. And she did, too. But how the hell could she tell Lauren that Vanhelm was dead and not tell her how she'd found the body, or where? How could they move him without possibly destroying evidence . . . ?

She hadn't really looked for evidence yet. "What about those fetishes and stuff you saw? Were they here?"

Oh, he really was a smug bastard. He tilted his head, smirked at her in that particularly irritating way he had. "Maybe. We havin a trouble on this one?"

She couldn't look at him as she replied. "No. No trouble."

"Aye, that's good, Tulip. Real good. C'mon, lemme show you what's on the finding."

His hand under her elbow helped her step over Vanhelm's corpse, then pulled her around the bend.

Magic hit her so hard that she stumbled, clutching at his arm like a drunk. Damn, every time she thought it was as bad as it could possibly get, it got worse. It filled her nose and mouth, a sludgy miasma of death and misery and dark clotting blood. So strong, so—

"You right, there?"

She barely managed to nod. "I'll be fine."

"Guessing pretty bad, aye?"

"Not fucking good."

He smiled, shrugged. "You know I ain't can tell, me."

"Yeah, I know." She'd never been jealous of his imperviousness to magic before, but she sure as hell was now. This was like death in vapor form.

Oh, and good; there were Vanhelm's lungs, dropped against the curved wall, out of the water. In between them sat the fetish, its body covered in sticky blood. It appeared to be leering at her, its toad lips stretched wide so she could see herbs stuffed inside like a mouthful of insects. That explained why the power was so much stronger here. Murdered blood combined with already nasty black magic equaled things she didn't even want to think about.

She grabbed her little camera, and a couple of Cepts while she was at it.

Lex leaned against the wall, watching her. "Thinking on something."

"Yeah? What's that?" The camera flashed. Those same awful thick crooked stitches up the toad's belly, like railroad tracks laid by a tripping lunatic. Carved on the toad's legs she noticed what appeared to be glyphs or runes.

She sighed and stepped closer, ignoring how her nausea increased as she moved in, tried to take some close-up shots to capture the individual glyphs in each frame.

"Maybe could move that body outta here, aye? Drop him off somewheres?"

"Really? You'd—" She turned, unable to hide her surprise. At least, unable to hide it until another thought occurred to her. One a lot more likely than the idea that Lex was simply being her helpful pal or something. "Wait, why?"

"Why not, aye?"

"Yeah, but—why would you want to help me?"

"Damn, Tulip. You ain't never stop bein mean. How's a man sposed to think, when you always like that?"

"Oh, come on. Like you're nice all the time or— What was that?"

"What?"

"Shh!" She waited, camera poised in her hands. Had she really heard that? Or had it been—

No. There it was again. A soft sound, a series of pattering noises. Like little bare feet running along the—

Oh, shit. "Lex," she said, stepping closer to him. Keeping her voice very low. "I think we need to get out of here, okay? Fast."

"Aye? Why? What's troubling you?"

"I think it's them, the vendor I told you about and his family—one of them, at least, and I really, really think we don't want them to find us here."

"You always so anxious and shit. Got my knife, me, and a gun—"

"No. This isn't—"

The laugh echoed down the tunnel and over her skin. Every hair on her body stood on end.

Lex's brows drew together. "One of em?"

"Yes, please, can't we just—"

A bang like a gong, loud and painful in the enclosed space. Another, a higher tinny ring.

The lights snapped off.

Chapter Thirty

> The Church makes the laws. The Church makes the rules. The Church expects to be obeyed.
>
> —*The Book of Truth,* Laws, Article 3

Every muscle in her body screamed *run*. They had to get out of there, away from Vanhelm's destroyed body, away from the lungs and the fetish, out of the tunnels.

But Lex's hand squeezed her arm tight, like he knew what she was thinking. She heard the sound of his gun cocked slow in his other hand as his lips pressed to her ear. "Ain't just go off now, Tulip. On the minute, aye? Let's us have a thought first."

Water splashed; how far away was it? Was that a foot? Something else? She pictured things dropped into the little stream, curse bags and gris-gris and fetishes, things the water would carry to them and drag against their feet. Her heart pounded so hard that she thought it might literally leap into her mouth.

"Ain't get that flash you got neither," he continued. "No draggin them eyes our way. Gimme a hold-on, aye?"

She nodded, knew he could feel her move.

"Know my way right, I do. Door ain't far, dig, back where we come. Stay on me, aye?"

She nodded again. Not enough air, there wasn't enough air in the tunnel, not enough in the world. Fresh air, clean air, air that didn't thrum with magic, lie thick and heavy in her lungs with it. Choking her. She clutched his arm, wiry and hard under her hand.

Gentle pressure forced her to step back, to turn slightly. Even her sense of direction started to fail her; had she turned all the way around, or just partway? Which way was she facing? The darkness around them was a solid thing, completely impenetrable.

Lex led her forward. Chess tried to keep her feet on the curve at the bottom of the wall, out of the water. Lex tucked her hand around his waist so her chest pressed against his back. It made walking difficult, but it wasn't as though they were just taking a stroll, and she had to admit it reassured her.

Which kind of pissed her off, but this wasn't the time to start wondering when she'd suddenly gone soft. People, she was discovering, were like cockroaches: If you allowed one in, more were sure to follow.

Another giggle, low and smooth. Her head whipped around, eyes straining to see something, anything, in the pitch-black air. Was that closer? Where were they?

Lex didn't stop. They took another step, another. Chess's foot hit something heavy, something solid and unyielding and yet somehow . . . somehow dull against her toes. Vanhelm's body. She swallowed hard, kept moving.

Something ran past them. She felt it stir the air against her skin and bit back a scream. Sweat trickled down her face, into her eyes; she wiped them against Lex's shirt without moving her hand. Without stopping. They had to get out, get out, get—

A sharp tug on her hair. A scream; not hers, not her voice. Hot foul-smelling breath on her cheek; Lex yanked her to the side and the gun went off in a flash of white light. Hot blood spattered on her skin.

And they ran.

No more secrecy now. No more hiding. Still they didn't use the light—all she saw were huge red spots before her eyes from the gun flash—but their feet splashed through the water, pounded the cement beneath them while voices screamed in rage and pain behind them. More than one voice, many voices, echoing around her, reaching into her and yanking out her soul.

Lex ran faster, pulling her along through the darkness. He was the only real thing in the world; this wasn't real, none of it was real, it was a nightmare she had to wake up from.

They were being chased. The screams turned to howls, catcalls. And then, horribly, to barks.

Dogs. Vicious ones. Baying in the tunnels, their low deep barks scratching her, hurting her, and it wasn't until her frantic mind realized they hurt that she realized why.

It wasn't real dogs following them. Not living dogs. It was psychopomps.

A dozen maybe, or a hundred. She had no idea, no way to tell. Didn't have the breath to tell Lex, and no point anyway; psychopomps couldn't be shot, couldn't be stabbed, couldn't be killed. Couldn't be stopped without magic, and even if she had time to get her supplies she somehow doubted these particular hounds would respond.

They hurtled around a corner with the baying getting closer, the unearthly howls of the psychopomps, sounds she'd never heard a psychopomp make before.

Her head turned to the left as they entered another tunnel, and she almost fell. Their eyes. She could see their eyes, their glowing purple eyes. Hundreds of them. Hundreds of eyes, oh shit oh fuck they were going to die, have their souls torn from their living bodies and devoured or savaged, those were not normal psychopomps holy fuck what were they she was going to die—

No! She ran harder. Pushed herself with everything she had, keeping up with Lex. She couldn't look back, didn't want to look back, couldn't stand to see them ready to bite.

Lex jerked her away, yanked her arm up. She stumbled on the steps, her right hand hit gritty cement. The dogs were right behind them, so loud she couldn't even hear herself scream.

He grabbed her, pulled her close and pushed them both out onto the street in one motion. Fresh air poured over her, moonlight blinded her. They had to keep running, she didn't know where they were or where to go, but they had to get away from those teeth gnashing behind them, those vicious jaws ready to snap shut on her legs—

Lex shoved her to the side; a staircase waited there, tucked off the sidewalk beside the tunnel door. She raced up it, her legs aching and heavy, Lex's hand on her back, the dogs howling in the madness of the— Wait. What?

No dogs.

All she heard was heavy panting, hers and Lex's, as they leaned over the splintery wooden railing of the stairs and peered down.

The tunnel door below slammed shut. Chess leaned over farther, trying to see—well, she didn't know what she thought she was going to see, but she felt the need to look anyway—but it was closed tight.

A few seconds later it flew back open. Vanhelm's body flew out, landing with a horrible squelchy thump on the curb.

The door closed again. This time it stayed closed.

Chuck's wasn't normally so crowded, but the Runouts were playing, so Downside's disaffected—which was pretty much all of Downside, at least all of the area around Fifty-fifth and Ace—turned out in droves.

Usually Chess would stand around outside to see if any familiar faces showed up to share a smoke and a few minutes of empty conversation. Tonight she didn't dare. She was wired to the gills and she was terrified, and a nice loud bar seemed like the best possible place to spend the next several hours.

Or most of the night. Chuck's stayed open until five, and she planned to be there at closing time and hopefully drunk enough that she wasn't scared anymore. A night home alone, jumping at shadows and staring at the front door, waiting for the knob to turn, did not appeal, and she had enough speed to get her through the Dedication ceremony at dawn and the day ahead.

"Safety in numbers" was one of those tropes she knew from experience to be utter bullshit. But she still felt better, pushing past the bouncer into the sultry, sweaty bar. She didn't stop to pay; she never did. Nobody charged Bump's Churchwitch, not if they didn't want trouble. Chess wasn't the type to cause any, but they didn't know that, and she had no compunction about using her job—such as it was—to get in free. Besides, she spent enough at the bar to make up for it.

The crowd shifted and flowed beneath the red-gel-covered blue lights, a small land mass in constant state of earthquake. Chess fought her way to the bar, pushing past girls in miniskirts and fishnets and guys with high spiked hair. Silver flashed at her from cheeks and eyebrows and lips, silver from chains connecting ears to noses and locked around skinny necks. All of them familiar, maybe not the individual faces but as a whole. The Lazy Cowgirls blasted through the speakers, and she relaxed inside for the first time in days, tapping her foot.

One finger to the bartender got her a beer. A few minutes of searching got her a seat in a booth against the opposite wall. The vinyl beneath her was sticky and torn, the tabletop covered with graffiti and grime. She lit a cigarette and slouched against the wall, scanning the crowd, picking out a few people she knew from around.

Yes. This was a good idea. None of Baldarel's people would be able to get in here, and even if they did—well, shit. If they did, they'd probably bring their dogs with them, and everyone would die. The thought was like swallowing a rock.

No. No, this wasn't a good idea. No matter how comfortable she was, she shouldn't be there. She was putting them all in danger by being there.

Except . . . Why had the dogs disappeared when they reached the street? Psychopomps didn't do that. They didn't just disappear; they were summoned, they retrieved whatever soul they were supposed to retrieve, and they took that soul back to the City. No Banishing needed, no nothing.

And nobody summoned a psychopomp for fun; it simply didn't happen. You couldn't play with a psychopomp. It wasn't like they chased sticks or shook hands or anything. Even in training no one had ever summoned a psychopomp without having a ghost for it to collect. The instructing Elders always had a few ghosts for them to practice on, in a special room devoid of anything that could be used as a weapon.

It was possible to summon a psychopomp without a ghost being present, and there were a few cases on the books of psychopomps being used as murder weapons, but it was rare, and the chances of getting away with it were virtually nil. A person killed by having their soul ripped from their body carried certain marks; it was easy to detect. And once detected, the energy signature of the one doing the summoning was tracked, and the murderer caught.

Either way, she'd never heard of a psychopomp simply disappearing without claiming a soul. Never.

So why the hell had Baldarel's done it? *How* had they done it? She hadn't heard any words of power spoken, smelled any herbs, or felt any sort of extra energy blast of the type that would come from magic like that. Of course, considering that she'd been terrified and frantic and overloaded with the power already in the tunnels, that wasn't saying much, even if you discounted the speed in her system.

At least it answered one question. She knew why they were underground. Ghosts were stronger there. If she were creating ghost bound spells she'd probably go there, too, for the extra power; it made sense that Baldarel would live there.

She stubbed out her smoke, drank her beer. Inspected for several minutes a flyer for a Poor Dead Bastards show. The idea of staying there still made her nervous; being the catalyst for mass murder by psychopomp wasn't something she particularly wanted. But the *life* around her, hot bodies crowded into the small blaring space, beer and sweat and smoke, smiling faces, dazed drugged-out faces, even the slightly queasy look of one or two people who would probably be puking in the alley soon—it made her feel part of something, just as much as working for the Church made her feel part of something.

So, yeah, she'd stay for a while. Think about things. Try to—

Terrible walked in.

Her stomach leapt into her chest. Should she— What should she do? Leave? Leave was probably the best idea, yeah, but to leave she'd have to walk right past the booth he'd just emptied with a jerk of his head and taken over.

With his . . . date. She guessed.

Amy was the only one of the girls he saw to whom she'd been introduced, and that had been a fluke. The girl now sitting beside him, her face bright with the slightly desperate chatter of the ignored, was new—new and, Chess thought a little meanly, looked as though she'd never had a serious thought in her dyed-red head.

Pretty enough, though. Especially if one's tastes ran to

heavy makeup and voluptuous breasts. Which Terrible's apparently did—well, what man's didn't, really. She must have been a real disappointment for him in that department. He must have—

No. No, and no. She was not going to do that to herself, not anymore. Whatever. He was on a date, fine. Out with some other girl—now draped over his chest like one of Dali's melting clocks—who didn't even have the grace to look a damn bit like Chess so she could comfort herself with the idea that he was hunting out some kind of replacement for her.

Not that that actually would comfort her, but at least she could think shitty thoughts about it. As it was, she just felt shitty, and that was infinitely worse.

She managed to make it to the bar for another bottle of cheap self-esteem without being seen, but as the bartender handed it to her, she felt it. Him. Felt his gaze on her. How she felt it she didn't know, but she felt it just the same, knew the second she turned around she'd catch him looking at her.

Sometimes she hated being right.

His face didn't move while he watched her walk back to her seat; not so much as a blink or a twitch of the lips to indicate he even knew who she was, that they'd ever shared a conversation, much less bodily fluids. Fine. She could do that, too.

And she didn't have to do it alone. She sat back down, threw a glassy smile at the guy sitting in her booth.

"Saved your seat," he said.

Terrible was still watching. She smiled wider. "Really? From a fate worse than death?"

It took him a second, but he got it. "Yeah, you could say that. Or maybe I saved me. You should have seen the guy who wanted it."

"Not your type?"

He shook his head, his expression solemn. He had a

nice face; any other time she would have studied it, would have wondered how he looked from the neck down. Would have considered finding out, if she had nothing else going on.

As it was he was nothing, just a face at which she could smile and pretend to be having the time of her life. She didn't think that if she blinked she'd recognize him again when her eyes opened. "I like them smaller," he said. "Makes me feel like a man."

"Do you not usually?" Terrible had looked away; now he glanced at her again, shifted in his seat. She leaned forward a little, keeping tabs on him out of the corner of her eye.

"Am I supposed to?" He didn't appear to notice her sneaky eye-corner spying.

"Well, it's usually—" Oh. Oh, no. The music changed. Chess recognized that song, heavy with bass, those sonorous opening notes . . .

The Stooges, "I Wanna Be Your Dog." The song that played the night she and Terrible first—that night at Trickster's, the night she'd fucked everything up for the first time. The most serious time. The night before she'd gone ahead and slept with Lex, sending all of them down the slippery road to hell.

"Usually?" The guy prompted, but Chess barely noticed. She wasn't looking at him. Couldn't look at anything or anyone but Terrible, because he turned to look at her and she knew by the way his brows drew together and his mouth turned down that he remembered, too.

His date took the opportunity to slide her hand over his chest, stroking her fingernails over his throat. His gaze faltered; he turned back toward the girl and her ample bosom, and Chess couldn't sit there for another second.

She mumbled something, she didn't know what, and got up, still clutching her beer. The music filled her head, swelling inside it, and the pressure was going to kill her in another minute, it hurt so fucking bad.

To get out of the bar she'd have to walk right in front of him. No way. Let him see her hasty and embarrassing retreat? Fuck that.

Her seatmate tried to stand up, reaching for her, but she ducked away and headed for the bathroom, using the sheer force of her embarrassed rage to propel herself through the crowd. They were in her way. They deserved to get shoved or elbowed.

It was early enough that nobody was waiting for the bathroom. Or hell, maybe she just didn't see the line. All she saw was the door and the promise of a few minutes of privacy. That was all she needed. Just a couple of minutes, just to get her head together, just until that fucking song ended and she could pretend it never came on in the first place.

It was also early enough that the bathroom itself—a cramped room only slightly bigger than a closet—was fairly clean, or again, maybe she just didn't see it. She couldn't see much, not with the tears blurring her vision.

The wall was cold, hard white tile. She pressed her forehead against it, wrapped her arms around herself. Shit . . . just . . . shit. Why had he come there, of all places? Why couldn't she grow a fucking pair and stop being such a baby? What was the matter with her that she couldn't just get over this—over him? She'd never done this before. Never had any regrets when something didn't work out. For that matter, she'd never had anything to regret, never had someone she wanted to keep around for any length of time.

It wasn't like she hadn't done this to herself. She had. Every step along the bastard trail had been made by her alone. She'd gone back to Lex's place that night instead of crashing at a friend's place like Terrible wanted her to—had tried to get her to do, he'd had his phone in his hand. She'd stood in Lex's bedroom and thought he looked like a good time, so why not have one? She'd lied to Terrible the next day, convinced herself that was the right thing to do.

And all of that she could maybe excuse herself for. Maybe.

Chess lied to herself every day; it was just something she did, like taking her pills or making sure she had a pen in her bag. Little lies, mostly. Insignificant. Of course there were big ones there, too, like telling herself that she was more than just a junkie who got lucky enough to possess a talent not everyone had. That she was alone by choice and that she was not terrified of other people because they couldn't be trusted, because they carried filth in their minds and pain in their hands and they would smear both all over her given half the chance.

But the biggest lie she'd ever told herself, the one she'd told herself for months after that night at Trickster's, was that she wasn't falling in love with Terrible, hadn't already fallen. That all those nights spent sleeping on the couch, shutting her eyes against the lamps because sometimes if Terrible saw her lights on he'd stop by, meant nothing; that he'd call and offer to buy her dinner and she always said yes even though she wasn't hungry at all; that their friendship was casual when, in fact, they saw each other almost every night.

Hell, wasn't that why she'd slept with Lex to begin with? To escape those feelings? So it was useless to pretend that continuing to sleep with Lex as time went on, that spending the evening getting itchy with Terrible and using Lex to scratch with afterward wasn't . . . twisted.

And now she was paying for it as the music pounded into the bathroom and she huddled against the icy tile and cried the tears she knew she deserved to cry.

Someone knocked on the door. Shit, couldn't they

even give her two minutes? The fucking lyrics had just started, she'd barely been in there for thirty seconds.

"I'll be right out."

They knocked again.

She swiped at her eyes with her hands, but the tears wouldn't stop. They'd been building up for so long, turning into a lake behind a dam, and now the wall had been breached and there was no plugging the holes. "Just a min—"

The door swung open, and Terrible slipped into the room.

Chapter Thirty-one

[It's always tempting to think you can get what you want by giving a man what he wants. Don't be fooled by this! And teach your daughters not to be fooled either.
—*Mrs. Increase's Advice for Ladies* by Mrs. Increase]

She tried to spin around and hide her tears, but he was too fast. One hand caught her arm and whirled her back to face him; the other hooked around her waist and pulled her against him.

Their eyes met. Oh, no. If he thought he could come in here and grab her and she would just drop her pants for him again, after all the things he'd said to her, after his fucking apologies, like he was ashamed of himself for wanting her—so fucking patronizing—and he'd changed his number and there he was with a date sitting in a booth outside—

Then he kissed her, and she caught herself in another lie. Dropping her pants was exactly what she was going to do, what she was doing, because without her telling them to be, her hands were already at his belt, tugging the buckle free, practically ripping his jeans open and shoving themselves inside. She wavered on tiptoe, straining to reach his mouth, unable to hold on to his neck or shoulders because there were other, far more important parts of him to grab, and his hands slid up and down her body, tangling in her hair, heating her breasts and neck and back.

Her jeans and panties fell to her calves, her back fell against the tile. He pushed her shoe and the bundle of fabric off one foot—his mouth left hers to bite the sensitive skin over her hipbone—and came back up, hooking his elbows under her thighs to lift her. Her jeans dangled from her right foot; it probably looked ridiculous but she didn't give a damn.

And apparently neither did he. His mouth took hers again, hard, stealing her breath and her sanity. She knew she should resist, should tell him he couldn't just storm in here and use her like that, but who was she kidding. She'd never been able to resist temptation—especially an unhealthy one—and at that moment he was another pill, another line; one she needed, one she would die if she couldn't have, and her entire body was already vibrating in anticipation. So she twined her arms around his neck, holding on tight, while he shifted her in his arms and drove himself into her.

She cried out, her voice echoing off the tile. Somewhere deep in her mind it registered that anyone standing outside the room would probably hear her, but she didn't care. Couldn't help herself anyway, because his fingers dug into her skin and his hips pounded her into the wall and it was just as it had been the day before, when she couldn't see or think or do anything but feel. Like electricity running through her body or the thick velvet of magic making everything tingle; she was hot and cold and shivering from both, her senses in total overload. He refused to give her a break, to slow down, to let her process what was happening. It terrified her. It made her want to scream with pleasure. She bit him instead, hard on the neck, the taste of his skin filling her mouth while he gasped and let his head fall back.

Behind him the door started to open. How he heard it over the sound of her voice and his own she didn't know but he did, swinging her around and using her to slam the door shut again. The thin wood rattled in its frame and kept rattling, booming along to his punishing rhythm. Dimly she wondered if the door would break; then his grip shifted again so his hand could slide between them and she didn't give a shit if it did.

His mouth left hers; he leaned back, looking down. Watching as he slowed his pace, rotated his hips, made breathless sounds fly from her mouth. And she let him, stretching her arms up to grip the top of the doorframe, stretching her back so her shirt rode up and pulled tight across her chest and he got a better view. She got a good view herself, watching his face; the same absorption on it she'd seen when he was fighting, when he was working. Total focus. On her. It was thrilling.

He came back to her. His lips found her throat, sucking hard enough to leave a bruise, crushing her to him again. She tilted her head, and clutched his shoulders so hard that her fingers were sore.

The door bucked and creaked behind her; fists on the other side added their own offbeat clamor. She and Terrible were together on their side of it, she completely in his power, unable to move, unable to do anything but let him have her and to glory in the fact that he was. She fisted the hair on the back of his neck, yanked his mouth back to hers, lights exploding behind her closed eyelids. Her body tensed, she was ready, she was so fucking ready, and she had to pull away because she had to breathe and when she did their eyes met—

It was too much. She couldn't take it, couldn't handle it, not when she knew he'd be able to see everything, all her feelings and stupid vulnerabilities plain in her eyes. She dragged her gaze away as her back arched and her head fell against the vibrating door and her body shook and clenched around him and somewhere in there she thought she screamed but she wasn't sure.

His low, thick voice danced over her skin. Her head

spun, she couldn't see, couldn't think. Only his voice, only his hands on her and his body inside hers and against hers told her she really existed, that this moment really existed. Somewhere in the back of her mind she thought if he hadn't been clutching her she might go through the door herself—which wasn't a totally unrealistic idea—and simply disappear.

But it wouldn't happen. She knew it wouldn't because he was there, because his strong arms held her up and his big chest pressed against hers and his breath heated her skin, because he shuddered under her hands and his body went rigid and she came back to awareness with her forehead resting on his shoulder and her arms aching from holding him.

This time there was no long dazed pause; he moved again almost immediately, setting her down on her unsteady legs. She braced herself against the wall. The cool tile shocked her back to reality, where the door was still bucking and angry shouts came through the wood.

He tugged his jeans back up and yanked the door open. From her position behind it she couldn't see what happened, but the sounds told her well enough; the strangled *gawk* of someone being grabbed by the throat, the dull crunch of a fist against flesh, the tumbling thuds of a falling body.

"Any else wanna bang the fuckin door? You bang that fuckin door again, I kill you. Dig?"

Apparently they did. Certainly she didn't hear anyone arguing. No surprise there.

He slammed the door behind him and leaned against it, staring at the floor like it was about to jump up and attack him.

She fastened her jeans, stuck her foot back in her shoe while an ugly certainty crawled into her brain to make a home. "If you apologize to me again, I will hit you."

His shoulders lifted; not a shrug, but a hunch, as if he expected her to hit him anyway. Which, given what happened the day before, she couldn't exactly say she blamed him for. "Aye, well . . . guessin I ain't can say that one again. Ain't like I come in here by surprise."

She dug around in her bag for her pillbox and pulled it out. The heavy silver filigree, rough against her palm, grounded her. Gave her whatever it was she needed to keep talking. "So why did you come in here, then?"

He shook his head.

"Terrible . . . come on, just—"

"Aw, shit. Ain't can do this, Chess. Fuckin speeches and shit. Whatany you're wanting, I ain't—ain't can give it. Not on the now, dig. Not after . . ." He shook his head again.

"After what you saw," she finished. "After you found out about—Lex."

"You ain't even quit seein him now." Light flared through the room as he lit a cigarette, the enormous flame on his black steel lighter blowing heat against her skin while he eyed her. "Givin you knowledge bout them tunnels, aye? Still seein him, and you wanting me to—"

"But that's different, it's work, and—"

"He ring you up, gave you the knowledge? Or he come at your place for ought else, just happen to drop it down while he there?" The darkness in his eyes, the bitterness in his voice, told her he already knew the answer. And why wouldn't he? He knew Lex—not as well as she did, but he knew him. Knew Lex wasn't the type to hand out chunks of helpful information out of the kindness of his heart.

Knew because when it came right down to it, he wasn't the type to do that either.

She looked away. Lit her own smoke, wishing it was something stronger than plain tobacco. "Yeah. He came for something else. But he didn't— I ended it. Really, really ended it, and he knows it."

"Only knowledge Lex got is what Lex wanting."

"Yeah, I know. I know that, that's why I never— It never meant anything. He never meant anything to me. And I never told him anything about you, never. But he did help me out, he helped me out when Kemp was killing hookers and he helped me out . . ."

Shit. What did it say about her that telling the truth always made her sound like such a liar?

"Earlier tonight he took me into the tunnels. He—"

"Earlier? You with—"

"No, just listen, please. He told me they found—*ow*— I needed to see the tunnels. And we were chased, we found a body, one of the— He was dead and they chased us with psychopomps and it was—You remember, who we saw yesterday. And I found out more about him, he isn't just—*ow!*—he's bigger than we thought. He's someone else."

Her beer still sat on the floor where she'd set it, by the sink. He scooped it up and took a long drink. "What the fuck, Chess, keep tellin me I gotta give you trust an then—"

"Because I can't lie to you, I don't want to hide things from you anymore. I'm trying to make it right, Terrible, and I can't help it if there's things you don't— Would you rather I kept lying and pretended I hadn't seen him and hadn't found out what I found out? I have a job to do and that's what it was, that was all it was, he had information I needed."

"Aye? Maybe I got some knowledge you need right, too. Lex trying to push Bump off Forty-third, aye? Sent he men just on the other night, start gunfights there on the border streets. Figure he tryin kill em all, stick he own in afore we—"

"What?"

"What?"

She shook her head. "Say that again. Say what you just said again."

His brows lifted, but he did as she asked. "Try an kill Bump's men on them border streets, put he own in."

"To push Bump out. To take over."

"He got he goals, aye, an having me an Bump dead at the top of he list. You *got* that fuckin knowledge, aye? You had it months gone, you know what he givin the try, an you still—"

"He's trying to push them out and take over." Her phone had fallen into the bottom of her bag; she'd forgotten to slip it back into its little pocket. She dug around for it, found it and pulled it out. "That's what he's doing. It's not the— Not *them,* I mean, maybe it still is, but it's him too, he's taking over their plan."

"What you chatter—"

"Maguinness. Baldarel." Pain shot up her arms; she gritted her teeth and ignored it. It was a warning shot, not serious yet. "From the tunnel. Yesterday, and tonight with Lex. He's killing them, whatever they were doing he's doing it now and they're running."

Where had she put Lauren's number? Had she even— No, there it was, in Recent Calls. Great. She hadn't solved the mystery, not entirely, but she had a big piece now. A *big* piece.

The phone threatened to slip away from her when she tried to cradle it between her shoulder and her ear; Terrible reached out to steady it while she cracked her pillbox and tossed three Cepts down her throat. Her body hummed with exhaustion; exhaustion mixed with that bizarre post-sex energy that sometimes hit her and made it impossible for her to sleep. Or rather, impossible for her to sleep without taking something heavier. She had plenty of those, and she might even take one—at least she would if she could convince herself it was safe to go back home.

For a fleeting moment she considered asking Terrible if she could crash on his couch, but no. He probably wouldn't let her, not just then; and if he did, he would feel imposed upon. Pushed. She wasn't stupid enough to think this conversation—the first real one they'd had in weeks—meant she was forgiven. Far from it.

What it did mean, though—at least she hoped it did—was that he was willing to talk to her. That maybe he was willing to start trying to get past her betrayal. Just the thought made her heart pound. She'd do whatever she had to do to make sure she didn't fuck that up, and pressing him for a place to stay would definitely be fucking it up. The last thing she wanted was for him to wonder if she was using him, or make him think she was after something. Something else.

No answer on Lauren's cell; no answer at her house—Chess had that number scribbled in her notebook. Shit. How long did it take to spend an evening with Daddy? Where could she— She could be dead, that's where she could be. She and the Grand Elder both. Not likely, perhaps, but definitely in the realm of possibility.

Chess turned to Terrible, standing behind her smoking with his back still braced against the door. Fuck, there was another problem. They were going to have to leave this bathroom soon, and given the door pounding, she imagined they were going to have a very interested audience when they did. Just what she needed.

"Lauren isn't answering. D'you think maybe . . ."

He looked at her as if trying to assess exactly what she was thinking or what ulterior motives she might have. Either he found none or he worked out some way to handle it, because he gave her a half-shrug, a lazy lift of one shoulder. "Aye, take you over if you're wanting."

"Thanks. Really, thanks a lot."

"Aye, well. Figure Sela ditch out, aye?"

Right. Oops. "That was your date?"

He nodded.

"Yeah . . . maybe you should go check, huh? Just to be sure?"

"What you do, wait up here?"

"Think I can get out that window?"

He considered it, smiled a little. "Let em all get the thought I were in here on my alone?"

"Oh. Right. That would be kind of—"

"Naw, ain't give a fuck what them got in them heads. Here." He crossed to the window, its glass long since replaced by plywood. It took him a minute to force it open; paint cracked and the entire frame screeched and shook. "C'mon."

He lifted her up, helped her squeeze out the window. "Go on out front, aye? Meet you up there."

She wanted to say something. Wanted to lean back in and kiss him, to touch his face or fix the strands of pomade-slick hair that had fallen over his eyes. But this new armistice was too delicate; she was acutely aware of it beneath her like a tiny storm-tossed raft. For the first time in weeks she had some hope, honey-poison sweet and thick on her tongue and in her heart. She didn't think she could stand losing it again.

So instead she just nodded and watched him push the window down until the slab of weathered plywood covered the hole where he'd been.

Chapter Thirty-two

> Not all danger comes from without. But most of it does.
> —*The Example Is You,* the guidebook for Church employees

The alley she stood in was bordered by a chain-link fence and full of Dumpsters and shadows. Maybe walking back through the club itself wouldn't have been so bad after all. So people would have seen her, would have known, so what? She wasn't ashamed of it.

Of course, it was entirely possible *he* was. Wasn't that a happy thought. She wrapped the edges of her cardigan closer around her and headed toward the street, picking her way through the garbage. It stank back there, of trash and puke and urine—typical alley smells, with stale beer thrown in for spice.

Things rustled as she walked past them; rats, other rodents. Bugs maybe. It was a little early for them yet, but Downside roaches were awfully hardy. Everything had to be, to survive.

Music drifted through the walls as the band started to play. They usually played a pretty good show; she kind of wished she could stay. Wondered if Terrible's date had. They hadn't been in the bathroom that long. Ten minutes? Fifteen? It was entirely possible that whatever-her-name-was—what bullshit, Chess knew her name—just thought Terrible was waiting in line or had gone off to talk to someone else, and was still sitting in the booth looking vacuous and waiting for him to come back so she could flop all over him again.

She sighed. What a stupid emotion hope was. And incredibly premature in this case. There was no reason to—

The growl stopped her in her tracks. Where had it— Surely it was just a dog. Just an ordinary stray. It always paid to be cautious around a stray, but it wasn't anything to worry about, not really.

She took another step forward. The growl grew louder. Something moved behind her, a clattering noise like a wooden box falling.

Her blood went ice-cold in her veins.

Okay. Okay, no need to panic. It could be anything. Anyone. It didn't have to be a psychopomp after her, right? Psychopomps didn't usually growl. It was just a dog.

But even a dog was bad enough. And combined with the sick, twisted energy slick with blood and mucus that invaded her, surrounded her, insinuated itself over her skin and into her hair and mouth in a curling black mist that tasted of sewage and death, it was especially bad.

Even as she started running she knew she probably wouldn't make it. The fence on her right was too high, the mouth of the alley too far, and they were behind her, she heard them racing through the garbage.

She wanted to scream but couldn't spare the breath. Didn't know if it would matter anyway—who would come to investigate a scream? Nobody. Maybe in other parts of town they might, but not here.

Her feet slipped on slick piles of trash and she stumbled, almost fell. The energy around her thickened, stealing her strength. She was going to be sick, the end of the alley didn't look any closer and she couldn't run anymore, she was going to be sick—

Another growl behind her, lower and louder, echoing in the small narrow space. She pushed herself as hard as she could, but it was like running through treacherous mud sucking at her feet.

She wasn't going to make it.

Terrible was going to hit the street soon, what would he think when she wasn't there? Did he trust her enough again to know something had happened to her? Or would he assume she'd ditched him?

She should drop something. Leave something. So he would know she hadn't ditched him, that she hadn't played another trick on him.

The street loomed in front of her, she was almost there. Behind her a snarl, the sound of panting—

She reeled around the corner of the building just in time to see Terrible's date slap him.

Ordinarily she would have ducked back out of sight, but nothing in the world would induce her to step back into that alley, not even the very good chance of being assaulted by a furious woman who'd apparently just found out what her date had been up to in the bathroom with another girl. With *her*.

Luck was with her in that, at least. Sela didn't turn around. Instead she did something much worse; stalked off on her five-inch platforms to where Terrible's Chevelle sat under a streetlight, and leaned against it with her arms folded over her chest. "Taking me home, you are," she called. "I ain't walking back alone."

Terrible glanced at Chess. "Ain't can just leave her—"

"I have to go with you. I mean, I can't stay here." Quickly she told him about the alley. "He's here, he's probably watching, if I don't get out of here—"

"Shit." He glanced at Sela, back at Chess. "Ain't gonna be a fun ride, aye? She pissed up right. Ain't can say I blame her, guessin somebody gave her the happening. . . ."

"It has to be better than sitting here waiting to be attacked."

"Ain't so sure you ain't gonna be," he muttered, but he jerked his head just the same for her to follow him to the car.

". . . and whoever the fuck you thinking you are, you runcy slut," Sela went on, glaring at Chess from the shotgun seat, "you want him, you fucking take him. See how you like it when he forgets calling *you* causen he too busy with some other dame. Thinking about some other dame. Amy don't even see him no more causen of it, you knowing that?"

"Hey," Terrible started, but Sela cut him off.

"So ain't you think just causen you in this car now means any damn thing. It ain't. He pretending it do, he lying and saying it do, but it ain't. Pretend that other dame just he friend, so he say, but ain't like it true."

Terrible turned up the music, trying to drown Sela out with Nashville Pussy. It didn't work. She reached over and snapped it off. "Some Churchbitch she is, too. Leastaways that's what Amy telling me. Amy say she met her once and she weren't shit."

Chess cringed. Not that this little monologue wasn't fascinating, but Terrible looked as though his head was about to explode.

He whipped the Chevelle around a corner with a squeal of tires; she checked the speedometer and saw they were doing about fifty-five. Well, she guessed she couldn't really blame him for wanting Sela and her mouth the hell out of his car.

Still, she almost found herself wishing the journey could last a little longer.

"Thinking I seen her too," Sela said. "Some Churchbitch, all her tattoos, thinking she so special. Seen her two weeks past, I did."

Two— What? "What did she look like?"

Sela snorted. "Ain't so fucking hot. Hair like mine, and she poking around some vacant lot. Betting she looking for more magic shit, trying to hurt people. Them all—"

"She had red hair?" It had to be Lauren. None of the other Church employees—at least none Chess could think of—had red hair.

But Lauren had supposedly just arrived in town the day Chess met her.

"Aye, red like mine. And she skinny, too, she like you, got no—"

"Two weeks ago? You're sure?"

Sela rolled her expertly made-up eyes. "I ain't stupid. Were two weeks past, causen I'd just got paid the day afore. I recall it causen I'd bought new shoes and I were—"

"What was she doing?"

"Why you care?"

Terrible was looking at her, too; she caught his eyes in the rearview. He snatched them away before she could see the expression in them.

"It might— I mean, I'm just curious."

"Just snooping around, she were. Like she looking for summat. I seen her and can't even take a guess why Terrible so—"

"She was snooping around in a vacant lot?"

"Aye. Freaky, iffen you asking me. But guessing that what Terrible like, aye? What he deserve, sneaking off into the bathroom with some rigmutton *cunt,* leaving me on my alones in the bar, and other men talking to me and me saying I got me a date there and he fucking some *whore* while everyone outside the bathroom hearing them—"

" 'S enough, Sela," Terrible cut in.

"—and ain't even got the balls to pay me my fair jannocks and gimme the tell he own self. Cocksucker."

They squealed around another corner. Terrible cut the Chevelle up sharply in front of a rundown house with a sagging roof.

Sela glared at him. At both of them. "Ain't wishing you luck, bitch. Or you neither. And ain't you call me again, dig? Done, Terrible. Bad enough I gotta hear that Churchbitch name all the damn time, now you pull this trick on me. No more. You go fuck yourself, aye?"

She threw open the heavy door of the car and flounced out, nearly slamming it on Chess's hand.

Chess barely noticed, though. She was too busy giggling, helpless snorts of laughter forcing themselves out from between her tight lips. She didn't want him to see she was laughing, to think she was laughing at him.

She glanced at him guiltily, expecting to see him frowning at her. But he wasn't even looking at her. Didn't appear to even realize she was still in the car. His shoulders were shaking, hunched over the wheel. His face was turned away.

Her laughter died. "Hey . . ." She stretched out her hand. Should she touch his shoulder or something? Shit, if he was that upset . . .

But he was laughing. He turned to her and she saw it, and her own giggles came rushing back, and she climbed over and collapsed into the front seat with tears in her eyes, she was laughing so hard. She couldn't even have said why it was so funny; it was horrible, what they'd done to Sela. She couldn't blame the girl for being angry or for saying any of the things she'd said. Hell, if Chess had been in her position she probably would have said a lot worse. But for some reason she couldn't explain it just struck her as endlessly amusing, funnier than anything she'd seen in ages, and it felt so good to laugh she didn't bother analyzing it. She couldn't even remember the last time she'd laughed, really, really laughed.

They laughed until her chest started to ache, and then suddenly they weren't laughing and his face was only a few inches from hers. Darkness hid his expression from her, she had no idea what he was thinking. What he thought of her now. It didn't make sense that everything could have changed in the course of one short drive or a few minutes of shared amusement, but how would she know? The sum total of her wisdom on the subject of emotional relationships could be written on the head of a fucking pin.

He cleared his throat. "Guessing we oughta move on, aye?"

"Yeah. I guess so." Was that her voice? It didn't sound like her.

For a second she thought he wasn't going to move after all; her entire body tightened. But then he did, pulling away from her, shoving the car in gear and nosing back onto the street. She gave him Lauren's address, and they rode the rest of the way in silence.

Damn.

There had to be a reasonable explanation. Had to be.

The Chevelle idled outside the modern apartment building where Lauren lived, its engine noise echoing off the cars around them until he switched it off.

Once the moment-that-wasn't faded, her mind returned to the Lauren question. Sela said she'd seen Lauren—well, she hadn't said "Lauren," but Chess couldn't imagine who else it could have been—in a vacant lot two weeks before. But Lauren shouldn't have been there, because Lauren should have still been in—well, whatever city it was she came from. New York?

Surely there was a reasonable explanation for it. It wasn't really a big deal. But it made Chess uncomfortable just the same.

"Want me give you the wait, or what?"

"Huh? Oh. No, I guess not. Lauren can give me a ride home."

His eyebrows rose. "You heading back your place? After them in the alley and what you tell me on the earlier, about—about them tunnels?"

"I'll have her take me to Church. I can spend the night there."

The minute she said it she wished she could take it back. She'd lied and told him that before, let him think she was spending nights in one of the cabins on Church grounds when, in fact, she was in Lex's bed. Told him that lie more than once. And he knew it; she saw it in the way his expression hardened, saw him looking back and remembering every time she'd said that, wondering if she'd been honest about it.

"No, I mean it. Really. Unless . . . could I stay at your place? On the couch, I mean, I'm not asking to—" Fuck. She should have stuck to her earlier resolve not to ask him.

He hesitated. "Ain't thinkin that a good idea, aye?"

"Oh. Right. Yeah, of course, I understand, it's no big deal. I'll be fine."

"Shit." His hands twisted on the wheel. "I give you a ring up an hour on, aye? Iffen you ain't got yourself a bed, you come to mine. My couch, dig. Ain't can have you crashin your place, not with them after you. Cool?"

"Yeah, that's— Thanks. Really."

He shrugged. "Better get you in, aye. Ain't early."

Before she could stop herself or talk sense into herself she leaned over and kissed him on the cheek. One more chance to breathe him in. "Thanks, Terrible."

He just nodded. She gave him one last look and got out of the car.

Chapter Thirty-three

[Church employees work together, united in their common goals: to protect humanity, to punish the guilty, and to live in the Truth.
—*The Example Is You,* the guidebook for Church employees]

Lauren's hair was as mussed as her apartment; it was obvious Chess had awakened her. Either that or she had a man in there, and somehow Chess doubted that that was the case. Even if it hadn't been for the events of the night before, she didn't think Lauren would allow a man to see her in stained sweatpants and a T-shirt with worn-out armpits. It was one of the most unappealing outfits Chess had ever seen in her life, about as sexy as an oozing sore.

The rest of the apartment wasn't much better. Lauren had obviously just moved in, so some mess was to be expected, but this place was all empty shelves and empty food containers. Worse than Chess's place, although Chess didn't leave food lying around. Even if she ate regularly at home she wouldn't have left food out like that; she could practically see the germs breeding in the congealed bits of yuck clinging to the sides of the cartons and bowls scattered on every surface.

How could someone who looked like such a tidy little bitch be such a slob? It just . . . didn't fit.

Like what Sela said didn't fit. "You haven't been here long, huh?"

"No, only—well—" Lauren lowered her voice, gave Chess a grin that might have been conspiratorial if she hadn't still looked off. "I've actually been here almost a month, but my dad doesn't know. I didn't tell him when I got in so I wouldn't have to go stay with him, you know? I wanted a little freedom first."

So much for that theory. Not that Chess had really believed it anyway. Why would the Grand Elder's daughter conspire against the Church?

"I'm going to go take a shower, okay?" Lauren dug into one of the boxes and pulled out a towel. It at least looked clean. "Sorry. I was at the gym and I was hungry so I threw on these old rags. They're comfy, you know? Let me just clean myself up and then you can tell me everything."

Chess didn't believe her, not for one second. The shadows under Lauren's eyes had not come from too much jogging or whatever the hell it was people did at gyms. There was something haunted about Lauren now, something furtive and hunched. As though the other woman was trying to hide inside herself.

Couldn't be done. Nobody knew that better than Chess. But who wanted to get into a discussion about it? Not her. So she did the next best thing and ignored it completely. "Oh, could you take me to Church after? I don't want to go home tonight, not after— Well, I'll tell you about it."

"Elder Griffin said they've been trying to get you moved back on grounds for a while. You're like bait for the Lamaru where you are, you know."

"I'm fine where I am."

"And that's why you need another place to stay tonight?"

Chess folded her arms over her chest. "Are you going to give me a ride or not?"

"Yeah, fine. You're really touchy, you know that?"

When Chess didn't respond, Lauren gave a dramatic sigh. "Whatever, I'll take you to Church. Or you can stay here if you want, I don't care."

With difficulty Chess suppressed a shudder. Stay there? And let all those bacteria crawl all over her while she slept? Ugh, no thanks. "I think the Church is best, really. I have a couple of things I want to look up and I need to talk to Elder Griffin before Elder Murray's Dedication."

"Oh? Why?"

"I just want to talk to him about the case. You know, keep him in the loop and everything."

"Do you have new information?"

Chess forced a smile. "Yeah, actually. Why don't you take your shower, and then I'll tell you about it."

"Yeah, I get it. I stink. Okay, just . . . make yourself comfortable. Here." The couch's pink toile fabric was covered with papers and files; Lauren stacked them up, clearing a hasty space. "Watch TV or something. I'll only be a couple of minutes. And I have some news, too."

Chess waited until the water started running before peeking at the files. Hmm . . . employee records for the slaughterhouse, that was good . . . preliminary reports on the cause of the fire . . . a slim file on Vanhelm with his birth certificate. Why hadn't Lauren told her she had that?

Well, she might not have had a chance. Files didn't always get put together as quickly as everyone would like. And Lauren had just said she had some news, too.

Okay. So, slaughterhouse records, Vanhelm's file, reports. A few pages on psychopomps copied from *Tobin's Spirit Guide*. An employee file—

CESARIA PUTNAM.

Her hand paused in the air above the slim, pale-blue folder. She supposed it was reasonable that Lauren would have her file. She'd already admitted she'd read it; making copies was unorthodox, to say the least, but . . . the Black Squad kind of did whatever it wanted.

That didn't change the dull, helpless anger rising in her chest. Bad enough Lauren had looked at it, read it. She brought it home to study, too? What the fuck?

She flipped open the cover; her eyes ran up and down the lines of print. Name, date of birth, address . . . training grades and test results . . . She turned the page. The commendation she'd received for defeating the Dreamthief, another commendation from a particularly sticky Debunking case in her second year.

It should have ended there, but . . . no. This wasn't her basic file. This was her personal file, her confidential one. Chess's hand shook slightly as she picked up Elder Banks's notes on the results of her fertility test. The edges of that sheet were softened by grubby fingerprints. Lauren had spent some time there, reading that one.

Next came a bundle of papers clipped together; the letter she'd written asking permission to live off-grounds, with comments from her instructors and the Elders—Elder Griffin. He'd been on her side; well, she'd known that. But some of the others, some of the comments they made about her lack of trust in her coworkers, her standoffishness . . .

She didn't want to look anymore. There was nothing she could do anyway. Lauren had a right to look at her file. And much as those soft edges and fingerprints bothered her, she couldn't do anything about it. Couldn't make Lauren unsee any of it or remove the knowledge from her head.

But . . . She flipped back quickly to the first page. There it was. Her picture. The same picture she had in her bag, the one taken from Vanhelm's apartment.

The Church only printed one copy of those pictures; it wasn't like they handed them out for employees to trade like they were kids in school. Well, at least Chess remembered other kids getting copies of those pictures in school and trading them. She'd never gotten any of her own.

So if her picture was still in the file, where had Vanhelm's come from?

The hair on the back of her neck prickled as she dug it out. Same picture. Same background. Same smile, same girl.

But now that she was really studying it . . . *was* that the same girl? The eyebrows were a little different, it seemed; the girl in Vanhelm's picture hadn't plucked hers quite thin enough.

This was crazy. She was crazy. But then . . . two weeks ago she would have said nobody could cast a glamour strong enough to fool a witch. Now she knew differently. At least one person had—she remembered Lauren's face changing when she touched that fetish—and who knew how long the effect of that would last?

Had Maguinness created another Cesaria Putnam? Had the Lamaru? And why?

Something wasn't right here. Her nerves weren't settling. They were getting worse. She didn't want to be at Lauren's place anymore, didn't want to be anywhere near her. Panic spread from her stomach up into her chest, thrumming into her brain. Exactly why, she didn't know, but she needed to get out of there. Needed to think. Instead of innocently messy, Lauren's apartment now looked booby-trapped; anyone, anything, could be hiding in the boxes and clutter.

She was being ridiculous. Lauren was the Grand Elder's daughter. But who gave a fuck. It felt wrong, and she was going with that.

The water shut off, leaving the room too quiet. Chess shoved the papers back in order and closed the file, setting it back the way she thought it had been.

She reached into her bag for her notebook and pen, intending to scribble a note for Lauren and haul her ass out of there before Lauren got dressed. Her finger caught on something; she pushed it aside, almost jumped out of her skin when the apartment filled with a loud, shrill, sustained beep.

Fuck! Lauren's tracker. She'd switched it on. Her hands shook as she dug it out, tried to find the off switch, and realized the sensors in her bag weren't lit up.

The tracker wasn't reading the sensors in her bag; they hadn't been tripped.

So where was the sensor that it had tripped? Number four?

One of the two she'd planted on Vanhelm.

The tracker's high-pitched beep throbbed in her head, a scream of panic she couldn't utter, while she dug around in Lauren's couch until she finally found it.

Stuffed under the cushion Lauren had set the files on; she must have shoved it in there when she saw Chess at the door. Must have been looking at it when Chess arrived and not had time to hide it.

Must have been looking at Erik Vanhelm's shirt.

Chess leapt off her knees, ready to jump over the couch to the front door and get the fuck out of there, but her leap came too late. Just a second too late, it had taken her just a second too long to find the thing, why the fuck had she even bothered, she'd known anyway . . .

Lauren stood in the doorway, her dark green bathrobe hanging open. Water dripped down her bare skin, over the pale curves of her round breasts and flat stomach.

The gun in her hand pointed right at Chess's head. In her other hand, raised to her ear, was her cell phone.

"Stop right there," she said unnecessarily, and then, into the phone, "Yes, now. Hurry up."

The door stood at least two strides away; there was no way Chess could reach it before Lauren pulled the trigger.

And given how cramped that apartment was, unless Lauren was the world's worst shot there wasn't a chance in hell she'd miss.

Okay, Plan B. Whatever that was. Shit! Shit shit shit. "Ha-ha, Lauren," she managed. "Very funny. Put the gun down and get changed. I want to hear your news."

Better come up with a Plan C, because no way was Lauren dumb enough to buy that.

Nope, definitely not dumb enough. She snapped the phone shut and slipped it into her pocket. "Shut up and sit back down."

Chess obeyed. What else was she supposed to do?

Laying her cards on the table might be a good idea. Well, she might as well, anyway. Her hand slipped into her pocket. She had her own cell, she could call . . . who? She still didn't have Terrible's number, and she'd probably get voicemail at the Church.

Which left Lex.

Of course even that semi-useless gesture required she be able to see the phone. And somehow she didn't think Lauren would miss that. Okay. Hold the phone anyway, and wait for a chance. And hope it came fucking soon, because reinforcements were apparently on their way. *Shit.*

She looked at Lauren. "Vanhelm is dead."

Even knowing what she thought she knew, she wasn't prepared for Lauren's reaction. Her face . . . crumpled, literally scrunched up and seemed to slide down; she was unrecognizable. "No. No, he can't be—no."

"I'm sorry, Lauren." The odd thing was, for a second she actually *was* sorry. It was impossible to stand in the presence of such grief and not be touched by it. Especially when she'd experienced something similar not long before.

She'd been lucky. She'd been able to save him. Lauren hadn't had that chance.

Lauren's voice was a harsh, bitter knife cutting through her thoughts. "You're lying."

"I'm not. I saw him. He's dead."

"What . . . what happened to him?"

"He was—" No. Wait. "He was murdered. Cut up."

Lauren knew Maguinness was after them, but she might not know he had his own psychopomp army below the city. Telling her Vanhelm had been killed by dogs might tip her off—might be playing the only card Chess had.

Tears fell onto the dark green terry cloth of Lauren's robe. "No. It wasn't him. It couldn't have been him. He was—he was—"

"He tried to rape me, Lauren." Something else had occurred to her, something that sent rage flying white-hot up her spine. "Or was that a lie? Just like what you told me happened to you. It was a lie, right? You thought you could, what, spook me with it? Distract me? What?"

"He wouldn't have raped you."

"Really? Because he sure was ready to."

The gun wavered in Lauren's hand. Chess had to admit she was impressed that Lauren had held the thing steady for this long; could she even see Chess through her tears?

Didn't matter. She could see well enough to know if Chess suddenly got up and made a run for it, and that was the important thing.

"He wouldn't have. He wouldn't do something like—"

"Something like what? Like pretend to be raped in order to get a rise out of somebody? What the fuck, Lauren? You unbelievable *bitch*." She stared at the gun. Watched it, forced herself to remember it was there so she wouldn't jump off the couch and attack. Lauren had lied. She'd actually *made that shit up*. Just to cause her pain, just to fuck with her. "What were you—"

"I wanted you to trust me."

Chess stared at her.

"What? I thought, if we had something in common, if I opened up to you, you'd—"

"Oh, for— Whatever." Stick to the case, she reminded herself. Get some answers, so that on the off chance she managed to escape she could do something about it. "Look. Vanhelm is dead. How many of you have died? How—"

"You should know. Who did you tell? Who have you been reporting to?"

"What?"

"Who did you tell?"

"I didn't tell anyone." A jolt of pain shot from her wrists up; shit, the Binding. It kept her from telling . . . and it forced her to tell.

Like she'd told Terrible and Lex both, in a roundabout way. Oh, fuck, no. No. She would not give them up to Lauren, absolutely not. All the Lamaru would need were their names; five minutes asking questions in Downside would be enough for them to find both men. And as much faith as she had in them and their ability to survive . . .

Lauren's eyes narrowed; she'd seen the flinch, knew what it meant. Fuck! "You're lying."

"I can help you, Lauren. We can help you. Come with me to the Church, we'll tell Elder Griffin, he can—"

Lauren laughed, a genuine laugh. One that would have been pretty if not for the edge of hysteria lying beneath it. "Are you serious? You think I don't know what the Church will do to me?"

"This is different, you're a Church—"

"It's not different, and you know it. What mercy does the Church show? What mercy did it—did *you*—show Randy Duncan?"

Lauren swept past, toward the door. Chess didn't turn

around, didn't bother to remind Lauren that she hadn't killed Randy Duncan. The Dreamthief had killed him. So she'd been right: This little plot wasn't just about psychopomps and the Church. It was about her. It was revenge.

That was how the Lamaru had known to show up on the corner that first night, the night Lauren had taken her to the vacant lot where the parts had been found; Lauren had told them where she was. It answered her question about why they hadn't come after her yet, when they knew who she was and where she lived. They'd wanted to torture her first, fuck with her. If she died, fine; if she didn't, they could fuck with her some more.

"You're the Grand Elder's daughter, for fuck's sake. Why would you . . . Why are you doing this?"

Lauren gave a harsh laugh. "You don't know anything about me, Cesaria."

The slow tingle of magic crawled over Chess's skin, etched in darkness. A jolt of power went through her. Blood magic. Blood wards. Lauren was locking her in, more effectively than even the most hardcore deadbolt could.

Tires squealed outside; Lauren relaxed. "Good, they're here. We can get this over with."

"Yeah, great."

"Oh, come on. Look." Still holding the gun, Lauren edged across the room and into the little open-plan kitchen, opened a drawer; when she brought her hand out of it she held a syringe. "It won't be bad. I promise. This isn't poison or anything painful. They wanted to— Well, after Randy Duncan you're not exactly popular with us. But you did save me in that fire. When that freak we got supplies from bombed the place and I couldn't get out, you came for me. So I convinced them to do this instead. I don't forget when people do things like that for me, so even though you have to die—"

They were outside, whoever was coming; Chess heard car doors slam in the parking lot outside. Warding hexes or not, gun or not, she had to try now. *Now!*

She vaulted herself off the couch, back toward what she assumed was Lauren's bedroom. There would be a window there, she was sure of it, Lauren's apartment was only on the second floor, and she'd take her chances—

Fuck, ow! Her head jerked back and she leaned into it, trying to loosen Lauren's grip on her hair; shit, it felt like her scalp was coming off. The gun hit the tile with a dull slap, but she couldn't see where it landed.

She drove her elbow backward into Lauren's stomach. The pressure on her hair lessened for a second, long enough for her to gain a few feet. If she could just get into the bedroom she could lock the door, she could scream, surely the neighbors would call the Squad—

Right. Lauren *was* the Squad. They'd call her first, and she'd use her authority to tell them everything was fine, and they'd believe her.

Lauren shouted something behind her and pain, pain like Chess'd never felt before, shot up her arms from the marks on her wrists and blood spattered from the rough edges of them and she fell, it hurt too much to stand.

Footsteps thundered behind her and shook the floor. Hands tangled in her hair, yanked her up onto her hands and knees. A heavy-booted foot caught her just below her throat. It felt like he'd kicked through her chest, through to her soul, they picked her up and she struggled against them, fighting their hard hands, fighting the horrible pain and the helpless dread creeping into her mind. They had her, five or six of them, big men, their skin crawling with filthy power as they dropped her on the couch.

She scrambled back off it, only to be surrounded by legs; they towered over her like a human cage. Without thinking she crawled backward and pressed herself against the wall, wedged herself into the dusty space next to the TV cabinet. She couldn't get out, she was stuck. *She couldn't get out.* For a second she contemplated flipping the cabinet onto them but discarded that idea almost instantly. She wasn't strong enough to move it.

But there had to be something she could do. Even six Lamaru men and Lauren . . . well, fuck, no, six Lamaru men and Lauren could turn her into a grease spot in less than a minute. But they might make a mistake. They'd already made one, involving Baldarel. And she just bet they were pissed about that.

But did they know they'd made it? Did they know that the man they were apparently taking orders from, letting mastermind their plan and informing of their every move, was the same man trying to kill them? That they were little more than puppets, servants to whatever plan he had?

She didn't think so, judging by how Lauren had referred to Maguinness. She just couldn't be sure, and she couldn't get it straight in her head, couldn't get the words and thoughts to focus properly.

"Cesaria." Lauren's voice cut through the panicky haze. She didn't want to panic. If she was going down, she wanted to do it with dignity; if she was going down, she'd do her damnedest to take them with her. The thought calmed her.

She couldn't get out. Whatever she faced now had to be faced; she had no choice.

"I'm sorry, I really am. It was . . . interesting, meeting you. Working with you. We've all wondered about you, you know."

"I can help you—"

"Oh, come on. You're not going to help us, and we all know it. No. Everything is in place, and we worked too long on this—but you can take comfort in something. You'll certainly be remembered."

"What—" Chess started, but she didn't get to finish.

"We need you to tell us now who you told. What you know."

Okay. Take a deep breath. Try to sound confident. "I'm not telling you shit."

"I don't think you have a choice."

She pressed her back against the cool wall, tried to look casual. Torture. She could handle that. She'd gotten good with it, hadn't she? A childhood like hers demanded it. She could leave her body if she had to, leave the pain behind, ignore it all. Once that trick was mastered it never left. "Pretty sure I do."

Lauren smiled and lifted her hands. The sleeves of her robe fell to her elbows, exposing her pale, unmarked inner forearms and wrists. "I think the First Elders would disagree with you."

Chapter Thirty-four

[Above all they demand loyalty, as the Church demands loyalty; and loyalty will be given no matter the cost, for this world is but a bridge to the next. And that is Truth.
—*The Book of Truth,* Rules, Article 426]

Chess didn't know how much time had passed. Twenty minutes? Or several hours? It was nothing more than a blur. Her stomach roiled and twisted. The First Elders would kill her. With pain. Consign her to a spirit prison; she'd be tortured for hundreds of years, roasted in fires, run through with iron . . . Who knew what other surprises they had planned for one who broke a Binding Oath?

They hadn't shown up yet. She knew they would. Sooner or later—probably sooner—she'd stop finding questions she could safely answer.

"You're being ridiculous, Cesaria." Lauren waved the syringe in front of her. "You don't have to die like this. And you don't have to go to spirit prison. Just tell us what we want to know and it can end so much more pleasantly."

"I didn't tell anyone," Chess said, and bit her lip hard enough to cut it when more pain shot up her arms. Her clothes and the carpet around her were soaked with her blood; the TV cabinet she'd huddled next to was spattered with it. She tried to remember that a little blood spilled looked like a lot, but it wasn't easy when the spilled blood in question was hers. "I don't know anything."

"But I think you do. You said you found Erik dead. You saw him. What happened to him?"

"You don't want to know."

"I think I do. I wouldn't have asked otherwise, right?"

What information could they get from that? They knew Vanhelm was dead. Would knowing about his posthumous—so she assumed—organ donation really make a difference?

It might. No way to tell. They'd asked her so many things, it was all starting to run together. She couldn't seem to keep straight what she'd told them and what she hadn't, what she should and what she shouldn't.

But she hadn't mentioned Lex or Terrible. And she hadn't mentioned Baldarel. She had no idea if she should.

Part of her thought it didn't matter, that she should tell them. Drop that bomb in their laps, let them fight it out. Maybe they'd kill one another and forget about whatever it was they planned to do at the Church.

But it didn't feel right. She kept thinking that if they didn't know what he was up to, who they were really dealing with, there was power in that. Power for her, for the Church. There had to be some way to use their ignorance against them, to lead them astray. To give herself enough time to escape—yeah, like that was going to happen—or for . . . for something. Anything.

In the end she could only go with what she felt was right. And something told her not to give them Baldarel. At least not at the moment. When the First Elders showed up she might change her tune.

"Was anyone with you?"

"No." Oh, shit . . . that was worse, it was so much worse, like being shot up with acid, searing up her arms. Blood spattered from the wounds, thicker, faster now. Some vague part of her mind thought it might be because that was a double lie; she'd betrayed the Oath by taking people with her into the tunnels, and now she was betraying it again by lying about it.

The rest of her mind didn't care because that was agony, tearing into her with relentless sharp teeth and ripping her apart like a lion with a raw steak. She threw up on the carpet, she was dizzy, she couldn't think . . .

"Who was with you, Cesaria? Who knows about us?"

"Nobody." She was going to die. Right there. Right then. She was going to die, because the insistent tone of Lauren's voice and the way she leaned forward made it very clear that Lauren knew she was on to something, that the question of who else knew was more important than Chess had originally thought.

Why did she care so much? If the Lamaru were engaged in yet another plan to destroy the Church and take over, why did they care if someone knew about it? Why not just kill her and start doing whatever it was they were going to do before anyone had a chance to warn them?

The answer came from somewhere outside her; the part of her still capable of rational thought, the part that had escaped her body. *They needed to know because they couldn't start yet.* For whatever reason, things weren't quite ready; they had to wait for something, and they were afraid someone would stop them before—

"Elder Murray's Dedication," she gasped, fighting the fresh pain in her arms and the hot gush of more blood from her wrists. Oh, it was so awful, she was filthy and disgusting and she didn't want to die like that. But the Lamaru men were in the room, they were not authorized to hear what she had to say, and it didn't matter that they knew already because she was talking to them and that was enough for the Binding to activate. "It's Elder Murray's Dedication, isn't it? What you're waiting for? Why you can't—"

Lauren's slap barely hurt; what was one more source of pain? "Who did you tell?"

"You planted that ghost at the execution. And the psychopomp, right? A test or something." Yes. It probably was Lauren—Lauren, who'd been in town earlier than she'd originally claimed and wouldn't have had to sign in to see— No, no, that didn't make sense, because Lauren's father hadn't known she was in town. Maybe it was someone else, someone whose name she didn't recognize, and Maguinness had been there simply to mislead.

Something flickered in the air to her right. Fresh energy flicked over her skin, tasting it. Ghost energy, making her tattoos itch and tingle.

The First Elders were coming. Yes.

Lauren saw it, too. "Who did you tell? If you tell us, you don't have to go to spirit prison—we'll let you live if you tell us. Just tell us. Who knows?"

"You planted the ghost so it would—would kill one of us." The last word turned into a scream. The pain was worsening. She had to finish. The First Elders would appear any second and they would take her. She didn't want to go, shit she didn't want to go and she was so scared. So fucking scared and alone but she didn't have a choice. She had to force an end to this.

Had to end it now before they got her to admit that Lex and Terrible both knew what was happening, or at least had some idea. That either one of them might go to the Church. They both knew Doyle; she'd told Terrible to go to him before. She knew he would if he realized something had happened to her. Knew that despite the awkwardness he still cared enough to do that for her.

Keeping the Lamaru from attacking the Church was one thing, an important thing. Keeping the Lamaru from finding Terrible or Lex—that was something else entirely.

That was something she had to do, and would die to do. Was *going* to die to do.

She clenched her fists, putting all the strength she had left into her hands to try to fight the pain so she could speak. "You had to kill one of us. Any one of us. You needed—you needed a Dedication, you needed that much power. Right? That was your plan, right?"

"Tell me who you told!"

"Who planted the ghost? Who planted that psychopomp in the executioner's bag?"

The First Elders burst into existence.

Chess's tattoos shrieked, power flaring over her skin so hard and hot that she thought she was going to explode into flames right then and there and that would be how they'd take her.

She flung herself sideways, knowing it was useless to try to hide but trying anyway. Lauren followed, grabbing for her, attempting to throw her back at the Elders, to serve her up to them.

So forbidding they were. Worse even than when she'd seen them at the Binding. Then they'd been cold and aloof, and bound from doing harm to the living by their own laws and the power of the cast circle and spellwork.

Now they were not bound. Their faces, those hideous ghost-white faces, translucent and eerily perfect, smudged with black circles around the eyes, glared at her. They reached for her, their bodies dipping and swaying like dancers.

Chess grabbed Lauren's hair and yanked. Hard. Hard enough to drive Lauren's face down into the floor with a satisfying thump.

Lauren screamed and hit back. The First Elders advanced slowly. They had all the time in the world.

Chess didn't. She was exhausted and her wrists still shrieked in agony; her head was too light and her body too heavy. Still she fought against Lauren's hands, catching glimpses of the Lamaru backing away into the hall.

Her phone rang.

She was so busy fighting she didn't realize what it was at first. Lauren didn't seem to realize either; she twisted Chess's hair in her fist and tried to stand, presenting Chess to the First Elders like some kind of doll.

"You heard her lie. You heard her break her Oath." Lauren's voice shook almost as badly as her legs. Chess didn't pay much attention to either. Her hand found her phone still in her pocket, slid it out enough to glance down to see who it was as she hit the button to answer.

TNL flashed on the screen. Lex? What was Lex calling her for?

No time to ask. She didn't bother. Didn't even bring the phone up to her ear. She screamed instead. It felt stupid and dramatic but she did it anyway; she screamed Terrible's name in desperate hope that Lex would get the message and that if he did he would do something about it.

Lauren's grip loosened; Chess figured she was looking for the phone, still on in Chess's pocket. Didn't matter. She took the opportunity to twist away—leaving a clump of hair in Lauren's fist, damn it—and headed for the front door. It was still warded but she might be able to get out, all the power in the air might snap the wards.

The Elders flowed around Lauren, their hideous angry gazes fixed on Chess. The door wouldn't open. It didn't matter much, they would simply follow her until they caught her, she didn't have any way to Banish them—

Or did she?

They were ghosts. Stronger and more powerful, but still ghosts, subject to the laws that ruled ghosts. She didn't know if a regular psychopomp would take them, and the thought of trying to use a psychopomp pumped fresh terror into her veins, but what the hell. So what if the psychopomp turned on her—she was going to die anyway, and at least if it did she could avoid the spirit prisons.

And maybe it wouldn't, and it would do its job. Maybe Lauren had some psychopomps that weren't tainted. Chess bet she did, since if the Lamaru took over they'd need a supply.

Her bag was by the door. She yanked the zipper—they were within touching distance of her now, she saw their hands raise, curled into claws, ready to strike her, to grab her.

Her own hands closed around the bag of graveyard dirt and the clump of mandrake. She dared to look down, grabbed the almost empty bag of iron filings and her black chalk.

She used it to sketch a warding sigil on the floor. No effect. Okay, she hadn't thought that would work, but the dirt might.

She flung a handful in an arc. The Elders paused when it hit them, their faces going from angry to furious, their energy increasing. Well, they were going to kill her anyway, right?

Lauren burst through the Elders and tackled her. The iron filings fell from her hand. Lauren's fingers closed around her throat.

No time to think. Just react. She shoved herself sideways, pushing Lauren off and punching Lauren in the face as hard as she could. More pain, in her bones, jolting up her arm. Ignore that, too.

Cold against her skin, the First Elders' hands, snaking over her. Their rage transmitted to her through her skin, oh, fuck, she was too late to stop them.

Her left hand found the iron filings but the confusion in her head, the pain and fear, made it almost impossible to know what to do with them. The graveyard dirt hadn't stopped them. Hadn't done much at all.

She rolled forward, hit the wall. They came at her again. She picked up the filings and, not knowing what else to do, dumped them over her head.

They had power of their own; she felt it merge with hers, give her strength. Not much, but a little, just enough to launch her forward through one of the First Elders' legs, like running through a freezer. Her heart jerked in her chest, shocked by the cold, the anger . . .

And they were really angry now, their faces growing harder, their eyes darker, narrower. If they caught her they were not going to make this pleasant, and they would keep trying. Even if she managed to escape now they would keep coming after her, they wouldn't give up—

She took one desperate second she didn't have to center herself, to open herself up. Where were Lauren's supplies? The Lamaru would have the sorts of things Chess didn't normally carry, items with extra power. Illegal power. She reached for that energy, tried to find it, while the First Elders moved toward her like slow mountains.

Something glimmered to her left. A door. She'd thought it was to a closet, but maybe it wasn't.

Lauren screamed. Chess didn't look back. She leapt to the door, flung it open.

Skulls. Dozens of them, up and down the walls on shelves, spreading out onto the floor. Dogs and pigs and birds . . .

She didn't have her Ectoplasmarker, couldn't have marked the First Elders even if she did. But she was covered with iron—that might be enough.

She didn't have a choice. Blood still oozed from her wrists and her head felt soft, too light for her body. The ghosts were right behind her, Lauren coming behind them, still screaming.

Chess scooped up five of the skulls on the floor and swiped her bleeding wrist along their tops; her hands left bloody fingerprints on the bleached bone. Shoved as much of her power as she could along with the blood, enough to make her voice hoarse and her vision blur.

"I call on the escorts of the City of the dead! Guardians I call you, come now! Come now!"

She threw the skulls.

The dogs formed in midair, glowing in a way she'd never seen before. In a way she did not like. Oh, shit, those weren't regular psychopomps—what the fuck were those things?

The Lamaru were shouting, Lauren was screaming, the dogs howled. Every hair on her body stood on end; they weren't psychopomps—what were they? They had teeth sharper than anything she'd ever seen and as she watched, one of them latched on to one of the First Elders and tore a chunk out of him.

A door slammed: the Lamaru locking themselves in Lauren's bedroom. The psychopomps she'd created kept tearing, *shredding* the First Elders. Chess stood rooted to the spot and forgot to breathe because the First Elders were screaming and fighting and it didn't matter. They were falling apart.

Disintegrating and giving up their power. The dogs grew as they tore, and Chess felt them growing, felt herself growing too because they were connected to her. That wasn't right, psychopomps didn't connect to their summoners. Didn't destroy ghosts, either. Pressure built in her chest, spreading through her arms and legs. What the hell had the Lamaru done, what the hell had they created?

Lauren shouted something. Words of power Chess didn't recognize but felt vibrate inside her. She watched Lauren set fire to a dish of herbs, she didn't know which ones or where they'd come from but fuck, if she was going to keep beasts like that in her house she guessed she'd be prepared to send the fuckers back to wherever they came from, too.

The smell of the herbs hit her nose. It hurt, like breathing poison. The dogs howled again, in agony this time.

They hadn't finished destroying the First Elders. Scraps of them, chunks of ghostly bodies, littered the floor, legless feet planted in place.

Lauren went on shouting, the dogs went on howling. Chess screamed, sinking to her knees. She almost wished she'd let the First Elders take her, because she couldn't do this anymore. She'd never been so exhausted in her life, and as the skulls fell back to the ground she looked up at Lauren and started to cry.

Shame rode those tears, streaming from her eyes and dripping down her cheeks. Not that it mattered. Lauren's face was red and twisted with rage; she stormed across the floor, grabbed Chess's hair, yanked her head to the side, and shoved the needle into her neck.

No more pain. Instead pleasure washed over her, raced up her veins and into her heart and mind, and just before she collapsed she wasn't sure if she should laugh or cry. She knew that feeling. Loved that feeling. Lived for it, thought of it, pined for it, begged for it. And now she might die for it, and wasn't that a fuck of a thing.

Lauren had shot her up with a massive dose of Dream.

Chapter Thirty-five

> Remember, through cleanliness and proper grooming you show others you respect yourself, and that's what makes them respect you. No boy wants to date a slob.
>
> —*Teen Truth,* the magazine for girls

Darkness cradled her, held her in soft arms and kept her warm. When she tried to open her eyes, light stabbed her and she shut them again, rolling over on the bumpy— Wait. She was supposed to be dead. Was she dead?

Silence made her think perhaps she was. The City was a silent place. If she was dead, she'd be there.

She didn't want to open her eyes.

But . . . the City didn't smell like garbage. At least she assumed it didn't. It didn't to living people, but as far as she knew, nobody had ever asked a ghost if the City stank to them.

The thought made her giggle. She tried to snuggle deeper into the— Wait.

Wait. No, she wasn't dead. She was definitely not dead, because newspapers didn't exist in the City, and newspaper covered her.

She opened her eyes. For one confused second she thought she was at the bottom of a hole of some kind, that she was wrong and she was in the City after all . . . until she realized she was looking at the gunk-spattered walls of a Dumpster.

They'd tossed her in there. Spiked her and thrown her body in the garbage. Fuckers.

Oh, shit, what time was it? What— It was still night, but what time was it?

It was Friday night—she hoped it still was, anyway. Saturday was the day of Elder Murray's Dedication. They'd all be heading into the City for the ceremony, the entire staff— Would Lauren be with them? Would the Lamaru be waiting for them, would Baldarel?

Was her— Yes. Okay, her bag was there. Her phone? Did she have . . . Something was in her pocket and she thought it was the phone but she couldn't tell for sure, couldn't get her stiff hand in there. Okay. She'd get out of the Dumpster first.

The fact that she'd ended up in a Dumpster with a Dream OD pumping in her veins would have given her cold chills if she'd been able to feel them. As it was, she focused on the lip of the Dumpster and on getting out, on what she'd learned and what she had to do, and pretended this little movie hadn't played in her head a few hundred times already with a much less cheerful ending. Not that this one was particularly happy.

Her muscles protested and her joints creaked as she pushed herself to a stand, clinging to the walls of the Dumpster no matter how sick it made her to do so. She didn't have a choice. Once that ceremony started . . .

She needed to get to the Church.

The edge of the Dumpster was more slippery than she'd thought. It took three tries for her to get her leg up over it, cringing all the while at the smell and the bits of rotten food clinging to her clothes. She tumbled without grace to the dirty cement below.

That hurt. And since she was already in pain she might as well go ahead and throw up, too. Her stomach thought it sounded like a good plan, and who was she to disagree?

The world spun around her, jittered and shook before her eyes. She needed to figure out where she was. She needed to get to the Church. Needed help.

Her legs didn't want to support her. They moved slowly, clumsily. It occurred to her that while she was still alive, she might not stay that way. It had been night when she'd gone to Lauren's place and it was night as she wove her way down the alley, but that didn't matter much; her system was pretty fucking loaded and so was she. The irony that her tolerance for Dream had saved her life—so far, at least—wasn't lost on her.

The mouth of the alley opened onto an unfamiliar street. It didn't look real; it was flat somehow, like a painting, or like the exhibits in the Church Archives made of plywood. People stood on it like they were talking but she couldn't see their lips move, couldn't hear them; their arms lifted in slow motion. She had the creeping sensation that if she walked too far into it she would be swallowed, turned into something flat and inhuman, too. It would trap her and never let her escape.

But the brick wall rubbed solid and rough against her palm. She stood in reality; she would stay in it.

Keeping her body in contact with that reassuring wall, she slipped out onto the street. Signs above doors made no sense. Shit, she couldn't read them. The lines were nothing but squiggles; they didn't form anything. She knew they must, she just couldn't see them—was too fucked-up to see them—but it didn't help. Her sluggish heart coughed in her ribcage.

Okay. Her hand slipped into her pocket— Yes! The phone was in there.

She braced herself against the wall and stared at it, trying not to see her blood-covered hands, trying to make sense of the buttons. Okay. Not being able to read created problems when trying to . . . Hell, she'd try them all. Wasn't like she had all that many people programmed in there, right?

Her fingers slipped off the buttons. Maybe she should take a nap first. Her eyelids were so heavy, her limbs felt rubbery. If she— Speed. She had Nips in her pillbox, right? She could take some. That might help.

The heels of her boots slid over the sidewalk; her ass hit the pavement with a thud she didn't feel. Her jeans were stiff with dried blood, still damp in places. Her arms were rust-colored with it. She didn't even want to imagine how she looked.

Okay, pillbox . . . pillbox . . . Her hands got tangled in her bag and she couldn't get them free. Long minutes passed while she struggled with it, almost crying except she couldn't feel anything enough to cry. Finally her hand closed around it and she yanked it free.

Stupid little catch! Why did she have a pillbox with such a dumb little catch on it, she couldn't seem to get it open . . . couldn't see it very well, her eyelids kept closing on her . . .

Voices. She opened her eyes and saw a gang of teenagers across the street. What the— Shit, she'd passed out, hadn't she. For how long?

What was that noise? Nobody on the street seemed to be making any, but it came from somewhere. And she knew that sound, it was a song, a familiar one, it— A phone call! Oh, shit, a phone call, that was awesome, that was what she needed. Okay. Gingerly she pressed the button, held it to her ear. "Hello?"

"Tulip? Tulip, shit, that you?"

"Lex?"

"Aye, where you at? You give us the tell now, aye, we all over lookin for you, you—"

He disappeared. Had she hung up? Or had she fallen

asleep again? Maybe she should just close her eyes and curl up. They were looking for her, they'd find her, right?

Wait, who was *they*?

Loud voices came through the phone. Arguing. And then another voice. "Chess? Chess, what they done to you? Where you at, you know where?"

"Terrible?"

"Aye. Lookin for you, dig? You got any knowledge where you at?"

"No, I'm— I don't know where I am, they threw me away and I don't know where I am. . . ."

"What?"

"They threw me away. I was in the Dumpster, I don't know where I am and they . . . they spiked me and I can't really . . . I can't really think very well, can you find me?"

Silence.

"Terrible, please . . ." She wanted to cry but couldn't. Couldn't seem to muster any tears, her mouth was so dry too, was her water in her bag? "I'm lost, I don't—"

"You see any signs?"

"I can't read them. I'm sorry."

"See anything? Got anything you can give me?"

"I'm so tired. I just want . . . I just want to go to sleep." That was wrong, she knew. This was important, she needed to stay awake, needed to tell them where she was. And what were Lex and Terrible doing together? There was no way in hell those two would ever be having a conversation that didn't end with blood and weaponry.

"Naw, ain't can sleep yet, Chessie. Hang on, aye? Got anybody around? See anything you know?"

"It . . . it all looks fake. Not real. They wanted me to tell them who you were." Pain in her wrists flared, but not too sharp. And this was important. She had to tell them what had happened. Why it was so important she wasn't sure but it was. "They wanted your names and I wouldn't. I didn't."

"Aye." Pause. "Aye, know you ain't. Later on that, aye? Just give us aught where you are. Anything?"

"No, there's a . . . Hold on." If she could get up she could walk to the end of the street. A sign at the corner, fuzzy white against the blurred streetlights.

Of course, she probably wouldn't be able to read it. But she might see something else there. A building she knew, anything. "I see a sign. It's a . . . I think it's a Stop Shop."

Yes. It was definitely a Stop Shop. The square green and white sign, its corner broken to reveal a strip of fluorescent light behind, stood alone on the street, guarding the small, empty parking lot.

"I think it's the one we were at before. Remember? I think it's that one." She'd know better if her eyes would work right, if she wasn't so tired and dry and moving through a fuzzy plastic world shrouded in dust.

Terrible and Lex murmured to each other; she didn't really hear them. Her legs ached again, she wanted to sit down, but if she did she'd pass out again and she didn't think she could do that yet.

Lex took over the phone. "Hey, Tulip. Sit you down where you at, aye? Ain't go closer to that shop, Terrible wants me to tell. You just sit and give us the wait, dig? We almost there."

"I can't get my pillbox open."

"No worries on it. Got straight for you, we do, you just give us the wait."

Her water was in her bag. Surely that would help? Her stomach couldn't seem to decide if water was a good idea or not but . . . anything, she was so dry, and shit she was filthy too. Covered in her own blood, covered in vomit—she didn't know when that had happened—and muck from the Dumpster. Wow, were they going to be glad they'd found her.

And she'd have to spend the day like that. What little urgency she was able to feel leapt in the back of her mind;

they had to hurry, the ceremony would start at dawn, she didn't know how many hours it was until then and what they still had to do . . .

She slumped back down on the pavement and started digging for her water. Damn, she'd left some of her supplies at Lauren's; the graveyard dirt, the mandrake and tormentil . . . It wouldn't be hard to get more—she could invade the Church supply room for most of it—but it was still a pain in the ass. Not that she could really feel her ass. Or anything else.

Her fingers didn't want to work the bottle top; she finally got it open. Water flooded into her mouth, through her body; she gulped it down desperately, ignoring her stomach's warning that it was too much, too fast. Water spilled from her mouth and dribbled down her chin and shirt and she didn't care. Honestly, it could only improve things, given how filthy she was. She was tempted to pour it over her head.

"Still there?" Lex's voice came from her lap.

"Yeah." Her stomach lurched, a warning she fought; after a moment it settled. Good. Now if she could just get her pillbox open, just to wake her up, she was so tired . . .

Her eyes closed. Whether she fell asleep she wasn't sure. All she knew was suddenly the world was flooded with light and noise. Terrible's Chevelle jumped the curb and came to a stop a couple of feet away.

Terrible and Lex leapt out. She didn't think she'd ever been so happy to see two people in her entire life. There was an awkward moment when both of them reached for her; they hesitated in unison, then Terrible knelt at her side and scooped her up.

"I stink," she managed. Not really what she wanted to say, but it came out anyway. Her fingers twisted in the fabric of his shirt, trying to get the signal to her brain that he was real, he was really there. "I was in the Dumpster."

"Naw, no worryin, now."

He set her in the car and she closed her eyes. When she opened them they were moving, speeding down the road so fast the streetlights looked like solid streaks of neon. Or maybe that was just her. She was acutely aware of how bad she smelled, how bad she looked, and acutely aware that she was drooling on Lex's shoulder. As if this whole situation wasn't humiliating enough.

"Get the wake on, Tulip," he said. In his hand he held a mirror, three fat lines stretching across its surface like tiger stripes in the reflected light. "Here. Gotta get you up, aye? Gots some knowledge for you. Got work, we do."

"What? What kind of . . ." She yawned.

"Here." He lifted the mirror carefully, tilted a chopped-down black straw in her direction with his other hand. "No time for holding up, it ain't."

Okay, that was worrying. Almost as worrying as the way her vision kept blurring and her fingers didn't want to close around the straw. It took her a few tries to pinch her nostril correctly. Lex held her hair back for her.

Her face went numb; the speed hit the back of her throat and flooded her mouth with that metallic acid taste, so familiar. So fucking welcome. Her heart bounced in her chest, stuttered into life, her eyes focused and her entire body tingled. She—

"What the hell are you guys doing? Together?"

Okay, that was an awkward silence. But she didn't care, because her blood purred merrily along in her veins and she felt lucky, so lucky and so glad to see them. Beneath the high something dark and uncomfortable stirred: This was a heavier dose than even she was used to. She had no idea how loaded that needle had been, but Lex must have chopped at least a gram for her, and tomorrow's hangover lurked, chuckling, waiting for her to crash.

But all that was later. For now she was alive in a speeding muscle car, high as a kite, safe.

"Gave you the ring up, iffen you recall," Lex said finally. "You shout me find Terrible, so I did. Thought he were killin you first, aye, but he weren't so we figured on you havin trouble, we did."

"You figured right," she said, regretting having asked. Because now it all flooded back; Lauren, the First Elders, the psychopomps, those awful psychopomps, and the pain and blood and . . .

Shit. The hangover would be more than worth it, because the only thing standing between herself and a total fucking breakdown was the hard shell of her high and the determination not to make herself look like even more of a pussy than she probably already did.

"Had the knowledge where you was," Terrible said. "Where I dropped you, anyroad. You ain't still there—checked all them rooms, aye? The whole building—so we guessed on them . . . dumpin you off somewheres."

"You looked in every apartment in the whole building?"

He shrugged.

Heat rushed to her face. After a second she said, "Wait. So nobody was in Lauren's place? Did you find her place?"

"Aye. All empty. Meaning, got furniture and all but them not in it. Lookin like they leave in a fuck of a rush, dig, all scraped. An—"

"What about the skulls?"

"Skulls?"

"Yeah, there was—she had a room full of—ow!"

Shit. And double shit, because she'd just caught the implications of Terrible's words. Yes, it was possible that when the two men had gotten to the building, Lauren and her Lamaru pals had been out making their fun little Dumpster deposit—she hadn't thought it was possible to be more pissed off at Lauren, but it didn't really surprise her to discover it was—but why would they all have gone along on that ride?

No. Better odds were that they'd headed off to the Church, to take their places before the Dedication ceremony.

"You right, Chess?"

"Huh? Oh, yeah, yeah, just—I need to make a phone call."

It was five in the morning; damn, she'd been out for, what, three hours? Four? Okay. The Dedication was scheduled to start at dawn, which was only a little less than an hour away. It was entirely possible Elder Griffin would be in.

His phone rang once. Twice. Three—

"Elder Griffin's office, Facts are Truth."

"Hi, I need to speak to—" Wait. There was something very familiar about that voice. "Dana?"

"No, this is Cesaria Putnam," said the girl on the other end.

Chapter Thirty-six

> To impersonate a Church employee is to commit as grave a crime against Truth as is possible, and the penalty is death.
> —*The Book of Truth,* Laws, Article 894

Her entire body went numb; for a second the phone threatened to slip from her grasp and get lost in the haze of red covering her vision. No. No, that wasn't possible.

"*Lauren?*" The name came out like a growl. "Lauren! Don't you dare, don't you fucking dare—"

"Cesaria? Shit, you're still alive?"

"I swear on fucking Truth, if you don't—"

Lauren gave a soft laugh. "Sorry, I have to go. The ceremony will be starting soon and, of course, I have to be there—I mean, *you* have to be there, since Inquisitors don't attend. Enjoy the rest of your day, though—I'm sure I'll be seeing you later."

"Lauren! Don't you hang up—*fuck!*" Chess pulled the phone away from her ear. She'd try again. She'd try all the extensions, she'd keep going until she got somebody, anybody, surely someone would believe her—

Except they wouldn't. Not if she wasn't standing right in front of them so they could see for themselves. Nobody she'd ever heard of had been able to cast personal glamours strong enough to fool a witch. Nobody in the Church would believe it was possible—hell, *she* still couldn't believe it was possible, even after hearing her own voice talking to her on the other end of the phone. Even after finding that fetish designed to cast glamours just like that, and seeing the picture of the girl who wasn't her.

No answer when she tried Elder Griffin's office again. No answer in Goody Tremmell's office. No answer for Elder Ramos, Elder Thompson, the library, the Archives, the Liaising office . . . She even tried the supply room, the prison, and the Grand Elder's office.

Nothing. Nothing but a recorded message informing her that due to the passing of a Church official, the offices were closed.

Fuck.

"What's troubling, Tulip?" Lex lit a cigarette, watching her drop the phone into her lap and rest her head on the back of the seat. Beside her, Terrible's arm tensed; she realized he was twitching every time Lex called her "Tulip," but couldn't figure out a way to tell Lex to stop it without calling attention to it.

"I can't reach anyone. They're all—they've all gone down to the City, and Lauren is—ow!—impersonating me!"

"What, like got she magic make her look like you?"

She nodded.

"Ain't knowing were possible, me."

"Yeah. I didn't think so either. Shit! The ceremony is about to start, they're all heading down to the City, and I don't know what they're doing but I have a feeling it's—ow—bad."

"Give you the tell what else bad. Them dogs? They all in my tunnels, dig, all over. Ain't can get down there."

"What?"

"Aye, why I gave you the ring up on the earlier, aye? When you screaming. Right before it them dogs started down there. Fillin all up, they are."

Her mind whirred. Okay. So the ceremony was about to start and the Lamaru were in on it, would be in the City, ready to unleash their crazed ghost-destroying psychopomps.

Meanwhile Baldarel must have had his own psychopomps in the tunnels. The tunnels that he knew led to the train platform—at least she assumed he did.

So what was he doing? Was he planning to burst into the City and—what? Kill the Lamaru and take over? Use his psychopomps to deliver the ghosts from the— No, because his psychopomps couldn't go above ground, right? Or at least they hadn't before.

"Tulip?"

"Yeah, I'm—I'm thinking. Shit." Her hand was cool on her forehead; she pressed her palm against it, hard, trying to squeeze the answers out.

Okay. The Lamaru's psychopomps tore up ghosts. If they were planning to set them loose in the City, the carnage would be— She couldn't even picture it. Didn't want to picture it.

"Where I takin you?" Terrible swung the car around a corner; they weren't far from her place, or from the highway.

She wanted to go home so bad. Take a quick shower, wash off everything that had happened and come out fresh and ready. Ten minutes was all she needed.

But it was ten minutes she really couldn't afford, and the state of her clothes didn't matter, not when— Oh, right.

"Are you planning to come into the City with me? I think the La—I think there's going to be some fighting down there."

Lex hesitated. Terrible didn't. "If you're needing, aye."

"Aye, me too, then."

"You'll have to wear robes. Over your clothes, but you have to wear them."

"Thought you tell me before nobody wearing clothes down there," Lex said.

"The Liaisers don't. This is for a ceremony, so it's a little different."

They shrugged. The car roared up the entrance ramp to the highway. They were coming with her, they would help her. She would have smiled with relief at any other time; as it was she didn't think she'd ever be able to smile at anything ever again. The image of the City grew in her mind, the City empty of all but her coworkers' screams.

It spread and got worse. A world without ghosts meant a world without the Church. A world of anarchy. It was easy to imagine humanity happily settling into freedom, celebrating its escape from the constant threat of spectral attack.

But Chess lived in Downside, a place where the Church's laws barely reached. She knew what happened when there was no authority. She saw factions battling for supremacy, using innocent people as cannon fodder or shields. She saw destroyed cities. Destroyed lives.

How many times in school had she been taught about the wars that had resulted from multiple governments? About racism and xenophobia and intolerance and everything else that existed simply because it could, simply because when cultures and belief systems clashed, no one wanted to give in or see the other side?

In the Church those things didn't exist. If the Church ceased to exist, would they return? Or worse?

She didn't want to find out. Didn't ever want to find out. So she took a deep breath, and prepared herself to break one of the Church's most ironclad rules—one she hoped they would forgive her for, because if they didn't she'd be executed. If she survived the fight, that was.

"Hey—maybe you guys have some more people you could call? Have them meet us there? I think—I think we're going to want an army of our own."

* * *

It wasn't an army, but it wasn't bad: twenty or thirty men, covered in weapons, with dangerous eyes and heavy boots. One or two she recognized. Most she didn't. And it didn't matter either way.

They stood outside the enormous iron-banded double doors of the Church, right by the pillory where Reckonings took place, waiting for her orders. For her to tell them what to do; both Lex and Terrible had stepped back. She was in charge.

Which made sense. She was the one who knew what they were facing.

Okay. She turned her back on them, grabbed her pillbox, and tossed another Nip into her mouth. Not the smartest thing in the world to do, probably; speed fucked with her power and her ability to sense ghosts. But then, her system was still struggling with the heavy Dream load and she needed to be as alert as possible. And as for interfering with her ability to sense ghosts? She was going to the City. Of course there would be ghosts.

At least she hoped there still would be. The sky was lightening above them. Time was running out.

As quickly as possible she marked them all with her black chalk, using the heaviest wards and sigils she knew. The risk of possession was high in the City, and none of these men would be able to fight it off. Hell, none of them would be able to fight a ghost at all. Maybe bringing them wasn't such a good idea.

No choice. She pushed up her sleeves and went to work on her tattoos, finishing the incomplete ones, an unwilling smile forming on her lips as power sizzled along her nerves and up her spine. A rush that never got old.

"Okay." She gestured for them to gather around her. Magic from their marks shifted in the air, adding to hers, a pleasant buzz in her brain over the speed and the still-present slow euphoria of Dream. "Guys, we're heading into the City of Eternity, so there are some things you should know. Don't approach any ghosts, or look at them directly. The wards I gave you should protect you, but be careful. They don't have weapons down there—at least they usually don't—but it's entirely possible someone might be . . . someone might have given them some. Keep your hands on your own weapons at all times. If you let go, they'll grab them, and they'll come after you first—but they can't harm you without a weapon. If you just ignore them, no matter how sca—no matter how uncomfortable it is, you'll be fine. Okay?"

General nods. She couldn't tell if they were overconfident or too scared to speak, or maybe they just genuinely didn't give a shit whether they lived or died.

"Civilians aren't supposed to enter the City. I need your word, all of you, that you won't tell anyone about this or about what you see down there. Nobody. Got it?"

More nods.

She looked at them for a minute, at the mixture of excitement and unease reflected in their expressions, in the tense poses of their bodies and the way their gazes kept darting around to see if someone was going to crack.

She wanted to say something else, to wish them all luck, or repeat her warnings, or . . . anything. But it was only a delaying tactic, and they couldn't afford it.

So she just nodded, turned around, and unlocked the double doors.

Inside, the hall waited, huge and silent. Energy buzzed in the air, stronger than usual, a combination of her fear and the ceremony now taking place.

"This way." Her voice echoed in the vast space around them, louder than usual without the low hum of voices in other rooms.

The men trooped along behind her past the offices, through the doorway under the main staircase, and into the supply room behind the chapel.

Here shelves were lined with everything a witch could ever need to defend against spectral attacks. Bins of herbs, rows of candles, their scent thick and spicy-sweet in the still air. Spare stangs. Iron filings, iron chips, iron blocks. Black and blue flowers for stang decoration; fire-dishes in every size from tiny to serving platter. Bulging sacks of graveyard dirt. And in the corner lay a stack of ceremonial robes. She slipped one over her head and handed out the rest.

Her cardigan was still smeared with filth. She took it off and tied the arms backward around her waist so the body hung down like an apron. There might not be time to dig around in her bag once they were down there; hell, there definitely wouldn't be. So she turned the sweater-apron into a pouch and loaded it up, choosing not just items that would fend off crazed psychopomps but anything she thought might have a use against the Lamaru or Baldarel and their particular brand of creeped-out, bloodthirsty black magic.

"If you guys want to carry some iron too, it might be a good idea," she said, reaching up to grab the wolfsbane bin. Its edge had just come off the shelf when Terrible's hand joined hers, lifting the bin away and bringing it down for her.

He didn't look right. Well, no, he looked fine—better than fine, just seeing him gave her strength—but he looked . . . uncomfortable. Unease hovered around him; his eyes glinted at her from his too-pale face.

"Hey, are you okay?"

"Aye."

She opened her mouth again, ready to press him on it, but something in the way his jaw set made her close it again. Not only was there not time; even if there had been, this wasn't the *right* time. Especially not in front of men who worked under him. Most especially not in front of Lex.

So she let it go, and focused on loading the men up with as many protective items as she could grab: amulets on iron-link chains, small totems, charm bags stuffed with herbs and stones. In their identical pale-blue robes with their spiked hair and scarred faces they looked like prison inmates putting on a show.

Silence prevailed as she led them through the chapel to the elevator and pressed the button. Her nerves were joining the game in a big way, her heart kicking in her chest, her stomach doing a tap dance beneath it. What was going on down there, in that silent place below the earth? The ceremony must have started; had the Lamaru already made their move? Had Baldarel?

What would they find when they reached the platform? Had Baldarel's dogs reached it yet?

The elevator doors slid open and they climbed in. For the first time, Chess was grateful the car had been designed with rituals like the one they were about to crash in mind; it was a squeeze, and it made her a bit nervous about the weight, but they all fit. Silently. No one spoke. Her hands were freezing. She clenched them together in front of her, twisting them, flicking her fingernails the way she always did when speeding out of her skull. She couldn't stop moving. Couldn't stop picturing the possible carnage that awaited them, those earlier visions of an empty City and a world at war searing themselves into her brain.

And beneath it all lay the old fear, the familiar one: of the City itself, of the silence and the spectral shapes and the dirt, of the empty-eyed ghosts sliding past her. Reminding her, always reminding her, that this was all that waited at the end: this desolation that everyone else seemed to find peaceful and comforting but that still caused her to wake up drenched in sweat a couple of nights a year.

They came to the bottom of the elevator shaft with a small jolt, and the doors slid open.

Chapter Thirty-seven

[I was certainly scared when I got on the elevator, and even more scared when it stopped and my Liaiser led me into the antechamber where I met the spirit of my dead great-grandfather. But there was no need to be afraid, and I managed to trace back four more generations of my family with his help!]

—"My Visit with the Dead," by Etherida Pilcher, from *It's You!* magazine, March 2000

Thick, powerful energy swirled into the elevator car, over Chess, through her, leaving her chest tight. They'd started the ceremony, they must have, and she practically leapt from the car. They had to get moving, get on the train and go. Thankfully, they didn't have to wait for it; it returned automatically after each journey. It was too dangerous to keep it near the City; bolts could be unscrewed, parts used as weapons. No foreign objects were permitted in the City.

She hit the switch that opened the train's doors and gestured the men inside, her heart pounding triple-time. Speed, and her fear of the City, dislike bordering on hatred. And above it all the absolute terror of what they might find when they arrived.

The men sat down. She didn't. Instead she forced herself to walk into the little booth in the front and press the button that brought the train to life. Dull blue lights glowed overhead, reflected off the Plexiglas windows, gleamed dully off the iron walls and fittings. Like sitting in an iceberg, it was; the heaters whirring overhead would kick out warm air in a few seconds, but for the moment it was cold and sterile inside the car, silent save for the dull grind of the first set of doors opening to admit them to the tunnel.

Chess leaned against the iron pole in the center. She couldn't sit down. Couldn't look at any of them as the floor lurched under her feet and the train carried them into the darkness. How many of them were about to die? How many of the men sitting there, close enough to touch, were living the last moments of their lives?

Her entire body buzzed so hard that she thought it might explode if she didn't focus on keeping it together. Her pouch full of supplies made an ungainly weight in front of her. She still stank. And she was probably about to die painfully, along with the rest of them.

This was her fault. If she'd caught on earlier, this might not have happened. If she'd paid more attention to Lauren and her suspicion that everything wasn't right there. If she'd sat down and thought about the clues, about Baldarel's tie to the smuggled ghost at the execution and the fact that the death of a Church employee in good standing automatically meant the entire staff would be in the City at the same time.

She should have been quicker. Should have been better. And if she died—if any of them died—she had only herself to blame.

Best of all, there was a very good chance that she was going to be killed by someone who was actually pretending to be her. Which reminded her . . .

Something clogged her throat when she turned around. She pushed her words out around it. "There's going to be a—*ow*—a girl in there who looks just like me. So . . . please be careful, okay?" She forced a smile; her face felt like a rubber mask. "Don't kill anyone with my face."

They nodded. A few of them smiled. Fear touched their eyes. Terrible's brows drew together, but he didn't speak. And she was glad. She didn't want him to talk to her, didn't want anyone to talk to her.

Outside the windows everything was black. The train with its motley load of passengers hurtled through the emptiness. With every second the power outside them grew, pressing against her skin, throbbing in her head. Her grip on the pole tightened. She could do this, she'd gotten through worse than this, dealt with power more intense than this, and she could do it this time, too. She held the thought in her mind, pictured it as bright red words against the black earth outside. Focused on it: *She could do this.* She had to.

Finally the train ground to a halt. The doors slid open, spilling them out onto the smaller platform. Their breath fogged in the icy air, glowed iridescent blue in the light from the lone bulb above the thick double doors.

The locked double doors. No big deal there. It actually felt good to handle it, to know that here at least was something she knew how to do. Something easy. Whatever else was happening, whatever other fears she had, whatever insecurities and blame and self-hatred and other freaky problems plagued her—at that moment it was about work, about doing something she'd been trained to do.

From behind her came the sound of the train's doors slamming back into place, the rush of wind as it began its return journey, but she ignored it. The train didn't matter. The work mattered.

First she inserted her key into the ornate lock, turned it counterclockwise three times until it clicked. Energy puffed out of the lock and licked her fingers, testing her. She waited, totally focused. Any second it would recognize her power, that elusive whatever-it-was that identified her as *witch,* and the power of the oaths and spells that made her Church. This was why the Lamaru needed a ceremony, or at least part of the reason; they could get onto the platform, but unless someone opened the door from the inside, they couldn't get in. The lock required a Church member to open it.

It happened. A flare of heat against her skin, there and gone in less time than it took for her speed-addled heart to beat once. As quickly as she could she pushed back at it. *"Harraskata berkarantus."*

The click would come next. She braced herself, set her feet more widely. Such a simple ward this one was, but so effective; a test of power, of reflexes, of knowledge.

She felt the click rather than heard it; her entire body clicked with it. A rush of heat slammed into her and rocked her backward, but she held her ground, pushed against it harder. Fighting it like she had the Binding, only a few days that felt like months before.

For a moment everything hung in the balance while she struggled with the load of magic threatening to blow the top of her head off. She gritted her teeth and fought harder, waiting, pushing.

And just like that, it disappeared. Her balance was off; her forehead hit the door, but she was too busy feeling totally triumphant to be embarrassed by that. And what the hell, none of the men knew how it was supposed to go anyway.

She turned to them, gave them one last inspection. "Remember what I said, okay?"

They nodded. Their fear drifted through the air to her. Another thing to fight. She had enough problems of her own without worrying about their feelings.

One deep breath for luck, one more to center herself. "Let's go."

She pushed the door open and stepped through the thick magical barrier and the wall of iron chains into the City of Eternity.

The men gasped. So did she, but for a different reason. The ceremony was in full swing; she could see the huddled mass of blue-robed figures a hundred yards or so away, could feel their power sweep through her like a nuclear blast and shake her just as hard.

She didn't want to be noticed, not yet. So she crouched down, motioned with her hand for the men to do the same, and started moving carefully across the uneven dirt floor, not taking her gaze off the Church group ahead.

They moved in a slow circle, chanting. Words of power bounced off the smooth dirt walls, rose hundreds of feet into the air and crashed against the distant ceiling. Some of the light came from the candles inside the salt circle the Church employees had laid; she knew how thick the line would be, knew that at least two Elders stood outside it, not participating in the ceremony itself, their only job to continue feeding power into that circle to keep it strong.

More dim light came from the wards crisscrossing every inch of the walls and ceiling, strengthening the power of the earth itself, glowing blue with that same power.

The strongest illumination came from the ghosts. Below the surface of the earth they glowed more brightly than they did above it, each of them a phosphorescent bulb in human form, flowing through the air. Ghosts milled around the enormous space, drifted through the vast emptiness, floated just above the ground. They clung to the blank uneven walls in unwelcoming clumps; they glared at the ceremony. Their anger was overwhelming, subdued though it was by the City's powerful wards and by the earth itself. Outside the City, ghosts below the ground were more powerful, more dangerous—the reason basements and underground structures were illegal. But inside the City they were neutralized—at least until someone made a mistake and provided them with a weapon, or the means to escape through either set of doors guarding the train tracks.

There was nothing to hide behind as Chess led the men toward the ceremony. No boulders, no ditches, no piles of dirt. The City contained no topography, possessed no visual interest. It was an ice-blue neon hell, so cold her nose felt numb, so enormous she had never seen where it ended.

They slid against the wall of the Liaising Station, its solidity behind her back a false comfort. In a minute they'd be past it, out in the open; they'd be seen. She had no idea how their presence would be welcomed.

Already some of the ghosts had noticed them. Furious as they were at the presence of Church employees, at the very idea that their home was being invaded by living people they could not touch, it had taken them longer than usual. Chess had hoped it might take even longer, but the life force she and the men carried with them stood out like a beacon, she knew, created waves that rippled through the empty air and brushed against the forms of the dead.

She halted at the end of the Liaising Station wall and turned around. Terrible and Lex hunched right behind her. Neither man appeared to notice the ghosts or the cold misery of the space; they watched her, waited for her, with an unshakable faith in their eyes that would have been comforting if she wasn't pretty damn sure they were all about to die. What would Lauren do when they arrived? What would the Lamaru do? Were they here already, hidden beneath pale-blue robes in the circle?

"In a second we'll be in the open," she whispered. "We'll need to run for it. But stop before we hit the circle, okay? Don't break—"

Too late.

Power flared like a thousand-watt bulb being switched on. Her words ended in a strangled gasp as she spun around and almost fell. Terrible caught her shoulders; she felt him squeeze, glanced back just long enough to meet his eyes. One second of eye contact—all it took to rupture her heart.

Another throb of power. She snapped away from him, righted herself.

Above the circle hung the spectral forms of Elder Murray and the executioner. It was the high point of the Dedication, the moment when the last vestiges of their humanity were magically returned to them so they could bid their farewells before being relegated forever to the City.

But it didn't take a Churchwitch to know something was wrong. As Elder Murray's head touched the top of the circle—she could see the thin white-light shell of power above it—another voice rose even higher. A voice that sent chills of rage up her spine and made her start running before she was even aware she was doing it.

Her voice.

Her own fucking voice, screaming words of power so tinged with black energy they were like vomit spewing into the air. That energy sailed through the circle and shattered it. Confused shouts and screams erupted.

Something else erupted, too: three psychopomp ravens. Lauren's psychopomps—or new ones, probably. They flew over the small crowd, through the thickening air, their eyes glowing red as they grabbed ghosts and lifted them. Carried them to the door, pushed the iron chains apart.

Chess felt the magical seal over the doors break, like a cable snapping.

Felt the doors open, and glanced back to see a black mass pour through the space and flow across the ground. The Lamaru. Saw ghosts begin to escape.

Not her problem—or rather, not her immediate problem. All she had time to worry about was herself, Lauren pretending to be her, smiling in triumph and raising a sword as the Elders and Church employees turned on her.

Some of her men passed her, heading for the black cloud of Lamaru almost at the broken circle. Her makeshift pouch bounced against her thighs, heavier than she'd thought it would be. She grabbed it and clutched it to her, her lungs ready to burst in her chest.

Her voice echoed again, impossibly loud. This time it was answered. Not just by the Lamaru joining in the chant—some of them, anyway, the ones who weren't already raising weapons to attack the defenseless Church employees—but by the dogs.

Hundreds of them, their howls filling the air, crashing off the walls and ceiling and into her ears.

Each Lamaru must have carried dozens of skulls, all those she'd seen at Lauren's and then some. What the fuck was the point of bringing in psychopomps when you were opening the City doors and letting the dead escape? What the fuck was— No, no time to think, it was too late for thinking.

The ghosts were moving, stirred and excited, blurring as they forgot their shapes and simply became masses of energy. Shit. Unshaped ghosts were incredibly dangerous; they grew extra arms or legs, merged with one another to form new beings, powerful ones. Was that the Lamaru's plan? To set them all— No, why have psychopomps, which destroyed ghosts, if you wanted to set the ghosts free?

The Lamaru had reached the Church employees now. Some of Lex's and Terrible's men had, too—she saw weapons flash, heard screams of a different tenor.

But she barely paid attention, because worse than that, worse than all of it, was watching the dogs attack the ghosts, tearing them apart, savaging them. They weren't setting the ghosts free, they weren't worried about leaving the doors open, because they were destroying the ghosts, ripping them limb from spectral limb.

She hit the fray. Took a second she couldn't afford to

figure out what to do first. Some of the ghosts had found the iron candlesticks and were trying to pick them up and use them as weapons. One gripped a burning candle and waved it slowly in an arc.

That's what she needed. Fire. The men were fighting the Lamaru already—shit, there were so many of them, more than she'd expected—but her fellow employees were still defenseless, without weapons of any kind or the types of herbs needed to truly subdue the dead. She had to find Elder Griffin or Elder Ramos, tell them what was happening.

The City was a bedlam of blue robes, black robes, dogs and ghosts and knives flashing like ice in the cold blue air. She ducked across the remnants of the salt line, grabbed one of the firedishes strewn on the dirt floor and righted it, yanking her lighter out of her pocket with her other hand.

Her pouch contained mistletoe, ground toad bones, and dried psychopomp flesh. She tossed them into the dish with some asafetida and fired them up, blowing gently to get them to catch faster and waving her hands in the smoke to spread it. She had no idea if it would be effective against the psychopomps now tearing their way through the hordes—

Pain exploded in the back of her skull. The scene before her disappeared; red lights flashed and dirt filled her mouth as she pitched forward. Her already burned thigh hit the firedish and glanced off. Feebly she cried out, tried to roll away, but hard hands held her there; one gripped her hair and shoved her face into the dirt. She had no idea whether it was the Lamaru or the Church.

With a stomach-churning effort she flipped herself over, swung her right arm in an arc. It connected, cracked so hard she thought her bones might have shattered.

More arms on her, fighting her. An iron candlestick rested on the ground nearby. She grabbed it and swung, not caring if it hit anyone but just thrilled to be doing something.

One of the Lamaru grabbed the candlestick, tried to yank it away from her. She let him pull her to her feet and kept going, ramming herself into him.

Her firedish blazed now, thick tingly smoke filling the air. She couldn't see if it made a difference to the psychopomps, couldn't see anything but the black-robed man before her. Couldn't think of anything but the intense and impersonal need to bash his head with the candlestick as hard as she could.

Instead she brought her knee up and rammed it into his balls, then swung away from him before he had time to fall.

Elder Griffin's head appeared, light shining from his pale hair. Chess tucked the candlestick under her arm and ran for him, using the thing as a spear to clear her path.

He'd acquired a ritual knife somewhere and was using it to slash at two Lamaru who were slowly trying to back him up against the wall. She charged at them, swinging the candlestick like a baseball bat. His face darkened when he saw her; the knife lifted.

"No!" She managed to duck away, holding the candlestick, not wanting to hit him but terrified he'd kill her before she could speak. A fist glanced off her cheek, she jumped back. Shit, there were too many of them, too many Lamaru.

Too many ghosts. Spectral hands closed over the candlestick and leapt back as the iron burned them. The thing turned rage-filled eyes on her, lunged at her; her tattoos screamed even louder, searing her skin as her blood turned ice-cold from the ghostly contact.

It tried to grab her, possess her. She felt it. Shit. Her tattoos held. What about the wards she'd inscribed on the men? What about—

Terrible. She took a chance and turned her attention

away from Elder Griffin for a moment, looking for him; saw him raising his bloody knife above his head and driving it down into a black-robed chest. Still fighting. Still alive, still himself.

Elder Griffin grabbed her by the neck, threw her to the ground. For a second she just stared at him, shocked. He'd never touched her in anger, never done anything to make her suspect he even had it in him. And the old reaction came back; she wanted to curl up into a ball, hide, make herself invisible, take the punishment and make it end faster.

But then he raised that ceremonial knife above her heart and plunged it down.

Chapter Thirty-eight

> It is not enough to know the Truth. You must speak the Truth.
>
> —*The Book of Truth,* Rules, Article 558

"It wasn't me!" No time to roll away, she raised her hands and grabbed his wrist.

He was too strong for her; the knife continued to descend, slowed but not stopped. "Elder Griffin, it's me, it's Chess, that wasn't me, it was Lauren—"

Desperately she tried to meet the cold blue chips of his eyes, to make him see her, who she really was.

It didn't work. Shit. Her stomach twisted; she brought her legs up and kicked his arm away from her. Kicked *him* away from her with a crunch that reverberated in her mind, digging itself down deep into that hidden place where guilt and shame constantly bubbled and seethed. His arms around her at the Binding, holding her, his soothing voice . . .

No time to stop, no time to try again. He was already staggering back toward her. Instead she ran through the thickening smoke, passing through ghosts, knocking against unfamiliar bodies. Dogs brushed her legs but ignored her, searching instead for their dead prey.

And the dead prey appeared, drawn by the tang of blood and life in the air, gathering in ever-deepening hordes and pushing their way through. Getting aggressive.

Cold hands reached for her, tried to grab her. The iron candlestick in her hand grew hot from the constant warding, so hot it was hard to hold.

This was useless. She could hope to defeat the Lamaru, but she couldn't hope to beat their ghost-mauling psychopomps, psychopomps behaving in ways she'd never seen, who felt like nothing she'd ever felt, whose purpose was the utter destruction of everything the Church was built on. The Elders and Church employees were gathered around the firedish she'd started, chanting, sending waves of almost unbearable power rolling over her, making every step she took a struggle, yet it barely seemed to have an effect on the murderous psychopomps. Ghost parts littered the ground; every step was like dipping her feet into icy water. Her eyes filled with tears. Now that she had a second to stop, she was exhausted; all the energy she'd exerted already, all she needed just to keep moving, was too much even for the speed she'd taken.

She stumbled over her own feet. Her stomach roiled, nausea overwhelming her. The fight went on around her and she pressed herself against the dirt wall, wanting to stay out of it. Or rather, not wanting to, but feeling she should. She'd been kidding herself that she could change things down there. Nothing she could do. She'd failed, she was a failure, and she'd—

Lauren.

What made her look she didn't know, but she did, and caught sight of Lauren—of herself—at the periphery of the fighting crowd. If anything could galvanize her, that was it, that bitch. There Chess was blaming herself, and it was Lauren's fault, Lauren's plan, Lauren's doing. And not only had she done it, she'd done it disguised as Chess.

Rage cranked her heartbeat back to a rapid pump and she took off past the ghosts and psychopomps, pushing bodies out of the way. Fuck them. At that moment she didn't give a shit what happened to anyone, anywhere, as long as she got to settle her hands around Lauren's miserable fucking throat and squeeze until she didn't have any strength left.

Lauren turned; their eyes met. Chess almost fell. Staring at herself, at this perfect doppelganger—a shiver of pure terror jerked through her body. Doppelgangers were harbingers of death. Bad luck. Every magical instinct she had, honed by six years of Church training and three as an employee, told her to turn the fuck around and get away as fast as she could, that to look at her doppelganger was to curse herself, that some things couldn't be unseen and that was one of them, forever hanging over her like the guillotine's blade.

But only for a second. That wasn't her, it was Lauren, and if one of them was going to die it sure as fuck wouldn't be Chess—at least not if she could help it. Her feet found their way again. She dashed around the mass of fighting men, glimpsed Lex a few feet away, kept going.

Lauren hunched down, spreading her hands, ready. At the last second Chess dodged to the side, pivoted around her, grabbed her hair and yanked it back as hard as she could.

Her left eye exploded as Lauren's fist shot straight up, stunning her. Her grip loosened, but just for a second. She still had that hair and she wasn't letting go. Lauren fell on her back onto the ground, and Chess, gripping her hair, spun around and yanked her knife from her pocket with her free hand.

The point pressed into Lauren's neck, her own eyes stared back at her. "Tell me how to stop them."

Lauren said nothing. Her eyes cut away from Chess, widened slightly; thus Chess turned her face directly into the fist.

She tumbled off Lauren, her entire body limp, her

brain short-circuiting. Lights flashed in her head, she couldn't think, dimly felt someone grab her by the throat and squeeze.

Her arms refused to move. Nothing would move, she could still feel her body but it refused to obey her commands. It took her a second to realize she was held down, that Lauren sat on her chest with a twisted smile that rendered her face—Chess's own face—unfamiliar as she choked her. Ugly power traveled down Chess's arms, a familiar power, something slithering and glutinous beneath Lauren's energy: the glamour she was using.

Panic replaced the air in her chest. She couldn't breathe. Struggled harder, to no avail. This couldn't be it, she refused to let this be it, suffocated on the floor in the City.

Limp. She forced herself to go limp, fighting every instinct she had. Lauren would relax, wait for it, she'd think Chess was dead and *oh, fuck* her lungs were about to explode and the need to move, to breathe, to fight hammered inside her like the worst withdrawals ever and her heart screamed and ached because she was about to die and there was something she hadn't done, something she hadn't ever done in her life, and she should have and she needed to and it was too late.

Lauren flew off her. Air rushed into Chess's lungs, she couldn't get enough, great gasping lungfuls of it flavored with herb smoke and blood and so fucking sweet she wanted to bottle it. For a moment she lay there gasping the dizziness from her head, until her vision cleared and she saw Lauren scrambling away from Terrible's heavy footsteps. How had he known it was her?

Lex's gore-spattered blue robe clung wetly to him; he looked like a ceremonial butcher at Festival time. Blood dripped off his hands as he quickly dispatched the Lamaru who'd helped Lauren hold Chess down. No time to thank him; she reached out, brushed his sleeve, turned away after Terrible. Her makeshift apron banged her knees; of course. She had that. Lauren didn't.

Terrible had caught Lauren; she was trapped beneath him, both her arms twisted behind her back and clasped in his fist. Her face was twisted in pain; shit, was that what Chess actually looked like? She'd never thought her nose was so pointy; it didn't seem so pointy in the mirror, but— She shook her head. This was not the time to get distracted.

Terrible wasn't distracted; his head moved constantly, checking everyone out, looking to see if any other Lamaru were around.

Chess settled her hand on his sweaty shoulder for a second, said his name. Were his eyes a little too bright?

No time to worry about it. She reached for Lauren's neck instead, aiming for the thin silver chain digging into Lauren's skin, certain she knew what it was.

She wasn't disappointed. Lauren struggled but Terrible held her fast so Chess could haul up the fetish, the talisman Lauren had used, the ugly stuffed toad-body full of filth.

The second the thing left her skin, Lauren's glamour disappeared, but what was left behind was a woman Chess had never seen before. Not Lauren Abrams, at least not the Lauren Abrams Chess thought she knew.

"Who the fuck are you?"

Lauren—the woman—whoever the hell she was—didn't reply. Terrible tugged her up from the ground by the arms; the woman's face went pale.

She had dark hair cut like Chess's, with the same heavy bangs and black dye; Chess assumed it was to assist the glamour. But the eyes meeting hers were blue, not hazel; the features heavier, the lips thicker. An unfamiliar face, but Chess had seen it before. It was the face she'd seen at Maguinness's place when Lauren touched the fetish. The face she'd seen in the executioner's kitchen, too.

Would this endless mind-fuck ever end? Only one way to find out, she guessed. She pulled her arm back and punched Lauren with all her strength, the crunching pain in her already aching knuckles making her entire body hum with satisfaction.

Blood flew from Lauren's mouth. Almost instantly ghosts appeared, swiping at it, trying to grab it and absorb energy from it. Chess's body turned from warm to icy and back again as parts of them passed through her. She'd long since stopped noticing the burning rush of her tattoos. Her entire focus at that moment was on watching Lauren and on trying to keep her body from flying apart under the heavy magic in the air, on keeping the fetish from touching her skin.

"Tell me what to say. Tell me how to call them off."

No reply.

"Tell me how to do it. Look! Look at them! You're losing, you've lost. Tell me how to stop it now and we won't kill you."

"You—you wouldn't kill me."

Chess smiled. Let Lauren see that smile, let her see how truly unpleasant it was. "I might not, but he will."

Right on cue Terrible nestled his bloody knife against Lauren's throat. She opened her mouth. Closed it again. Chess drew her fist back—

"Reklatia halkebirto," Lauren spat. Power blasted from her with the words. Behind Chess, the dogs began to howl.

The sound stirred the ghosts up further, if that were possible. They darted and spun, their mouths opening wider and wider, their movements frantic.

One of them grabbed the fetish. Chess yanked it back, but not fast enough. The fetish, loaded with power, fed the ghost. Translucent glowing arms became solid, glowed brighter. The ghost's face twisted into a leer, its hand raised, ready to strike. She pulled her own hand back, her vision narrowing until all she saw was the ghost's fist, calculating when the blow would come and how she could deflect it—

A flash of movement to her left as Terrible knocked Lauren out. He grabbed the fetish before Chess could stop him.

His entire body stiffened. His already too-pale skin went even whiter, as though he were a ghost himself. Chess remembered how it had felt to touch the fetish, the twisting horrible sickness of it—and she'd been prepared for it, had felt its like before and knew how to handle and fight it. What he might be feeling, what might be happening to him, especially with that sigil carved into his chest, making him more vulnerable, she had no idea. She reached for him with her arms and her power, trying to find what was happening to him and absorb it somehow.

He crumpled. Just fell in a heap at her feet. She screamed and dropped to her knees, stuffing the fetish into her makeshift apron. She'd destroy it in a minute.

In a minute—fuck, so much to do. Speak Lauren's incantation, check on the dogs and the ghosts, on the fight. It felt like they'd been there forever. A lifetime beneath the earth. They would never escape.

Her watch told her it had been barely fifteen minutes when she glanced at it as she tried—unsuccessfully—to pull him into her lap.

Terrible's head lifted. His dazed eyes found her, stared at her for a second, as if he'd never seen her before in his life, while her heart jerked then flooded with relief when recognition replaced confusion. He glanced away, checked that Lauren was still out, then pulled away from her to get up.

But she hadn't forgotten her resolution in those dark seconds when she thought her life had ended. And whether this was the right time or not, it was the only time she had; she needed to get back to the Church employees and tell them the incantation, to chase the dogs away, to soothe the ghosts.

Hours of work ahead, if she even survived to do it. Some Lamaru still fought, screams and howls still filled the air, ghosts swirled around them in blazing streaks of pale light. She put her hands on his shoulders and locked his dark eyes with hers, thinking she would very probably throw up in another minute, but if she died without ever having done it she'd never forgive herself:

"Terrible. I love you."

He blinked. She couldn't read his eyes, had no idea what he was thinking. Equivocations sat on the tip of her tongue, bottlenecked in her throat in their eagerness to fly out and pretend she hadn't said it, hadn't meant it, shit, she felt so stupid—

The City doors exploded in a ball of blue fire and iron.

Baldarel had arrived.

Chapter Thirty-nine

> Into that great empty space beneath the earth's surface the Church placed those angry souls, and calmed them; and peace reigned above and below through the Church's power.
>
> —*The Book of Truth,* Origins, Article 75

Silence so loud it hurt her ears followed the blast, a heartbeat moment in which everyone—Church, Lamaru, gang members, ghosts—stared at the enormous hole, at the cloud of choking black smoke rising to the ceiling, and at the crowd gathered where the doors used to be.

Baldarel's power followed the flame a second later, ripping through the City. Chess's hair blew back from her face, her grip on Terrible tightened as Baldarel's magic threatened to blow her away.

The psychopomps disintegrated. Just—turned into clouds of black dust and evaporated where they stood, wiped out of existence in the time it took her to realize what was happening.

Baldarel's voice boomed at them, invaded her body, thundered in her head until she couldn't hear anything else, couldn't see anything at all. Fuck, that was bad, he was so strong, too strong, what the hell were they going to do, how the hell could they fight a being that powerful—

But then another voice rose, a familiar one, rolling over her and soothing her terrified mind. Elder Griffin, at first alone, then joined by the Grand Elder, by Elder

Ramos, Elder Thompson. Tears started in her eyes without her realizing it, and without making the decision to do so, she stood up and joined them as well.

They were reciting the *Vakterum Alagarum,* a string of power words she'd never been allowed to speak. They were required learning for all Church employees, but like sigils, couldn't be copied whole without risking a cast, so the *Vakterum* was not spoken until necessary. She'd written it out for her exams, all forty-five lines of it.

They drowned out Baldarel's voice, buried it under a thick shower of pure Church magic. Chess's heart lifted. It couldn't be that easy, she knew it wouldn't be, was waiting for the other shoe to drop; but for that one second she just wanted so fucking badly to believe it was possible, that they could win, that Baldarel would be subdued so quickly and easily.

Her own power rose again in her, coming from she didn't even know where. Certainly she didn't feel as though she had any left, as if she had anything left at all; the speed was wearing off and she was crashing and she smelled of garbage and puke and Terrible hadn't replied. She felt as though a fire had ravaged her insides and left only charred lumps where her soul and power used to be.

But still it rose in her, and still their voices rose around her.

At least until Lauren leapt on her from behind and dragged her down again.

Terrible was already moving, his big body a blur as he reached for Lauren. Lauren's arm tightened around Chess's neck.

Chess threw herself forward with every bit of strength she could summon and some she couldn't. Her knees hit the ground with a painful crack, but it worked. Lauren flipped over Chess's back and landed in front of her.

She was so fucking tired of Lauren suddenly, the bone-deep exhaustion the woman had engendered in her from the very beginning. "I'd ask you to help us stop him but you won't, will you?"

Shrieks and howls from the doorway interrupted her, and the last vestiges of bright soft hope left her. Baldarel's family, dozens of them, their bodies low and fast, covering the floor, weapons raised in their mutant fists.

And worse. An army of psychopomps, more of them. Not like the oversized Lamaru hounds; these were larger, their ears stood high off their heads and their noses pointed up, their eyes glowed a bright unholy red and their black fur rippled with terrifying blue fire.

They didn't howl. Their silence made the hair on her arms and the back of her neck stand up. Not dogs. Jackals.

They moved like a black ocean over the ghost-littered ground, sucking them up. Eating them. Eating the ghost parts, absorbing them, and with every bit they sucked into themselves they grew brighter, their eyes redder. With every part they absorbed, Baldarel's power shook the air harder.

The Elders' voices still sounded, the words of the *Vakterum* still pounding off the walls, but they were losing. Chess felt them losing, knew Baldarel felt it, too, and he started to glow and rose into the air. Grew above them, flew above them. A wraith.

He was a wraith.

How the fuck had she not sensed it, known what he was? He'd touched her, he'd reached into her head like a bank robber grabbing cash from the till and she hadn't known, hadn't recognized the spirit attached to him or seen it. His toad-magic was too strong, the same toad-magic that powered Lauren's glamour. Transformative magic, the magic of the shifter.

Silhouetted against his green-blue glow were the bodies of the men. The Lamaru had stopped fighting, were screaming and running, staring in confusion. Of course. They recognized Maguinness, thought their enemy had arrived and had no idea why.

Lauren got up, glanced at Chess with a sick, hideous leer of panic. "What is he doing here, was he the one you told?"

"He's Baldarel, you stupid bitch, he's known who you were all along."

Lauren's face went utterly white, her mouth fell open. Triumph rose in Chess's breast, and damn did it feel good. "He double-crossed you and you were too—"

The first shouts turned her away just in time to see Baldarel's family start slicing the Lamaru to shreds.

Lex's and Terrible's men reacted immediately. Chess almost smiled to see it, might have smiled if she hadn't been so frozen with terror. They were there to fight, they were trained to fight—fight they would, and who or what they were killing didn't matter.

Ghosts rose from the Lamaru, tried to keep fighting but couldn't. Instead they spun around, heading for Baldarel, swinging at his feet. As Chess watched they disappeared, devoured by Baldarel, their energy fueling him and making him larger still, brighter still. How to defeat that? How the fuck did one destroy a destroyer, something that seemed to have no vulnerability, something neither living nor dead, that treated ghosts like chewable vitamins?

Lauren got up and ran. Chess let her, was glad to be rid of her. She had to find an Elder, any Elder, anyone who would listen to her.

She ran as fast as she could—which wasn't very fast, with all that magic making the air heavy—back to where the circle had been. On the way she almost stumbled over Bruce Wickman's body, eyes wide open and staring, blood soaking the front of his robe. Bruce was—had been—a Liaiser. How many more of her fellow employees had died?

She looked around for Terrible, found him cutting a swath through Baldarel's children with a knife in each hand. Didn't see Lex. Fear stabbed at her.

The psychopomps were getting closer, heat blasted from them. She didn't dare glance back. Caught sight of Elder Ramos leaning against a wall with blood soaking his sleeve, his mouth still moving, reciting the *Vakterum*. She couldn't feel the spell anymore, couldn't feel any Church magic in the air at all. Her hand tightened around the handle of her knife.

Her firedish was still burning, the flame almost dead. Quickly she reloaded it. Asafetida, tormentil, ajenjible, and melidia, the most powerful herbs the Church had. Powdered bones of crows and toads. She'd grabbed almost everything in the supply room and she used it now, flinging it into the firedish, trying desperately to summon her own power and force it into the dish as well.

Baldarel might be connected to his body, but he wasn't in it at that moment; that's what made him a wraith and not simply a Host.

So where was his body?

Being able to return to it might grant him protection, at least somewhat, but it would limit his power. At that moment he was out of his body, he and whatever that thing was he'd hooked up with, that thing that combined with whatever soul-killing magic he'd worked to enable him to do what he was doing.

She ducked to avoid a fist, struggled to think past the ghosts speeding around her and the shouts and the sound of flesh against flesh, the smell of blood so thick in the air she could taste it. She had to be able to do something, had to be able to— *Psychopomps*.

Again. He had control over them, was able to somehow make them turn on the ghosts, to remove their careful training to make them harm ghosts instead of aid them, or to make them out of beasts whose instincts were to harm. Most animals weren't used as psychopomps because they weren't always effective in ritual, weren't gentle or familiar, showed up early or late or failed to recognize the passport etched on the ghost's skin and took the wrong spirit . . . but anything could be trained to be a psychopomp, in theory. All creatures had the capability to do it.

A heavy body fell into her, knocked her down. One of Lex's men, locked in battle against a rabbity-looking man with a hole where his nose should have been and no chin. His arms, ending in bright knives clutched in his many-fingered fists, windmilled and spun, slashing the air, slashing the gang member's robe. Chess interrupted her thoughts long enough to swing herself out of the way and drive her own knife into the enemy's back. She caught the brief nod of thanks from Lex's man and ducked back down to the firedish.

Anything could be a psychopomp. Psychopomps always beat ghosts, always.

To beat Baldarel they had to separate him from his ghost.

And what the fuck, it wasn't like she had a lot of other options.

"I call on the escorts of the land of the dead!" Her voice barely registered in her ears. Shit, she had so little power left, all she had was adrenaline, and that might keep her awake but it didn't do shit when it came to powering magic.

But magic was all around her, thick in the air. Baldarel's magic. Could she . . .

Again. No other options. She closed her eyes, opened herself up, and started pulling at the energy around her, drawing it in, choking and gagging on it. It tasted like death and rot and sent horrible shivers down her spine, it burned her soul like acid.

But it was power, and when she tried again, her voice

rang clear and loud in her ears. "I call on the escorts of the land of the dead! By my power and the power of the Church, by the power of air and earth, I call on you to take this man Baldarel back to his place of silence!"

A few of the beasts near her turned, looked at her. Was it her imagination or had the red light in their eyes faded?

"Escorts, I call you! By my blood and by my power, by my command you will take this man!"

She lifted her knife and sliced her palm over the firedish, barely feeling the pain through everything else. Her blood sizzled onto the burning herbs and raised thick clouds of purple smoke; her Bound blood, blood dedicated to the Church and mixed with the Church's power.

Holy shit, she hadn't thought of it before, hadn't realized. By being Bound she had the Church in her, all of it, the power of the First Elders, the power of tradition, the power of every person in that room and of a magical system so complex and beautiful it brought her to tears.

Her blood was the Church's blood. Her body was its body. Her power was its power, her soul its soul.

She raised her hand again, clenched her fist hard. She didn't want to die. *Did not want to die.*

The blade of her knife, cold against the Binding scar. Searing, flashing, gut-wrenching pain as she sliced at the mark, digging deep so her blood spurted from the wound and into the fire, a thick pumping gush of it.

"By the Church and by my power I call the escorts! I command the escorts! Obey me now and take this man to his place of eternal silence!"

Power blasted through her like a lightning strike, a huge bright flash of it that stole her breath, stole her vision and voice. She floundered in it, struggling to keep her focus while the world shifted and the power erupted inside her like a geyser. She wasn't Chess. She was the Church, every member, every employee, from its beginnings as an underground magic study group to that moment when it reigned supreme, and she would reign with it until her heart stopped pumping.

The tiny speck of consciousness that remained inside her brain knew that moment could be imminent. So much blood, so much smoke, the fire so bright it hurt.

The Binding marks burned ice cold. Through the blur of her tears she saw something move on her wrists, not just the lacy pattern but something else, oozing out with her blood, spectral forms: the First Elders. They'd put part of themselves into her. She'd thought the psychopomps at Lauren's place had stolen their power and fed it back to her, but she'd been wrong, it had been the parts of them living in her blood that regrew and strengthened, and they formed themselves whole and towered over her, turned to join the crowd with a dignity that made her want to cry before another blinding rush of power tore into her flesh.

Baldarel pushed back. She felt herself flying, opened her eyes incuriously to see she *was* flying, her body twisting and turning on a wave of purple-black magic. Her apron fell off, spilled herbs and the fetish onto the ground. She ignored it. Who cared? Not she. She was too high to care, that was it—the ultimate rush, the ultimate high, the ultimate forget-it-all-fuck-it-all moment, and she didn't want it ever to end. She pushed back at him, so easily, directing that tremendous force toward its creator and adding her own to it, and the First Elders joined her, all of them together. She felt the rip, felt the toad-magic break, felt him separate from his ghost with a shiver that kept going, running all over her body.

Screams rose from the ground below. She slammed against the smooth dirt wall, fell, didn't feel it, didn't care. To the screams were added howls, psychopomp howls: Baldarel's beasts. She had no idea if that was a good sign or not.

And above it all, suddenly, came the Elders, chanting

again. She felt each of them join in, felt all of them as a unit.

Another explosion.

The power disappeared in a flash. It . . . evaporated, left her there on the ground with tears running down her cheeks and blood still pumping from her wrist. She smelled ozone. Every nerve in her body felt fried to a crisp. She was a husk, the shed exoskeleton of an insect left to crumble into dust after its owner had outgrown it.

Around her the fight went on, but even she could see these were the last desultory stragglers, still forcing themselves to move in the haze of smoke and frantic ghosts. From where she sat all the way to the ragged hole in the City wall the ground was littered with bodies and ghost parts. The psychopomps were gone.

Baldarel was not. A flurry of movement near the hole drew her eye in time to see Elder Griffin and what looked like the Grand Elder tackle him to the ground. Elder Ramos whipped off his robe and used it to bind Baldarel's wrists to his feet. Even from her seat she felt the emptiness around him.

Could she move? She wasn't sure. Didn't want to try, either. It was so comfortable there, her back nestled into a divot in the dirt wall, her legs bent in front of her. A good place to sit and watch. She was fine there, really.

At least until Elder Thompson, Dana Wright, and Agnew Doyle appeared before her, their faces twisted with rage.

Chapter Forty

> At the end of a case, all you can take with you is the knowledge that you did your part, that you acted as the Church would desire and defended the Church against those who sought to defile it. If you did those things, you have succeeded, no matter how you may feel.
>
> —*Debunking: A Practical Guide,* by Elder Morgenstern

"It wasn't me!" she cried, but Dana slapped her so hard across the face that she literally saw stars. By the time she felt capable of speech again it was too late—a chunk of dirty robe had been stuffed into her mouth and her wrists and ankles bound, blood still seeping into the fabric from her wrists.

Her eyes picked out Lex, still standing, talking to a few of his men; relief flooded through her. She scanned the small clumps of people, one or two still fighting, most of them not. She didn't see Lauren. Didn't see any Lamaru still standing. Saw a few of Baldarel's children but they huddled together crying, their fear and unhappiness somehow more appalling on their unformed faces.

In the middle of everything she felt sorry for them, was pleased she could. It wasn't their fault what they were, what he'd made them, any more than her upbringing had been her fault. She hoped the Church would take care of them.

Two Elders stood by the hole Baldarel had made; their voices carried to her, chanting. Rebuilding the magical seal, stretching it to cover the opening. Workmen had already been called, she assumed. The Church didn't waste—

Terrible appeared. Breath she hadn't realized she was holding escaped her. He was gathering his men into a small circle, fewer than there had been. She wondered how he felt about that, if he thought it had been worth it or was angry or . . . what. She hoped she'd get to find out.

"Cesaria."

Elder Griffin stood over her, his face stern but his eyes unbearably kind. He knew. He knew it hadn't been her, knew she'd come to stop it, she saw it in his eyes and felt it when he knelt beside her and tugged the wadded fabric from her mouth, untied her wrists and ankles.

"It wasn't me," she said again. It seemed to be the only thing she could force out. "It was a glamour, she got Baldarel to make it for her, he—"

"Worry not, Cesaria."

"The fetish is over there. I think." Her arm was so heavy; had it always been that heavy? "I'm sorry. I found out last night what he was doing—betraying them, trying to take over their plan and using them—and I went to tell Lauren but she wasn't really Lauren, did you know that? Shit, did— Oh, sorry, sir."

He smiled. "Go on."

"Did you get her? Did you find out who she is?"

"Elder Thompson has her, yes. But whether he has discovered her identity I know not."

"They wanted to destroy the ghosts. They thought if there were no ghosts they could take over, they thought he was helping them but he was using them. Planning a double-cross."

He nodded, his eyes lighting up. "So that is why. He needed them to get into the City. Needed the woman pretending to be Lauren, and the Lamaru's knowledge of Church ritual."

He'd needed their hints about the tunnels as well, but Chess didn't mention that. A deal was a deal.

They were silent for a minute, watching the vast space clear. The Liaisers—save for Bruce Wickman, of course—were busy around another firedish, sending sweet-smelling mullein smoke into the air to calm the ghosts. It appeared to be working.

Others were cleaning up, crawling across the ground in search of anything that could be used as a weapon and grabbing it.

Lex caught her eye; he was by the hole, about to leave. He held up a hand when he saw her, slid past Elder Ramos and out onto the platform.

"Cesaria . . . if I may ask, my dear, who are all those men?"

So many answers flew through her mind that she didn't know which to pick, aside from the obvious truth that "My drug dealer's enforcer and his rival who I used to fuck" was definitely not it.

So instead she said the one she thought was the closest to true, the one she hoped was true: "They're my friends."

Just thinking of going to Church made her tired.

In the two days between the battle in the City and the present moment when she threw a couple of Cepts into her mouth, fired up a cigarette, and tucked her tattered blanket over her legs, she'd been either there or asleep, with nothing in between. Hours of testimony. Hours watching Lauren—or rather, Cassie Benz, as her name turned out to be—testify. The Grand Elder had gone into seclusion when he learned the Lamaru had killed his daughter before she even arrived in Triumph City; Elder Ramos had been acting in his stead.

Now, finally, she had a day off. The next day she'd have to go in again to testify about Maguinness/Baldarel and his connection with the Lamaru, but for now, nothing.

Really nothing: she'd gone to the Market earlier to score instead of agreeing to Lex's plan to come by her place. She didn't want to see him. Well, no, she wanted to see him, but not then. Not yet.

Stupid of her, really. She didn't want to admit even to herself how stupid it was: that she didn't want him around, in case . . .

How was it possible to be totally red-face humiliated and yet proud of the same thing? For one short sentence, three short words, to create such a reaction in her soul?

Pride was a new one for her, at least pride that wasn't related directly to her job. She'd always been proud of that, proud and aware that she was lucky and that she owed something for that luck.

This was different. She shifted on the couch, watched the smoke drift from her cigarette into the air. It killed her that she hadn't heard from him. Killed her that she'd blown it. Embarrassed the fuck out of her that she'd actually said what she said, right to his face, staring right into his eyes.

At the same time, that pride was still there. Yeah, she had done it. She *had* said it right to his face. She'd been terrified but she'd done it, she'd said those words that she'd never said before—at least, never said them and meant them.

And nothing had come of it. And she guessed nothing would.

Thinking about it made her chest hurt. She put out the cigarette and grabbed a kesh instead. Nowhere to go, nowhere to be, why not? Anything to get her thoughts off that track and onto something else.

She'd just picked up her lighter when the knock at the door came.

Probably a neighbor wanting to ask if she'd gotten their mail. Possibly Edsel; he hadn't seemed too pleased that she hadn't stayed to chat that morning. Maybe Lex had decided to come by after all, despite her telling him she'd see him the next day after work.

Wrong, and wrong again. Terrible stood outside, his

hands deep in his pockets, his shoulders hunched in that way he had when he felt uncomfortable.

Yeah, well. She didn't exactly feel comfortable herself. What else was new?

"Hi," she managed, stepping back to let him in. His presence literally went to her head; she had to lean against the wall for a second. Of course, that could have been her Cepts, too, kicking in nicely enough for her to attempt a smile.

Bruises decorated his jaw and neck, a jagged cut started on the back of his hand and disappeared up the long sleeve of the shirt he wore under his bowling shirt. It stood out angry red as he pushed the door closed and leaned against it.

"Hey. You right?"

"Yeah, um, right up." Okay. What should she do? Invite him in to sit down? Why was he there? Shit, she was not good at this. "You? How are you?"

He shrugged. Stared at the floor.

"Hey, I didn't get to say thanks. For, you know, for finding me and bringing those guys in to help me and everything."

"Ain't need for thanks. All right there, now? Got the City locked up an all?"

"Yeah. New doors and everything. They had some already made, I guess. Elder Griffin said—" She hesitated for a second, anticipating pain in her wrists, but none came. They'd removed the Binding the second they'd left the City. She hadn't fully allowed herself to wonder if part of the reason they'd been in such a hurry was because they hadn't realized what kind of power it would give her, any more than she had until the moment she used it. Anyway, the end result was the same. No more marks, no more Binding. "Elder Griffin said they had some spares waiting just in case, so really it was just the wall that needed to be repaired."

"Any of them ghosts get free?"

"A few, we think. It's hard to tell because so many of them were absorbed. But we're pretty sure only a few got out. And we'll find them. They might have to pay a few settlements, but that's nothing compared to what might have happened if we couldn't use psychopomps, or if Baldarel had managed to absorb all the ghosts and take over. So . . . it's not that bad, really."

He nodded. "Aye, cool then."

"Yeah." She bit her lip. Was that why he was in her kitchen, in her apartment? Just to find out how the situation had resolved itself?

He had a right to ask. A right to know. That didn't make it hurt any less.

"Hey, you want a beer or something?"

"Aye, be good."

She fled to grab two beers from the fridge and set them on the cracked countertop. A threadbare dishtowel hung off the door of the unused oven, its sole purpose to protect her hands from the rough edges of the bottle caps. She used it now, flipped off one cap, reached for the other beer—

"Thought you was dead."

She glanced back at him. He hadn't moved. Well, they might as well talk about something, right? Even if that subject was a bit odd for him to pick. "Yeah, actually, I was kind of worried a few times myself, I mean—"

"Naw. Ain't my meaning." He cleared his throat; it didn't seem to help much, because when he spoke his voice sounded dry somehow. Strained. Still the same deep gravelly rumble she knew so well, but . . . tense. She realized she'd never, not once in the entire time she'd known him, heard him sound scared or nervous until that moment. Her heart gave a little crank as she opened the other beer and turned to face him.

"Thought you was dead when Lex come found me,

dig. An us tryin to give you the ring up, you ain't answering . . . drove around hours, we did. All that time I had the thought you was dead. An finally catch you, pulled up on that curb an you there so white, so fuckin *white,* Chess, all bloody an weren't moving. Thought it again."

He paused. His eyes flashed toward her for a second before turning away again, so fast she could almost have believed she'd imagined it.

"I ain't . . . Shit. Ain't liked it. Thinkin you gone."

"I knew you'd find me," she said softly, not wanting to interrupt but feeling the need to reassure him somehow. To say something. She knew how that felt, to look at someone and think they were gone. Would never forget seeing him on that broken sidewalk with his eyes closed and his chest silent and still, and how it had felt like her soul had been ripped from her body as well.

"But I weren't so certain, aye, an it . . . Fuck. I ain't good on this shit, aye? Ain't can say it up right. Fuckin killed me thinkin you dead, is all. Thought seein you with—with Lex weren't even so bad, not—"

"I'm not with—"

He shook his head. "Ain't sayin you is. Saw you with him, knew you gave me the truth. Just had the thought I better see you with that, aye? Than be gone. An you . . ." He took a deep breath, slow and loud, while Chess's entire body buzzed.

"What you say me, dig. 'Dyou mean it? True thing?"

Fuck.

It was one thing to be brave when the world was tumbling down around her ears and she was pretty sure she was about to die. It was another to be brave when he leaned against her door and her hands shook ever so slightly and she knew—*knew*—that this changed everything. Not just everything between them, but her life. That telling the truth would mean giving up privacy and security; that she might get hurt. *Would* get hurt, the way her luck ran.

Fear tempted her: say no, end the conversation, send him away. But she couldn't. It would destroy him, and she couldn't stand the thought of doing that again. It would be a lie and she'd told enough of those, especially to him.

She took a drink, swallowed hard. "Yeah. I mean it. True thing, Terrible."

He didn't move. Neither did she. Should she go to him? What was she supposed to be doing? Panic fluttered in her chest and she fought it down.

"Wanna believe you," he said finally. "Been . . . been missin you hard, aye. But I ain't for certain I can."

Shit. She wished she could say she was surprised, but she wasn't. Couldn't blame him, either. She'd have a hard time trusting herself, too; hell, she *did* have a hard time trusting herself.

It seemed to take a very long time to cross the sticky linoleum floor of her tiny kitchen, still clutching the beers in her stiff fingers. She watched herself stop a foot or so away.

"I never got to tell you what happened." She wanted to look up at him but couldn't, aware her face was flaming. "The night you got shot, I mean, the night at that house. I didn't know what was going on, I was on the ground, and I saw you. You weren't moving or anything, and a psychopomp was coming for you . . ."

She shook her head. "I killed it. Oliver Fletcher tried to stop me but I held the gun on him, I almost shot him too, because . . . because I couldn't stand it if you died, and I didn't care if they executed me for it—"

His hand cupped the back of her neck, pulling her to him in one quick, forceful movement; she barely had time to register it before his lips met hers.

No anger lurked in that kiss, none of the confusion

she'd felt from him before. It was like the first kiss at Trickster's, like the second on the rooftop: just the two of them, with nothing in between. Nothing in the way.

Both bottles fell from her hands; dimly she heard them land, heard foam spread across the floor and felt it licking cold on her bare feet. She couldn't have cared less. She wound her arms around his neck and pressed herself against him, solid and warm and real. His hands fisted in her hair, pulling it back so he could stroke his fingers over her collarbone, sending little shivers through her.

He lifted his head to look at her. Giving her his eyes, giving her what was behind them. "You know I do, aye? Love you right, Chessiebomb."

"Yeah. Yeah, I do, shit, Terrible, I really love you—" She didn't wait to finish the sentence, not when his face was so close to hers, when she could kiss him instead of talking.

Words were inadequate. No matter how good they sounded, or how good it felt to say them, there were other ways, better ways. It might take a while for him to trust her again. He might not ever forget about Lex; hell, she knew he wouldn't, knew it would probably come back to bite her on the ass one day. Could feel it lurking there, another dirty secret to add to her store of them, another shame to stockpile in her soul.

But he wanted to try, wanted to be with her. And she *had* to try. Was desperate to try. If that meant she was barreling toward another painful episode in a life full of them, it was nothing new, right? Because there was still the chance, the off chance, that she wasn't. That she could finally do something right. And if anyone could give her hope, it was him.

So she let him pick her up from the puddle of sticky beer they stood in and carry her to the bedroom. Suddenly the day ahead didn't seem nearly long enough, not for all the things they had to say.

Acknowledgments

As always, huge thanks go to my husband, Stephen, and our two little girls for their unending support and patience; to my agent, Chris Lotts; to Liz Scheier; and to Shauna Summers. Working first with Liz and then with Shauna has been an amazing experience, and I'm incredibly lucky. Big warm thanks go also to Jessica Sebor and April Flores and everyone else at Del Rey for making me feel valued and very, very welcome every step of the way.

I want to send enormous piles of gratitude to Emma Coode and Natalie Costa Bir in England and Australia, respectively, for getting behind the series so strongly.

Of course, I'd be nowhere without the friends who have helped and supported me and calmed me down when I freaked out. Cori Knell, Caitlin Kittredge (from whom I borrowed the Poor Dead Bastards), Stacey Jay, Richelle Mead, Mark Henry, Jackie Kessler, Jaye Wells, Shannan Palma, Ann Aguirre, Yasmine Galenorn, Kaz Mahoney, Synde Korman, and the entire League of Reluctant Adults, thank you. Also big thanks to Mike Mignola, and, of course, to all my blog readers and Twitter pals.

And last but not least, thanks to Charlaine Harris and Karen Marie Moning for picking up a book by a random stranger and liking it enough to recommend it to their readers. I am overwhelmed.